Professor Bernard Knight, CBE, became a Home Office Pathologist in 1965 and was appointed Professor of Forensic Pathology, University of Wales College of Medicine, in 1980. Now retired, he is able to devote more time to his writing career. The author of ten novels, a biography and numerous popular and academic non-fiction books, he has also written extensively for the BBC and ITV, both for dramas and documentaries.

D0366081

CROWNER'S QUEST

A Crowner John mystery

Bernard Knight

POCKET
BOOKS

LONDON · SYDNEY · NEW YORK · TOKYO · SINGAPORE · TORONTO

First published in Great Britain by Pocket Books, 1999
An imprint of Simon & Schuster UK Ltd
A Viacom Company

1 3 5 7 9 10 8 6 4 2

Simon & Schuster UK Ltd
Africa House
64–78 Kingsway
London WC2B 6AH

Simon & Schuster Australia
Sydney

A CIP catalogue record for this book is available
from the British Library

ISBN 0–671–51675–2

Typeset by Palimpsest Book Production Limited,
Polmont, Stirlingshire
Printed and bound in Great Britain by
Caledonian International Book Manufacturing, Glasgow

Author's note

Any attempt to give modern English dialogue an 'olde worlde' flavour in historical novels is as inaccurate as it is futile. In the time and place of this story, late twelfth-century Devon, most people would have spoken early Middle English, which would be unintelligible to us today. Many others spoke western Welsh, later called Cornish, and the ruling classes would have spoken Norman-French. The language of the Church and virtually all official writing was Latin.

Part of this story, most of whose major characters actually existed, is set against the rebellious behaviour of Prince John towards his elder brother, Richard the Lionheart. This was a very real threat in this last decade of the twelfth century, John's first attempt being made to usurp the Crown when Richard was imprisoned in Germany on his way home from the Third Crusade. Then John did homage to Philip of France and a French invasion fleet for a Flemish army was made ready. The mother of the brothers, the redoubtable Eleanor of Aquitaine, mustered a defence force of 'rustics as well as knights on the coasts over against Flanders'. This was perhaps a medieval precursor of 1940, Home Guard included – had it failed, we might now have all been speaking French!

Acknowledgements

The author would like to thank the following for historical advice, though reserving the blame for any misapprehensions about the complexities of life and law in twelfth century Devon; Mrs Angela Doughty, Exeter Cathedral Archivist; the staff of Devon Record Office and of Exeter Central Library; Mr Stuart Blaylock, Exeter Archeology; Rev Canon Mawson, Exeter Cathedral; Mr Thomas Watkin, Cardiff Law School, University of Wales; Professor Nicholas Orme, University of Exeter; to copy-editor Hazel Orme and to Gillian Holmes and Clare Ledingham of Simon & Schuster for their continued encouragement and support.

'Ay marry, is't crowner's quest law!'
Hamlet, Act V, Scene I

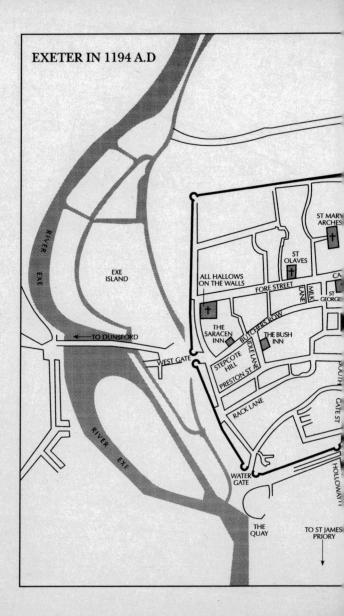

EXETER IN 1194 A.D

RIVER EXE

EXE ISLAND

ST MARY ARCHES

ST OLAVES

ALL HALLOWS ON THE WALLS

FORE STREET

CA

MILK LANE

ST GEORGE

BUTCHERS ROW

THE SARACEN INN

IDLE LANE

THE BUSH INN

← TO DUNSFORD

WEST GATE

STEPCOTE HILL

PRESTON ST

RACK LANE

SOUTH GATE ST

RIVER EXE

WATER GATE

HOLLOWAY

THE QUAY

TO ST JAMES PRIORY

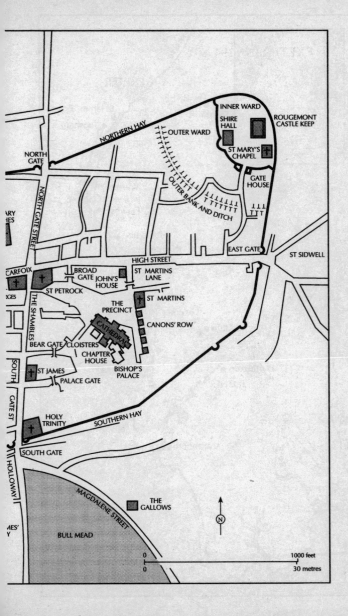

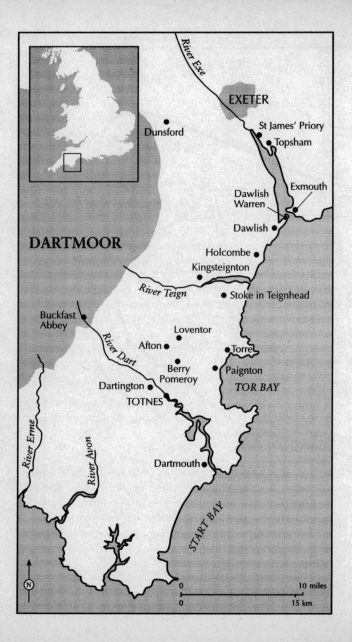

Glossary

ABJURER

A criminal or accused person who sought sanctuary in a church and then elected to 'abjure' by confessing his sin to the coroner and leaving the realm of England for ever, to avoid being mutilated or hanged. He had to proceed on foot, dressed in sackcloth and carrying a wooden cross, to a port nominated by the coroner and take the first ship abroad. If there was a delay, he had to wade out up to his knees in every tide, to show his willingness to leave.

ALB

A long garment, often elaborately embroidered, worn by priests when celebrating Mass, under a shorter garment called the chasuble (*q.v.*).

AMERCEMENT

A fine imposed on a person or a village by the coroner, for some breach of the complex regulations of the law. The coroner would record the amercement, but the collection of the money would be ordered by the King's Justices, when they visited at the Eyre of Assize (*q.v.*).

APPEAL

Unlike the modern legal meaning, an Appeal was an

accusation by an aggrieved person, usually a close relative, against another for a felonious crime. The remedy was either financial compensation, trial by combat or undergoing the Ordeal. Historically, it preceded (and in the twelfth century, competed with) the Crown's right to prosecute.

ARCHDEACON
A senior cathedral priest, assistant to the Bishop. There were four in the diocese of Devon and Cornwall, one responsible for Exeter.

ASSART
A new piece of arable land, cut from the forest to enlarge the cultivated area of a manor.

AVENTAIL
A chain-mail neck armour, similar to a balaclava, attached to the edge of the helmet and tucked in to the top of the hauberk (*q.v.*).

BAILEY
The outer enclosure of an early Norman castle of the 'motte and bailey' type. An artificial mound was thrown up and a wooden tower erected on top (donjon *q.v.*). Around its base, usually asymmetrically, a ditch and stockade demarcated the bailey, in which huts were erected for living quarters, kitchens, etc., the donjon being used as an inner refuge during siege.

BAILIFF
Overseer of a manor or estate, directing the farming and other work. He would have manor reeves under him and in turn be responsible to either his lord or the steward or seneschal.

BALDRIC
A diagonal strap over the right shoulder of a Norman soldier, to suspend his sword scabbard on the left hip.

BURGESS
A freeman of substance in a town or borough, usually a merchant. A group of burgesses ran the town administration and elected two Portreeves (*q.v.*) as their leaders, later replaced by a mayor.

CANON
A priestly member of the Chapter of a cathedral, also called a prebendary, as they derived their income from their prebend, a grant of land or a pension. Exeter had twenty-four canons, most of whom lived near the cathedral, though unlike the majority of other cathedrals, the canons were paid a small salary and had a daily allowance of bread, candles, etc. Many employed junior priests (vicars and secondaries) to carry out some of their duties.

CAPUCHON
Man's headgear, consisting of a long length of cloth wound round the head like a loose turban, the free end hanging down to one shoulder.

CHAPTER
The administrative body of a cathedral, composed of the canons (prebendaries). They met daily to conduct business in the Chapter House, so-called because a chapter of the Gospels was read before each meeting.

CHASUBLE
A thigh-length garment, usually embroidered, with wide sleeves, worn over the alb (*q.v.*) by priests during the celebration of Mass.

CONSISTORY COURTS
The ecclesiastical courts, which had the right to try priests, rather the secular courts. Anyone who could read and write – even just sign their name – could

claim to be tried by this court, as literacy was virtually confined to the clergy.

CONSTABLE
Has several meanings, but here refers to a senior military commander, usually the custodian of a castle – sometimes called a castellan. Appointed by the King in royal castles such as Exeter, to keep him independent of powerful local barons.

CORONER
A senior law officer in a county, second only to the sheriff. First appointed in September 1194, though there are a few mentions of coroners in earlier times. Three knights and one clerk were appointed in every county. The name comes from the Latin *custos placitorum coronae*, meaning 'Keeper of the Pleas of the Crown', as he recorded all serious crimes, deaths and legal events for the Royal Justices in Eyre (*q.v.*)

COVER-CHIEF
Headdress of a Norman woman, more correctly called a *couvre-chef*. In Saxon times it was known as a head-rail and consisted of a linen cloth held in place by a circlet or band around the forehead, the ends hanging down over the back and bosom.

CROFT
A small area of land around a village house for vegetables and few livestock, used by the occupant (cottar) who was either a freeman or a bondsman (villein or serf).

CUIRASS
A breastplate or short tunic, originally of thick boiled leather but later of metal, to protect the chest in combat.

DEODAND
Literally 'a gift from God', it was the forfeiture of anything

that had caused a death, such as a sword, a cart or even a mill-wheel. It was confiscated by the coroner for the King, but was sometimes given as compensation to a victim's family.

DONJON
The central fortified tower in early Norman castles, later called the keep. Originally of wood, it was soon replaced by masonry. The word dungeon, meaning a prison cell in the base of a castle tower, is a later derivative of donjon.

EYRE
A sitting of the King's Justices, introduced by Henry II in 1166, which moved around the country in circuits. There were two types, the 'Justices in Eyre', the forerunner of the Assizes, which was supposed to visit frequently to try serious cases, and the General Eyre, which arrived at long intervals to check on the administration of each county.

FIRST FINDER
The first person to discover the corpse of a slain victim or to witness a crime, had to rouse the four nearest households and give chase to the culprit (the hue and cry). Failure to do so would result in an amercement (*q.v.*) by the coroner.

HAUBERK
Also called a byrnie, this was a chain-mail tunic with long sleeves, to protect the wearer from neck to calf; the skirt was usually slit front and back to allow him to ride a horse.

HIDE
A medieval measure of land, which varied from place to place, but was usually 120 acres at the time of the Domesday survey, but later quoted at anything between

30 and 80 acres. A hide was supposed to be enough to support a family and was divided into four virgates. Another land measure was the carucate, about 100 acres, the area that one ox-team could plough in a season.

HONOUR
A holding of land from the King, baron or Church. It might be a large estate or a single manor and many honours consisted of numerous separate holdings spread over many counties. A manor might be one village or several, under the same lord. Some villages were split between different lords.

HUE AND CRY
When a crime was witnessed or discovered, the First Finder (*q.v.*) had to knock up the four nearest houses and give chase to any suspects.

JURY
Unlike modern juries, who must be totally impartial, the medieval jury included witnesses, local people who were obliged to gather to tell what they knew of a crime or dispute. The coroner's jury was supposed to consist of all the men over the age of twelve from the four nearest villages, though this was often a practical impossibility.

JUSTICIAR
One of the King's chief ministers in Norman times. In the reign of Richard I, the most effective was Hubert Walter, who was Richard's military second-in-command in Palestine, before he returned home during the Lionheart's imprisonment in Austria to help raise his ransom. Richard made him Archbishop of Canterbury and Chief Justiciar, and he virtually ruled the country after Richard's permanent departure from England in May 1194, only two months after returning from captivity.

KIRTLE

A woman's gown, worn to the ankles, with long sleeves, wide at the wrists, though fashions changed constantly. The kirtle was worn over a chemise, the only undergarment.

MANOR REEVE

A foreman appointed in each village, either by election of the villagers or by the manor lord. He oversaw the daily farm work and though illiterate like the vast majority of the population, he would keep a record of crop rotation, harvest yields, tithes etc., by means of memory and notches on tally sticks.

MARK

A sum of money, though not an actual coin, as only pennies were in use. A mark was two-thirds of a pound or thirteen shillings and fourpence (now equal to sixty-six decimal pence).

MOTTE

The artificial mound on which the wooden donjon (q.v.) tower was erected in early Norman castles, surrounded by the bailey (q.v.). An excellent example is Totnes Castle.

MURDRUM FINE

An amercement (q.v.) levied on a community by the coroner when a person was found dead in suspicious circumstances and no culprit could be produced – unless the villagers could make 'presentment of Englishry' (q.v.).

ORDEAL

Though sometimes used to extract confessions, the Ordeal was an ancient ritual, abolished by the Vatican in 1215, in which suspects were subjected to painful and often fatal activities, such as walking barefoot over nine red-hot plough-shares, picking a stone from a vat of boiling water, licking white-hot iron, etc. If they suffered no injury, they were judged innocent. Another common ordeal was to be bound and thrown into deep water; if the victims sank they were innocent; if they floated they were guilty, and were hanged or mutilated.

OUTLAW
Literally, anyone outside the law, usually escaped prisoners or fugitives lurking in the forests. They ceased to exist as legal persons, and anyone was entitled to kill them on sight to collect a bounty, as if they were the 'wolf's head'.

OUTREMER
The four Christian kingdoms in the Levant at the time of the Crusades, including the kingdom of Jerusalem.

PEINE ET FORTE DURE
'Hard and severe punishment', a torture used for the extraction of confessions from suspects.

PHTHISIS
Tuberculosis, rife in medieval times.

PORTREEVE
One of the senior burgesses in a township, elected by the others as leader. There were usually two, later superseded by a mayor, the first mayor of Exeter being installed in 1208.

PREBENDARY see CANON

PRECENTOR
A senior canon in a cathedral, responsible for organising the religious services, singing, etc.

PRESENTMENT OF ENGLISHRY
Following the 1066 Conquest, many Normans were covertly killed by aggrieved Saxons, so the law decreed that anyone found dead from unnatural causes was

presumed to be Norman and the village was punished by a murdrum fine (*q.v.*) unless they could prove that the deceased was English or a foreigner. This was usually done before the coroner by a male member of the family. This continued for several centuries as, even though it became meaningless so long after the Conquest, it was a good source of revenue to the Crown.

RULE OF ST CHRODEGANG
A strict regime of a simple communal life, devised by an eighth-century bishop of Metz. It was adopted by Bishop Leofric, who founded Exeter Cathedral in 1050, but did not long survive his death. The canons soon adopted a more comfortable, even luxurious lifestyle.

SHERIFF
The 'shire reeve', the King's representative and principal law officer in a county, responsible for law and order and the collection of taxes.

SURCOAT
Either a light over-tunic or a garment worn over armour, to protect it from the sun's heat and to display heraldic recognition devices.

TITHE
A tenth part of the harvest and all farm produce, demanded by the Church. Stored in large tithe barns in each village.

TUNIC
The main garment for a man, pulled over the head to reach the knee or calf. A linen shirt might be worn underneath and the lower sides or front and back would be slit for riding a horse.

UNDERCROFT
The lowest floor of a a fortified building. The entrance

to the rest of the building was on the floor above, isolated from the undercroft, which might be partly below ground level. Removable wooden steps prevented attackers from reaching the main door.

VERDERER
A judicial officer who supervised the royal forests and applied the harsh laws of the verge.

VICAR
A priest employed by a more senior cleric, such as a canon (*q.v.*), to carry out some of his religious duties, especially attending the numerous daily services in a cathedral. Often called a vicar-choral, from his participation in chanted services.

PROLOGUE

December 1194

The morning was ravaged by the sound of axe on tree and the crackle of flames as branches were hacked off and burned. A dozen men were slowly but surely pushing back the forest edge from the strips of cultivated land that lay on the valley slopes around the village of Afton, a few miles from Totnes. Already this month, in spite of interruptions caused by angry disputes with men from Loventor, the next village beyond the trees, they had advanced the new ground won from the woods by a dozen acres.

Alward, the Saxon reeve from Afton, was walking around the ash-strewn ground, counting the trees felled that week. He recorded them by notches cut with his dagger on a tally stick to show to the bailiff of his lord, Henry de la Pomeroy, who would inevitably complain about the amount of work done, whatever new area they had managed to add to his manor. Alward was well aware that they were on disputed land and that, with every tree dropped, they were getting deeper into the property claimed by Sir William Fitzhamon, who included the tiny hamlet of Loventor within his honour.

He disliked having to argue with the men from Loventor. When they had come to shout abuse at his team for trespassing the week before, it had come to blows: he had suffered a cut head and one of his men was knocked out during the scuffle. Following this, the bailiff had sent a couple of men-at-arms to escort the felling team, but after two days of peace, they were sent back to Berry Castle, the Pomeroy stronghold high on a ridge a mile away.

But that had proved to be the quiet before the storm. Today they had been at work for barely two hours when suddenly, from out of the trees opposite, came a yelling horde of men, waving cudgels and staves. Some of the Afton men immediately dropped their tools and ran downhill towards the village, which was visible in the distance. Others held their ground, encouraged by Alward, who tried to halt the attackers by shouting and waving his arms. The next moment a ragged figure felled him with a blow on the shoulder from a staff and another wild-looking peasant began kicking him. Similar scenes took place all over the despoiled area, with hand-to-hand fights going on amid yelling and curses.

Before long the rout was over – half the Afton men had fled and the rest were on the ground, nursing sore heads and bruised ribs, though no one was seriously hurt. Alward sat up painfully and saw that the raiders were now ignoring his men and collecting up all their tools. Within minutes, every axe and cleaver had vanished along with the marauders, who melted back into the forest as suddenly as they had appeared.

The reeve climbed to his feet, realising that, without their tools, there could be no more work that day – and that the bailiff and Lord Henry must be informed without delay. The message he must take to them was plain: this nibbling away at Fitzhamon's land was no longer going to be easy.

CHAPTER ONE

In which Crowner John is disturbed on Christ Mass Eve

For once, Matilda was happy. Flushed with pleasure and self-importance, she sat at one end of the long table in the high, gloomy hall of their house and urged her guests to take more drink, capons' legs and sweetmeats from the jugs and platters set in front of them.

At the other end sat the brooding figure of her husband, Sir John de Wolfe, the King's coroner for the County of Devon. Tall and slightly hunched, his black hair matched the thick eyebrows that sat above deep-set eyes. Unlike most Normans, he had no beard or moustache beneath his great hooked nose, but his dark stubble had helped earn him the nickname 'Black John' in the armies of the Crusades and the Irish wars.

This evening, though, even his usually grim face was more relaxed, partly due to the amount of French wine he had drunk but also because he had a good friend on each side of him. To his left was Hugh de Relaga, one of the town's two Portreeves, a fat and cheerful dandy. On the other side was John de Alencon, Archdeacon of Exeter, a thin, ascetic man, with a quiet wit and a twinkling eye.

Around the rest of the table were a dozen other Exeter worthies and their wives, from the castle, the Church and the Guilds. It was about the eleventh hour on the eve of Christ Mass and they had not long returned from the special service in the great cathedral of St Mary and St Peter, only a few hundred paces away from the coroner's home in Martin's Lane.

Their timber house was high and narrow, being only one room from floor to beamed roof, with a small solar built on the back, reached by an outside staircase. The walls were hung with sombre tapestries to relieve the bare planks and the floor was flagged with stone, as Matilda considered the usual rush-strewn earth too common for people of their quality.

The guests sat on benches along each side of the heavy table, the only two chairs being at either end. Light came from candles and tallow dips on the table and from the large fire in the hearth. The guests were sufficiently filled with ale, cider and wine to be in prattling mood, especially at Yuletide, when a strangely contagious mood of bonhomie infected the community.

'Matilda, I thought you usually patronised that little church of St Olave in Fore Street, not the cathedral?'

The high-pitched voice was that of her sister-in-law, Eleanor, wife to Sheriff Richard de Revelle. De Wolfe was not sure whom he detested more, his brother-in-law or the wife. Eleanor was a thin, sour-faced woman of fifty, an even greater snob than Matilda. Spurning the usual white linen cover-chief over the head, Eleanor wore her hair coiled in gold-net crespines over each ear. Her husband was also elegantly dressed, a man of medium height with wavy brown hair, a thin moustache and a small pointed beard – a complete contrast to his brother-in-law, who dressed in nothing but black or grey.

'Why, in God's name, is it called St Olave's?' drawled de Revelle, leaning back on the bench, the better to display his new green tunic, the neckband and sleeves worked elaborately in yellow embroidery.

'It's certainly in God's name, sheriff,' replied the Archdeacon, with a wry smile. 'Olave was the first Christian king of Norway, though I admit it quite escapes me why one of our seventeen churches in Exeter is dedicated to him.'

The conversation chattered on, the noise level rising as the contents of the wine keg lowered. Matilda, her square pug face radiant with pleasure at the success of her party, looked around the hall and calculated her resulting elevation on the social scale, to be gauged when she next met her cronies at the market or in church. For once she had persuaded her taciturn husband, who had been made county coroner only three months earlier, to open up a little socially and invite some people to the house after the Mass on the eve of Christ's birthday.

Rather to her surprise, even he appeared amiable tonight. At least the party had kept him at home, she thought, with momentary bitterness, and he was not down at the Bush tavern with his red-headed mistress, that Welsh tart Nesta. Outside the unglazed shutters the night was freezing, but a fire was roaring in the big hearth, which had the modern luxury of a stone chimney. Brutus, John's old hound, was stretched luxuriously in front of the flames, twitching now and then as a hot spark spat out at him.

The wine and food were constantly replenished by Mary, their house-servant and cook, while old Simon,

the labourer, carried in fresh logs to stoke the fire.
Matilda's own maid Lucille, the poisonous French
hag, as de Wolfe thought of her, was too grand to
serve at table and was lurking in the solar, eavesdropping through the high slit window, waiting to
help Matilda undress for bed when the party was
over.

Between joining in the gossip and scandal, Matilda
stole frequent glances at her husband, willing him to
do something socially elegant, such as standing to
propose a toast – to Jesus Christ, or the prosperity
of Exeter, anything to make his mark and reflect
some more glory upon her. Several times, she saw
him move as if to get up and she waited expectantly for him to raise his glass to the assembled worthies. But each time she was disappointed, as all he
did was reach across for a chicken leg or a jug of
Loire wine. Then the opportunity was lost, as her
brother jumped up and brandished his beaker, tapping imperiously on the table with the handle of his
dagger.

'We must give thanks to our host and his good wife
for inviting us to this most convivial gathering,' he
brayed, the long cuff of his tunic dangling as he waved
his cup back and forth. 'To Sir John de Wolfe, lately
appointed crowner to this county, and his good wife,
my little sister Matilda!'

As they stood and responded to his toast, John
thought that 'little sister' was the greatest exaggeration
of the twelfth century, as Matilda's square figure was
a good many pounds heavier than de Revelle's. Then,
charitably, he assumed that his brother-in-law had
meant little in years, as she was four less than her
brother's fifty. The coroner himself was only forty,

though the lined skin stretched over his high cheek-bones weathered by more than two decades of campaigning in Ireland, France and the Holy Land, made him look older.

Matilda's irritation at her husband's failure to match Richard's social graces was slowly subsiding, when another blow fell upon her ambition to become one of Exeter's premier hostesses. Suddenly she saw Mary, whom she rightly suspected of being another of John's amorous conquests, come up to him and whisper urgently in his ear. He looked over his shoulder at the door to the small vestibule that fronted on to the street. Following his gaze, Matilda glared in annoyance at a large face that peered around the door. It was fringed with unruly red hair and, below a bulbous nose, a huge moustache nestled, its ends merging with carroty side-whiskers before hanging down past his lantern jaw almost to his chest. It was Gwyn of Polruan, her husband's bodyguard and coroner's officer, a Cornishman for whom her Norman soul had even more contempt than for Saxons.

With growing apprehension and annoyance, she heard her husband's chair grate across the flagstones as he rose and walked across to the door. As she watched him whispering with Gwyn, her concern mounted into fury. 'If he leaves now, I'll kill him, God help me!' she muttered to herself.

Her worst fears were realised when John walked back across the hall, his head slightly forward, looking like some great bird of prey in his grey tunic and long black hose. Bending down to John de Alencon, he murmured something into the Archdeacon's ear. The emaciated priest stood up immediately.

The coroner cleared his throat and, in his deep,

sonorous voice, excused himself from the festivities for a while. 'I hope it'll not be long! I have but a few yards to go and hope to be back soon. So, please, eat, drink and be merry until then.'

Now furious, Matilda hurried around the table and caught her husband's arm as he walked with the Archdeacon across to the door, where Gwyn still waited. 'Where are you going?' she hissed venomously. 'You can't leave me like this now, with all your guests still here!'

'It'll not be for long, wife,' he grunted. 'This won't wait, I'm afraid, but I'll try to get back soon.'

Fuming with rage, she hissed again, into his ear, 'What can be more important on a Yuletide Eve than entertaining some of the most important citizens in Exeter?'

'What about a dead canon in the cathedral Close, woman?' he suggested, and slipped out of the door without another word.

De Wolfe and the Archdeacon strode on either side of the Cornish giant as they left the coroner's house. Martin's Lane was a short passage leading from High Street into the cathedral precinct. It took its name from St Martin's Church on the corner, from which a line of houses stretched along the north side of the Close. Here lived many of the twenty-four canons of the cathedral, along with some of their vicars, lesser priests and servants, all male, for officially, women were forbidden in their dwellings.

As they hurried through the still, frosty air, the coroner's henchman told what little he knew of the incident. 'An hour ago, that miserable clerk of ours came running to me at my sister-in-law's dwelling in

Milk Street. My wife and children are lodging with her tonight, as the city gates are shut until morning.' Gwyn lived outside the walls, at St Sidwell's, beyond the East Gate.

'What did Thomas have to tell you?' demanded de Wolfe. Thomas de Peyne was the third member of his team, a diminutive, crippled ex-priest who had been unfrocked for allegedly interfering with a young female novice in Winchester.

'He said that at about the tenth hour there had been a great uproar in the canon's house near where he lodges and someone came to fetch him out. Being the nosy little swine that he is, he went to see what was afoot.'

De Wolfe was used to Gwyn's leisurely way of telling a tale, but John de Alencon was less patient. 'So what *was* afoot, man?'

'The house steward was standing at the front, screaming that the canon was dead. With some others, our clerk ran through to the back of the house and found the prebendary hanging by his neck in the privy.'

By now the hurrying trio had entered Canons' Row, with the huge bulk of the cathedral on their right. A full moon shimmered on the great building, which hovered above the disorder of the Close, with its muddy paths, piles of rubbish and open grave-pits.

'He was undoubtedly dead?' growled the coroner.

Gwyn pulled up the hood of his shabby leather jacket against the chill air. 'Dead as mutton, Thomas said. The others felt his heart to make sure, then he ran to fetch me, while a servant went off to take the news to the Bishop's Palace.'

The Archdeacon, sweeping along in his long black cloak, clucked his tongue in irritation. 'And the Bishop is away at Gloucester, leaving me as the most senior cleric at this tragic time.'

They had arrived at the fifth house in the terrace, marked by a cluster of people around the narrow passageway that led through to the backyard. One short figure detached itself from the throng and limped towards them. Thomas de Peyne was blessed with a good brain and cursed with a twisted body. Old phthisis had bent his spine into a slight hump and damaged a hip to shorten one leg. As if this was not enough, the Almighty had given him a slight squint in his left eye. 'Thank God you're here, Crowner,' he squeaked, crossing himself nervously. 'These people are running around like chickens with their heads cut off!'

'Where's the corpse?' demanded John gruffly. He never wasted breath on niceties of speech.

Thomas pushed through to the passageway and the little crowd opened up deferentially for the other men, the servants and secondaries bobbing their knees as the Archdeacon passed. The alley was dark and narrow, running alongside the tall timber house roofed with wooden shingles. It was similar, though not identical, to the other buildings in the row, some of stone, some slated and some thatched.

At the back, the passage opened into a yard with several rickety outbuildings. One was the kitchen, another a wash-house and one a pig-sty. Furthest away, against the back fence, was a small shed that acted as the latrine for the whole house. It was built up on several stone steps, a deep privy-pit dug beneath it.

'He's in there, Crowner,' said Thomas, his thin, pointed nose wrinkling in anticipation. De Wolfe loped across to the shed, lit by the moon and the horn-lanterns of several residents who had followed them into the yard. He pulled open the crude door, whose bottom edge grated across the rough flagstones.

'Bring more lights here,' he commanded, as he stepped inside. The stench was strong after the cold night air outside, but as everyone had a stinking privy the coroner took no notice.

Gwyn, the Archdeacon and the clerk pushed in alongside him, holding tallow tapers taken from the servants. Along the back wall was a wooden bench with two large holes cut in it, in case more than one resident was taken short at the same time. Beneath it was a four-foot drop into an odorous pit, which was cleared from the rear by the night-soil man, who came around with his donkey and cart once a week.

But their gaze was fixed on a figure hanging in front of the seat, toes all but touching the floor. It was rotating slowly in the draught coming up from the faecal pit. Eerily, the face revolved close to de Wolfe's, the eyes just level with his, due to the coroner's greater height. Staring sightlessly ahead, tongue protruding, the corpse slowed down and stopped, then reversed its mindless study of the privy walls as the cord untwisted again.

For a moment there was shocked immobility, broken only by the clerk spasmodically crossing himself.

'For God's sake, cut the poor man down!' muttered the Archdeacon.

Gwyn started forward, pulling a dagger from his belt, but the coroner laid a restraining hand on his arm. 'Wait, until I look at his neck.'

Leaving the other three jammed in the doorway, de Wolfe stepped to the side of the dead man and held up his thin tallow candle. He saw that the corpse was a rather slight, elderly man with a rim of white hair around a bald crown. He was dressed in a long robe of thick black wool, similar to a monk's habit. The thin face was congested and purple, prominent blue eyes glimmering in the flicker of the candle-flame. Even in that poor light, pinpoint bleeding spots could be seen in the whites of the eyes. John grasped a drooping arm as the body turned slowly and stopped the rotation so that he could look at the side of the neck.

'What type of cord is this, John?' he asked his priestly namesake.

De Alencon, visibly distressed but keeping a firm grip on his emotions, was glad of the chance to divert his thoughts from the death of a colleague. He looked at the ligature, which was around the neck and vanished into the darkness above. It was a twisted rope of brown and black flax, the thickness of a man's little finger. 'It looks like a monk's waist cord, probably from the habit that covers him.'

'But a canon isn't a monk,' objected de Wolfe. He had little interest in the hierarchy of the Church, but knew that canons, or prebendaries as they were often called, were ordained priests and that Exeter was a secular cathedral, not a monastic house.

'Many people have a monk's habit,' piped up the all-knowing Thomas from behind. 'I've got one myself. They make fine wrappings to get out of bed or go to the privy on a cold morning.'

The Archdeacon shook his head. 'Poor Robert de Hane had a better claim to one than just the need for a warm robe. In his younger years he was an Augustinian from the house of Holy Trinity in London's Aldgate.

This is probably his habit from his days as a Black Canon.'

Gwyn's large, shaggy head was peering around the privy. 'I suppose he stepped off the seat after tying the cord to a rafter.' Looking up into the gloom, he could just make out where the rope was knotted around one of the rough supports for the thatched roof.

John de Alencon shook his cropped grey head sadly. 'I cannot believe it. Self-destruction is a mortal sin. What man of the Church, especially a senior canon, would take his own life – and on the eve of the birthday of his Saviour, above all times?' He passed a hand over his eyes in genuine distress. 'I just cannot accept it, John.'

The coroner had been silently studying the corpse, his hawk-like face drawn into a scowl of concentration. 'I don't think you need accept it, my friend,' he growled. 'Gwyn, come and look at this.' He beckoned his henchman to look more closely in the dim light at the side of the cadaver's neck. The monk's girdle-cord cut deeply into the left side under the angle of the jaw, then passed around to the right, where it was pulled sharply upwards and away from the skin in an inverted V-shape to reach a knot placed alongside the ear. From there, the cord stretched tautly up to the roof-beam. 'We'll see better when we cut him down, but look here,' he commanded, pointing a finger at the skin below the ligature.

Gwyn of Polruan put his face closer until his bulbous nose almost touched the corpse. 'There's another mark around the neck, lower down.'

The coroner looked grim. 'It can happen. I remember when King Richard executed all those Moors at

Acre, and again at Ascalon, some hanged fellows had two marks. But it's unusual.'

The Cornishman cast his mind back more than three years to when he had been with de Wolfe at the Third Crusade. At the fall of Acre, hundreds of Saracen prisoners were massacred, most by the sword, lance and mace – but many had been hanged.

'True, the rope can bite first lower down, then slip up with the weight of the body.' He sounded reluctant to agree.

The coroner's finger moved to the back of the cadaver's neck. 'But it can't do this!' he snapped.

The Archdeacon and his officer craned their necks to look, and Thomas de Peyne was almost jumping up and down behind them to get a better view.

On the nape of the neck, just below the monk's girdle-cord, the lower ligature mark crossed over itself, two short marks lying above and below the brownish-red line. John de Alencon looked questioningly at de Wolfe, his horror temporarily overtaken by curiosity.

'He's been garrotted – the cord was thrown over his head, the two ends crossed and pulled tight,' grated the coroner. He stepped back and motioned to Gwyn. 'Cut him down – gently now.' He pulled the Archdeacon back to the door to make room, while Gwyn sliced through the cord high up and took the weight of the dead priest easily in his other brawny arm. The clerk stood watching in fascination, furiously making the Sign of the Cross.

'Bring him into the house, where there's a better light,' ordered de Wolfe, and strode off ahead to the back door of the canon's dwelling. Gwyn carried the corpse in his arms like a baby, the head lolling back, the fatal rope trailing on the ground.

With the Archdeacon, Thomas, a few junior priests and some servants following, they went through a door and up a passage into a chamber that had a simple bed as the only furniture, apart from a large wooden crucifix on the wall. The canon's steward, a fat, middle-aged man with tears streaming from his eyes, stood wringing his hands alongside the bed, as Gwyn gently laid the body upon it.

'Get more lights, Alfred,' commanded the Archdeacon, and the steward hurried out, gulping orders at the other servants.

De Wolfe stood at the foot of the narrow bed and laid a consoling hand on his friend's shoulder. 'You knew him well, John?'

The senior cleric nodded. 'Even before I came from Winchester eight years ago. I had met him in London when he was still at Holy Trinity. A good man, very learned in the history of the Church.'

As they waited for more illumination, John asked more questions. 'What did he do in the cathedral community?'

'He was a regular canon and had a prebend, like the rest of us, but held no particular office. Most of his time away from daily worship was spent in the cathedral library. I'm not quite sure what he was doing – you would need to ask Canon Jordan de Brent, the archivist.'

The coroner stroked his long jaw, dark with black stubble. 'Was he politically active? I mean, in the Church hierarchy. Could he have made enemies?'

De Alencon's lean face wore a sad smile, in spite of the tragic circumstances. 'Never! He was quiet and retiring, hardly said a word at the chapter meetings. An unworldly man, his mind was lost in books and manuscripts.' He waved a hand around the bare room. 'You see this, a Spartan life, unlike some of our fellows, I'm afraid. Too many canons have forgotten the Rule of St Chrodegang and relish lives of comfort and even luxury. But not poor Robert de Hane here.'

The steward and a servant came back with a three-branched candlestick and a pair of tallow dips, which greatly improved the lighting. De Wolfe seized the candelabrum and advanced to the bed, with Gwyn on the other side. 'Let's have a good look at this. How much of the cord did you leave attached to the beam?'

Gwyn held his hands about a yard apart. 'About this much. Another few inches were sticking out from the double knot around the rafter.'

De Wolfe held up the cut end of the rope that was still around the canon's neck. 'Another half yard here. Could he have reached from the privy seat to tie it to the roof?'

The Cornishman pursed his lips under the luxuriant cascade of ginger moustache. 'He's not very tall, but perhaps he could just do it on tiptoe.'

De Wolfe turned his attention to the knot in the monkish girdle. It was a pair of simple half-hitches, not a slip-knot. He pulled on the cord and the knot lifted well away from the skin. 'There's a gap in the mark under that, as would be expected,' he muttered, half to himself. The upper mark, tight under the front and right side of the jaw, was a clear groove with a faint spiral pattern corresponding to the twist of the flaxen cord. But slightly lower was a similar, less pronounced mark, with narrow reddened margins, that circled the whole circumference of the neck. As he had pointed out in the privy, near the back of the neck this lower mark showed a blurred blob of abrasion on the skin, from which two short tails projected, one in either direction. He used a bony finger to point it out to the Archdeacon. 'That's not a hanging mark, John. Someone has dropped the cord over his head and pulled the two ends tight from behind.'

'Are you sure?' asked the worried cleric. A dead canon was bad enough, but a murdered one was ten times worse.

'No doubt about it – it's almost horizontal and there's no gap where the rope pulled upward to the roof, like the other false mark. And those red swollen edges mean that it was done during life. They can't be seen on the upper line, so he was dead when that was caused.'

Thomas was hovering behind like a bumble-bee, stealing glimpses from beneath the larger men's elbows. He was desperate to be included in the affair and, despite the squint, his sharp eyes could see something in the candlelight. 'His mouth, Crowner! Surely that's bruising on the upper lip.'

Gwyn prodded him with a muscular elbow. 'Leave this to the men, dwarf,' he grunted, half teasing, half serious.

The coroner, though he often joined with Gwyn in making the disgraced priest the butt of their humour, had learned a sneaking regard for Thomas's powers of observation. He looked at the florid face of Robert de Hane and confirmed that even within the pinkish-blue hue of the skin, there were a couple of small patches of a deeper shade below the nostrils. Taking the lips in the fingers of each hand, he turned them back to expose the gums and brown, decayed teeth. 'Ha, the plot thickens!' he exclaimed.

On the inner surfaces of the upper and lower lips, there were angry red patches and a small tear where the lining had been forced against a jagged front tooth. Under the middle of the upper lip, the little band of membrane that anchored the lip to the gum was ripped and had bled. 'His mouth was either struck or violently squeezed,' declared de Wolfe, an authority on injuries after twenty years on a variety of battlefields.

'Held across the mouth to stop him crying out?' hazarded the clerk, emboldened by his successful contribution to the investigation.

'Let's have a look at the rest of his body, Gwyn,' commanded the coroner.

Under his black habit, the prebendary wore only a white linen nightshirt and a pair of thick woollen hose. The coroner's officer began to wrestle off the outer robe, helped ineffectually by Thomas. 'He's starting to stiffen up – and he's cold, except in the armpits,' observed Gwyn.

De Wolfe nodded. 'I noticed his jaw was tight when I turned his lips. He's been dead a few hours.'

Soon they had all the clothes off and the sparely built priest lay pathetically naked on his own bed. Instinctively, John de Alencon reached across and, for the sake of decency, draped the nightshirt across the lower belly and thighs.

The trunk was dead white, but there was a purplish discoloration of the legs below the knees. 'He's been hanging for a while, the blood has had time to settle in the lowest parts,' commented the coroner.

'So he was hung up soon after death as he still has a little heat left in him,' reasoned Gwyn.

John turned to the steward, hovering in anguish

near the door. 'When was your master last seen alive, Alfred?' he snapped.

'He came back from vespers, sir, at about the fifth bell. He ate his supper in the dining room – I served him myself.'

'Did he seem his normal self then?' asked the Archdeacon.

'Yes, sir, he was reading a small book as he ate.' Alfred snivelled and wiped an eye. 'Then he went to bed. As it is Christ Mass, he should have been going to the special service, some two hours earlier than the usual matins at midnight.'

De Alencon looked at the coroner. 'He was not there. I noticed, as I must keep track of who is absent.'

John de Wolfe grunted, his favourite form of response. 'He couldn't have been there as he was dead by then, if the stiffening is coming on now.' He scowled at Alfred. 'Did anyone visit him this evening?'

'Not that I know of, Crowner. Once he retires to this room, he is left in peace to sleep or study. His vicar or the secondaries might know better than I, but I doubt it.'

The ranking of the ecclesiastical community below the twenty-four canons consisted first of the vicars-choral, minor clergy over the age of twenty-four who deputised for their seniors so that their perpetual attendance at services was reduced. Then came the secondaries, adolescents over eighteen training for the priesthood, and below them, the choristers, young boys who might stay on to enter holy orders later.

The coroner turned back to the corpse and leaned over the bed to study it intently.

'The arms – look there,' squeaked Thomas.

His master glared at him. 'I can see for myself, damn

you!' he muttered testily, motioning to Gwyn to lift up the left arm. On the white skin, between the shoulder and the elbow, was a scatter of blue bruises, each half the size of a penny.

'They're on the other arm, too,' volunteered Gwyn. 'And they look fresh to me.'

De Wolfe gestured to his officer to turn the body over on to its face. 'Let's see the back of his neck.'

At the centre of the nape, a deep groove began and passed around the left side of the neck. On the right side of the neck, the groove imprinted by the noose rose towards the ear, then vanished. Below it, another continuous groove passed around the right side to the voice-box in front and joined the common groove on the left.

'What do those marks on his arms imply, John?' asked the Archdeacon.

The coroner stood back while Gwyn rolled the canon face-up again. 'Grip-marks, where he was seized. Those round bruises are from hard pressure by finger-tips.'

De Alencon's lean face was a picture of grief. 'What terror and pain he must have suffered. He was such a mild man, with never any exposure to violence – and then to end like this. What's to be done, John?'

A new voice answered him from the doorway. 'A hunt for his killers, with no effort spared, Archdeacon.' It was the sheriff, the coroner's dandyish brother-in-law. He strode into the room and looked down at the dead priest with more indignation than sorrow. 'What a thing to happen on the eve of Christ Mass!'

Almost on cue, the great bell of the cathedral opposite began tolling for the delayed matins. 'I must go. I cannot miss the service even for this tragedy,' explained the Archdeacon. 'And I must tell the other canons what's happened.' He went towards the door, then turned back to the coroner and sheriff. 'I will send word to the Bishop as soon as the gates open at dawn. But I know that although this happened within the cathedral precinct, he would want you secular authorities to deal with it.'

Although they were inside the city walls, the whole of the cathedral Close was outside the jurisdiction of the burgesses of Exeter, which often gave rise to friction. But murder was against the King's peace and even a bishop would be unlikely to exclude the law officers.

'I suggest the dead man lies here until the morning,' said de Wolfe. 'There's little point in setting up a hue and cry in the middle of the night, especially as he's been dead for hours and the trail is cold.'

Richard de Revelle waved an elegantly gloved hand at the Archdeacon. 'Tell Bishop Marshal that the sheriff will spare no effort to bring these devils to justice. They'll be dangling from the gallows by the time he returns from Gloucester.'

At this the coroner caught Gwyn's eye, but his henchman's face remained impassive, though de Wolfe could read his thoughts about the sheriff's arrogance. As de Alencon left, followed by the anxious steward and most of the residents, the two main law officers of Devon faced each other across the corpse, flanked by Gwyn and Thomas de Peyne.

'So what's this all about, John?' demanded Richard. He stood with one hand on his hip, his fine green cloak thrown back over one shoulder to reveal his richly embroidered tunic of fine linen. The smooth skin of his rather narrow face was pink, both from the cold air outside and from John's best wine.

Grudgingly, the coroner told him what little they knew so far. De Revelle seemed unconvinced, although he had just assured the Archdeacon that the killers would soon be found. 'You find a man swinging by his own girdle-cord in his own privy, yet you immediately claim he's been murdered?'

As always, his tone of patronising criticism made de Wolfe itch to punch him on his sharp nose but, with an effort, he held his temper in check. 'A senior priest is hardly likely to jeopardise his entry into heaven by taking the life God gave him – especially almost on his Saviour's birthday! But we don't need theology to prove that. Just look there.' He pointed at the still figure on the bed. 'Does a suicide bruise his own arms, strike himself in the mouth and then, before he hangs, throttle himself from behind?' he asked sarcastically.

The sheriff sniffed delicately. He had no interest in the state of the body, only in any political implications that might involve him. He needed to avoid trouble, but also to milk the best advantage for himself with influential people like Bishop Henry Marshal, brother to William, Marshal of England. 'Cover the fellow up, for God's sake!' he snapped imperiously at Gwyn, flicking a glove at the folded blanket at the foot of the bed. Then he turned to leave. 'I'll send up to the castle to get Ralph Morin to send men-at-arms to search the town.'

Morin was the constable of Rougemont, the castle perched at the highest point of the city in the north-east corner of the walls. It took its name from the colour of the local sandstone from which it was built.

De Wolfe was scornful of this useless gesture. 'What are they going to do after midnight? Beat every passer-by into a confession?' Knowing de Revelle's methods, he thought that this was not as fanciful as it might sound.

The sheriff gave John another of his pitying looks, as if humouring a backward child. 'And how would my new coroner handle it, then?'

John angrily opened his mouth to shout that he was the King's coroner, not de Revelle's, but bit back the words: they had been through these arguments time and again. The sheriff resented the establishment of coroners in England four months previously, but he was in no position to defy the edicts of Hubert Walter, Archbishop of Canterbury and Chief Justiciar to Richard the Lionheart. 'We need to know *why* Robert de Hane was killed,' he said tersely. 'Then that should tell us *who* killed him. Rushing aimlessly around the streets will get us nowhere.'

'Was it robbery? Some of these prebendaries are rich men,' asked de Revelle, going off at a tangent.

For answer, de Wolfe waved a hand around the bare room. 'Not this one. He has a reputation for a modest, even Spartan way of life. There's little worth killing for here.'

The sheriff seemed to lose interest. 'We'll leave it until the morning, then. I must get back to my good wife.'

John straightened his back until his head almost touched the ceiling beams. 'I'll walk back to my house with you, then.'

De Revelle pulled on his gloves. 'Lady Eleanor has gone back to Rougemont. I sent her with an escort when I came here. Your guests have dispersed, I'm afraid.' He said it with a certain spiteful glee, knowing that his sister would blame her husband stridently for the collapse of her cherished social occasion.

The sheriff was right, for when John arrived in Martin's Lane ten minutes later, he found the hall deserted, the table scattered forlornly with empty cups, tankards and scraps of food. Brutus still lay before the dying fire and gave him a slow wag from his bushy tail, the only welcome he was to get that night.

When he climbed the wooden stairs from the backyard to the solar chamber, he found a grim-faced Matilda sitting in the only chair. The rabbit-toothed Lucille was unpinning her hair and helping her off with her new kirtle of stiff brocade and laying out her bed-shift.

There was an ominous silence until the ugly Frenchwoman left for her cubicle under the stairs. Then the storm broke. 'You've done it again, husband,' Matilda snarled. 'You seem to delight in spoiling every effort I make to increase your standing with the better folk in this city.'

'Increase my standing, be damned!' he retorted. 'I'm the King's coroner, I don't need to kiss the arses of any burgesses or bishops. If you want more social life, so be it – but don't pretend it's to advance my career for I'm quite content as I am.'

Matilda had never been one to duck a fight and she counter-attacked with relish, her solid, fleshy face as pugnacious as that of a mastiff. 'You're content, are you? I should think so! You spend most of your time in taverns or in bed with some strumpet. You use this new job as an excuse to avoid me. You're away from home for days and nights at a time – God knows what you get up to!'

'A senior canon of this cathedral has been murdered, Matilda. You're so thick with the clergy of this city, surely you know what a scandal this will be. Did you expect me to tell the Bishop when he returns that

I was sorry I couldn't attend to it but my wife was having a party?'

They had had this particular argument so often that de Wolfe was bored with it. Her accusations were always the same, and none the less objectionable because there was some truth in them. Married for sixteen years, he had spent as much of that time as he could away from her, campaigning in England and abroad. Now forty years old, he had been a soldier since he was seventeen and rued the day his father had insisted that he marry into the rich de Revelle family. 'If I'm often away, it's because the responsibilities of being coroner force it upon me, woman,' he growled. 'You were the one who was so insistent on me seeking the appointment. You nearly burst a blood vessel canvassing on my behalf among the burgesses, the priests and your damned brother.'

Had she but known it, her efforts had been unnecessary. Both Justiciar Hubert Walter and Richard Coeur de Lion himself had been more than happy to give the post to a Crusader knight whom they both knew well – in fact, John de Wolfe had been part of the King's escort on that ill-fated journey home when he was captured in Austria. But once the bit was between her teeth, Matilda wanted no excuses from her saturnine husband. Angrily she flounced on to the low bed and struggled to change from her chemise into her nightshift under the sheepskin covers to hide her naked body from him. This was no punishment for John, who had long given up forcing his husbandly duties upon her. Six years older than him, she had never been keen on consummation, which was perhaps why they had remained childless all these years.

'Being coroner doesn't mean you have to live in the

saddle of that great stallion of yours – when you're not riding a two-legged mare, that is,' she added nastily. Pulling out her thin chemise after wrestling on the nightgown, she threw it at the chair and returned to the fray. 'My brother is the sheriff of all Devon, yet he doesn't spend his days tramping across the county. He has men and stewards to do his bidding. But you have to pretend to be needed everywhere, just to get away from home.'

De Wolfe's thick black brows came together in a scowl. 'I don't have a constable and men-at-arms and a castle full of servants at my beck and call like your damned brother! All I have is my officer and a clerk.'

She laughed scornfully. 'That hairy Cornish savage and a poxy little priest! They were your choice. Richard would have given you two better men, if you'd accepted them.'

'I owe my life to Gwyn, several times over. There's no more trustworthy man in England. As for Thomas, he writes a better hand than anyone in this city – and you know damned well that I was obliging the Archdeacon when I took him on, for John de Alencon is his uncle.'

Sitting up in bed, the heavy fleeces clutched to her breasts, Matilda glowered at him. With that white linen cloth wound around her hair like a turban, she reminded him of a Moorish warrior he had fought hand-to-hand at the battle of Arsouf.

Also like the Moor, she threw something at him suddenly, not a spear but a half-eaten apple that had been on the floor alongside the mattress. 'Oh, go to hell, you miserable devil!' And with those final words, she slid down the bed and violently pulled the sheepskins over her head.

Slowly de Wolfe took off his own outer clothes, blew out the tallow dip that lit the room, then slid into the opposite side of the large bed. Lying back to back, there was only a yard between their bodies, but a mile between their souls.

Listening to her regular breathing, as she feigned sleep, he sighed. 'And a merry Christ Mass to you, too!' he muttered bitterly.

CHAPTER TWO

In which Crowner John talks to the canons

Unless occupied with other duties, it was the habit of Sir John de Wolfe to enjoy a second breakfast with his two retainers at about the ninth hour, after the cathedral bell had tolled for the services of terce, sext and nones, which preceded high mass. He had already eaten at seven that morning, alone in the dank, empty hall in Martin's Lane. Mary had given him hot oaten porridge, to keep out the winter cold, followed by slices of salt beef and two duck eggs on barley bread. She was a buxom, dark-haired woman of twenty-five, born of a Saxon mother and a Norman soldier who had not stayed for the birth.

As she stood near de Wolfe to pour him more ale, he absently laid a hand on her rounded bottom, more for comfort than in lust. In the past, they had enjoyed more than a few romps together in the hut she occupied in the backyard. But Mary, keen to keep her job, had refused him for some time past, sensing that her arch-enemy Lucille was suspicious of them. 'I'm in disfavour again, Mary,' he announced in a low voice, looking up furtively at the narrow window high on the inner wall that connected the hall to the solar.

'She had her heart set on that party last night being a great event,' murmured the maid. 'When you left with

the Archdeacon – and especially when her brother
followed you – the whole thing went flat and they
all drifted away. She'll not forgive you that for a long
while yet.'

Matilda pointedly failed to appear at the table, and
after his breakfast and a visit to the privy, John had a
perfunctory wash in a leather bucket of cold water in
the yard: it was Saturday, his day for such ablutions,
though not for his twice-weekly shave. Mary had set
out his weekly change of clothing in front of the
smouldering fire and he slowly climbed into a linen
undershirt and a plain grey serge tunic that reached
below his knees. Thick woollen hose came up to his
thighs – he wore no breeches or pants unless he was
going to ride a horse – and a pair of pointed shoes
reached to his ankles. Buckling on a wide belt that
carried his dagger – no sword was needed in the city
streets – he swung a mottled grey wolfskin cloak over
his shoulders and pulled on a basin-shaped cap of
black felt, with ear-flaps that tied under his chin. Then,
yelling farewell to Mary, he left for the castle, where the
sheriff had grudgingly given him a tiny room above the
gatehouse for an office.

At the drawbridge of Rougemont, the solitary sentry
greeted him by banging the stock of his lance on
the ground, a respectful salute for a knight whom
every soldier knew had been a gallant Crusader and
a companion of the Lionheart himself.

He climbed the narrow stairs to the upper floor
of the tall gatehouse, which had been built, like the
rest of the castle, soon after the Conquest, by King
William the Bastard, who had demolished fifty-one
Saxon houses to make space for it. His office was a bare
attic under the roof-beams, bleak and draughty, with

a curtain of rough sacking over the doorless entrance at the top of the stairs. There was no fireplace and the miserable chamber reflected the scorn with which Richard de Revelle regarded this new-fangled office of coroner. He considered it a slight on his monopoly of law enforcement in the county – a view shared by most sheriffs across England.

The coroner's team gathered here every morning to discover what calamities had occurred overnight, and today, though it was Yuletide and a religious holiday, the death of Canon Robert de Hane was high on the agenda.

De Wolfe sat himself on the bench behind his crude trestle table, with Thomas hunched on a stool at one end. The clerk was carefully copying a list of last week's executed felons on to another parchment, his quill pen almost touching his thin, pointed nose as he scribed the Latin words in an elegant script, his tongue protruding as he concentrated.

Gwyn of Polruan, named after the Cornish fishing village where he was born, perched in his favourite place, on the stone sill of the small window opening. As he looked down at the narrow street that led to the steep drawbridge below, he cleaned his fingernails absently with the point of his dagger.

The coroner sat with his long dark face cupped in his hands, elbows on the table. He usually spent this time of the morning struggling with his Latin grammar, as belatedly he was learning to read and write, under the tuition of one of the senior cathedral priests. But today his mind was on other ecclesiastical matters, trying to fathom who would want to kill an apparently innocuous old scholar.

'Thomas, you know much of what goes on in the

Close,' he said suddenly, in his deep, sonorous voice. 'Have there been any whispers or scandals there recently?'

The clerk, always eager to air his ecclesiastical knowledge, put down his quill. His bright button eyes fixed on the coroner and his head tilted like a bird. Like his master, he always wore black or grey, though his long tube-like tunic was shabby and worn, as he was poorer than the most penurious church mouse. 'Nothing about Robert de Hane, Crowner. He was the quietest of all the canons. He had no mistress or secret family placed in a distant village, like some of his fellows.'

'As far as you know, toad,' trumpeted Gwyn. 'I wouldn't trust any priest out of my sight with half a penny – or with my wife!'

De Wolfe had never discovered the cause of the Cornishman's antipathy to the clergy, in spite of being daily in his company for the past twenty years. 'Is there nothing these days to set tongues clacking about the cathedral?' persisted the coroner. 'With all those servants, vicars, secondaries, choristers, surely there must be some jealousies and intrigues afoot!'

Thomas racked his brains to dredge up some scandal to satisfy his master and bolster his own reputation as a source of inside information. He slept rent-free on a straw mattress in a servants' hut behind one of the canon's houses, thanks to the intercession of his uncle, the Archdeacon. He ate sparingly, either at food stalls in the streets or sometimes cooked a little of his own food in the kitchen hut in the backyard. On a salary of twopence a day, which came from the coroner's own purse, he would never get rich, but at least he would survive. That was more than he could have said of the previous two years, when he had almost starved to death in Winchester. The youngest son of a Hampshire knight, his spine and hip had been afflicted as a child by the disease that had killed his mother, but an aptitude for learning had directed him into the Church. After ordination, he had become a diocesan clerk and junior teacher at Winchester, where he had become valuable as an excellent writer of Latin. His teaching duties had been his downfall, as his pupils included some young girl novices from the nunnery. His physical faults, such as the bent back, the limp and the lazy eye, had made him so unattractive to women that he had no experience of them at all. When one precocious novice amused herself by making eyes at him, his clumsy attempts to embrace her had resulted in a charge of attempted rape. Poor Thomas had been arrested by the cathedral proctors and only the fact that he was a priest and that the alleged offence had occurred in the precinct saved him from the sheriff's justice and a probable hanging. As it was, the Consistory Court had tried him and summarily ejected him from the priesthood, which meant that his stipend and lodgings vanished. He had tried to eke out an existence by writing letters for tradesmen, but after a year or so, he had been virtually in rags and starving.

Desperate, he had walked to Exeter to throw himself on the mercy of his father's brother, Archdeacon John of Alencon. His uncle gave him a little money to keep him alive and promised to look out for some suitable employment. In September, the newly appointed coroner had needed a clerk to keep his inquest rolls and the Archdeacon had prevailed upon his friend John de Wolfe to take the disgraced priest on probation.

In spite of the largely assumed scorn with which the two big fighting men treated the stunted clerk, the arrangement worked well and Thomas's undoubted skill with a pen was reinforced by his value as a seeker-out of information. He was incurably inquisitive and had a knack of worming information from people and sifting gossip, which the coroner had found invaluable in the tightly knit communities of Devonshire.

Now, however, as Thomas tried to recall any recent rumours that might in any way be connected to the murder of the canon, nothing came to mind. 'The only hints of intrigue I've heard in the Close concern outside matters – and they were political, rather than ecclesiastical,' he said thoughtfully, tapping his chin with the end of the feathered quill.

Gwyn, who was lifting a stone jar of cider on to the sill, was scornful of the clerk's efforts to be useful. 'We've got a dead canon to deal with, so what's politics got to do with it?'

'Let's hear about it, anyway,' countered de Wolfe. 'We've nothing else to follow up.'

Thomas made a rude face at the Cornishman before continuing. 'It's only a glimmer of a rumour, really, but I overheard it several times from different people. They were guarded and spoke in a roundabout way, but I had the impression that some of the barons and, indeed, some prominent churchmen are chafing at the way the King seems to have abandoned England for Normandy and left William Longchamp as Chancellor and Hubert Walter as Chief Justiciar.'

De Wolfe was indignant. 'King Richard would never abandon his country, for Christ's sake! He has to fight that yellow-bellied Philip of France to keep Normandy intact, after John – that fool he has for a brother – tried to give it away when he was imprisoned in Germany.' The coroner was almost obsessively loyal to Richard, after serving him so closely at the Crusade: he took any criticism of his monarch as a personal affront.

Thomas was immediately on the defensive. 'I'm only repeating the gossip, Crowner. Everyone hates Longchamp and though Archbishop Walter,' he paused to cross himself, 'is not himself unpopular, these crushing taxes he has imposed to support the King's campaigns certainly are.'

Gwyn joined in the argument as he reached for the loaf and hunk of cheese that were sitting in a stone niche in the bare wall. 'People have always grumbled about their rulers and their taxes. It's only natural.' He hacked off a culf of bread for each of them with his dagger and chopped the hard cheese into three portions. 'So what's this to do with our dead canon?' he asked, handing round the food.

'Nothing, I suppose. I was only repeating what tittle-tattle is current,' squeaked Thomas.

De Wolfe stared suspiciously at his clerk. 'Is it just idle talk, Thomas? I know you, and your crafty mind wouldn't have brought this up unless you knew something more.'

The scribe wriggled on his stool. 'Not so much what is said, Crowner, as the way some people around the cathedral are talking. They look over their shoulders and lower their voices – or change the subject if they sense me eavesdropping.'

'That's no wonder, everyone knows what a nosy little turd you are!' growled the Cornishman, pouring rough cider from a stone jar into three mugs set on the table.

Thomas made a vulgar gesture at him with two

fingers, borrowed from the archers who had escaped having their bowstring digits chopped off by their enemies. 'More than that, Sir John, I overheard, at a small feast for St Justinian the other day, two vicars-choral who had their heads together over the wine. It seems one had heard the cathedral Precentor, Thomas de Boterellis, talking to another canon after Chapter. They were discussing some imminent meeting with the Count of Mortaigne, at which Bishop Marshal was to be present. They broke off when they saw they were being overheard.'

The coroner chewed this over in his head. Prince John was the Count of Mortaigne: it was one of the titles – to a Normandy province – that the King had recently restored to him, as part of his forgiveness for having plotted against him. The Prince had been across the Channel for most of the time since Richard's release last March, but he was reported to have been seen back in England recently.

'Why shouldn't the bishop talk to his sovereign's brother?' Gwyn always contradicted the clerk on principle.

Thoughtfully, de Wolfe washed down his bread and cheese with a swig of the sour cider. 'It bears keeping in mind, though. Both Bishop Marshal – and his Precentor – were supporters of John's treachery last year, though I can't see any connection with our dead priest. But keep your ear to the ground, Thomas.'

When their morning repast was finished, the coroner spent a few laborious minutes at his Latin lesson, silently mouthing the simple phrases from the parchment supplied by his mentor. Thomas watched him covertly, wishing he could use his considerable teaching skills to help his master, but conscious of the coroner's sensitivity over his inability to read and write. Before long, de Wolfe dropped the vellum roll impatiently and stood up, stooping slightly as his knuckles rested on the table. 'It's too early to go down to the cathedral – the priests will still be at their high mass. I'll walk across to have a word with our sheriff and see if I can get any sense out of him about how we pursue this killing.'

He pushed through the sacking and stumped down the narrow stairs, bending his head to avoid the low roof of rough stone, built by Saxon masons under Norman direction. Rougemont had been erected on William's direct orders in 1067 after he had captured Exeter following an eighteen-day siege. It was said that the Conqueror had personally paced out the foundations for the keep and it was towards this that John made his way. The castle occupied the high north-eastern part of Exeter, cutting off a corner of the city walls, first built by the Romans. Outside this inner ward, beyond a deep ditch, was the wide zone of the outer bailey, itself protected by an earth bank and a wooden stockade. Here, a jumble of shacks and huts housed soldiers, their families and their animals – a cross between an army camp and a farm.

De Wolfe's loping strides took him across the inner ward, surrounded by crenellated walls of red sandstone. As he walked through the frozen mud towards the keep, he heard chanting from the tiny chapel of St Mary on his right, where the castle chaplain was celebrating Christ Mass. On his left was the Shire Court, a bare stone box where the sheriff held his county court and the King's Justices came at intervals to hold the Eyre of Assize. His destination was straight ahead, almost against the further curtain wall, which ran along the edge of a low cliff above Northernhay. The keep was a squat structure of two storeys above an undercroft, a semi-basement that housed the castle gaol. The entrance was up wide wooden steps that led to a door on the first floor. In times of siege, the stairs could be thrown down to prevent attack from ground level, though Rougemont had not been at war for almost sixty years.

As John walked across the inner bailey, familiar sights, sounds and smells assailed him – the neighing of horses in stalls built against the walls where tattered huts also housed kitchens, wash-houses, and the shanty dwellings of senior soldiers and castle servants. Chickens, pigs and goats wandered through the mire, adding their ordure to the rubbish trodden into the mud, where hardly a blade of grass survived. The Yuletide holiday seemed to make little difference to the usual chaotic routine of life. Smoke rose from a score of cooking fires, while men-at-arms, their women and a few ragged children criss-crossed the busy area.

A soldier, wearing a thick leather jerkin and a round helmet with a nose-guard, stood at the foot of the staircase to the keep. Like the man at the gatehouse, he stiffened and saluted the King's law officer.

In the hall above, there was a scattering of people, fewer than on a normal working day. Most were castle servants, clerks and squires, who were clustered around the great fireplace as the morning was raw and frosty. De Wolfe ignored them and marched across to a small door where yet another man-at-arms stood: Richard de Revelle liked to display his importance with a full contingent of largely unnecessary guards.

Nodding absently to the soldier, de Wolfe pushed open the heavy studded door and walked into the sheriff's chamber. This was the room de Revelle used for his official duties, and beyond it were his living quarters. He spent most of his time here, going home at intervals to Lady Eleanor at either Tavistock or Revelstoke near Plympton. His wife rarely deigned to stay in Rougemont's bleak accommodation, but at the moment was reluctantly in residence for the festival of Christ's birth.

When the coroner entered, the sheriff was seated behind a large table near the fireplace, reading a parchment roll. A clerk was hovering at his shoulder, murmuring and pointing out something on the document. Richard ignored de Wolfe's arrival, took a quill pen from the table, impatiently scratched out a word and wrote something alongside. John felt a stab of jealousy at the casual literacy of his brother-in-law, who in his youth had attended the cathedral school at Wells. The clerk took the corrected roll, bowed and scurried out, leaving his master to acknowledge the coroner's presence. 'No more dead prebendaries this morning, John?'

'It's no matter for levity, Richard,' snapped the coroner. 'That nest of churchmen down there has a great deal of power.' He pulled up a stool to the opposite side of the table and sat glowering at his brother-in-law. 'I'm going down to the Close shortly to hold an inquest, not that it's going to advance us much.'

De Revelle smoothed his pointed beard with a heavily ringed hand. 'The deceased seems an unlikely candidate for murder. Are you quite sure it wasn't a *felo de se*?'

De Wolfe groaned silently at the sheriff's persistence in pursuing the suicide theory. 'And strangled himself

first and gripped his own arms enough to bruise them?'
he reminded his brother-in-law.

The sheriff was silent. He would have had little
interest in the death except that he was a close friend
of Bishop Henry Marshal and Thomas de Boterellis,
the Precentor, whose job it was to organise all the
services at the cathedral. They would want a full investigation of this sudden demise of one of their canonical
brethren.

'Do you know anything of the man, Richard?'

'Nothing at all. To my knowledge, I never saw him
alive. He sounded a very retiring man of God.' He
looked across at the dark, bony man opposite. 'Have
you any idea why he should have been killed? If, in
fact, he didn't die by his own hand.'

The coroner shrugged. 'God knows – presumably!
Have any of the town watch or your men-at-arms
heard of any undesirables in the city at this holiday time?'

De Revelle laughed derisively. 'Undesirables? Half
the bloody population of Exeter is undesirable! Just
go around the taverns or take a walk at night into
Bretayne, if you doubt me.' Bretayne was the poorest
district, down towards the river, named after the original British who had been pushed there centuries
before when the Saxons invaded Exeter. 'But I'll ask
Ralph Morin if he has any recent intelligence.' He
yelled for his guard.

A few moments later the constable of Rougemont
entered the chamber. He was a large, powerful man,
with a weatherbeaten face above a forked grey beard
and moustache. They discussed the killing for a time
with this Viking-like figure, but the constable had
nothing to suggest. 'The usual riff-raff are in the

town, but no one who is likely to strangle a respectable priest. Nothing was stolen, as far as you can make out?'

De Wolfe shook his head. 'He lived a modest life, unlike some of his fellow canons. There seemed nothing worth stealing in his house.'

De Revelle stood up and paced restlessly to one of the narrow slits that did service as a window. He looked down at the inner ward, where two oxen were laboriously hauling a large-wheeled cart through the mire. 'Personally I don't give a clipped penny for the life of some idle old cleric, but the Bishop is going to want answers when he gets back from Gloucester in a few days' time.'

Morin pushed himself away from the fireplace on which he had been leaning, the huge sword that hung from his baldric clanking against a bucket of logs. 'I'll send Sergeant Gabriel out with a couple of men to twist a few arms – but if nothing was stolen, it's useless making the usual search for men overspending in the taverns and brothels.'

John uncoiled himself from his stool and moved to the door. 'I'll talk to as many of the holy men as I can today, before the inquest. And my sharp little clerk is trying to ferret out any episcopal gossip for me – he's picked up a few hints already.' The coroner looked pointedly at the sheriff, but de Revelle met his eye without a flicker.

De Wolfe and his two acolytes stood at the great west end of the cathedral as the crowd streamed out after the high mass on this special morning of the year. Matilda had returned to St Olave's for her devotions. John sometimes wondered if she fancied the parish priest there, even though he was a fat, unctuous creature.

After the worshippers had dispersed from the cathedral steps along the many muddy paths of the Close, the clergy came out, eager for their late-morning lunch. With black cloaks over their vestments, they walked in small groups back to their various dwellings. Some went towards Canons' Row, others to houses and lodgings scattered throughout the precinct. Many of the vicars and secondaries walked down to Priest Street* on the other side of South Gate Street, not far from de Wolfe's favourite haunt, the Bush tavern, whose landlady, Nesta, was his mistress.

The coroner was lying in wait for several of the senior clerics, to question them about last night's events. The Archdeacon had promised to collect those canons who had best known Robert de Hane and deliver them to him before they vanished for their midday meal.

'What about the inquest?' demanded Gwyn, whose duty it was to round up a jury, whose members would include anyone who might have information about the sudden departure of the canon from this earthly plane.

'Better let them eat first – half have disappeared already,' replied de Wolfe. 'Catch them before the next service begins. That'll be vespers.'

The priestly staff of the cathedral were supposed to attend no less than seven services every day, beginning at midnight matins. The longest period free of devotions was between late morning and mid-afternoon.

'There he is, with a few canons in tow,' piped up Thomas, quickly making the sign of the Cross at such

* Now Preston Street.

a concentration of senior clerics. Although he had been ejected from the priesthood, he ached to remain accepted as one of the brethren and he never missed an opportunity to be in their company and included in their conversations.

The Archdeacon came out on to the wide steps, his spare figure enveloped in a hooded cloak, which hid the rich alb and chasuble underneath. As he moved towards the coroner, a trio of cloaked men sailed behind him. First was the Precentor, Thomas de Boterellis, then two other canons talking together, whom de Wolfe recognised as Jordan de Brent and Roger de Limesi. They were all residents of the row of houses where the death had taken place the previous evening.

John de Alencon greeted the coroner gravely, as did his three companions. 'Let us go to the Chapter House for our discussion. It will be more private,' he suggested.

Before they turned to re-enter the cathedral, de Wolfe told Gwyn to go back to Canons' Row, question any servants he could find and arrange the inquest there for two hours after noon. Then, motioning the delighted Thomas to accompany him, he followed the four priests inside. The congregation had now left and the vast, flagstoned nave was empty except for a few sparrows and crows that had flown in through the unglazed windows to pick up the crumbs left by the hundreds who had gathered for Christ Mass before the great choir-screen that separated them from the choir and chancel.

The Archdeacon strode across to the south side of the building, where between the outer wall and the great box of the choir a passage passed the base of the south tower. Here, a small door led out to the Chapter House, a small two-storey wooden building. There was talk of replacing it in stone, once the Bishop had agreed to give up part of the garden of his palace, which lay immediately to the east.

'We can use the library above,' said de Alencon. 'It is quiet – and most fitting, as poor de Hane spent most of his time there.' He led the way into the bare room, the walls lined with pews, where the daily Chapter meetings were held. In one corner was a wooden staircase, leading to the upper floor, which acted as the library and archives of the diocese. They climbed up to find a musty chamber half filled with high writing-desks, each with a tall stool.

Thomas de Peyne made himself useful by opening two of the shuttered windows to let in some light along with the keen east wind. It allowed them to see that shelves around the walls were crammed with parchments and vellum rolls, with more on the desks and piled in heaps on the floor. There were some sloping shelves along one wall, with heavy leatherbound books securely chained to rings screwed into the wood.

The Archdeacon clucked in concern. 'This place needs attention,' he murmured.

Jordan de Brent sighed. 'The place is too small, brother. It's high time it was rebuilt and enlarged. Last year we had a great influx of old manuscripts from many of the parish churches, sent here for safe-keeping. It was on these that Robert de Hane was working.'

Roger de Limesi nodded agreement. 'I helped him when I could, but it was a hopeless task without proper storage.' He waved a hand around the untidy chamber. De Limesi was a thin, almost cadaveric man, with two yellow teeth that protruded from below each end of his upper lip, fangs that gave the unfortunate man an almost animal-like appearance.

'Find a seat, if you can,' invited John de Alencon, clearing a space for himself on one of the stools.

When they were all settled in a ragged circle, with Thomas standing dutifully at his master's shoulder, de Wolfe began his questions. In deference to his rank, he addressed himself first to the Archdeacon. 'We need to find some reason for the death of this mild-mannered colleague of yours. Can you throw any light at all on this?'

De Alencon threw back his cloak, although the unheated room was as cold as the Close outside. 'Even a few hours' reflection has failed to bring anything fresh to my mind. Let us ask someone nearer to him if he has any comments.' He turned his nobly ascetic face to Jordan de Brent, who was a complete contrast to his fellow canon Roger de Limesi: he was plump and had a round moon face with a rim of sandy hair around a shiny bald head. He wore a permanent smile of vague beneficence and it was something of a surprise to hear his deep, booming voice when he spoke.

'He was indeed a gentle soul, devoted to the study of his beloved Church.' De Brent waved a fat hand around the library. 'For over a year he spent much of every day, when he was not at his devotions, sorting and studying the old records here, from all over Devon and Cornwall.'

De Wolfe shifted impatiently on his stool. 'But why should such a man come to an evil death?'

Jordan de Brent lifted his ample shoulders in a Gallic gesture. 'God alone knows, Crowner! But I will say that recently his manner seemed to change somewhat.'

The Archdeacon's lean face inclined towards him. 'In what way, Brother Jordan?'

'For several weeks now, he had been – what shall I say? – well, excited. Normally he was quiet to the point of being withdrawn, a dreamy, contemplative fellow, his mind locked in the past.'

'And do you know the reason for this change?' demanded the coroner.

'No, I can't tell you that. But since, say, the first Sunday in Advent, he worked even longer hours. He was brisker, his eye shone – though sometimes he seemed almost furtive when I passed near his desk.'

'You are in charge of this place?' asked John, lifting a finger to point around the archives.

'"In charge" is, perhaps, putting it too strongly. But for eight years the responsibility of caring for the books and parchments seems to have devolved upon me, for want of anyone else to do it.'

The Archdeacon broke in. 'Brother Jordan is too modest – he is looked on by the Bishop and the rest of us as the cathedral archivist. He has a thankless task – but, then, we need no thanks on this side of the grave.'

'Have you any notion as to what he was working on that might have wrought in him this change?'

De Brent lifted a hand to smooth the non-existent hair on his shiny red pate. 'I can only assume that he found something of historical interest in the old rolls he was studying. He had written a few tracts on old churches from Saxon times, so I suspect he had made some new discovery.'

Again de Wolfe looked around the cluttered room.

'Have you no idea what he was working on, to become so elated?'

De Brent glanced at Roger de Limesi, but the haggard canon regarded him blankly, although he said, 'We could look through his parchments, I suppose. He always sat at that desk.' He indicated one in the far corner, piled with vellum rolls and loose sheets.

'That will take us a day or two,' observed the rubicund de Brent. 'His main interest was the early foundation of Norman parishes and how they were taken over from the previous Saxon incumbents.' He looked around rather warily, then relaxed when he had confirmed that no Saxons were present.

The coroner scowled at the lack of progress he was making. Then, deferentially, Thomas spoke up. 'I could examine all the documents to see if they hold any clue to this matter – or help the canons to do so,' he added hastily, afraid that in his enthusiasm he might have spoken out of turn.

Before they could either approve or deny his offer, the Precentor spoke for the first time. Thomas de Boterellis had a round face, with an unhealthy waxy sheen, in which were set small, cold eyes. 'I have something to add, though it may not be very helpful. I refrained from speaking before as the matter concerns the confessional – but as poor de Hane is dead I suppose no harm can be done.'

Five pairs of eyes swivelled towards where he sat astride his stool as if on a horse, his chasuble flowing down to the floor on each side.

'Carefully now, brother, if it is a sensitive issue of religious faith,' warned the Archdeacon.

The other canon shook his head. 'It is not that – and may have some slight bearing on this affair. Some weeks ago, I cannot recall exactly when, Robert de Hane came to me after a Chapter meeting, as I am – I was – his confessor.'

John de Alencon broke in to explain to the coroner. 'Each of us – even the Bishop himself – is allotted a fellow priest to take his confessions. Often we pair up to take each other's sins and give absolution.'

De Wolfe thought this a convenient system and was glad that the heretical Gwyn was not there to give one of his scornful grunts at these ecclesiastical tactics.

The Precentor continued with his story. 'We went as usual to kneel before the altar of St Richard and St Radegund at the west end of the cathedral. He confessed a few minor sins, which need not concern us, but then he unburdened himself of a more specific matter.'

'Have a care, Thomas,' cautioned the Archdeacon again, concerned about the inviolacy of the confessional.

Locked in his obsessional habit, the coroner's clerk crossed himself jerkily in anticipation of some dread revelation, but no heinous sin of the flesh was forthcoming.

'De Hane said that he had been guilty of greed and covetousness, but that he had seen the error of his ways in time so that his actions now would be for the glorification of God through his Church in Exeter.' De Boterellis stopped abruptly. 'That is all that was relevant but, coming from someone with such a lack of avarice as de Hane, greed and covetousness seemed rather incongruous.'

There was silence for a moment. 'And he was never more specific about what he meant?' asked de Wolfe.

'No, he refused to elaborate, saying that all would be made clear in the fullness of time. But people do say odd things under the emotion of the confessional.'

The Archdeacon had been staring at the cobwebbed roof-beams with an air of abstraction, but now brought down his bright grey eyes to fix them upon the coroner. 'I wonder if another small fact fits into this puzzle,' he mused.

The others waited expectantly.

'A week ago, I was discussing our finances with the Treasurer, John of Exeter, partly to forecast our income in the new year that is about to begin. Among many other matters, he said that he had had a rather vague promise of a substantial sum from one of our canons. I didn't press the matter to ask from whom it had come, as it is not uncommon for the more affluent of our brothers to make such donations – but it may tie in with de Hane's promise to his confessor.'

Privately, the coroner felt all this talk of canonical riches too vague to be of any use, but so far it was all he had by way of background on the dead man. 'So do you think that Robert de Hane had some hidden wealth, in spite of his outwardly modest style of living, and that he was killed in furtherance of its theft?' he suggested.

De Boterellis shook his pudgy face. 'When he confessed to me in such an indefinite way, the matter seemed in the future, that he was regretful for aspiring to keep what was going to come to him, rather than what he already possessed.'

There was another thoughtful silence among the circle of men perched on their high stools, until Jordan de Brent's deep voice broke it. 'One trivial matter,' said the archivist. 'Our brother Robert rarely left the cathedral Close. He was either at his devotions in the cathedral, or home, or here in the library. Yet in the past three weeks he vanished several times for a day on the back of a pony and returned with mud-spattered feet at dusk.'

'And you say that was unusual?' asked de Wolfe, who spent half his life on the back of a horse.

'Very much so – he was a most sedentary person. I've no idea where he went, he merely told me that he would not be here in the library on those few days. His vicar-choral and secondary must have stood in for him at services. They or his manservants might know where he went.'

This added scrap of information seemed to exhaust the meagre pool of knowledge about the late Canon de Hane, and after de Wolfe had arranged with Jordan de Brent for Thomas to sift through de Hane's manuscripts the hungry priests dispersed to their midday meals. The coroner and his clerk walked across to the house where the death had taken place. In it, there was an air of sadness that ill-befitted the festival of Christ's birth. The body still lay on the bed as the coroner had yet to hold the inquest. Afterwards it would be removed to lie in reverence before the high altar in the cathedral.

Gwyn was in the kitchen, a lean-to built against the back of the house, projecting into the narrow garden. Most of the canons' houses, originally wooden, had been refashioned in stone. They were long, narrow dwellings, one room wide with a main hall in front, then several small bedrooms, and various nooks and crannies for lodging guests and accommodating the resident secondary priest. The few male servants slept either in passages or in the shacks in the garden, which also had a stable, as well as the wash-house and the privy where the body had been found.

With the coroner's officer were two servants of the deceased canon, as well as a young secondary and a vicar who deputised for de Hane at many of the daily services. They all looked uneasily at the swarthy coroner as he swept into the kitchen.

Gwyn eased his huge frame off the corner of the table where he had been sitting. 'No one seems to have any light to shed on this affair, Crowner,' he growled, scratching his crotch vigorously, a habit he had akin to Thomas's tic.

De Wolfe's black brows descended as he scowled round the assembled faces. 'I've heard that the canon made some unaccustomed excursions on horseback out of Exeter these past few weeks. Did any of you accompany him?'

One of the servants, a young man named David, with muscles bulging through the sleeves of his plain hessian tunic, took a step forward. 'I made his pony ready for him, sir, and offered to go with him, but the Canon was most insistent that he went alone.'

'Was that unusual?'

'It was unusual for him to go anywhere at all, Crowner,' replied David, who seemed too bright and intelligent to be a lowly yard-servant.

Then, unwilling to be left out of the picture, his older colleague cut in, 'Though we have two good horses and a pony in the stable, they are hardly ever used. Their hoofs have to be trimmed for lack of wear on the road.'

'Have you any notion of where he went?' demanded de Wolfe.

'It couldn't have been very far,' said David. 'The

Canon, God rest his soul, was a timid horseman. The nag usually walked for him and rarely got up to a trot. On these trips, he never left the Close until the ninth hour of the morning, and he was back before the city gates shut at dusk, which is early this time of year.'

John glanced across at his bodyguard. 'Gwyn, what distance would a slow pony travel in that time?'

The Cornishman pulled at the ends of his shaggy moustache. 'Not far – perhaps to the edge of Dartmoor or down to Exmouth and back, I reckon. Depends on how long he stopped to conduct his business when he got there.'

The coroner turned back to the sturdy young groom. 'Do you know which way he went?'

David shrugged. 'Only on one of the three occasions did I see him leave the city, sir. I was buying fish in Carfoix and I saw him making down the hill towards the West Gate.'

De Wolfe made the usual grunting noise in his throat. 'That could lead him to half of Devon. You've no idea where he went or what he was doing?' he persisted, his eyes roving across the others, to be met with sorrowful shakes of their heads.

'He always took a roll of parchment in his saddle-scrip,' volunteered the younger man, hesitantly. 'And though the pony came back fairly clean, the Canon's boots and the hem of his robe were caked with red mud, for I had to clean them.'

'So he must have been walking somewhere away from his horse,' put in Thomas. This obvious interpretation was received by Gwyn with a pitying scowl.

As with the meeting with the canons, further questions led to no useful answers and the coroner became impatient. 'Now that it's daylight, let's look again at the place of his death,' he commanded. He led the group out of the kitchen into the cluttered yard, where chickens and ducks flapped from under their feet. The stench of the privy was no less in daylight, but de Wolfe climbed the rough steps and pulled open the rickety door. The remains of the girdle-cord still hung down from a gnarled rafter, the frayed end swinging gently in the cold breeze.

The coroner's gaze went to the edge of the planks that formed the seat of the privy, worn smooth by several generations of canonical buttocks. 'No scratches or mud there, Gwyn,' he observed. 'If he had hanged himself he would have had to stand on there to tie the rope above, then launch himself into eternity.' John turned and dragged Thomas forward. 'Get up there and see how far you can reach to the roof-beams.'

As the lame clerk scrambled awkwardly up on to the seat, Gwyn grabbed his leg and pretended to push him down one of the twin holes into the malodorous pit below. The clerk shrieked in terror and tried to kick him in the face.

'For God's sake, stop it, you pair of fools!' snarled de Wolfe.

'But the little runt is too small to reach,' objected Gwyn.

'The canon was only a hand's length taller, so lift him up a little,' snapped the coroner.

With a grin, the officer grabbed the clerk around his waist and hoisted him up a few inches. 'About there?' he demanded.

'Can you reach the knot now?' demanded de Wolfe.

Thomas waved his hands in the air, but they fell well short of the knot tied around the rafter that supported the woven wattle under the thatch.

'Is he high enough?' asked Gwyn again.

John stood back in the doorway to check Thomas's elevation compared to the dead man's height. 'Plenty high enough – so there's no way he could have tied the rope up there. Somebody much taller did it for him, standing on the seat.'

He motioned Gwyn to put Thomas down and his officer again resisted the temptation to drop the clerk into the ordure below.

'No more to see here,' grunted de Wolfe, and turned to face the handful of servants and priests who stood at the bottom of the privy steps. 'Did any of you see anything untoward out here last night? Any strangers in the yard or the house?'

There was a chorus of denials. Then the old steward spoke up. 'Most of the servants from the Close were either at their homes or at Yuletide revelries in the taverns, and the priests were either in the cathedral or celebrating at each other's lodgings.'

'And anyone can come to this yard down the side passage,' added the resident secondary, a pale young man with a hare-lip. 'From there they can come into the house through the back door.'

De Wolfe paced the yard, but could think of no way to further the matter. 'Right, the inquest will be held here at the second hour of the afternoon. All of you will be present.' He strode off up the side lane, making for home and a confrontation with his wife.

When he reached the house in Martin's Lane, however, only Mary was there. 'The mistress has gone off to St Olave's', she informed him archly, 'then to eat with her cousin in Fore Street, she said.' She wagged a finger at him. 'You're still in disgrace. Last night was a great disappointment to her.'

De Wolfe snorted in disgust. 'The bloody woman! The party was almost over – and only I and the Archdeacon left them.'

'It doesn't need much for the mistress to take umbrage,' observed Mary, sagely. 'Now then, Master John, do you want me to make you a meal?'

De Wolfe picked up his cloak again. 'No, dear Mary, I'll go down to the Bush before the inquest – I'll have a bite to eat there.'

As he marched out, the buxom maid murmured under her breath. 'I'll wager you're hoping to get more than a bite at the Bush, my lad!'

His favourite tavern, run by his favourite woman, was built with empty plots of ground on either side. This gave the name Idle Lane to the short cross street that joined the top of Stepcote Hill to Priest Street in the lower part of the city. The inn was a square, thatched building with frame walls filled with wattle-and-daub.

John pushed open the door, ducked his head under the low lintel and went into a hubbub of sound, smell and smoke. The fire glowing on a wide stone hearth had no chimney, but vents under the edge of the thatch allowed the fumes to filter out between the ends of the beams that supported the attic-like upper storey. As it was Yuletide, the place was full with men and a few women, making the most of the chance to drink during the day.

His usual place at a small table on the other side of the fire was occupied, but as soon as the old potman saw him with his one good eye, he unceremoniously pulled two youths off the bench and waved de Wolfe across. 'Morning, Cap'n, I'll tell her ladyship you're here.' Edwin was an old soldier half blinded in Ireland,

where he had also lost most of a foot. He always called
de Wolfe by his military rank, to acknowledge his
reputation as a fighting man.

The coroner slipped off his wolfskin cloak and
hung it behind his table across a screen, a wattle
hurdle hammered into the earth floor to keep off the
draughts. Within half a minute, Edwin was stumping
back to slap a quart pot of ale in front of him. 'She's
coming directly, Cap'n. Do you want some food?'

'Yes, and plenty of it, Sergeant. I could eat that old
foot of yours, if you'd still got it!'

The ancient cackled with glee, rolling the white,
collapsed eyeball horribly, then stumbled away to the
kitchen.

As he drank the warm ale gratefully, John looked
around at the throng. He nodded and spoke to a few
nearby, all of whom were well aware of his intimacy
with the landlady of the Bush. Many were tradesmen –
of all types, from tanners to wool fullers, from butchers
to tinsmiths. There were some off-duty men-at-arms
from the castle and a few burgesses, the upper echelon
of the merchants and traders in Exeter. The women
were either the mistresses of some of the men – never
their wives – or whores: their business never stopped
for festive days.

He heard Nesta's high voice shouting at her serving-
maid and cook somewhere at the back of the big room,
where Edwin was now busy drawing ale and cider from
casks wedged up against the wall. As trade was brisk, the
pottery mugs received only a token swill in a crock of
dirty water before he refilled them under the spigots.

This was life as John liked it, even though he
appeared a morose, solitary man. He was happiest in
the company of men, despite his appetite for women's

charms. After a few mugs of ale his tongue would loosen and he enjoyed telling tales of past campaigns, of travel in foreign parts and hearing the latest scandals from Winchester or London. To sit by a warm fire in a busy tavern and listen to the bustle of life around him, to exchange greetings with men he had known for years, was a comforting change from the sterile hours of silence or stilted conversation he suffered in the house in Martin's Lane. As he reflected on these things, he was suddenly and pleasantly interrupted. A warm body slipped on to the bench and pressed against him, a soft arm sliding through his. 'How is my favourite law officer today? I hear you had a busy night in the cathedral Close.' The owner of the Bush was a one-woman intelligence service: everything that took place in Exeter seemed to be common knowledge in the tavern within minutes of its happening.

John de Wolfe looked down at her with a rare smile of pleasure and affection. He saw a pretty auburn-haired Welsh woman of twenty-eight, with a heart-shaped face, a high forehead and a snub nose. Slightly under average height, Nesta was curvaceous, with a small waist and a bosom that was the object of many a man's dreams in the city. 'You are the best thing I've seen so far today, sweet woman,' he said, with mock-gallantry.

The redhead pretended to pout. 'As you've spent your time with the corpse of a strangled prebendary, that's no great compliment, sir!'

He squeezed her thigh with a big hand. 'If you know so much about my business, madam, maybe you'd like to tell me who are the culprits.'

She leaned across to take a drink from his mug, using the opportunity to press her breast against him. 'Give me a few clues and I'll solve it for you, John. But what else has been happening to you this past day or so?'

He sighed and slid an arm around her shoulders. 'I'm in disfavour with Matilda, once again.' He told her what had happened during her party last night.

He got little sympathy from his mistress. 'Poor woman! Fancy having such a husband as you! If you'd left my entertainment like that, I'd have blacked your eyes – and then banned you from my bed for a month.' She was only half joking, for though she had no particular liking for Matilda, she knew there was fault on both sides and that, when he chose, this man could be as awkward and stubborn as a mule.

He grinned at her as one of the maids arrived with his food. 'If she banned me from her bed for a month the only penalty would be that I was spared her snoring – for no other activity occurs on our couch, I can tell you.'

Nesta prodded him in the ribs in mock-outrage. 'A fine story! You couldn't keep your nightshirt down even if you were in bed with Bearded Lucy.' This was a repulsive hag, reputed to be a witch, who lived in a hut alongside the river. All the same, Nesta was secretly pleased to know that he claimed to keep his virility for her. 'Eat your victuals, Sir Crowner, and stop talking such nonsense.'

As he tucked into his food, for which the Bush had the best reputation among all the taverns in Exeter, Nesta was called away to settle an argument between the cook out in the yard and one of the maids. Using his dagger and his fingers, de Wolfe tucked into a slab of boiled bacon and fried onions that rested on a thick trencher of bread laid directly on the scrubbed boards of the table in lieu of a platter. The juices soaked into the trencher, which would be collected with all the others and given at the end of the day to the poor in the Bretayne district. As he ate his meat and spread yellow butter on to bread torn from a wheaten loaf, he felt calm and contentment spread though him, though the death of the canon still niggled in the back of his mind.

At the last mouthful, Nesta came back with a fresh quart of ale for him. 'Tell me about this poor man in Canons' Row,' she demanded. Although she was a prodigious source of information and gossip, he knew that his confidences were safe with her – not that much was ever confidential in this small city, where everyone considered their neighbour's business common property.

He told her what little he knew of the death of Robert de Hane and the lack of any apparent motive. He spoke in Welsh, as it was her native language and the one his mother had used with him as a child. Even when Gwyn was with them they talked in Welsh, for his own Cornish was similar, as was the Breton spoken by many visiting traders and shipmen.

'Why kill a harmless old man like that?' she asked, full of sympathy as always for the defenceless and the underdog. 'You say he had no wealth or possessions to steal?'

De Wolfe took a deep draught of his ale. 'There was some talk of his coming into wealth, which he was giving to the Church, but he had nothing that could be stolen from his house or his person.'

Her hazel eyes studied the strange man alongside her: he was not handsome, with that long gaunt face and beak of a nose, but he was tall, sinewy and utterly masculine. Though usually gruff and sparing with words, he could be loving and tender and she knew, to her great delight, that when roused he was a lover without compare, his long body a relentless machine for giving them mutual pleasure.

She had known him for six years, since her late husband Gruffydd had given up soldiering and bought the Bush Inn. John and Gruffydd had been together on several campaigns, the Welshman a master archer from Gwynllwyg* in south Wales, the home of the long-bow. Within two years, though, Gruffydd had been dead of a fever and Nesta was left with an inn and substantial debts. De Wolfe had loaned her money and paid for help in the tavern, until her own hard work had turned it into a successful business. It was only then that friendship had become passion, but she was well aware that it would never go beyond that: it was unthinkable that a Norman knight would leave his wife – especially a de Revelle – for a mere alehouse-keeper. Nesta also knew that he had other women tucked away around the county, but once again she settled philosophically, if reluctantly, for what she could get and was content to believe that she was his favourite.

She was silent long enough to make him look down at her and give one of his smiles, which was all the warmer for its rarity. 'Sweet woman, you know most of the gossip in this city. Are there any new whispers?'

She pretended to pout at his lack of romance. 'Crowner John, do you only want me for a spy? Am I of no use any longer to warm your bed – though it always seems to be my bed that you try to wreck in your frenzy?'

He slid a hand on to her plump thigh, smooth

* Present-day Gwent.

through the green woollen kirtle she wore under a white linen apron. 'I've no time today to warm your bed, more's the pity, my love. Gwyn will be chasing me before long for this inquest. But I wondered if your sensitive – and very pretty – nose had smelt any intrigues that may have a bearing on this murder. It seems like the work of men who knew what they were about, to make such an attempt to conceal murder as self-destruction.'

The Welsh woman grew serious. 'I know nothing remotely to do with dead canons, John. But there has been a strange atmosphere abroad these past few weeks, even for a month or two.'

'What do you mean – strange?'

'All manner of men come in here, from the city and further afield. From Cornwall going east, and from Southampton and London going west, as well as shipmen from Normandy and Brittany. I listen to all their chatter – many a contract is made in here and not a few dark plots, I'm sure.'

'What are you trying to say, woman?'

'Lately, there have been more furtive conversations, ones that break off when you pass their table. And more among the soldiering class, knights, squires and a few mercenaries, who would sell the use of their sword for a couple of marks.'

'How can you tell, if you can't hear what they say?' he objected.

Nesta turned up her hands in supplication. 'Just a woman's instinct – or maybe an inn-keeper's instinct. This doesn't affect the merchants and workmen but a higher class of customer, especially those who have a sword clanking under the table. Even old Edwin has noticed it, he says. He's the nosiest man this side of

Windsor and he tries to eavesdrop on people's talk, but he has been warned off more than once.'

'By whom, for instance?' persisted the coroner.

'There are some mercenaries, out-of-work squires, who sometimes pass through. They go to Plymouth or the eastern ports, seeking recruitment for wars in France or even from barons this side of the Channel. One threatened to cut off Edwin's ears if he persisted in hanging about their table.'

De Wolfe considered this, his black brows lowered in thought. 'This is interesting, though for different reasons than our deceased canon,' he murmured. 'Keep your ears open, Nesta love, this may be a return of the old trouble that afflicts England.'

CHAPTER THREE

In which Crowner John holds an inquest

A few minutes later, de Wolfe was back in the cathedral Close, where Gwyn and Thomas waited for him at the front of the dead canon's house.

'There are too many folk to fit inside so I moved the cadaver out into the backyard,' explained his officer. 'I've laid him on a bier we borrowed from the cathedral porch.'

They walked through the house and out at the kitchen door. Gwyn had taken a chair from the hall and set it against the wooden fence. In the centre of the yard was the bier, a stout wooden stretcher with four legs and handles, on which lay the mortal remains of Robert de Hane, decently covered with a linen bedsheet. In a wide circle around it stood the servants from the house, the vicar-choral, the secondary priest, two choristers and several similar residents from nearby houses.

As John took his solitary seat, a convoy of priests, their black cloaks billowing, hurried down the alleyway from the Close to join the throng. They included the Archdeacon, the Precentor, the Treasurer and half a dozen canons, including the two who had been at the meeting that morning. De Wolfe noticed that the sheriff was not among them: he had no legal obligation to be present.

Gwyn started the proceedings in the traditional way, enjoying his chance to bellow at a group of senior churchmen. 'All persons having anything to do with the King's coroner for the county of Devon, draw near and give your attendance!'

The buzz of conversation died down as those present gave their attention to the coroner.

'This is the inquest into the death of Robert de Hane, lately a canon of this cathedral,' began de Wolfe formally, his hard voice cutting incisively through the cold air of the winter afternoon. 'It is not the usual procedure as we are on ecclesiastical ground, which strictly is within the jurisdiction of the Church. However, Bishop Henry Marshal has agreed that whenever there is an unnatural death in the cathedral precincts he will defer to the secular authorities, embodied in the King's sheriff and coroner.'

He paused to look sideways at Thomas de Peyne, who was squatting on a small stool with a roll of parchment, quill and ink spread on a box before him. 'Normally, a jury would be gathered from all who might know anything about the death – in the countryside every man above twelve years of age from the Hundred or the four nearest townships should be summoned – though that is often an impossible task. Here we cannot drag half the population of Exeter into the Close, so I will make do with those who may have any information by virtue of their nearness to this house.'

He paused again, to let Thomas write a summary of what he had said, then went on. 'Where a corpse is found in the countryside it is also usual to demand presentment of Englishry. Here this is pointless, as we all well know the late Robert de Hane for a Norman.

And as there is no village or town to amerce for the death of a Norman and as this is Church ground, I will dispense with that aspect.'

'Not a lot left to say, then,' murmured Gwyn to himself, under cover of his huge moustache.

The coroner scowled around the expectant throng. 'Let the First Finder step forward.'

The servant who had discovered the body when he visited the privy the previous night trod hesitantly forward. He described in a few words that at about two hours before midnight he had found the canon hanging by the neck when he pushed open the door. When the shock had passed, he had run to the house and roused the older steward, then they had raced to the adjacent houses to raise the alarm. One of the servants remembered that Thomas de Peyne, the coroner's clerk, lodged in a nearby house. As they had a vague idea that this new official called the coroner had to be told about sudden deaths, Thomas was sought and he had taken control of the situation.

One by one, the servants from de Hane's house were called but, as John already knew, there was virtually nothing they could add.

'He was in his room from about the sixth bell,' quavered Alfred, the old steward, near to tears at the sight of his master lying still under the sheet in front of him. 'After that, I didn't see him again – alive.'

'Was that at all unusual, for him to stay alone all evening?' asked the coroner.

'Not at all, sir. He was a great one for reading and praying, or sometimes writing about his old churches. And he went to bed very early, as he was used to getting up at midnight for matins.'

The other servants all told the same tale, as did

Robert de Hane's vicar-choral and his secondary. De Wolfe avoided the matter of historical research and the canon's trips into the countryside, as he could not see that the inquest was the place to delve into those. When all who might have had anything useful to say had been heard, he rose from his chair and advanced with Gwyn to the bier.

'It is necessary for you, the jury, to examine the body, before coming to a verdict based on what you know, what you have heard and what you see on the corpse,' he said. He nodded to Gwyn, who pulled down the sheet to expose the cadaver as far as the waist. The Cornishman usually flicked off the death shroud to expose the whole body, but de Wolfe had warned him that in the presence of a gaggle of senior cathedral canons, he had better be a little more reverential. Even so, there was a communal sigh as the pallid skin of the dead priest was revealed. Reluctantly, the jury shuffled a step or two nearer at John's impatient gesture.

The coroner stepped to the side of the wooden stretcher and began to demonstrate to the onlookers. 'The victim had a cord around his neck, which sat in this upper groove.' He ran his finger around the deep valley under the left side of the corpse's chin. At the same time, Gwyn held up the offending ligature and showed it to the jury, like a mountebank conjuror about to perform a new trick. 'But that had not killed him,' barked de Wolfe. 'Here you also see a mark, lower down, which does not rise behind the ear.' Gwyn lifted the head and the coroner jabbed at the skin of the nape of the neck. 'Here there is a cross-over mark. A cord – no doubt the same one – was pulled from behind to strangle him.' Gwyn lowered the head and at a sign from his master held up the arms. 'On both arms, betwixt shoulder and elbow, there are fresh blue bruises, where he was gripped – see?' Finally, after Gwyn had replaced the arms by the sides, the coroner pointed at the dead man's mouth and turned out the lower lip to show the bruising inside. 'He was struck in the mouth – there!' Then de Wolfe stepped back and Gwyn pulled up the sheet with a flourish.

'Now, you jurymen, I suggest that you have little choice as to a verdict, given what you have heard and seen. It was not an act of God, like an apoplexy. It was not a misadventure, as no one is strangled accidentally in a privy. The taking of his own life would be extra-ordinary in a man of God who wishes to preserve his immortal soul – especially so near Christ's birthday. And, in any event, he could not assault himself then strangle himself before he hanged himself!'

There was a single nervous snigger among the jury, which attracted ferocious looks from the clergy.

De Wolfe glared around the assembled men and fixed on one, a servant from next door. 'I appoint you the spokesman. What is your verdict?'

Surprised, the man looked hurriedly around at his fellows, who all nodded vigorously, anxious to be compliant. 'We agree it was a killing, Crowner. Somebody else done it.'

John nodded briskly. 'I therefore declare that the death of Canon Robert de Hane was a homicide by persons as yet unknown. There is no question of amercing anyone. The First Finder seems to have done his duty correctly by immediately raising what amounts to a hue and cry. The surrounding four households were alerted, as the law demands. The coroner was notified without delay and the body was not moved or buried, so all these requirements were met. As I have said, the matter of presentment does not arise and, although he was a Norman, there is no question of a murdrum fine as the ground belongs to the Church.' He bowed his head perfunctorily to the canons in the back row before declaring the inquest closed.

As the jury and audience dispersed, the coroner went across to John de Alencon, who was standing with the Precentor, Thomas de Boterellis and the Treasurer, John of Exeter. 'The corpse is now yours. The legal processes are finished,' he said sombrely.

The Archdeacon stepped forward and laid a hand on the shoulder of the still form under the linen sheet. 'Poor Robert. We will arrange for him to be taken straight away to the cathedral. He can lie there with candles at his head and feet until we can bury him with due honour.'

Thomas de Boterellis fastened his small, beady eyes on John and demanded to know what was being done to arrest the perpetrators.

'That is the sheriff's task,' replied de Wolfe, 'but we both feel an obligation to seek out the killers. There are some pointers, but we have a long way to go, I fear.'

The cathedral Treasurer shook his head sadly. 'What a way to have to spend part of Jesus's birthday,' he said. 'We should all be celebrating, not mourning.'

After a few more minutes of commiseration in a similar vein, the group drifted away and de Wolfe told the house steward to have the body taken back into the house and to dress it in whatever was appropriate for a priest lying before the high altar.

The rest of that Yuletide day was an anticlimax, as far

as de Wolfe's coronial duties were concerned. After the inquest, he made his way slowly and reluctantly back to Martin's Lane, but was relieved to find that Matilda was still absent. He assumed she was deliberately shunning him, for which he was thankful, so he walked back to the Bush and spent a few hours in pleasant dalliance with Nesta, first in her bed upstairs then, in the early evening, over another good meal before the hearth downstairs.

When he eventually trudged home it was snowing fitfully, and this time he found his wife sitting grimly before a small fire in the gloomy hall. Matilda responded to his attempts at conversation with monosyllabic curtness, so John gave up trying to heal the breach and sat silently fondling his hound's ears until Mary came in to see if they wanted food or drink. Matilda shook her head sulkily, but her husband, determined to dull his smouldering resentment, called for mulled wine.

However, while this miserable holy-day evening was being endured in the coroner's household, others were pursuing the mystery of the canon's death: his clerk in the cathedral and his officer in another tavern.

Thomas de Peyne, eager as ever to prove his worth to his master, had already started his researches in the cathedral library. He had taken the Archdeacon's consent literally, and had obtained the key to the Chapter House from one of the cathedral proctors. With the light of a few candle ends from one of the side altars, he was poring over the parchments scattered on and around de Hane's desk. They were in total disorder and Thomas thought that either the old canon had been utterly disorganised in his way of working or that someone had been rooting though the rolls and sheets.

By the dim light of the guttering candles, the little clerk began to sort the documents into some kind of order, trying to match up separate sheets so that they followed a pattern. There were long rolls of sewn vellum, which were easier to deal with as the text was continuous, but sorting the many single sheets needed the patience of Job. Thomas, perched on a high stool, carefully compared sheet after sheet of parchment, checking the subject matter and the last few lines of Latin script, to match them where possible with other leaves to make continuous text. Some were single pages, but others were fragments of incomplete narratives. Many of the parchments were ancient, dry and brittle, often faded and discoloured, to the extent that they were virtually indecipherable. Some were ragged and frayed, or even torn in half. Many were palimpsests, sheets that had been used more than once previously, the old writing having been scraped off and the surface chalked so that they could be re-used. Parchment was sheepskin that had been laboriously treated to take ink – the best quality was vellum, the soft skin of young lambs. But all this effort was a task in which Thomas delighted: parchment and ink were more to him than food and drink and his exceptional literacy, in an age when fewer than one person in several hundred could read, made him the ideal choice for a nosy coroner's clerk.

In a couple of hours, he had made as much order as was possible among the material on the desk and the nearby floor and had a score of neat piles and rolls in front of him. During his sorting, he had gained a cursory impression of the subject matter and, as the archivist Jordan de Brent had said earlier, it was apparent that Robert de Hane's main interest had been in the early history of the parish churches in Devon, especially the transition from Saxon to Norman control soon after the Conquest.

There was much reference to the Domesday survey of 1086, and most of the parchments seemed to have been written by priests and canons in the decades after this. They were of all degrees of quality, both in penmanship and literacy; some were of fluent and elegant prose, others of a crude doggerel, written by country clerics with little learning apart from the ability to put quill to parchment to record bare facts.

That evening Thomas sat in the lonely archive room for hours, lighting one candle stump from another as the flame flickered down to the last blob of wax. He was fascinated by the stories of the days when a few thousand Norman invaders had subjugated two million Saxons and imposed a whole new administration, secular and religious, upon them.

But his task was to find something in these records that might shed some light on the canon's death. He sat back in the icy room to try to assemble his thoughts on what he had read so far. Most of the texts were factual records of the names of priests, both Saxon and their Norman successors, changes in manorial tenancies that affected the gift of the curacies and lists of grants, tithes and largess from new Norman lords who had ousted the Saxons from their lands.

But which one, thought Thomas anxiously, held a clue to the current tragedy? The coroner seemed convinced that de Hane's death was connected with his researches in the archives. As the clever little man reviewed in his head the parchments he had just scanned, he failed to see anything that might have had a financial aspect, such as was hinted at by de Hane's confession and the vague promise to the cathedral Treasurer.

The only faint clue he had found was a pen mark in the shape of a cross in the margin of one parchment. Many of the documents were so creased and stained that marks were abundant, but Thomas's expert eye saw that the ink on this little crucifix was fresh. The mark was on a single sheet of aged parchment which had a few paragraphs about the original Saxon landowners of some land west of Exeter – and about those Normans who had acquired it after the Conquest. Thomas recognised the parchment as one of a number of sheets that between them covered most of the county. Unfortunately the little ink mark was not against any particular parish or hamlet, but was at the start of a line in Latin that contained the word 'Saewulf'. The clerk knew this to be the name of a Saxon earl who had been a substantial landowner in the county and whose name cropped up time after time in the Domesday survey. Thomas also noticed that the mark had been made against the first of many entries of Saewulf's name in the parchments that he had sorted, so he reasoned that whoever had drawn the cross had a particular interest in the long-dead noble. The fresh look of the mark strongly suggested that it must have been made by Robert de Hane as, according to the other canons, no one had looked at these dusty archives for many years.

The little clerk sat back on his stool in the gloom and pondered his find. It did not seem to help much, as it gave no clue as to where geographically de Hane's interest might have lain. He turned over the sheets following the marked one and saw that Saewulf's name was attached to many manors and villages, which he had owned before 1067. There was no indication by any other fresh marginal mark of which of Saewulf's possessions might be singled out for special attention and, even after another hour of squinting in the flickering illumination of the remaining candles, the coroner's assistant failed to make any other discoveries.

Twenty miles from Exeter, another Yuletide celebration was being held that evening in Berry Pomeroy Castle, a square tower perched on the edge of a lonely crag two hundred feet above the Gatcombe brook. Around it on the other three sides was a bailey, protected by a wooden palisade with a central guard-tower and massive wooden gates. Henry de la Pomeroy had invited a number of his more noble neighbours to a banquet, which was in the last stages of preparation in the kitchens outside. In the hall, which occupied the whole of the first floor of the donjon, sixty people were already sitting at long tables being regaled with drink and entertainment from musicians, mummers and jugglers as they waited for the food. The walls were decorated with holly, fir branches and mistletoe, and two huge fires burned in chimneyed hearths to keep at bay the cold wind that moaned up the narrow valley below the castle.

The upper table was for the host and his most favoured guests, but the three centre chairs remained empty until the meal began. The absentees were in an upper chamber, on the floor divided into solar, chapel and guest rooms. They were drinking wine, standing around a glowing fire in the hearth. This was their host's first Yuletide as lord of Berry, following the violent death of his father earlier in the year – an incident his guests were careful to avoid mentioning.

Henry de la Pomeroy was a thick-set, short-necked man of thirty years, though he looked older. His large, drooping moustache was of the same mousy brown as his long hair, but he sported no beard. Henry wore a permanently aggrieved expression, as if the whole world were conspiring to annoy him. He had worried one wife into an early grave and was working on the second.

'This retaliation you promised to arrange for me, Bernard. You say it is fixed for tomorrow?' He waved his wine cup at his cousin, Bernard Cheever, who held several manors along the lower reaches of the river Dart. Cheever, a dapper man of more placid nature than Pomeroy, smiled amiably. 'Don't fret about it, Henry. I told you days ago that I would arrange it – and I did. It's not the most important thing you have to worry about.'

Pomeroy, dressed in a yellow tunic with a short red cloak pinned around his shoulders, still looked unhappy. 'It was that damned bailiff's fault, I should have his hand chopped off. I told him to leave a couple of men-at-arms with the felling team, but the idiot took them off after a couple of days because nothing happened.'

The third member of the group smiled wryly. He was a namesake of the host, Henri de Nonant, Lord of Totnes, whose burly joviality concealed a hard heart and a scheming mind. 'You sound outraged, friend, yet it's you who are stealing the man's land! Are you surprised that he shows his disapproval?'

Pomeroy threw the dregs of his wine into the fire and picked up a flask from the table to refill all their cups. 'It's a moot point, whether that land is his or not, Henri.'

'You mean, we're not sure which of our families stole it from the Saxons?' drawled Cheever mischievously.

'Conquest is not stealing, Bernard,' snapped Pomeroy, who had not a trace of a sense of humour. 'William the Bastard had a better claim to England than Harold – and he won. So his followers had a right to all the land and William gave this honour to Ralph, our grandfather four times removed.'

'The Domesday commissioners were not at all clear on where his boundaries lay,' commented de Nonant.

'Then I'll clarify it for them – at the point of my sword if needs be! If you look at the lie of the land, those three virgates in the valley between Afton and Loventor obviously belong to Afton. Cleared of forest, they make a continuous sweep of ploughland.'

'But William Fitzhamon thinks otherwise – and he says he has four generations of occupation to uphold his claim,' said Cheever mildly.

'And I've got five generations that say he's wrong – so to hell with him!' retorted Pomeroy. 'I need a strong arm or two to keep him from interfering again. My reeve says that Fitzhamon used ragged outlaws to assault his team. What does it matter if we kill a few to make our point?'

Henri de Nonant held up a cautionary hand. 'Have a care, we don't want to start a private war here, not at this delicate time.'

Pomeroy was dismissive. 'Who's to censure us, eh? We are the law in these parts. The only one who could cause us problems is the sheriff – and Richard de Revelle's not going to bother us, is he?'

'What about the new coroner, this former Crusader?' asked Bernard Cheever.

'That's John de Wolfe, from over at Stoke-in-Teignhead,' supplied de Nonant.

'Coroner! Who the devil takes any notice of a coroner?' said Pomeroy derisively. 'Just a glorified tax-collector recording the pennies of dead felons for the Exchequer.'

Henri de Nonant was not so easily convinced. 'There is talk that this crowner has the ear of both Hubert Walter and even the King.'

'They've got a bloody long ears, then,' cackled Cheever. 'I wager that Richard will never set foot in England again.'

The more cautious Nonant shrugged. 'So be it, then. But be careful – for the sake of a few acres of land, we can't risk drawing attention to ourselves, until everything is in place.'

Pomeroy swallowed the rest of his wine and moved towards the door. 'Let's go and eat and drink our fill. And, Bernard, I trust I will hear tomorrow that these fellows have done their job. I want that felling completed and the stumps pulled out before the end of January.'

While Thomas de Peyne was indulging in his lonely labours in the cathedral, Gwyn of Polruan was mixing business with pleasure in another hostelry in the city. Not far from the Bush was a less reputable tavern on Stepcote Hill, called the Saracen. It was run by a fat, surly landlord known as Willem the Fleming and attracted a rougher class of customer, many from the Bretayne district just across Westgate Street, as well as dubious strangers entering the city through that gate.

However, Willem brewed good ale and it was also the place to pick up criminal gossip, as well the pox from the many harlots who used it as a business address.

This Christ Mass evening, the burly Cornishman was sitting in the Saracen with a quart pot of best ale, talking to some acquaintances and listening to the buzz of conversation around him. He had already eaten heartily with his wife and two children at her widowed sister's house in Milk Street. They had left their own small dwelling in St Sidwell's to spend the festive day there. Gwyn, tiring of women's gossip in the tiny room, where the children slept on a straw mattress in the corner, had wandered out for a drink and some male company. He knew every tavern in the city, both as a customer and as coroner's officer, for many of the inns were the scene of fights, assaults and even killings. Only last month the Saracen had been the scene of a fatal robbery for which two men had been hanged – and Willem was still bemoaning the ruination of one of his mattresses from the blood of one of the victims. Gwyn sat on a bench against one wall, sucking the ale from his bushy moustache and listening to one of his companions complain about the cost of living since the King had restarted his campaign against Philip of France. 'With a pair of working shoes now almost threepence, how can we live?' he whined, but Gwyn's attention was suddenly elsewhere.

He noticed a face across the room that he could not quite place, though he had seen it recently. Then he realised that the young man's clothing was different from what he had worn that afternoon: his priest's garb was shrouded in a dun cloak that enveloped him from neck to ankle. He was one of the vicars from Canons' Row in the close, who had been at the inquest and had been hovering around on the previous evening when the body was discovered. Gwyn did not know his name or to whom he was a vicar, but certainly he was not Robert de Hane's: his had been a pasty-faced man with a pug nose; this was a dark fellow with acne scars on his cheeks. He was talking animatedly to a tall young man with very blond hair and beard, and a large sword at his belt. Between them was a very attractive, if bold-looking, woman of about twenty-five, her long dark hair rippling unbound over her shoulders.

Though some priests were dissolute, both in drink and womanising, they were usually discreet in the cathedral city and did not publicly flaunt their lifestyle: normally they kept their mistresses indoors and did their drinking in relative privacy. It was strange to see a vicar, even in plain clothing, in a seedy tavern like the Saracen, especially in the company of a woman who looked as if she might be 'of a certain character'.

Gwyn watched them for a few moments, heedless of the continuing complaints of the man sitting next to him. He saw the vicar talking quickly to the fair man, his head close to the other's in an attitude of confidentiality. His hands waved in nervous gestures and he darted frequent glances about the large room as if suspicious of an eavesdropper. The coroner's officer dropped his head and looked across the inn from under his bushy red brows, not wanting to be recognised. The low, smoky chamber was full of people, drinking and talking loudly, so there was not too much chance of the vicar spotting him – even though Gwyn was a giant of a man, he was sitting behind a shifting throng.

The blond fellow was listening attentively to the priest, nodding every now and then but saying little. The woman's handsome face looked from one to the other, her full red lips pursed in a somewhat anxious expression. Gwyn recalled having seen her about the town before – he had a healthy appreciation for an attractive woman – but he did not know her name. She was not a common whore, as far as he knew, but there something about her manner that spoke of easy sensuality.

He interrupted his companion, a leather-worker from Curre Street, who was still prattling on about the cost of living. 'Who's that good-looking dame there, Otelin?' he asked.

The man lowered his jar from his lips and craned his head around a bystander to see across the smoky room. 'The woman with the big dugs? That's Rosamunde of Rye, who's no better than she should be – but, like most of the men in Exeter, I'd not kick her out of my bed.' Otelin licked his lips with futile desire.

'Is she from the city? And who is the man with her?' demanded the coroner's lieutenant.

'She follows the younger knights and squires about the country, so I hear,' Otelin answered. 'The likes of you and me wouldn't get a hand into her bodice – she fancies the bright young fighting men, and some of the older ones, too. No doubt that yellow-haired fellow is one of them, by the way he flaunts his broadsword.' Otelin peered across the inn again. The tall young man was now taking over the discussion, the priest and raven-haired woman listening intently. 'I don't know his name,' he said, 'but I've seen him with others of the same type. I think he is squire to one of those mercenaries, from down Totnes way.'

A group of drinkers moved across their field of view, and when they had a sight across the room again the priest had moved away in the company of another girl, with a pallid face but a gaudy kirtle. They went across to the ladder in the corner, which, like the Bush and most other inns, led up to the primitive sleeping accommodation on the floor above.

As they pushed their way through the throng, the blond squire and Rosamunde of Rye went hand in hand towards the street door and vanished. Gwyn of Polruan spent the next hour sitting in the Saracen, drinking his ale and pondering on whether what he had seen had any significance in the case of the murdered canon.

CHAPTER FOUR

In which Crowner John learns some history

By the next morning, Matilda had thawed sufficiently to appear in the cold light of dawn to join her husband at the breakfast Mary set before them in the bare hall of their house. Over hot bread, cold pork and mulled ale, they sat each side of the long table, silently avoiding the sharing of each other's thoughts. His wife could sulk for days on end, which de Wolfe found worse than an outright fight – the latter gave a better excuse to flare up and clear off to the Bush, where he could enjoy the pleasant company of his mistress. But when Matilda was merely sullen, he felt that he had to try to wean her back at least to a state of neutrality, for the sake of his own relative peace of mind. Although John did not enjoy her company, even at the best of times in this loveless marriage, he found outright warfare, niggling bickering and silent antipathy about as welcome as a festering open wound.

Unable to leave her, due to the social obligations of a Norman knight and a King's officer, he had to endure the *status quo* with as good grace as he could muster. Yet although he had ample opportunity to relieve his sensual needs, mainly with Nesta but also with a couple of other ladies around the county, he still had to live in Martin's Lane with a wife obsessed with her position in the social hierarchy of the county.

De Wolfe was the only coroner in Devon: the mandate from Hubert Walter had required each county to appoint three knights and a clerk, but here only two had been found to accept the unpaid post, and the other, Robert Fitzrogo, had fallen from his horse in the first fortnight and been killed. De Wolfe had been left to cover the huge expanse from Barnstaple on the Severn Sea down to the south coast, with Exmoor and Dartmoor included in a vast tract of country that on horseback took three days to cross.

As he sat chewing the rind on his pig-meat and crunching the crusty bread, he tried to take stock of his own state of contentment. A soldier since the age of seventeen, he was now forty and put out to grass, as far as foreign campaigning was concerned. Although he could have gone to join his beloved Richard Coeur de Lion in France, an old wound in his left hip, from a spear thrust in Palestine, made him wary of long sojourns in the field, living in tents or filthy castle barracks. He had wearied of endless killing, and the massacres in the Third Crusade, from which he had returned two years previously, had sickened him of outright war. When he was young, he had been in the Irish campaigns and often in Normandy and France, but the Holy Land had been a different world. Also, though he hardly admitted it even to himself, he still felt responsible for the King having been captured in Austria. Gwyn and de Wolfe had been part of Richard's small bodyguard during their attempted journey across the continent after being shipwrecked in the Adriatic. Through no fault of de Wolfe, the Lionheart had been seized while he and Gwyn had escaped. The King spent almost two years in the clutches of Leopold of Austria and Henry of Germany. It had been the huge ransom that England had to pay, a hundred and fifty thousand marks, that had helped to impoverish the country since, and which had driven Justiciar Hubert Walter to squeeze every penny in taxes from the hard-pressed population. Indeed, the creation of coroners had been part of the drive to extract as much money as possible from both rich and poor.

Yet de Wolfe found that he enjoyed the job: it gave him the chance to get out and about on a horse, sometimes to become involved in a fight when things turned nasty – and, above all, to escape from Matilda with a legitimate excuse to be away from home for days on end. She had thought that becoming coroner would give them increased prestige in the county pecking-order, without too much labour, that the coroner would merely officiate at local courts, hobnob with the King's Justices when they came, and oversee the formalities at inquests. She soon learned, with dismay, that it meant her husband had to spend most of his time away from home on the back of his old warhorse Bran, in company with the red-haired Cornish savage and an evil little gnome, who was both a sexual pervert and a disgraced priest.

A state of grumbling hostility had developed between de Wolfe and his wife, fuelled mostly on her side by his stubborn obstinacy to carry out his duties with faithful dedication, born of his conviction that it was his duty to his king. Another source of friction was her awareness of his infidelity, though the knowledge that virtually every Norman in the country had a mistress or two made this a lesser evil. Matilda herself had had a flirtation or two with men in the past, when John was away at his wars, but she had done it partly from pique and partly from boredom, rather than any passionate desire. In fact, she had found the affairs embarrassingly sordid and had long been chaste.

Though this morning she had condescended to sit with her husband at the table, the silence was almost palpable enough to be cut with his dagger. His feeble efforts at conversation were met with stony indifference and he soon gave up, with a glowering sense of familiarity with the situation.

As soon as he had finished eating, he threw on his cloak and whistled down the passageway to the yard for Brutus, deciding to give the old hound a walk up to the castle. The snow had stopped overnight, but there was a couple of inches of slush on the ground, dirty and stained in the middle of the lane and in the high street where people threw out their slops. Brutus was not too happy at being brought out of Mary's warm kitchen to plod through the cold streets, but he faithfully followed his master, enjoying the various smells at each corner and the opportunity to cock his leg every few yards. At the castle gatehouse, he darted ahead of de Wolfe and ran up the twisting stone staircase, knowing that the dog-loving Gwyn would throw him a piece of his breakfast cheese.

Up in the spartan chamber, Thomas de Peyne was in his usual place at the rough table, scribing away at duplicate rolls for the judges when they came to the January Eyre of Assize. Gwyn was perched on his window-ledge, chewing at the remains of a loaf, with Brutus already sitting at his feet staring up hopefully for a share.

De Wolfe settled himself behind his table as Thomas put down his quill pen and waited expectantly. Before he could start telling of his archive researches, Gwyn broke in with his own story about his visit to the Saracen the night before. When he had finished, the coroner leaned forward on the table. 'Did you learn this fellow's name?' he demanded.

The Cornishman nodded. 'I made it my business to question Willem the Fleming afterwards, miserable devil that he is. He told me that the fair man was named Giles Fulford, squire to a young knight from the Welsh Marches, who is currently living in this county.'

'Do we know his name as well?'

'Yes. The Fleming told me grudgingly that it was Jocelin de Braose. His father is a Marcher lord from somewhere near Monmouth.'

John de Wolfe chewed his lip as an aid to memory. 'I heard of that family when we accompanied Archbishop Baldwin around Wales on his recruiting campaign for the Crusade in 'eighty-eight. They had a bad reputation, as far as I recollect – every Welshman spat on the ground when their name was mentioned.'

Thomas couldn't resist airing his extensive knowledge of recent history. 'William de Braose was the one who invited a dozen Welsh chieftains to a banquet at his castle at Abergavenny – and stabbed them all to death!'

Gwyn grunted, to indicate that he saw this as typical Norman behaviour, but forbore to say so in as many words: although his master was half Welsh, he was still a Norman official.

De Wolfe pulled his mind back to the present. 'So what of this Giles fellow? Why should he be gabbing to a cathedral priest in a low tavern with a doxy at his elbow?'

His officer shrugged. 'The devil alone knows. Willem

said that both he and this Jocelin, whom he serves, are both now mercenaries, hiring their arms for anyone who will pay them.'

The coroner's eyebrows hauled up his forehead. 'Mercenaries? I heard some tales of them only yesterday. It seems that they are frequenting Exeter a great deal lately. Are these men former Crusaders like us?'

Gwyn grimaced. 'I very much doubt it. The Fulford fellow was too pale to have been in Outremer. Probably they've been in France for their fighting.' He threw a piece of stone-hard cheese in the air. Brutus caught it effortlessly and swallowed it in one gulp.

'What of this black-haired wench who seems to have caught your fancy? Do you think this vicar has her in his bed?'

'I doubt it. She looked too much of a handful for such a weed as that boy. It was this Giles that had her by the arm. The vicar took some drab of his own up to the loft of the Saracen.'

'Is this Rosamunde just a common harlot, then?'

'Not according to Otelin, the leatherman. I gathered she was a camp-follower to these hired soldiers, a cut above an ordinary whore.'

John picked up a parchment roll and absently looked at Thomas's inscription under the tape that tied it. His new literacy just allowed him to make out the name of the deceased person to whom it referred, a man who had fallen from a roof a week ago. But his mind was elsewhere.

'Is any of this at all to do with our dead canon?' he muttered. 'Only the presence of the next-door vicar has the slightest possible connection.'

'He is the deputy for Roger de Limesi,' the astute Thomas reminded him. 'That might be a slight strengthening of the connection, as there are twenty-one other canons who have nothing to do with the archives.'

Having got a word in between the two bigger men, he continued by telling of his sole discovery of the fresh cross against Saewulf in Robert de Hane's parchments. His announcement was met with blank silence by the other two in the chamber. Abashed, he murmured, 'I know nothing of this Saxon, but I will find out. It may be a pointer to something, as the mark was made in the same colour ink as that on the canon's desk in the Chapter House.'

Gwyn snorted, which made Brutus recoil. 'A mark on a roll of sheepskin! Is that all your night's labour can turn up, midget?'

De Wolfe held up his hand to forestall a squabble between his assistants. 'No matter! The next task is to shake some information from this vicar, but first I'll see what's to be learned about Jocelin de Braose and his squire.'

A few moments later, having left Brutus in the safe hands of his officer, the coroner was in the sheriff's chamber. This time, the sharp-faced Lady Eleanor was there, dressed for travelling, an elderly handmaiden hovering behind her. A harassed-looking Richard de Revelle was shouting orders at a steward and at Sergeant Gabriel, who was leading a small escort for his wife on her journey back to Revelstoke.

The coroner greeted the woman civilly. She replied with cold ill-grace, and de Wolfe retired into the shadows of the room until his brother-in-law had ushered the party out and had seen them depart from the keep of Rougemont on their slow four-hour journey to his main country residence near Plympton.

On his return, Richard was almost affable in his relief at having seen the back of his wife for a week or more. 'Wives are all very well in their place,' he said cheerfully, 'as long as that place is a long way from their husbands.' He sat behind the heavy oak table that served as his desk. 'Now, what can I do for you, John?'

The coroner came straight to the point. 'What do you know of a man called Jocelin de Braose? And his squire, for that matter.'

De Revelle looked warily at his brother-in-law. 'Almost nothing – why?'

'Just tell me, man. Do you know of him at all?'

The sheriff, dressed in his favourite pale green, pulled rather nervously at his beard. 'I know his name, of course, and generally of his family. But I've never met him, that I can recollect. Again, why do you want to know?'

De Wolfe had a distinct feeling that the other man was being evasive, if not actually lying, and wondered why this should be. 'He may be involved in the death of our old prebendary. It's only the faintest of possibilities as yet, but any glimmer of light is welcome in this obscure affair.' He related Gwyn's story of the meeting with Canon de Limesi's vicar, feeling that it had only the most tenuous connection with Robert de Hane.

His brother-in-law was obviously of the same mind: he scoffed at the idea. 'For God's sake, John, how can you make a conspiracy out of this? The damned priest was probably trying to buy a night's lechery from this squire's woman. You know what some of these clerics are like – their celibacy is the biggest joke in the city.'

De Wolfe had to admit that he was probably right

but, like a dog with a bone, he wouldn't give up worrying the matter yet. 'This Jocelin fellow, I hear he is one of those who sells his sword to the highest bidder.'

'There are plenty of them about, John. Think of all your Crusader comrades who have returned home to find nothing to occupy them or fill their purses. They can't all find wars in France.'

'So this man is one of those hired warriors, then,' persisted the coroner. 'I have heard that they have even formed some sort of confederation in these western counties.'

The sheriff became cautious at once. 'I know nothing of that. Any baron or manorial lord is entitled to employ men in his service, be they cooks or men-at-arms. It has always been so.'

He refused to be drawn further and John changed the subject slightly. 'What about this Rosamunde wench? Is anything known of her?'

Richard de Revelle's narrow face twisted into a leer. 'I've certainly heard of her – she has a reputation as the most talented doxy between Penzance and Dover. Not that I have any personal knowledge of that,' he added, with such haste that de Wolfe knew he was lying. It was little more than a month since he had caught his brother-in-law in bed with a harlot in the very next room.

'She is a whore, then?'

The sheriff put on a sanctimonious expression. 'I have heard that she started as one. She was thrown out of her birthplace of Rye for it and then worked the Kentish ports, until her good looks attracted some of the noble travellers crossing the Channel. Since then she seems to have sold her favours only to those she fancies, usually good-looking fighting men with money at their belt.'

The coroner noticed that Richard seemed as happy to discuss the woman as he was reluctant to talk about Jocelin de Braose. He also wondered how the sheriff was so familiar with the history of a woman of no virtue, when he claimed never to have met her. Now he tried to get the conversation back to the young knight: as the King's representative for the county, the sheriff should have been the best authority on all the Norman establishment in Devonshire. 'Jocelin de Braose comes from the Welsh Marches, I hear?' he said.

De Revelle's lips tightened in annoyance at the return to an unwelcome subject. 'So I assume. That family has been trying to subdue the damned Welsh in that area for more than a century.'

'So why is the son here in the West Country now?'

'How the devil should I know?' snapped the Sheriff. 'I presume he uses his sword in the service of someone. If he's a junior son of his father, he may have no prospects at home, especially if he has been away at the wars for some years.'

'So where is he selling this sword at the moment?' persisted John.

De Revelle scowled at him, but could hardly feign ignorance of what went on in his own county. 'I believe I heard that he has been in the company of Henry de la Pomeroy or his kinsman Bernard Cheever – but whether he is still there now, I couldn't say.'

De Wolfe knew that Pomeroy was a baron who held large tracts of land in central and western Devon as well as many manors in Somerset and Dorset. He also knew a lot more about Pomeroy's father. 'Doesn't it worry you, Richard, that these men are attached to a family who are reputed to be traitors?'

The sheriff looked sullenly at John. 'What concern should it be of mine?' he growled. 'Henry's father is dead, and that's all behind him.'

'And we all know how and why he died, Sheriff!' said de Wolfe sarcastically. It had been the scandal of Devon earlier that year. Pomeroy's father, also a Henry, had been a leading supporter of Prince John's revolt. When the Lionheart had returned from captivity last March and crushed the remnants of the rebellion, he had sent a herald to Berry Pomeroy Castle with his felicitations. Once inside, the herald announced that he brought a warrant for Pomeroy's arrest for treason against the King, whereupon Henry stabbed him to death. Fearing retribution, he abandoned his castle and rode with his troops to St Michael's Mount, the rocky island in Cornwall, which he had previously seized for Prince John by disguising his soldiers as monks. His constable there had already dropped dead of fright on hearing of the King's release from Germany, and when Henry de la Pomeroy was besieged by Archbishop Hubert Walter and the sheriff of Cornwall, he committed suicide by slashing his wrists. Sardonically de Wolfe reminded his brother-in-law of this salutary tale of treachery, but it seemed he would gain nothing more from de Revelle so he eased himself from the edge of the table where he had been leaning. 'I think I'll have a strong word or two with this vicar. Perhaps the knowledge that he's been seen in a tavern with women of easy virtue will loosen his tongue.'

De Revelle, though glad that the talk had left Jocelin de Braose, became uneasy in case the Coroner went off now to upset the Bishop by exposing one of the cathedral priests as a rake. De Revelle was close to the head of the Church in Exeter and the last thing he wanted was for his brother-in-law to start a new scandal in the precinct. All things considered, his sister's husband had become a damned nuisance since being appointed coroner a few months ago, upsetting Richard's cosy monopoly of the intrigues that went on in the county. 'I wish you would just let this matter of the canon rest, John,' he said. 'He was obviously killed by some opportunist robber – that is, if you were right in claiming that he didn't do away with himself. Why make such a great mystery of it? If you need a solution, accuse one of the servants. I'll hang him for you and the whole affair can be forgotten.'

De Wolfe was scornful of what he considered to be the sheriff's immoral attitude to justice and, after a few tart words, he left de Revelle's chamber and marched back to the gatehouse, muttering under his breath at his brother-in-law's unsuitability to represent the King. The Lionheart was de Wolfe's idol. If pressed, though, he would have had to admit that, as far as England was concerned, Richard Coeur de Lion left much to be desired: he had spent only a few months of his reign in the country, and showed no sign of ever returning now that he was at war in France. He had not bothered to learn a word of English, and his queen, Berengaria, had never so much as set foot in England, not even for Richard's second coronation earlier that year – to which she had not been invited! The King looked on Normandy as his true home, and England as a mine from which his ministers, notably Hubert Walter, hewed money and goods to support his armies.

As he strode across the inner ward, the east wind whistling around his legs, John felt nothing for his monarch but loyalty, born of the camaraderie of the arduous campaigns in the Holy Land and the stresses of their escapade between the Adriatic and Vienna. To see his brother-in-law twisting his royal appointment endlessly to suit his own advantage made the coroner even more determined to confound de Revelle by making every investigation as complete and honest as possible.

He stamped into the room at the top of the gatehouse and snapped instructions. 'Gwyn, get back to the tavern on Stepcote Hill and find out all you can about that squire and his master – and the woman from Rye. Threaten Willem the Fleming if you have to, tell him we'll have him up at Rougemont to sit in the gaol for a few days and maybe suffer *peine et forte dure* unless he comes up with some information.' This was a bluff on de Wolfe's part, but the threat might loosen the surly inn-keeper's tongue. 'And you, Thomas, come with me to the Close. We need to have words with this young priest who seems to have difficulty in keeping his chastity intact.'

The clerk tipped his head sideways like a sparrow. 'You have two hangings to attend at midday,' he reminded his master.

De Wolfe scowled: he had forgotten that, Yuletide or not, the twice-weekly executions still took place at the gallows tree on Magdalen Street outside the city. He had to be present to record the event and to confiscate the property of the dead felons – if they had any. 'We'll be finished by then, if we get down to the precinct straight away,' he snapped.

But Thomas had another objection. 'The priests will all be at morning services until about the eleventh hour.'

'Then we'll pull him out to talk to us. His immortal soul won't suffer too much for missing an hour's chanting.'

Equipped with new axes and with their bruises fading, Alward's men had gone back to their clearing of the woods between Afton and Loventor. For several days they were unmolested. Those in Fitzhamon's village must have known that the work had resumed, as the smoke from the burning debris reached above the tree-tops and the sound of axes rang out to a great distance in the frosty winter air.

The Afton team had one additional tool this time: a horn slung on Alward's belt. The sound of this, driven by his powerful lungs, could reach far down the face of the forest along which they were felling their trees. On this morning of the day following Christ Mass, when work began again after the festival, the expected attack resumed. Once more, another dozen roughly clothed men charged from the woods and began to belabour the villeins and freemen from Afton, although this time the workers were even quicker at running away.

The instant the assailants appeared, Alward began to blast away on his cow's horn, which caused the ruffians to slow up to wonder what was going on. Within seconds of the trumpeting, there was a thunder of hoofs in the middle distance and from the tree-line, two hundred paces away, half a dozen horsemen emerged and bore down on the combatants. Though half the number of the assailants, the mounted men cut through them like a knife through butter, scattering the men on foot in panic.

This time, there was no attempt to avoid serious

injury. The riders swung swords with professional skill and two of the men from Loventor fell at once, with lethal wounds gushing blood on to the ground. Pulling their large horses around, the six men began chasing the would-be attackers, felling another with a blow on the back and inflicting lesser wounds on two more. Even one of the Afton workers was mistaken for an aggressor and given a deep cut on the head, which fortunately did not prove fatal.

After the second sally, the men from both villages were hopelessly intermingled in their hapless attempts to escape to the shelter of the trees. The leader of the horsemen, a stocky young man with red hair visible under the rim of his round metal helmet, raised his sword and yelled at his companions to follow him. Expertly wheeling their steeds, the avengers galloped off down the edge of the woods and out of sight, leaving the Loventor men to creep slowly out of the bushes to collect their dead and wounded, watched silently by the peasants they had come to attack.

Thomas de Peyne was sent into the great cathedral to find the vicar, who was called Eric Langton. Thankfully, his task was easier than he had expected – the ex-cleric looked on disturbing a sacred service as a sin worse than blasphemy. In the event, he found that Roger de Limesi was himself present at the devotions so his deputy was dispensable. Thomas was able to sidle along the back of the choir stalls, where the more junior officiants stood, and tug at Langton's robe without disrupting the proceedings.

The mystified vicar allowed himself to be drawn into the shadows of the arches between the chancel and the side aisles where the coroner's clerk hissed in his ear that he was wanted urgently at Robert de Hane's house in the Close.

Eric Langton recognised Thomas as someone who lived in Canons' Row – presumably a priest, as the little clerk had never denied it – and followed him without protest, mildly relieved that he had escaped the next hour of boring worship.

In the bare hall of the dead prebendary's dwelling, the coroner was waiting, sitting on a bench at one side of the oak refectory table. He motioned Langton to stand opposite him and launched straight into his interrogation, his long dark face glowering at the young vicar. 'What were you doing in the Saracen tavern last night, associating with a hired adventurer and a painted whore?' he demanded. Both descriptions of Eric's companions were a little exaggerated, but the coroner believed in the power of over-statement when confronting a witness.

Langton was normally pallid, but now the remaining blood drained from his scarred cheeks. Between his dark hair and the black cloak he had thrown over his church robes, his pinched face was ashen and his lips quivered, but no words emerged. Eventually, though, after de Wolfe had harshly repeated his questions, the story came out, reluctantly and hesitantly.

'Canon Roger sent me with a message to Giles Fulford,' he said, in a low voice, his eyes avoiding John's. 'It was urgent, so I had to seek him out in one of the taverns he often frequented.'

'One that you also often frequented,' snapped the coroner. 'You went upstairs with a drab, so you must be well acquainted with the Saracen.'

The vicar's white face suddenly flushed scarlet. 'I have a – a friend I see there sometimes, yes.'

De Wolfe gestured impatiently, his black brows lowered scornfully. 'I don't give a damn about your morals, priest, though your archdeacon and bishop might have a word or two to say to you after this. I want to know what was going on between your master and this man Fulford.'

The wretched cleric, staring ruin in the face, twisted in anguish. 'I know little of the reasons, Crowner, I swear. Some weeks ago, the canon took me aside and asked me if I knew any bold man who might help him in a private venture that would need strength and determination. I took it that he meant someone who would act for him in some enterprise unfit for a man of the church.' He looked down at his pointed shoes. 'Canon Roger knows that I have some weaknesses – he is a tolerant man and has overlooked my lapses in the past.'

The coroner could not be bothered to explore Langton's 'weaknesses'; he was not concerned with this erring priest, but with what lay behind his story. 'So what followed?' he demanded.

'I had this friend in the town – a woman I knew. I asked her if she knew any persons who could aid Canon Roger. She took me one night to meet Rosamunde of Rye.'

'A harlot's coven!' observed John sarcastically.

'In turn, she brought Giles Fulford, and I arranged for him to meet my master.'

De Wolfe grunted at this sanitised version of a vicar's nocturnal activities in the less savoury streets of Exeter. 'Where did they have this meeting and what was discussed?'

'Giles came to the cathedral one day, after the morning services. They talked in the nave after everyone had left. It seemed a safe and private place. I have no knowledge of what they discussed. I was told to keep well clear of the meeting.'

'Did your canon meet him on other occasions? And was anyone else involved?' grated the coroner.

Langton shook his head energetically. 'I cannot tell – I heard nothing more of the matter at that time.'

'What about your doxy in the town? Surely, between your bouts of carnal lust, you discussed this unusual happening,' asked John cynically.

'Yes, I asked her about it – naturally I was curious. But the girl said that Rosamunde had told her to mind her own business or it would be the worse for her.'

There was a ring of truth about this that de Wolfe accepted. 'So what about this latest meeting last night?'

The vicar looked even more furtive and downcast than before. 'The canon took me aside yesterday, after the inquest you held. He told me to seek out Fulford at once, to tell him that everything was over between them, whatever that meant. He said that he did not want to see him or hear from him again as all their plans had been confounded by the death of Canon de Hane.'

'And you claim to know nothing more about the matter than this?' snapped the coroner. 'I find that hard to believe!'

Eric's face was a picture of abject misery. 'It is the truth, Crowner. I swear by God and the Virgin and every saint in the calendar! I was but a messenger in this, I have no idea what lies behind it. You must ask the canon himself. After this I am finished. I care not what happens to me now.'

This struck a sympathetic chord with Thomas, himself an unfrocked priest, and he laid a comforting hand upon the vicar's arm. But the coroner was in no comforting mood: though he believed Langton's story, he was now grimly determined to discover the whole truth – and Langton had just suggested the obvious way.

'Indeed, Canon de Limesi will need to answer a few questions – and that very soon! As for you, just get out of my sight. You should be glad that you have the benefit of clergy or you'd soon be languishing in a cell in Rougemont. But, no doubt, your Archdeacon and the Bishop will have a few scores to settle with you in the near future.'

The wretched vicar slunk away and the coroner turned to his clerk. 'What do we make of that, Thomas?' he asked, in a rare show of familiarity with his underling.

The little man was confused: he was overjoyed that his master had actually asked his opinion about something, an unusual honour indeed, but he was also grieved that a colleague in his own beloved Church, of which he still felt an integral part, in spite of his own scandal, should have been caught out wenching and frequenting taverns. He hedged. 'We don't yet know that Canon de Hane's death has anything at all to do with Roger de Limesi. Odd though this story is, it may have some innocent explanation.'

De Wolfe made a rude noise with his lips. 'For God's sake, Thomas, you must be able to see the facts clearer than that, even with your swivel eye! De Limesi hires a thug and then, on the day of the murder of a colleague who sits with him in the archives every day, makes a panic call to the said thug to call off whatever was being plotted!'

Put like that, even Doubting Thomas had to admit that de Limesi had a great deal to explain.

'As soon as those priests come out from their endless singing and chanting this morning, I want Roger de Limesi brought here for me to question. Get yourself over to the cathedral steps and catch him before he vanishes to fill his stomach.'

'What if he refuses me? I am nothing compared to the rank of a prebendary in this cathedral.'

'Thomas, stop thinking of yourself as a derelict priest. You are my servant, a deputy of a royal law officer. You will insist that he comes. If he refuses, go to your uncle the Archdeacon and tell him that I say it is of the utmost urgency that de Limesi comes to see me. And tell John de Alencon that he might wish to be present when I interrogate his fellow prebendary to see that there is no impropriety.'

Reluctantly the clerk went off on his unwelcome errand and waited at the west front of the huge church until the morning devotions were over. These religious services, though open to anyone who was content to stand at a distance in the nave, were really for the benefit of the cathedral staff in their endless glorification of God rather than for public worship, which was the function of the seventeen parish churches in the small city. Thus there was virtually no exodus of a congregation through the doors, the services having been confined to the canons, vicars, secondaries and choristers assembled in the choir just below the chancel.

But now the saga took a fresh and unexpected turn, as the first person to emerge was a young secondary.

He hurried across the steps towards de Peyne, whom he recognised as the coroner's clerk, lodging in the next house. 'Well met, Thomas! I've just been sent to find your master. The Archdeacon wishes to speak most urgently with the Crowner. He wants him to come to the Chapter House without delay.'

'But I've been sent here to command Roger de Limesi to come to the coroner,' countered the clerk.

'I think it's in connection with that particular canon that the meeting's required,' replied the young priest, tapping the side of his nose as a hint that something serious was going on.

Unsure of what to do now, Thomas hurried, as fast as his lame leg would allow, back to John de Wolfe. He found that Gwyn of Polruan had also just returned from his visit to the Saracen.

A few minutes later, the three arrived at the Chapter House on the south side of the cathedral, where they found John de Alencon sitting on one of the benches, with Jordan de Brent and Roger de Limesi on each side of him. De Limesi sat some feet away from the Archdeacon, looking very subdued indeed.

The benches were arranged in two rows on three sides of the bare room. A lectern for reading chapters from the scriptures took up part of the fourth side, where there was also a tall-backed chair for the Bishop, though he rarely attended.

The coroner stood in the centre of the room and stared at the three priests. 'I was just about to seek out Canon Roger to ask him some very direct questions,' he said ominously, in his bass voice.

John de Alencon motioned de Wolfe to sit down and, with his assistants on each side of him, he dropped on to a front bench exactly opposite the coroner's party. 'This is a private and delicate matter, John,' said the Archdeacon gently, his grey eyes flicking meaningfully to the men on either side of the coroner.

'It is also a matter of royal jurisdiction, as granted to us by your bishop,' responded the coroner. 'It may be such a serious matter that even the protection of the Church towards its members may not be sufficient.' Guessing that the Archdeacon was reluctant to have the discussion aired before two servants, he said, 'Sooner or later my clerk will have to write down all that transpires, so he needs a complete grasp of what is being said. And my officer is always at my side. He is as much a part of me as my arm or leg.'

Both his assistants glowed internally at this expression of his trust in them, and their silent devotion to their master became deeper than ever.

John de Alencon nodded his acceptance, and began his explanation. 'Roger de Limesi has come to me with a strange and disturbing story. He wished to make a confession in the religious sense, to obtain my absolution, as I am his regular confessor. But, in the circumstances, I had to refuse him, as the inviolability of the confessional would make it impossible to divulge what he wished to say.'

There was a silence in the room that had a breathless, suspended quality, as the coroner's team waited for what was to be revealed.

'I have therefore advised him to tell this story to you, Crowner, as the matter is one of grave secular importance. And, as you said, we know that Bishop Henry has devolved the rights of the cathedral to you in such circumstances.' The thin yet serene face turned towards the discomfited de Limesi. 'Your confession in religious terms will be heard later, but that is none of the business of John de Wolfe. Unburden yourself now, Roger, and say what you must say.'

The canon, a black cloak over the alb and chasuble which he wore during the morning services, slowly raised his drooping head. 'My shame is almost more than I can bear, though my motives were not bad, Crowner. That they may have contributed to the death of my brother canon is the bitter part, from which I fear my immortal soul is in danger.'

'We will deal with your immortal soul later, Roger,' said the Archdeacon, with the merest trace of irony in his mellow voice. 'For now, let's have your story.'

De Limesi gave a great sigh and plunged into his narrative. 'It began here, upstairs in the library. I became intrigued by Robert de Hane's increasing activity and enthusiasm during the past month or so. I've known him for years, poor soul, and I was surprised by this sudden burst of energy, the long hours he spent here and the mysterious trips he began making into the countryside.'

Jordan de Brent's deep voice broke in. 'This is just what I described before. De Limesi is right, our late brother became a changed man.'

'One day I asked him what he was working on,' continued de Limesi. 'He was evasive and this made me all the more curious. So, God forgive me for my deceit, I took the opportunity of his absence at prime one day, when my vicar was performing my own duties, to go through the parchments on his desk. It was clear that he was searching old records from the early churches in Devon. Eventually I came across a double sheet of ancient vellum that he had hidden under a sheaf of palimpsests, away from the bulk of the other documents.' He paused to press his brow, as if a ferocious headache had struck him. 'It was in poor Latin, written in an ugly hand by a village priest, a Saxon. From the context, he must have written this in early ten sixty-nine, a couple of years after we Normans first spread into these parts.'

The coroner spoke for the first time. 'What village was this?'

'It was Dunsford, a small hamlet some eight miles west of Exeter.'

Thomas whispered excitedly, into his master's ear, 'One of the holdings of Saewulf, whose name bore the inked cross I told you about!'

Almost immediately, his comment was confirmed by de Limesi. 'This priest was setting down something that had been confided to him by his Saxon lord, Saewulf, who held much land and property in Devon before the Conquest. Saewulf was afraid – quite rightly, as it turned out – that his lands would be confiscated and his property taken from him when our armies came into Devon. There was nothing he could do about his land, but he was determined to try to save at least some of his wealth. Shortly before the arrival of our conquerors from Wessex, he hid a large quantity of gold and silver, in the form of coin and ornaments, in the vicinity of Dunsford, hoping to retrieve it if a Saxon rebellion was successful.'

The Archdeacon nodded sagely. 'There were such rebellions, as we know. In 'sixty-eight, King William had to put this city under siege for eighteen days until the locals came to their senses.'

Thomas could not resist airing his historical knowledge. 'And later that year, the three bastard sons of King Harold tried to seize Bristol – then came into Somerset and defeated the Norman militia there.'

The coroner was more interested in treasure than history. 'So what of this gold and silver?' he demanded.

'It seems that Saewulf had great trust in this local priest and confided in him the location of this hoard, in case he was killed or captured in the fighting. The priest, whose name is not recorded, was charged with trying to restore the treasure to Saewulf's family or, failing that, to give it to the Church.'

There was a silence, in which the brains of those present could almost be heard weighing up the relative rights of the ecclesiastical versus the secular authorities to a great pile of gold and silver.

'So what did you do next?' de Wolfe grated.

'I read all the manuscript, which contained other topics about the church and parish which were not relevant. I knew now what had been exercising the mind of Robert de Hane to make him so excited.'

'And what of the location of this treasure? Did the parchment explain that?' asked the Archdeacon. He almost succeeded in keeping the excitement from his voice.

'No, there was nothing. The text suggested that the directions to find the hoard were on another document. I read it, then placed it back carefully where I had found it.'

'Then what did you do?' rumbled de Wolfe.

'I was intrigued, naturally. Buried treasure fascinates us all, surely. I wanted to know more, but I could hardly ask Robert, who had already shown himself to be very secretive about it.'

'What did you think about the prospect of recovering a valuable hoard of precious metal?' asked the Archdeacon.

'I thought it would be a great honour to be able to

hand such a gift over to the Church,' replied de Limesi virtuously. 'For that was what Saewulf had commanded his priest to do, if it could not be returned to his family.'

'So you secretly recruited a mercenary to recover it for you?' said the coroner sarcastically. 'Why not go to the Archdeacon or even the Bishop and enlist the powerful aid of the Church?'

The canon flushed, either from shame or anger, de Wolfe was not sure which. 'That was my sin. I wanted to have the praise of the chapter and the Bishop. It was arrogance and pride, driving me to overtake poor Robert de Hane in finding the treasure. But it was the sin of vanity, not of my own greed.'

John held his tongue, but thought that anyone who believed that was either a saint or a fool.

'So why go to a man of fortune, if you didn't know where the hoard was hidden?' asked John de Alencon.

'I did that after I had found such directions,' replied the canon. 'The day after reading the Saewulf story, I arranged to be in the archives when de Hane was absent at devotions. I searched high and low, but found nothing. Later that day, when he had returned to the library, I went to his house on some pretext and hunted around there – we canons often visit each other's dwellings and the servants are used to other clergy being in and out – but again there was nothing. The hiding-places in his Spartan dwelling were few indeed.'

'Get to the point, man!' snapped the coroner, wearying of this slow tale.

'I found it eventually, carefully hidden in his high desk in the archives. He had sewn two old parchments together at three edges, forming a pocket. It was a single half-page of old vellum, with obvious directions to the spot where Saewulf had secreted his wealth. I copied this on to a new page, then returned the original to its hiding-place.'

'Where is that copy now?'

'I destroyed it – and the original has vanished too, for I looked yesterday. De Hane must have taken it away before his death.'

At this news there was a collective sigh.

'You had better explain,' said de Wolfe grimly.

De Limesi moved uneasily on his bench. 'The directions were to a certain spot just outside the churchyard at Dunsford. No doubt this was where de Hane went when he took those rides on his pony, to survey the scene. I went there myself, during the first days of this month. The directions were clear, but when I looked over the hedge of the churchyard, so many paces from the church and so many from one of the ancient yews, many small trees and bushes had grown over the spot. I realised that Robert could not have recovered it alone and I soon saw that it was also beyond my capabilities. I needed help to dig at that place and that is why I asked my vicar to find me a man who would do the task.'

The Archdeacon looked askance at his brother canon. 'Yes, Eric Langton! He will have to answer to the Consistory Court over this affair. But that's another matter. What came next?'

'Giles Fulford came to see me privately. He is distantly related to the Fulfords who come from near Dunsford, but that was a mere coincidence. We agreed that for recovering the hoard he would receive a tenth part of its value. This seemed appropriate as it is the same share as our tithes, if the wealth was to go to the Church.'

The stony silence that greeted this repeated assertion of his virtue spoke eloquently of the scepticism of his listeners.

'Surely you were not so naïve as to believe that a mercenary recruited in a tavern would play honestly by you?' De Wolfe had a scathing lack of belief in de Limesi's truthfulness. 'What was to stop Fulford recovering the treasure and making off with the whole lot?'

'I promised him excommunication and to be damned to eternal hell if he betrayed the Church in that way,' answered Roger earnestly.

John snorted in derision. 'Then you must be a bigger fool than you are a rogue, sir, if you believe that a man like that would care more for his soul than even a handful of silver. But carry on with your unlikely tale.'

De Limesi showed the first signs of defiance. 'Not so, Coroner! I intended going with him myself, to make sure he handed over what we agreed.'

'And I suppose you were going to make him submit by disarming his sword with your walking-stick!' retorted the coroner.

The Archdeacon raised a hand to stop the squabble. 'Let's hear the rest of your story.'

'Two weeks ago, we met outside the city and rode to Dunsford together. If we had met the parish priest I would have said that I was interested in church history – I had enough knowledge of Canon Robert's work to make it sound convincing. But in the event it was not needed. We saw no one but local peasants who were of no account.'

This dismissive attitude to those of the lower orders

in his pastoral flock also registered in the minds of his audience.

'We surveyed the churchyard, and the field and wood beyond it. The directions pointed to a patch of wasteground just over the hedge. Fulford said it was an impossible task for one man, due to this overgrowing of vegetation. It's well over a century since Saewulf buried his treasure and the place has changed.' The canon mopped his face before continuing. 'Fulford said that he would need two strong men to help him, and that made a discreet operation all the more difficult. He demanded a quarter of the proceeds instead of a tenth, and I had to agree.'

'You could have dismissed him and sought the ample help of the chapter,' said the Archdeacon, with a steely look at his colleague. 'We have more than enough strong servants in the close here.'

De Wolfe was less reticent. 'You fool, he could as easily have said he would do it for free, for he had no intention of giving you anything at all – except perhaps a few blows from the flat of his sword.'

'Let him have his say, John,' advised de Alencon.

'Fulford then forbade me to accompany him on the next visit, to keep his accomplices unidentified. He said that he would bring whatever he found to my house at night, when he and his friends had finished their digging.'

'What about the parish priest at Dunsford – and, indeed, the lord of the manor? How was he to avoid their attention?'

'This didn't seem to worry him. When I had first told him the place was Dunsford, he had laughed and said there would be no problem. Maybe because he claimed kinship with his namesakes there.'

'And did he turn up at your dwelling with a sack of gold?' asked John sarcastically.

'He did, in a manner of speaking. A week ago, he came slyly to Canons' Row in the evening, bearing an earthenware jar.'

De Wolfe's eyebrows rose in surprise, but his cynicism was soon restored.

'He was in a high temper, for after many difficulties, he said, all he and his men had unearthed was this pot. On opening it, he had by no means found the expected treasure.'

'What was in it?' cried Jordan de Brent, unable to contain his curiosity any longer.

'A single brooch – admittedly a very fine one, of Saxon workmanship, made of gold with inset jewels. It was of some considerable value, but hardly a treasure hoard as expected.'

'Anything else?' asked the Archdeacon.

'A slip of parchment, much faded and covered with mould, even though the jar had been tightly stoppered and sealed with wax. Fulford could not read so he had to bring it me. It was just about legible when I unfolded it, a short message to the effect that the brooch had been overlooked "when his treasure was hid", so that it could not be buried in the same spot as described "in the other document".'

John de Alencon exhaled softly. 'So there must have been another parchment giving directions to the main hoard?'

De Limesi nodded, his face a picture of misery. 'Undoubtedly! But search as I did, all last week, I could find no trace of it.'

'Where is this brooch now?' demanded de Wolfe. 'And the parchment?'

The canon scrabbled inside his cloak and produced a soft leather pouch. 'The brooch was kept by Fulford, in spite of my protestations. He never even let me touch it. I had to study it gripped in his fingers. But he gave me the parchment from the pot.'

He opened the pouch and took out a scrap of vellum, faded and discoloured. He unfolded it and held it out to the coroner, who passed it quickly to Thomas.

'It is covered in grey rings of dried mould,' observed the clerk with distaste. 'The writing is faint, but just readable.' He paused a moment, screwing up his eyes to decipher the words. 'It is as the canon says, telling that the brooch was buried afterwards, not where the first message described hiding the main treasure.'

'Are you sure this man had not found the main cache as well and was not just fobbing you off with this story?' suggested de Wolfe fiercely.

De Limesi turned up his hands in supplication. 'That message tells the truth – there was only the brooch. And Fulford was in a rage, threatening me for wasting his time. He demanded that I search again for the missing parchment, but there was no sign of it. Meanwhile, he said that he would keep the brooch and sell it to defray his own costs. He gave me two days to find the missing parchment. A few days before Christ Mass, I had to send him a message that I needed more time. I would try to get Robert de Hane to tell me if he had the original map and maybe go half-shares with him.'

'What's this about half-shares?' snapped John de Alencon. 'I thought you were retrieving this treasure for the glory of God in the cathedral church of Exeter?'

'Of course, brother – I meant each sharing equally in the honour of presenting it to the Bishop,' stammered de Limesi unconvincingly.

'What next?' ventured de Brent.

'Three days ago, Robert de Hane went off on his last pony ride, obviously to Dunsford again. He came back early and when I saw him in the library he was most agitated. I tried to talk to him, in the hope that he might tell me the whole story and even reveal if he had the other document. But he refused to say what was wrong and would only ask repeatedly when Bishop Marshal was due back from Gloucester as he had the most urgent news for him.'

'So what do you think had occurred?' asked de Alencon.

De Limesi's small eyes flickered from the senior priest to the coroner and back again. 'He must have seen the signs of digging among the trees and bushes on the spot described by his parchment. Disturbed earth and broken vegetation would have told him straight away that someone must have discovered his secret.'

John mused on this for a moment. 'So we still don't know if de Hane had discovered the directions to the main hoard?'

They all looked back to de Limesi for enlightenment, but he only shrugged. 'How can I tell what he knew? But I sent a message through Eric to Fulford to let him know that Robert de Hane now knew that his treasure site had been looted. I assumed that he was eager to tell the Bishop, to unburden himself so that an official search could be made, either to recover the newly stolen brooch from Fulford or to excavate for the main hoard, depending on what he already knew.'

'And that message undoubtedly led to his death!' snarled de Wolfe. 'This man and his accomplices would immediately have to silence de Hane before he gave away his secret to the cathedral authorities – and also to kill two birds with one stone, by forcing the poor canon to divulge whether he had the original parchment with the directions to the main hoard.'

'That explains the bruises on his face and arms,' exclaimed Thomas.

De Limesi buried his face in his hands. 'May the Holy Trinity forgive me! I have tried hard to convince myself that his death was either by his own hand for the shame of trying to conceal his discovery from the chapter or that it was a coincidence, a robbery and a murder unconnected with this affair. But now I see that I have been deluding myself.'

'What is to be done, John?' asked the Archdeacon. 'Are we to set the sheriff upon this young brigand right away?'

De Wolfe pondered for a moment. 'We have no proof to connect Fulford with the corpse in the privy. Indeed, we have only the story from this sorry prebendary's mouth that there is any substance in the whole affair. However, Richard de Revelle, I know, would be happy to hang Fulford, as he is less concerned with natural justice than most of us. But if Giles Fulford did get the missing parchment from the dead canon, then subterfuge, rather than execution, might be a better way of killing two different birds with one stone.'

It was late afternoon when three riders galloped along the track from Berry Pomeroy village towards the castle, set lonely on its cliff above the fishponds and mill below. There was thick forest between the village and the fortress, but a wide area had been cleared of trees around the bailey to aid defence, and the horsemen emerged from the woods well before they reached the dry ditch around the castle. The drawbridge was always down these days and they cantered across it into the bailey to draw rein before the entrance to the donjon. They did not dismount and the leader, a thin, erect man in late middle age, called imperiously to a servant leaning over the railing at the top of the wooden stairs: 'Tell your master that William Fitzhamon wants words with him – at once!'

The man scurried inside like a frightened rabbit, leaving the lord of Dartington, whose honour included Loventor and many other manors in Devon and Somerset, sitting immobile on his large stallion. He had a long chin and a high-bridged nose, giving him a haughty appearance that well suited his manner. A shock of crinkled, prematurely white hair was visible under the rim of his thick leather helmet. An equally thick leather jerkin protected his chest, over which flowed a voluminous brown riding cloak. The two horsemen behind him were his son Robert, a thirteen-year-old edition of his father, and a squire, a burly fellow from the Somerset Levels.

In a moment, the servant reappeared with the Pomeroys' seneschal, a mature man who had served the old lord for many years and was now steward and general factotum to his son. He had been expecting a visit from Fitzhamon since the rout of the Loventor men that morning and had been primed as to what to do. First, he attempted to soothe the irate neighbour with an invitation to enter the hall to take some wine, but Fitzhamon was in no mood for social niceties. 'Tell Henry de la Pomeroy to come out here and speak to me, face to face!' he snapped. 'You know full well what brings me here.'

The old seneschal, who dealt with most of Pomeroy's business, knew the score exactly, but feigned ignorance. 'I regret, Sir William, that I have no knowledge of what you mean. My master is not here. He left this morning for Exeter and then he is riding on to Tiverton.'

This was a bare-faced lie, as Henry was upstairs in his bedchamber with one of the serving-girls, his wife having left that morning to visit her sister in Okehampton. But Fitzhamon, whatever he might have suspected, had no way of challenging what the steward said and had to be content with leaving a threatening message. 'When he returns, tell him that I have had enough of his thieving ways. If so much as another twig is cut from my forests, I shall ride to Winchester – or London, if need be – to seek out the Chief Justiciar and put the matter before him. Is that understood?'

The seneschal blandly played the innocent. 'I have no notion as to what you mean, sir, but I will certainly carry those words to my lord.'

Impatiently Fitzhamon pulled round his horse's head to aim it at the gate, but then relaxed the reins to launch another tirade at Pomeroy's right-hand man. 'You can also tell him that those two men murdered by his mercenary thugs today will be investigated by Sir John de Wolfe, the King's crowner, to whom I have already sent a messenger. He also may have a thing or two to tell Hubert Walter about how they came to their deaths!'

As he dragged on the stallion's bit again, Fitzhamon made one last parting shot. 'And tell Pomeroy that I can give the Justiciar some other damning news about him and his treacherous friends!'

With that, he dug his prick-spurs into the horse's belly and hammered across the bailey, his silent companions close behind.

As they vanished over the drawbridge and into the gloom of the trees, the old steward leaned on the rail and rubbed his wispy beard thoughtfully. If he had ever heard a direct threat, this was it. And it was a dangerous one for quite a few nobles in this part of England.

CHAPTER FIVE

In which Crowner John visits a lady

In the late afternoon of the day after Christ Mass, a lone rider came through the West Gate and made his way up to Rougemont. He was unfamiliar with Exeter, having been to the city only once before. Unsure of where he should deliver his message, he dismounted at the drawbridge to the inner bailey and asked the guard for directions to someone in authority. The man-at-arms stuck his head into the door at the foot of the gatehouse, and Gabriel, the sergeant of the castle guard, soon appeared.

'My name is Ulf, bailiff to Sir William Fitzhamon at Dartington, near Totnes, come to report two dead bodies in Loventor,' declared the man. 'Who should I speak to about them?'

Gabriel, a rugged old veteran of many campaigns, was glad of an excuse to visit his friends on the top floor and led the bailiff up the narrow stairs to the small upper chamber. Here, John de Wolfe was silently mouthing the Latin phrases set by his tutor for tomorrow's lesson. Gwyn was squatting on his window-ledge, peeling an apple with his dagger, and missing the opportunity to bait Thomas, who was still in the Chapter House, searching for the missing parchment.

Gabriel announced Ulf as one of Fitzhamon's bailiffs, then subsided on to Thomas's vacant stool to eavesdrop on any news. The bailiff told his story about the sudden descent of the avengers upon Loventor's attempt to repulse the assart-cutters. 'Those men were professional soldiers, Crowner. They were well armed and cut down two of our men without warning. Though we wished to teach de la Pomeroy's woodsmen a lesson, we only intended to cause some sore heads and a few bruises – but these men slew two of ours as you would swat flies.'

'When did this happen? And what have you done with the bodies?' demanded de Wolfe.

'This very morning, sir,' replied Ulf, a heavily built Saxon with a hoarse voice. 'Sir William's steward knew that we have to report such violent deaths to the crowner so he sent me in haste to tell you.'

'You've not buried them?' growled Gwyn, knowing that the disposal of embarrassing bodies was usually a first priority of villages.

'Indeed not!' replied Ulf virtuously. 'We have put hurdles around them to keep off the dogs, who showed a great interest in the smell of blood.'

'Do you know who attacked your men?' asked de Wolfe.

'I was not there myself, but two reliable men who were leading the outlaws we hired said that one man was Giles Fulford, though the leader was a fellow with red hair, a darker shade than your man here. They did not know his name.'

The coroner looked at Gwyn enquiringly, then back at the bailiff. 'Does the name Jocelin de Braose mean anything to you?'

Ulf looked blank. 'No, never heard of him. Our men may have, but not me.'

After a few more questions, John arranged to meet the man early next morning to ride to Loventor, and Gabriel took him away, with the advice to seek a penny bed and meal at the Bush, the best inn in the city.

When they had gone, the coroner pondered the reappearance of Fulford in this incident, but felt it was impossible to relate it to the death of the canon.

'This red-headed leader, Gwyn,' he demanded of his officer. 'We must discover if this man is Jocelin de Braose. Who would know if he has the same coloured thatch?'

The Cornishman lifted a hand to his own unruly ginger hair. 'There are plenty of us about! But I'll ask at the Saracen tonight to see if anyone knows him – his squire seems to visit the place often enough.'

As it was getting dusk, before long John trudged home to Martin's Lane, to spend an evening of sullen silence with his wife, relieved only by mulled wine and dozing by the fire until it was time to stumble to bed.

In the grey light of dawn next day, the coroner rode his great stallion Bran down Fore Street to the West Gate, with Gwyn close behind on a big brown mare. The usual chill wind was blowing from the east, but there was no fresh snow. Both men wore heavy woollen tunics down to mid-calf, divided front and back to allow them to sit in the saddle. De Wolfe had a black leather hood, pointed at the back, over his long riding cloak, while Gwyn had a hessian sack wrapped around his head, the ends tucked into the frayed collar of his thick leather jerkin.

Ulf of Dartington was waiting for them inside the gate, which had just opened for the day. It was a hanging offence for a porter to allow any gate to be opened between dusk and dawn, except in some rare emergency sanctioned by the sheriff.

The three mounted men moved through the gate against a milling crowd pressing the opposite way. These were mainly countryfolk, laden with baskets of vegetables, eggs and chickens or pushing handcarts piled high with such produce. They came to sell to the city-dwellers, setting out their wares on the edge of the street or supplying the established stall-holders with fresh stock.

Once out of the gate, the riders crossed on to Exe Island, the marshy area reclaimed from the river, which supported mean huts clustered around the fulling mills for washing and preparing wool. At the other side of the island, de Wolfe led them into the cold water of the Exe, to splash across the shallows. There was a flimsy wooden bridge for travellers on foot, but the long stone bridge stood unfinished, as the builder, Walter Gervase, had again run out of funds.

Once up the opposite bank, they took the main highway west towards Plymouth and Cornwall. The going was good as the usual muddy morass had been hardened by the frost into a firm surface. Clipping along at a trot, they reached Chudleigh in less than two hours and turned off the main track southwards, to head towards Totnes on the river Dart.

Another hour or so brought them near the village of Ipplepen, when they branched off again on to tracks through the scrub and forest that lay between the villages. John knew this area well: he had been born and brought up at Stoke-in-Teignhead, a manor in a small valley south of the Teign estuary. Here his mother, brother and sister still lived and he resolved to call upon them on the way back to Exeter. Eventually they reached the hamlet of Loventor, where Ulf led them behind a tithe barn near the small wooden church. A few curious villagers trailed up to them as they slid from their horses and lashed the reins to a fence. Behind the barn, a leaning structure of wattle walls and a thatched roof, was some wasteground on which several hurdles of woven hazel-withies had been stuck in the ground to form a square against the back wall of the barn.

'We kept them in here for you, Crowner,' said Ulf proudly, aiming a kick at a scraggy dog sniffing at the enclosure.

The bailiff pulled aside a hurdle and ushered de Wolfe and his henchman inside. On the ground were two bodies, laid side by side. They were dressed in clothing so rough as to be little better than rags. 'These were outlaws?' The coroner's remark was more a statement than a question.

'They were. We gave them some food and a few pence to teach those woodcutters a lesson. They are always hanging about the villages along the edge of the moor and forest, looking either to rob and steal or to do some occasional work for a pittance.'

De Wolfe well knew that although outlaws were supposed to be hunted like vermin, they often crept back into society, either to perform casual labouring work or even to settle permanently and take up a trade. Officially they were outcasts, usually escaped prisoners, suspects on the run or sanctuary-seekers who had promised to abjure the realm but who had melted away into the forests instead of seeking ship at a port. Anyone could slay an outlaw on sight; in law, they were considered 'wolves' heads', and a bounty of five shillings could be claimed for their

amputated head, if brought as proof to the sheriff
or coroner.

'Were all your gang outlaws who attacked the assart-
makers?' snapped de Wolfe.

'All but two, who were our own men, including the
reeve. Sir William decreed it should be done, so his
steward found the men.'

De Wolfe bent over the corpses and saw that the
right arm of one had been severed at the shoulder –
the bloody limb was lying on the grass alongside him.
The other had a massive wound in the neck and the
coroner unhesitatingly stuck his fingers into the slash
to gauge its depth. He looked up at Gwyn. 'The neck
bones are chipped by the blade. It was a good blow,
almost took his head off,' he said conversationally. He
considered himself an authority on methods of killing
and maiming, after a score of years on a multitude of
battlefields. He wiped his fingers on a tuft of frozen
grass and stood up. 'I suppose I must hold an inquest
on them, Gwyn.'

The hairy assistant looked dubiously at the still
figures on the ground. 'Is there any need?' he asked
grudgingly. 'If they are outlaws, they don't even exist
in the eyes of the law. Why bother?'

The coroner rasped a hand over his black stubble –
he was due to have his shave tomorrow. 'I'm not sure.
Nor do I think that anyone else knows the answer.
The instructions are far from clear as to the duties of
coroners.'

The only mandate they had was a single sentence
issued by the meeting of the King's justices held
in Kent last September. This merely said that, in
every county, three knights and one clerk were to
be appointed to 'keep the pleas of the Crown', which

meant all legal events that took place in the county had to be recorded for presentation to the Justices when they made their visits, which were noted for their infrequency and irregularity. As part of this 'keeping of the pleas', the coroner had to investigate all sudden deaths, assaults, rapes, finds of treasure, wrecks, catches of royal fish, such as whales and sturgeon, and perhaps even robberies. He had also to attend all hangings, mutilations, ordeals, trials by combat and any other legal happening that might come along. Yet the instructions for how to deal with such matters were vague in the extreme. De Wolfe knew that if he tried to seek clarification as to whether he need investigate the deaths of non-persons such as outlaws, he would wait months for a response from the royal court, if the judges of the King's council could be bothered to consider the matter.

'Let's do it, to be on the safe side,' he muttered to his officer. 'There may be some political aspect to this. I suspect that a couple of dead men are but a symptom of some feud between Henry de la Pomeroy and William Fitzhamon, over land tenure, apart from this assart business.'

As if some heavenly ear had overheard him, a diversion occurred. Gwyn's head went up and he almost sniffed the air. 'Horsemen, coming this way – at least three of them,' he said.

It was a minute or so before de Wolfe's less keen ear heard the hoofs, but soon horses appeared at the end of the track through the village and four riders cantered up to the tithe barn. 'It's Sir William Fitzhamon,' said Ulf, hurrying out of the hurdles to pull his forelock to his master.

The leading horseman was a thin, erect man whom

John had met somewhere in the past, but with whom he was barely acquainted. Fitzhamon dismounted, walked across to the coroner and greeted him abruptly, giving hardly a glance at the bloody cadavers on the ground. 'This is my son, Robert,' he said jerking his head at the lad, who had also slid from his horse, leaving two squires mounted to guard their rear. 'I assumed rightly that you would come here this morning, in response to the message I sent with my bailiff,' he said, with a touch of arrogance that irritated John. 'These dead rogues are of no account in themselves, but I wanted official recognition of the harm and insult that Pomeroy has done to my estate.'

De Wolfe, half a head taller than Fitzhamon, glowered at the older man. 'I gather this comes about from some land dispute?'

'There is no dispute, Sir John. The land is mine and has been in our family for generations. It is flagrant robbery on the part of Pomeroy, who is trying to push back my boundary by several hides, hacking and burning my part of the forest where it abuts on to his land, between this village and Afton.' He smacked his leg in anger with a riding crop. 'It's not the first time he's tried this.'

He took the coroner by the elbow and pulled him away from the others, while his son followed uncertainly behind him. 'I have a number of manors scattered over the western counties and I cannot be everywhere at once. But this has gone too far. I have threatened Pomeroy that I will petition the King if he does not stop cutting my trees and withdraw back to his own boundaries.'

'The King is a hard man to petition, these days. He is ever abroad,' observed de Wolfe, though without any hint of criticism of Richard the Lionheart's disregard for England.

'I know that, and resign myself to not seeing him in person – though I wish I was still young enough to assist him in his war against that milk-sop in France, the unspeakable Philip.'

De Wolfe's heart began to warm to Fitzhamon, after their first cool encounter. Anyone who was such a staunch supporter of the King was a man to admire, in his eyes.

'I can – and will – go to see the Justiciar over this,' continued Fitzhamon. 'I regret that I missed the chance to meet him last month when he was in Exeter, but I had a week of the bloody flux and could not get from my bed or the privy.'

'Hubert Walter is a fair-minded man and would consider your complaints seriously,' advised de Wolfe.

Fitzhamon gave a quick look over his shoulder. 'I could tell him a few other things as well, beyond my complaints about my land boundaries, if I had a mind. Things he might well pass on to our sovereign.'

Intrigued, John tried to lead him into more detail, but Fitzhamon seemed to feel that he had said too much already and would not be drawn further. They walked back to the barn and Fitzhamon prepared to remount his horse. 'I wished to bring these deaths to your notice in the proper manner, Crowner, so that Henry de la Pomeroy is in no doubt that he has done wrong in setting a pack of rogues upon my own men who are defending my land.'

As he swung himself into the saddle, de Wolfe went up to him. 'Your bailiff said that a man called Giles Fulford was among those who attacked your men, but that the leader was a red-headed fellow. Have you any idea who that might be?'

Fitzhamon shook his head. 'I am not acquainted with the mercenaries of this county, sir. I know that many hot-blooded young men are putting themselves at the disposal of those who need strong arms and long swords to further their ambitions. I myself was invited to join them, but I considered it infamous! But, as to names, I can't help you. I leave that to my servants.' With this arrogant snub, he swung his horse round and cantered off, his silent son and two guards close behind him.

The coroner stared after them, until they vanished around a bend in the track. 'I wonder what it was he almost told me,' he mused.

The inquest that followed was a simple, hurried affair. Gwyn rounded up the two Loventor men who had accompanied the outlaw pack that had attacked the woodcutters. The surviving outlaws had vanished: no forest-dweller was going to risk being in the proximity of the King's coroner if he wanted to keep his head on his shoulders.

As Thomas was not there to pen a record on to his rolls, de Wolfe had to remember the few relevant facts so that he could relay them to the clerk when they got back to Exeter. With a handful of village men as a jury, the coroner rapidly recounted the circumstances of the killings. Though there was obviously no way to 'present Englishry' on a pair of nameless outlaws, he was reluctant to amerce the village with a murdrum fine, salving his legal conscience with the excuse that as the men were legally non-existent, it did not matter from what race they came.

Within ten minutes, the circle of uncomprehending men standing around the corpses had been told by the coroner to bring in a verdict of murder by persons unknown. They were allowed then to shuffle away, reluctantly going back to their tedious labours after this unusual diversion from the endless drudgery of village routine.

'I had thought to name Giles Fulford as one of the killers,' said John to his officer, 'but there's no proof other than the word of a villager – and little good it would do anyway. But we must keep a closer eye on Master Fulford when we get back to Exeter.'

It was gone noon when they left Loventor, and although they could have got back to Exeter before curfew closed the gates, de Wolfe took the opportunity to visit his family. Though they travelled through lonely countryside, along narrow tracks well suited to ambush, the two old fighting companions felt no threat from wayside brigands. John's steed patently advertised the fact that he was a warrior, for Bran was a giant of a horse, his size and hairy feet proclaiming him for a destrier, a warhorse used to carrying the weight of arms and armour. As for Gwyn, it was the man rather than the brown mare that would have given any footpad cause to hesitate. The wild, hairy giant, with his leather cuirass, shoulders protected with metal plates, had a ferocious look that strongly suggested he would be quite happy to use the huge sword hanging from one saddle-peg or the hand-axe swinging from the other.

An hour and a half took them the nine miles from Loventor, through Kinkerswell to Stoke-in-Teignhead, a well-ordered village with a neat manor house, nestling in a green valley a mile or so from the sea. The house was solidly built in stone, one of the last acts of his father, Simon de Wolfe, before he went off to the Irish wars where he was killed. Years of peace had allowed the defences of the house to be relaxed, and though there was a wooden stockade around the yard, its drawbridge had not been raised for as long as John could remember. They clattered across it to be greeted with genuine pleasure by the servants, some of whom had known John since he was a child. Gwyn was also a favourite, as he had been there many times. Both serving-wenches and the men enjoyed his boisterous good humour, which gave the lie to his wild looks. He went off to the kitchens to pinch the cook-maids' bottoms and be fed until he could eat no more, while de Wolfe went in to his family.

The steward, an old Saxon called Alsi, met him on the stairs from the yard, beaming his pleasure at the visit. 'Your brother is at Holcombe today, Master John, but your mother and sister are up in the solar.'

The rest of the day was spent in eating, drinking and gossiping around a roaring fire in the hall. His mother, Enyd de Wolfe, was a sprightly, still attractive woman of sixty-three, with auburn hair, which now, however, contained some silver threads. Small and dainty, her vivacity made everyone love her, from the lowest servant to her three children. The eldest was William, today at their other manor a few miles north along the coast at Holcombe, near Dawlish. He was two years older than John, but looked much like him – tall, dark and lean, like their father. But William's nature was different: he had no interest in travel, fighting or foreign wars. His passions were farming, sheep-rearing and running the two manors. When their father had died, he had inherited the estate, but equal shares of the income came to Enyd and the two other children, the third being Evelyn. She was the baby, now thirty-four, an amiable, gossipy woman. Evelyn had wished to become a nun, but after her father's death, Enyd had asked her to stay at home and help run the household.

This cold evening, they delighted in fussing over John, extracting all the news and Exeter gossip that they could get from him – even that concerning Matilda, whom they disliked as much as she disliked them. Privately, Enyd always regretted her son's marriage into the de Revelle family, which had been engineered by his father as a socially advantageous move that would enable John to become a county notable. However, Simon had not foreseen his own early death – nor that John would spend two decades away from Devon at the wars, mainly to keep away from his unpleasant wife. That his mother was Celtic, with a Welsh mother and a Cornish father, was anathema to Matilda, to whom anyone less than full-blooded Norman was on a par with the animal kingdom.

Eventually, almost dizzy from too much food, wine and chatter, de Wolfe stumbled off to a mattress stuffed with goose feathers set out for him at the side of the hearth and slept as well as Gwyn, who had a blanket thrown over a pile of hay in the warmth of the kitchen hut.

In the morning, the twenty-eighth day of December, after a huge breakfast, they left Stoke and rode gently up to the mouth of the Teign. At low tide they waded their horses across the narrow river where it passed the sand-bar to reach the sea. On the other side, John led the way up the coast track, then turned slightly inland to reach the village of Holcombe. Here he found his brother supervising the building of a barn, part of which was to store the wool from an increased flock of sheep that helped to sustain de Wolfe's income.

William came down a crude ladder to greet his brother, and the two men embraced warmly. 'I couldn't pass by without giving you my wishes for a prosperous New Year, brother!' exclaimed John. 'Especially as my own prosperity depends so much on your efforts.'

They talked for a while about the manors and the wool trade, which was the economic strength of England. Gwyn watched from a polite distance, marvelling again at the similarity in the appearance of the brothers, and in the difference between their personalities. After family talk had been exhausted, William asked about the coroner's work, which seemed to fascinate him. De Wolfe related his current problems, then asked if his brother knew anything of Giles Fulford and Jocelin de Braose, but William had never heard of them.

Gwyn waited patiently for half an hour until the two men had had their say. Then, after mutual slaps on the back, de Wolfe climbed aboard his great horse and they set off again northwards. It was not yet mid-morning as they cantered along the coastal track towards Dawlish, a few miles further on. They could have reached Exeter by early afternoon, but from past experience Gwyn suspected that they would just make the city gates as they were closing at dusk.

Fishermen's huts along the beach indicated that they were in Dawlish, though the centre of the village was a little inland, up a small creek where boats were beached on the banks. John slowed Bran to a walk as he turned up the path alongside the little river and seemed to be staring intently at them as if seeking a particular vessel. Then he prodded the stallion into a trot and moved up the track to where a number of houses, both wooden and stone, formed the nucleus of the hamlet. He reined up outside a new dwelling, built of grey stone with two round arches facing the road, enclosing a sheltered arcade in the Breton style. He turned in his saddle to speak to his officer. 'Gwyn, I have a call to make, so find yourself the alehouse and have some food and drink. I'll see you later.'

The Cornishman grinned under his bushy moustache: his earlier prophecy had been confirmed. As he plodded away for some welcome meat and ale, de Wolfe dismounted and tied his horse to a rail at the side of the new house. There was a closed door at the front, under the arches, but he walked down the side towards the yard at the back, seeking the rear entrance.

'Are you a thief who tries to sneak into my house unobserved?' came a voice from behind him.

He swung round and a smile of pure pleasure transformed his usually sombre features. An attractive lady was standing there, having slipped out of the front door and followed him round. 'Hilda! By God, you look more lovely every time I see you.' The sincerity of his greeting brought colour to her cheeks and she stepped forward to kiss his lips. Her oval face was made brilliant by two large blue eyes and a full red mouth, but her glory was the cascade of pale blonde hair that fell below her shoulders. The usual cover-chief of white linen was absent and her long neck was bare of any wimple, though it carried a heavy-linked gold chain. She wore a simple kirtle of cream linen with blue embroidery around the high neck-line. A blue cord was wound twice around her waist, the long tasselled ends falling almost to her feet.

She linked her arm in his and pulled him towards the gate into the yard. 'You may as well come in by the servant's entrance, if you were so reluctant to use the front door,' she teased.

'I couldn't see Thorgils' boat in the river, but he might have changed it, for all I knew,' he explained sheepishly.

As they made for the back door, she told him that her husband was away. 'As usual, so I see him about one day in twenty. He has taken wool to St Malo and will not be back until next week.' Probably some of my own wool, thought de Wolfe, as he had both the partnership with his brother and another with one of the Exeter portreeves, Hugh de Relaga.

The ground floor of the house, which was large by local standards, was a storeroom for Thorgils' trade and was piled high with bales, boxes and casks. A girl was searching for something among them, and smiled archly at John and her mistress as they made for the stairs to the upper floor. Hilda gave her a light clip around the ear and ordered her to bring some food from the kitchen for her guest. Grinning even more widely, the girl scuttled out to take the latest gossip to the other servants.

The upper floor was the living quarters, with a stone chimney, a table and chairs and a sleeping area with a large palliasse covered in sheepskins. The room was warm from a glowing fire and Hilda struggled to pull off John's cloak and hood. He released his clumsy sword scabbard and dropped the massive weapon with a clang on to the floorboards. He sank down thankfully on the edge of the palliasse and waited for her to pour some wine from a stone bottle into two shallow cups.

As they drank, the pert serving-maid came carefully up the steep stairs with a board carrying bread, meat and fish. She put it down, then left, and, for the next few minutes, the blonde woman watched him eat, as they caught up with each other's news.

De Wolfe had known Hilda since she was a child, as she was the daughter of the former manor reeve in Holcombe. He was eight years older than her, but even before he left home for the wars when he was seventeen, she had been a budding beauty. At every homecoming afterwards they would flirt and by the time she was fifteen they were lovers. Both knew that it would never progress beyond happy tumbles in the hay, as she was from a lowly Saxon family who served the Norman lord of the manor and his family, of which de Wolfe was a member. One day, when John returned from France, he found that Hilda had been married to a much older man, Thorgils the Boatman in nearby Dawlish. She was not unhappy at that: he was a good man with an excellent business who could give her most things in life – this new house was evidence of his prosperity. De Wolfe thought that, years ago, he might have been in love with Hilda, but long separations and her marriage had rendered his feelings to genuine affection and a healthy lust. He suspected that Thorgils knew he was being cuckolded – and maybe by others than himself – but nothing was ever said. Perhaps the sixty-year-old mariner accepted that leaving ashore a beautiful wife half his age carried inevitable risks.

Hilda poured more wine and sat down next to him on the bed. He told her of the current goings-on and the problems with both the dead canon and the land dispute not far away in Loventor. When he mentioned Giles Fulford, her face darkened. 'That man and his master – they are a pair of lecherous swine!'

John looked at her in surprise. 'You know them?'

'Hardly know them, but they came here some weeks ago, to meet Thorgils' boat when he returned from Caen. He was two days late because of contrary winds so they stayed in the village. Both of them tried to seduce me – to pass the time, it seemed, even though they had their own doxies with them.'

'What was his master like? You know his name?'

'Of course. It was Jocelin de Braose. Those two were more like brothers than lord and squire. I suspect they took it in turns with the same women. One was a black-haired harlot – Rosamunde of Rye, they called her.'

'What does he look like, this Jocelin?'

Hilda leaned back to look at him quizzically. 'Why are you so interested, John? Are you going to challenge them for trying to lie with me?'

'We know this Giles is involved in several dubious escapades, but de Braose is more elusive. What's he like?'

'Good-looking, I must admit, though he has none of your mature charms, John.'

He tapped her shapely bottom in rebuke. 'I asked what he looks like.'

'Red hair – a dark auburn, in curls. Quite a lady's man, if you fall for that sort of pretty boy.'

'By all accounts he's pretty handy with a sword. Yesterday I held an inquest on two men he and his friends had hacked to death.' De Wolfe threw back the rest of his wine. 'Why should they want to see Thorgils, anyway?'

She tossed her long hair with an elegant swing of her head. 'He was bringing half a dozen men from France. They came to meet them from his boat.'

'What sort of men?'

'Soldiers, I'm sure. Not ordinary men-at-arms, but well-dressed, well-armed knights. They were Normans – I mean, men from Normandy itself, for they had not a word of English between them.'

'Has this happened before?'

'Yes, both Thorgils and some of the other boatmen along the coast have been ferrying such men for the past couple of months. I don't know where they go, but someone brings spare horses for them and they gallop off into the countryside somewhere.'

She put down her wine cup and snuggled closer to de Wolfe. 'I'm tired of talking about my husband's cargoes. Are you only here to spy on me, John, and wheedle out the secrets of Dawlish?'

He grinned his rare grin again, and held her by the shoulders to look at her smooth, lovely face. A purist might have thought her nose a trifle too long, but for a woman of thirty-two she was as near perfection as any man could want.

He leaned forward and they kissed again, then slowly slid sideways on top of the sheepskins.

As Gwyn had predicted, they reached Exeter with little time to spare before the city gates creaked shut. Gwyn carried on outside the walls to reach his hut in St Sidwell's, while the coroner plodded his tired stallion up to the livery stables in Martin's Lane. When he had seen Bran safely fed and watered, he walked across to his own house and cautiously entered the hall. There was no sign of Mary to give him early warning of any domestic strife so he had to cross the flagstones to the hearth, where he could see a pair of feet projecting from one of the cowled monks' chairs.

'You've deigned to come home at last, have you?' a high, hard-edged voice snapped. Matilda was huddled against the draughts with a woollen shawl over her kirtle. 'You stay away for two days and a night with no message for me whatsoever. How am I supposed to know where you are and when you'll be back?'

'Does it matter?' he grunted. 'You'd never have a meal waiting. If it wasn't for Mary, I'd starve to death in this miserable house.'

'That's what serving-girls are for, you fool. Though perhaps you can find other uses for them, that Saxon included!'

For a moment, he thought she meant Hilda, whom he hoped was still unknown to his wife – but then he realised that her remark had been directed at Mary, whose mother was a native.

'You've been in every tavern in Devon, I suppose, since I last saw you.'

This rankled with de Wolfe, as he had not set foot in an inn since Christ Mass. 'I have been to see two dead outlaws, then stayed with my family, held an inquest and then travelled home.' He reversed the order of the inquest and his visit to Stoke to account for the time spent that day, but whatever he said, Matilda would use it as grounds for complaint.

She ranted on for a few more minutes, managing to get in a few spiteful remarks about his family, then grudgingly gave him a message. 'That evil little clerk you employ is sitting in the kitchen, as far as I know. He came here two hours ago, pestering us to know where you were. He says he has an urgent message for you – though what can ever be urgent in your business is quite beyond my understanding.'

Eager both to escape her and to hear what Thomas de Peyne had to say, de Wolfe loped away to the vestibule and turned down the earth-floored passageway to the backyard. In the lean-to shanty on the left, which was both the kitchen and Mary's home, he found his crooked clerk perched on a stool. He was eating heartily, for the motherly Mary, suspecting that the little ex-cleric was half-starved, was stuffing him with good food.

When Thomas saw his master, he gulped the last mouthful and slid off the low stool next to the cooking fire. 'Crowner, I have some news from the Close. Canon Roger de Limesi's vicar came to me this afternoon at his master's behest. The man Fulford has sought Langton, and demanded that he hand over the parchment that reveals the site of the main treasure. He threatens to kill de Limesi if he fails to deliver it. The canon does not know what to do, as he has no such document, as we know.'

The coroner adjusted his mind to this new and unexpected turn of events. 'Does the Archdeacon know of this?'

Thomas nodded. 'The canon went directly to see him, in fear for his life. I think the Archdeacon is awaiting your return to discuss what is to be done.'

De Wolfe rasped a hand thoughtfully over his chin, the stubble now well overdue for attention. 'Go to the Close, arrange for Roger de Limesi and his vicar to attend upon John de Alencon at his house at the seventh hour, then go to the Archdeacon and say that we will all be there at that time.'

The little clerk hurried away self-importantly, and

the coroner turned to Mary, who had been silently listening to these exchanges.

'I'll have something to eat out here, my girl. The atmosphere in the hall is colder than an easterly gale.'

He failed to mention that he did not feel like going to the Bush for a meal that night: there, he would have to meet the landlady's eye after his visit to Dawlish that day.

The Archdeacon lived in Canons' Row in the same way as many of his fellow prebendaries. Among the twenty-four priests some had specific appointments and duties, but this gave them no special privileges. There were four archdeacons – John de Alencon for Exeter itself, the others for Cornwall, Totnes and Barnstaple. There were also the Precentor and the Treasurer, but all had similar houses and lifestyles, either in the Close or in houses elsewhere in the city.

De Alencon, named after the town in Normandy from where his family originated, resided in the second house in the Close from St Martin's church, almost within a stone's throw from the coroner's dwelling. After he had finished a hot, filling meal quickly provided by Mary, de Wolfe had made a token visit to the hall to emphasise to Matilda that he was going out on duty, to meet senior members of her beloved priesthood.

He walked across to the Close and found Thomas waiting for him, shivering in his thin cloak outside the Archdeacon's house. Inside, Roger de Limesi and his vicar Eric Langton were already there, both looking subdued and uneasy. Indeed, the canon was afraid for his very life after the murder of de Hane and the threats of Giles Fulford.

The room in which they met was almost as spartan as Robert de Hane's bare chamber further down the road. John de Alencon was another austere priest who took the Rule of St Chrodegang literally, as far as worldly goods and comforts were concerned. They sat around a bare table on rough benches, the only light coming from three tallow dips hung on the wall, which also carried a large crucifix.

'We could have this villain seized by the sheriff, I'm sure,' began de Alencon. 'Richard de Revelle would be happy to indict him on the sworn evidence of Langton and the canon here. Threatening the life of a man of God – or anyone else – must surely be a hanging matter?'

Remembering his brother-in-law's strange attitude to Fulford, de Wolfe was not so sure, but kept his tongue still on that matter. He said, 'Maybe, but what would it achieve? There is not the slightest proof that he was involved with the death of Robert de Hane, though the circumstances point that way.'

'De Revelle is not noted for his affection for proof,' said the Archdeacon wryly.

'No, but it would be far better to catch this man red-handed, for it may also trap any associates he may have. His master is a knight called Jocelin de Braose, and I have good reason to think that both of them were involved in some other bloody venture. Maybe this de Braose is in on the treasure hunt as well.'

'So what do we do, John?' asked de Alencon. 'We have no map or directions to give him.'

John looked sideways at his stunted scribe. 'But we

could always manufacture one. How would he know the difference?'

De Limesi's small eyes had almost vanished into his podgy cheeks. 'Surely he could tell an ancient parchment from a new one? It's my life that's in danger if he suspects he is being hoodwinked.'

Thomas spoke up. 'I could use a piece of old parchment taken from some of the blank skins that abound in the archives. I can thin my ink to make it faint like old writing. And remember, he cannot read.'

'So how does he hope to find any treasure, if he cannot decipher the directions?' asked the Archdeacon, reasonably.

'This vicar will have to translate it for him. Is that what happened last time?'

Eric Langton nodded. 'He committed what I said to memory. It was not difficult, only a number of paces and a landmark or two.'

The coroner looked grimly at him. 'You'll have to go with them this time, to interpret the instructions on the spot.'

As he realised the hazards, the vicar paled. 'When they find there is no hoard, they will undoubtedly turn nasty,' he stuttered.

'That can be part of your penance, brother,' observed de Alencon drily. 'Albeit a very small part, considering the evil you have done.'

De Wolfe brought the meeting back to practical matters. 'My clerk will produce a false parchment. Thomas, it should have complicated instructions, so that Langton will inevitably have to go with Fulford to translate them. Otherwise, we have no means of knowing when they will attempt to recover the treasure.'

He looked at John de Alencon. 'We need to ambush

these fellows and catch them in the act. For several reasons, I do not wish to involve the sheriff at this stage. Afterwards though he will need to take into custody any perpetrators.'

'What are you asking, John?' responded the Archdeacon.

'We don't know how many adventurers or ruffians Fulford will bring into this escapade. I have only one fighting man to assist me so we need a few strong arms to capture anyone who tries to dig for this treasure. Can you help there?'

There was some discussion between the two canons, and it was arranged that several of the younger servants from the Close would be recruited, including David from de Hane's household. Thomas would go straight away that evening to the Chapter House library and write some fictitious account of where the main hoard could be found in the vicinity of Dunsford church. Eric Langton would take this to the Saracen late that evening; if Fulford was not there, he would try again tomorrow, insisting that he had better be present at the digging, to interpret the instructions accurately.

With much misgiving on the part of both Roger de Limesi and his vicar-choral, the meeting broke up so that the priests could prepare for their nightly services, and de Wolfe could go home to his frosty welcome at his own fireside.

CHAPTER SIX

In which Crowner John lurks behind a hedge

When there was no war, revolt or insurrection in England, the nobility had to find other ways to pass the time and release their aggression. The usual surrogate for armed conflict was hunting, where the urge to kill and maim was transferred from fellow men to animals. In Devon, the wolf, the wild boar, the fox and, above all, the stag were the victims of this pastime, which in the case of some Normans was almost a full-time occupation. The forests were sacrosanct, either to the lord of the honour or to the King, who reserved to himself vast areas for hunting. It might be a capital offence for any commoner to poach on these lands and a complex system existed to protect the hunting by means of verderers and even special courts for the punishment of offenders.

But on the day before the eve of New Year, the hunting on the lower reaches of the River Dart was untroubled by poachers: a score of the local aristocracy were scouring the heavily wooded valley in pursuit of their sport. The event had been organised by Henri de Nonant, the lord of Totnes, who had invited many of his friends and neighbours to hunt on his lands, as well as in the forest owned by Bernard Cheever and on the estates of other manorial lords whose domains were continuous with theirs.

De Nonant had started the day with a lavish breakfast for all the hunters in Totnes Castle. A remarkable fortress, it had been built by Juhael soon after the Conquest; hundreds of men had toiled to raise a high mound, on which he built a circular stockade. At one side was a large bailey, itself protected by a deep ditch, the whole edifice looking down on and dominating the little walled town that stretched down to the Dart. To his surprise, as he was not the most sociable of men, Sir William Fitzhamon was one of those invited, though his son was not. Being as fond of chasing the stag as any other man, he accepted the invitation, which had come at short notice the previous day. It was delivered by word of mouth by de Nonant's bailiffs, who travelled around the district recruiting the guests.

The hunters assembled soon after dawn, none having to travel more than a dozen miles to reach Totnes. As many of the participants had their own squires, the company amounted to more than thirty men, and after eating and drinking, the already raucous throng set off from the castle bailey into the dense woods that rose on each side of the valley. There was no set route or organisation: the hunters dispersed into the forests and scrubland as they wished, some in small groups, others in pairs or with their squires. All had their own hounds running alongside, darting hither and thither, looking for the scent of deer or boar. Most hunters carried a long-bow and a supply of arrows, though a few relied only on lances.

Within minutes, the yelling and horn-blowing around

the castle subsided, though occasionally the gate-keeper could still hear a distant blast or the yelp of a hound up on the hillsides. The weather had improved slightly and the wind was not so keen in the deep vale of the Dart, though there was still frost on the ground to keep the mud at bay.

Deprived of his son, William Fitzhamon had brought with him one of his reeves, a man called Ansgot, renowned for his prowess with the bow. His lord suspected him of being an accomplished poacher, but as long as he did not practise on Fitzhamon's own land, he was not bothered – if the fellow wanted to risk a hangman's noose elsewhere, that was his business.

With the Saxon close behind him, Fitzhamon cantered away from the castle with the rest of the crowd, but gradually they all diverged and when well into the trees, the two were alone. Ansgot had with him a pair of large hounds, loping along one each side, but so far they had shown no sign of raising a quarry.

Fitzhamon pushed ahead, along the east bank of the river, then splashed across and started to climb the other side of the valley. Although he knew more than half of the other hunters, who were either acquaintances or neighbours, he deliberately kept away from the distant sounds of the pack, preferring to hunt alone. Soon one of the hounds shot off to the right and, nose to the ground, vanished into the trees.

'He's taken a scent, master,' called Ansgot, and for five minutes or so, they pushed their way through thickening forest to keep the hounds in sight – the other had chased away to join its companion. Then the reeve called again, shouting urgently at his master's back. Impatiently, Fitzhamon reined in his horse and looked over his shoulder. Ansgot had stopped and was dismounting to feel his horse's back leg.

Cursing, he trotted back to his servant to see what was wrong.

'He's lame. I thought there was something wrong a while back, master.' The reeve picked up the animal's hoof and held it between his thighs, the better to examine the lower leg. 'There's a cut here, in the fetlock,' he exclaimed. 'What bastard would do this to a fine mare?'

His master, anxious to follow the hounds, looked down impatiently from his saddle. 'Was she sound when you left home?'

'Yes, sir. This is a fresh wound. It must have been done when we ate at the castle. While you went to the hall, we serving-men were fed in the kitchens. The horses were left tied up in the bailey.'

Fitzhamon sighed in exasperation. 'Then you'll have to walk her back to the castle. I'll see you there when the day's sport is finished.' He wheeled his horse around and hurried after the hounds, who were whimpering at the edge of the small clearing, anxious to follow their scent. Cursing, Ansgot began the long trek back, leading his lame mare by a rein.

While the nobles of south Devon were crashing through the forest in search of their quarry, a second meeting was taking place in the Archdeacon's house in Exeter. Once again, the late-morning meals usually enjoyed by the clergy were being postponed by the need to devise a plan of action.

'I gave Thomas's false document to Giles Fulford late last night,' muttered Eric Langton. 'He wanted to know where I had obtained it so I told him I found it among de Hane's papers in the archives.'

'Did he accept it as genuine, do you think?' demanded John de Wolfe.

'I'm sure he did. The greed showed on his face and he was in no frame of mind to question it.'

Thomas allowed himself a congratulatory smirk. He was proud of his forgery, which he had laboured over the previous evening. On a piece of vellum torn from an old hymnal, he had penned long-winded instructions to an imaginary site where the treasure was buried, using old ink he found in a stone bottle in the cathedral library. He had diluted this with dirty water from the yard outside, rapidly dried it over a candle flame, then rubbed and creased it until it looked genuinely old.

'And you say Fulford will go to Dunsford to make the search tomorrow?' confirmed the coroner.

The scar-faced vicar nodded gloomily. 'He will be there at noon, he said. He was riding off somewhere at crack of dawn today, but will be back at Dunsford tomorrow.'

'And he accepted that you must be there also?' asked John de Alencon.

The vicar sighed. 'Yes, sir, to my peril. In fact he gave me back the parchment. He said it was no use to him without me to read it. I am to meet him just outside the village at midday.'

'Did he say who will be with him?' demanded the coroner.

'I tried to discover that, Crowner, but he told me to mind my own business. He's not a man you can ask twice.'

John turned to his officer. 'We will get there well

before him and conceal ourselves somewhere within sight. Thomas is not needed. He can continue to look for this real document.'

The clerk had mixed feelings about this. A self-admitted coward, he was happy to avoid any violent confrontation, but he would have liked to witness the climax of the affair, preferably from a safe distance.

'Archdeacon, we may take the two men you mentioned from these houses to add strength to our arms?' asked de Wolfe.

The ecclesiastical John nodded, though his lean face looked worried. 'I hope no harm will come to them. As cathedral servants, they do not expect to act as warriors.'

'Look upon it as them policing the safety of the canons, John. This all stems from the murder of one of your brothers.'

This satisfied de Alencon's conscience and he looked hard at Eric Langton. 'If you conduct yourself well in this, it will go in your favour when you are judged by the Bishop. He returns tomorrow night and will have to be informed at once of all these unfortunate happenings during his absence.' His grey eyes strayed to Roger de Limesi, who tried to look both virtuous and contrite.

'How long did it take you to ride to Dunsford?' the coroner snapped at the vicar.

'My poor nag is broken in the wind and she can move at little more than a walk. But on your steeds you could reach the village in just over an hour – it is but seven miles away.'

The coroner arranged for Gwyn to make sure that the cathedral servants were well mounted and armed, and to meet himself and his officer at the ford beyond the West Gate three hours before noon the following day. Then the meeting broke up, but the Archdeacon took John aside as the rest were leaving. 'Why are you avoiding the sheriff's participation in this?' he asked.

De Wolfe replied, in a low voice so that the others would not overhear, 'There is something going on that I do not understand yet. This man Fulford – and, I suspect, his master de Braose – keeps appearing in various places, yet de Revelle seems reluctant even to question them. That is partly why I hope to catch at least one of them red-handed tomorrow. Then the sheriff can hardly avoid taking some official notice.'

The two Johns eyed each other steadily and each felt sure their thoughts were similar. 'Are the old troubles starting up again?' asked the priest cryptically.

The coroner sighed. 'I have no proof, but my guts tell me that something is brewing. Let's just watch and wait, old friend.'

Henri de Nonant's breakfast, though lavish in quality and especially quantity, did not last the hungry hunters many hours. Chasing around the countryside, even on horseback, was an effective way for large, muscular men to use up energy – and when their quarry was nearby, they would dismount and chase on foot with their long-bows, working up both a sweat and an appetite. By noon, they were making their way back to Totnes, their throats dry from shouting and horn-blowing, their stomachs rumbling with hunger. In dribs and drabs, the score and a half men came back into the castle bailey, a few with deer draped across their squire's saddle-bows and one or two with dead foxes. The sport had not been too good – most of the animals of the upper Dart valley had had the sense to keep out of range of the hunters and their hounds.

Once again, the lord of this honour had laid on plenty of food and drink, and soon the hall was resounding with noisy chatter, coarse laughter and the sounds of eating, drinking and belching. De Nonant was acting the perfect host, going from group to group, slapping backs, making jokes and listening to the interminable exaggerations of the hunters about the one that got away.

But outside, one man was not so cheerful and became more worried as time went by. Those who were not landowners or their squires were fed in the kitchens, a dozen or so men, usually far better hunters than their masters. Among them was Ansgot, whose eyes kept turning to the gateway in the bailey as he waited for his master to return. He began to question the others as to whether they had seen Sir William Fitzhamon after he himself had had to return with his lame mare. He was met with shaken heads and blank expressions – some of them wouldn't have recognised Fitzhamon. Eventually, Ansgot left his food and climbed the wooden stairs to the entrance to the hall. He put his head in at the door and looked for de Nonant's steward. After a while he managed to attract his attention – the older man was supervising the servants taking food, ale and wine around to the hunters.

'Is my master here, Sir William Fitzhamon?' He wondered if, in some unlikely way, he had arrived unseen.

The steward shook his head. 'Not in here, brother. I haven't seen him since breakfast.'

The bailiff became more worried than ever, for although his lord was a stern, unbending man, he was not feared or disliked. He was always fair with his people, both freemen and villeins. His wife, too, was a good woman, who did her best to help the more unfortunate of the villagers, especially sick children. He had no desire to see Fitzhamon lying injured in the forest, perhaps gored by a maddened wild boar. Ansgot went back to the kitchen and spoke to a few men he knew, reeves and falconers from other villages. Two left their pots of ale and cider, and went out with him to look for his master. He borrowed a sound horse and the three men rode quietly away over the drawbridge and down through the town into the woods. The Saxon led the way along the path he had taken that morning, before his horse went lame, then continued on to the river, which was the way Fitzhamon had said he was going. At the other side of the small ford, the three men separated and went off at parallel routes, a few hundred paces apart.

Ansgot was now alone and carried on for the better part of a mile before he heard urgent blasts of a horn to his right, followed by the plaintive baying of hounds. The man on his left came crashing through the undergrowth to respond to the summons and Ansgot joined him. The three were soon together again, and Fitzhamon's two hounds bounded to the familiar figure of the reeve.

The falconer slung his horn back over his shoulder and slid from his horse to approach something hidden by a clump of withered ferns covered in hoar-frost, with trees on every side.

'It's Fitzhamon, Ansgot. And he's dead.'

Matilda was in a half-way mood, as John described it to Nesta later that evening. She was not raving at him or throwing shoes, as she sometimes did, but was distant and sullen, replying to his attempts at conversation with polite disdain, not using two words where one would curtly suffice. Thankfully, she managed enough speech to tell him that she was going to one of her interminable services at the small church of St Olave, at the top of Fore Street.

They had already eaten their evening meal, boiled belly of pork with cabbage and onions. The supper was a silent, strained affair, but Mary gave de Wolfe a broad wink every time she passed behind Matilda to show that she was sympathising with him. As soon as she had cleared the debris of the bread trenchers and spilt gravy from the scrubbed boards of the table, John retired to the fireside with another quart of cider, whilst his wife marched up to the solar for Lucille to dress her for church. Her maid was a refugee from the Vexin, north of the lower Seine, which Prince John had lost to Philip of France while the Lionheart was imprisoned in Germany.

When mistress and maid had left for St Olave's, the coroner lost no time in leaving for the Bush, giving Mary a crushing hug and kiss of thanks on the way out.

In the tavern in Idle Lane, business was quieter than it had been on his last visit. His customary bench was empty and, after a few words with a couple of acquaintances on his way across, he sat down and waited for Edwin to bring over a jar of ale. As the old soldier slid it on to the table, he failed to make his usual salutation, but rolled his one good eye towards the back of the room and made a grimace that de Wolfe took as some sort of warning. Puzzled, the coroner took a few mouthfuls and waited for Nesta to appear, but after five minutes there was still no sign of her. He turned around and saw the Welsh woman standing at the door that led to the kitchens. She had been looking across at him, but as soon as their eyes met she turned abruptly and vanished through the door.

Edwin passed him, collecting empty tankards from the tables. 'You're in the shite, Cap'n. You want to keep your legs crossed for a bit,' he muttered conspiratorially.

It dawned on John what had happened. 'How in hell did she find out?' he muttered to the old pot-man.

'A carter from Dawlish came in this morning. He started talking about warhorses and the fool let drop that yesterday he had seen your Bran tied up outside the house of Thorgils the Boatman. Mistress Nesta was not amused!'

Never one to shirk a confrontation, he got up and pushed his way through the stools and benches to the back, followed by knowing glances and nudged ribs among the patrons, most of whom seemed to know exactly what was the problem.

He bent his head to go out into the cold darkness of the yard behind the inn. As well as the usual stables, privy and wash-house, there were two kitchen huts, each throwing out red light from their cooking fires. Silhouetted in the doorway of one was the trim form of Nesta, standing motionless. He strode over and grabbed her around the waist, pulling her into the gloom of the yard.

She jerked away, but let his hands remain on her, leaning back to stare up at him in the flickering light. 'You bastard!' she said. The light was just sufficient for him to see the glint of a tear in each eye.

He sighed and pulled her against his chest. Again

she resisted, but the strength of his arms was overpowering and she suddenly relaxed against him. 'I'm sorry, John. I can't help it.'

He rocked her from side to side, ignoring the serving-girls, who were peeping from inside the kitchen door. 'I'm the one who should be sorry, love,' he said contritely, 'but you know what I'm like, you've known it from the start.'

The redhead sniffed, rubbing her face against his tunic. 'I get jealous, now and then. It's stupid, I've got no claim on you, John.'

He bent to kiss the top of the linen cap that covered her auburn curls. 'You are the one I love best, Nesta,' he said in Welsh. 'The one I always come to, my best friend as well as lover.' She slipped her arms around him in the darkness, but said nothing. 'The others are just a passing dalliance, Nesta. A rare adventure that I can never resist when the chance arises. I admit, Hilda is a girl from my youth, I like her very much but she knows I'm a leaf in the wind that passes her door now and then and blows away as quickly. It's not like that with you.'

She raised her face and managed a smile. 'You're a lecherous old ram, Black John.' She used the name by which he was known on campaigns and the battlefield, told her by Edwin, who was proud of de Wolfe's military reputation. She moved away and took him by the hand, drawing him back to the lighted door of the inn. 'You're a disgrace, John, but I'll have to put up with you, I suppose. I'm going to see the blacksmith tomorrow, to see if he can forge me a chastity-belt for you!'

'He'll need to stock up on iron, then, to make one to fit me, woman!'

Now all smiles, they went hand in hand into the taproom and, for a moment, John feared that the assembled patrons, who had been watching the back door, would break into a round of applause. After another quart of best ale, and some beef and bread taken before the fire, the reconciled pair climbed the wide ladder in the corner to the upper floor, where they spent a hour in Nesta's bed, partitioned off from the common lodgings where pallets or bundles of straw accommodated the guests of the Bush Inn.

At around midnight, Devon's coroner crept up to the solar in his house in Martin's Lane to slip under the blankets and furs at one edge of their bed and listen to the snores of Matilda on the other.

The next morning, the ambush party set out from Exeter. Eric Langton went out of the city at the same time but, as he had claimed, his slow nag would get to Dunsford well after the others. De Wolfe wanted to be in place before Giles Fulford arrived, to get the best vantage-point to see what he did.

Dunsford was almost directly west of Exeter, on the road to the stannary town of Chagford, where tin-mining was carried on right under the edge of Dartmoor. Dunsford was in fertile farming land, which climbed up and down small steep valleys, with wood-land and forest breaking it up into many separate manors and villages. The coroner's party consisted of Gwyn and the two servants from Canons' Row, the stocky young groom David and another powerful Saxon called Wichin. Decent horses had been allotted to them by John de Alencon from among the pick of the stables in the Close, and Gwyn had seen to it that they were armed with thick staves and daggers. The only swords were with John and his officer, clanking at the sides of their saddles. The coroner wore a round metal helmet with a nose-guard over an aventail of chain-mail that tucked under the collar of the thick leather cuirass that he wore under his cloak, but he had no other body armour, feeling that a full mail hauberk was too much for the arrest of a couple of adventurers.

The day was crisp and cold, but the wind had dropped and thin clouds scudded high in a pale blue sky as they trotted along. As the vicar had estimated, they came within sight of Dunsford in about an hour and a half. The church was just below the crest of a ridge above the valley and was visible from a distance. Gwyn wondered how they were to avoid becoming a public spectacle and maybe frightening off their quarry. The same problem had occurred to de Wolfe and he reined in at the side of the track before they reached the village. 'We'll split up here, not to be so noticeable,' he said. Privately, he was not confident that this would help: most hamlets were so isolated and self-contained that the appearance of a solitary stranger, let alone four, would rapidly become a matter of considerable curiosity to the inhabitants.

The two servants, closer to village life than the coroner, had a suggestion. 'We can say we're miners on our way to Chagford,' said Wichin. 'We could stop for some ale and a piece of bread – there's surely some old dame who sells suchlike here. That could pass the time until they come without causing too much suspicion.'

'What about us?' asked Gwyn of his master.

'We can either ride into the woods and wait outside the village for a time or maybe seize the bull by the horns and go into the church, pretending to be officials.'

'We *are* officials!' pointed out his henchman. 'But maybe we should have brought that little runt Thomas. He's good at worming his way in with parsons.'

De Wolfe decided on the bolder course and sent the two servants ahead to carry out their tin-miner impersonation. He and Gwyn stayed out of sight in the trees for another half-hour, then walked their horses slowly into the village, which straggled along the upper slope of the ridge above a valley. The church had a simple nave and squat tower of old wood and evidently had not changed since the days of Saewulf. The usual tithe barn sat on an adjacent plot, the customary symbol of the people's beholdenment to the power of the Church as well as to their manorial lord.

As the ground was frozen, there was little work going on in the field strips that ran up and down from the road, but in the distance, the coroner could see men clearing ditches and repairing the fences that kept livestock off the arable land. On the crest of the ridge opposite, smoke was drifting from the inevitable forest clearance. As in Loventor, the manor was cutting new assarts to increase the farmland at the expense of trees.

They dismounted at the church and tied their horses to fencing alongside the gate into the churchyard. There were a few inquisitive inhabitants about and several women with children were watching them as if they were visitors from the moon, but no one approached. The presence of two heavily armed men in the village, one wearing a Norman helmet, was not good news in any hamlet and it was best to keep clear.

Gwyn was uneasy. 'We can't leave the steeds here.

This Fulford will smell a rat at seeing a pair of war-horses in the very place he's come to rob.'

De Wolfe chewed his lip. His officer was right, as usual. 'Thomas drew those fanciful directions to the treasure so that the search will be made in that copse above the church, between it and the open pasture beyond,' he said, pointing to some trees a hundred paces away from the church tower. 'If we bring the horses into the churchyard and shelter them behind the chancel, they will be well out of view.'

The villagers were rewarded with the unusual sight of a pair of large horses being walked though the gate and up the steep slope from the road, around to the back of the church, where Gwyn tied them on long head-ropes to a low branch of an ash tree, where they could crop the grass.

Then the coroner and his helper went into the church to keep out of the way. It was a bare hall, with a beaten earth floor. There was no seating in the nave, only a pair of benches at the further end, at right angles to the altar. This was a plain table covered with a linen cloth, carrying a large tin cross flanked by a pair of candlesticks.

'Seems a poor sort of place,' muttered Gwyn, as he sat himself on a window-ledge near the door. 'They can never have recovered after this fellow Saewulf hid all their wealth a century ago.'

De Wolfe wandered restlessly about, looking at the church's lay-out. There were two window openings on either side of the nave, closed by shutters in the usual absence of glass. In the small square room at the base of the tower, which seemed to be used to hang the modest vestments of the parish priest, there was a single slit window at head height, which John found ideal for keeping a watch on the copse where the fictitious treasure was buried.

Gwyn pushed open a shutter on the nearest window and peered through the crack down on to the lane through the village. 'Those two fellows from the cathedral are better placed than us,' he complained enviously. 'They are sitting outside a hut opposite, with a pot of ale and a hunk of bread each.'

An hour went by, and the four men still waited. John prayed that Fulford had not had second thoughts about risking another search in broad daylight. The only diversion was the appearance of the parish priest, who must have been warned by a villager that strange men had invaded his church. He was a short, elderly man, who approached with some trepidation and hesitantly asked their business.

The coroner thought that at least part of the truth was the best policy, rather than fiction. He explained that they were waiting to arrest some miscreants who were looking for valuables that might belong to the diocese of Devon and Cornwall. The presence of agents of the Bishop, as he described the two men opposite, was more than enough to satisfy the priest.

'I suppose this explains those men who came the other day and began digging in the hedge behind my church,' he said, with some relief. 'When I challenged them, they offered to break my head if I didn't go away. I watched them from a distance as they dug several large holes, but I failed to see if they found anything.' He seemed glad to take the coroner's advice to scuttle off home before any violence began.

'I hope these swine do come after all this,' grunted Gwyn, hunching himself into his jacket in the dank air of the old building. 'I would far rather be in the Bush or the Saracen with a quart of cider than sitting in this damp bloody church!'

As if in answer to his prayer, Wichin, one of the men sitting opposite, suddenly motioned to Gwyn with his hand and pointed up the road. Then, with his companion, he vanished into the hut to keep out of sight.

'Someone's coming. Let's see who,' said the Cornishman, in satisfied anticipation of a fight.

The coroner came to join him at the window crack and they watched as four horsemen trotted past the church then turned off the track to go up towards the copse.

'Eric the vicar was the second man,' muttered Gwyn, 'and the third was Giles Fulford – I recognise him from the Saracen.'

De Wolfe hurried back to his slit in the tower and peered out. 'And the first is a fellow with curly red hair. We've got our Jocelin de Braose at last!'

His eyes followed a burly young man dressed in a red cloak and, on his head, a green capuchon, a length of cloth wound like a high turban, the free end hanging down stylishly over one shoulder. From beneath it curly russet hair showed, much the colour of Nesta's. A fringe of beard the same colour ran around the edge of his jawline, joined by a wispy red moustache. The four men had pushed into the stand of trees, around which was a confusion of scrub, but the bare branches allowed them to see some movement inside the copse.

'Let's get nearer to see what they're doing,' commanded the coroner. They let themselves out of the church and Gwyn waved to the two men lurking in the doorway opposite to join them.

There was a thick hedge of rank brambles and small ash trees between the churchyard and the copse, which easily concealed John and his companions as they stealthily crossed the frosty grass from the church. They moved towards the further corner, where there seemed to be a gap in the hedge, and peered cautiously between the dead blackberry fronds.

In the distance, they could see figures moving inter-mittently between the trees and bushes. Scraps of speech came across on the cold, still air. They could not distinguish the words, but de Wolfe recognised the higher pitch of the vicar's voice. Then came the swish of a sickle as brush and undergrowth were slashed. The coroner bent further to put his mouth nearer Gwyn's ear. 'We'll wait until they start digging. That's better evidence that they are actually searching for treasure trove.'

A few moments later, he was rewarded by the sounds of a heavy hoe and a shovel. Whenever the iron blades struck a stone, there was a sharp crack, and once a muffled curse suggested that one of the diggers had hit his own foot.

Gwyn was impatient to get into action, but de Wolfe laid a restraining hand on his arm. 'There's plenty of time, they're not going to give up now. And who is the third man, I wonder?' he murmured.

'Some peasant or outlaw to do the hard work, I suspect,' grunted his officer. 'Digging would be below the dignity of a knight.' From the sounds, thought John, there were two men at work, so presumably the other was Fulford, the squire, as the weedy vicar would be of little use. If two were busy with spade and hoe, then they could not instantly use their weapons when it came to a fight. He decided to satisfy Gwyn's eagerness for action. Slowly sliding his sword from its sheath, inching it out to avoid making a tell-tale noise, he jerked his head towards the gap in the bushes and led the way at a crouch. The hole in the hedge was not complete, but the undergrowth was much lower and they could step across the crisp dead brambles. The continuous clash of iron on earth and stones covered any faint crackling made by their feet and soon they were creeping forward over grass and weeds between the trees.

De Wolfe motioned Gwyn to go to the left with Wichin, while he and David circled the other way, to come on the diggers from both directions.

As he got within twenty paces of the bushes beyond which they were excavating, a face was suddenly raised and a pair of eyes met his. It was Eric Langton and, for a tense moment, John was afraid that the fool might cry out in surprise. He raised a finger to his lips, then motioned with his hand for the vicar to move away from the others.

A voice from behind the thicket said, 'Where the hell d'you think you're going, priest?'

'To have a piddle, that's all,' came the vicar's tremulous reply.

'Well, have it here, we're not particular. And check that damned parchment of yours. There's no sign of anything yet and we're down well over two feet.'

As de Wolfe crept even nearer, the sound of digging started again, and a moment later, there was a loud clang and another curse.

'There's a bloody great stone down here. Give me a hand to heave it out, will you?'

The coroner heard the tools being dropped as the men struggled with a boulder set in the red earth.

It seemed the ideal moment to surprise them, so John stood erect, gave a great yell for Gwyn and crashed round the bush that separated them from the diggers.

He had a momentary impression of the four men frozen in utter surprise, two of them knee-deep in a hole in the ground, then confusion erupted. The first to react was the red-haired man standing on the other side of the hole, who pulled out his sword and, holding it two-handed, advanced on de Wolfe with a roar of defiance.

The coroner picked de Braose as the main adversary and, in a second, their steel blades had clashed with arm-tingling impact. But before de Wolfe could pull back for another strike he felt a numbing blow on his left leg, which threw him off balance. One of the men in the hole, probably Fulford, had seized his discarded shovel and swung it almost at ground level to strike the coroner on the shin, giving him the chance to scramble out of the hole and join the fight.

De Wolfe came within an ace then of being killed, as the auburn-haired leader poised himself for a chopping swing with his broadsword, but David, the groom, swung his thick stave in the path of the blade. The stout wood was splintered by the blow, but it turned the swing away from de Wolfe, who had fallen sideways, supporting himself with one hand on the ground.

Gwyn and his cathedral companion Wichin had been delayed a few seconds by a thicker wall of undergrowth on their side, forcing them to run a few yards to the left to get through. Now, with ferocious yells, the wild Cornishman crashed across to the mêlée, his first thought being for the safety of his master, whom he saw almost on the ground under the menacing blade of de Braose. But the latter had been diverted by the intervention of David and his staff and, in anger, Jocelin turned his blade on the groom. He swung his great sword again, but fortunately for David the flat of the blade, rather than the edge, caught him on the side of the head. He fell as if poleaxed and took no further part in the fight.

As Fulford scrambled out of the hole, John recovered sufficiently to face de Braose again, but he found that both knight and squire were now coming against him, as the other digger, far from being a menial labourer, showed himself an experienced combatant. Ignoring his discarded hoe, he seized a long spear lying on the grass and, almost before his feet were out of the excavation, lunged forward with it at Gwyn. Though the officer had his sword at the ready, its reach was far less than that of the spear and the hairy giant had to hop back and chop sideways at the shaft to avoid being skewered. Eric Langton had taken to his heels and was out of sight of the yelling, thrashing group of men, but the battle was not to last long.

As Fulford and de Braose advanced on de Wolfe, Gwyn backed around to try to stand by him, dodging repeated short jabs from the unknown man's spear. The coroner was now facing a sword and a long-handled spade, waving his own sword slowly from side to side.

For a few seconds, there seemed to be a stand-off, until the canon's man Wichin, who had been obscured behind Gwyn, gave a great yell, swung his stave over his head and brought it down on the shaft of the spear. He forced it to the ground, but before he could lift his stave again, the spearman had pulled back his weapon and jabbed it into Wichin's shoulder.

The leaf-shaped point dug deeply into the muscle, and blood welled immediately through the leather jacket. Wichin screamed, dropped his staff and, as the lance was pulled out, fell to his knees with the pain and shock.

But the intervention had given Gwyn his opportunity. He reversed his move towards the coroner and, raising his great sword, swung it in a whistling horizontal arc at the spearman. The blade connected with the side of his neck and the man collapsed in a welter of blood and agonal convulsions.

With hardly a glance at the man whose life he had just taken, Gwyn leaped back to John's side. Within two minutes of the fight beginning, three of the combatants had been eliminated and now it was two against two, all seasoned warriors. However, the coroner and his officer had twice the number of years' experience on the battlefield than the younger men, and Fulford was armed only with a shovel – his sword lay sheathed on the ground where he had left it to go digging.

'Give in, both of you,' yelled de Wolfe. 'We don't want to kill you!'

For answer, Jocelin de Braose, his capuchon unwound and fallen down his back, swung his sword back and forth to form a zone of protection in front of him and tried to move forward towards the coroner. That old campaigner dropped his own massive blade at an angle, holding the hilt above waist-level, then suddenly moved it forward into the path of de Braose's weapon. There was a clang as metal hit metal and when de Wolfe jerked his hands forward again, the other blade was deflected towards the ground. But the younger man leaped backwards and freed his sword before John could make a swing at him.

As this duel was going on, Giles Fulford was attempting to use the longer reach of the shovel to hit Gwyn on his sword arm. One blow landed, but the coroner's officer merely grunted and waited his opportunity. As the tool swung again, he sidestepped and hacked down on the wooden shaft just above the heart-shaped blade. Though it was too thick and hard to be severed, a deep chop mark appeared, which then split several inches up the centre of the handle. With a roar, Gwyn opened himself deliberately to another blow, which landed with a thwack on his leather-covered ribs. As he had anticipated, the split handle gave up the ghost instantly and the shovel-head fell off on to the ground.

'I've got the bastard!' he yelled, and dived on Fulford, knowing that the coroner would prefer these two alive rather than dead. As Jocelin and de Wolfe entered another cycle of striking and parrying, Gwyn became over-confident of seizing the squire. He tossed his sword behind him to grab Fulford in a bear-hug. But Giles still had half the shovel-shaft in his hands. With it he gave Gwyn a bone-shattering crack on the temple, which made the big Cornishman stagger and put his hands to his head in a temporary stupor, though he wasn't knocked out. Fulford put a hand to the back of his belt and whipped out an eight-inch dagger. The flash of the blade caught de Wolfe's eye. In desperation he brought down his sword with a sledge-hammer of a blow that skidded down de Braose's weapon and struck the hilt-guard with such force that it was twisted out of his hand. Before the sword had even hit the ground, John made another swing at Fulford, trying to strike his knife arm. He missed as the man jumped aside, but by then Gwyn, though groggy, had recovered enough to grab his attacker's arms and the pair began to wrestle with the dagger waving dangerously a few inches from Gwyn's ribs. De Wolfe was trying to watch both adversaries, afraid that Fulford would manage to stab his officer and that de Braose would retrieve his sword and return to the attack while the coroner's attention was divided.

But the reflexes of an old soldier and a good share of luck saved the day. De Wolfe jumped towards Fulford and jabbed the tip of his sword forward. At the same time he felt an impact on the sole of his foot. He had trodden on the cross-piece of de Braose's sword as he pricked Fulford's upper arm. The big two-handed swords were designed for slashing, not fencing, and the tip was broad and rather blunt, but it penetrated the thick leather of Fulford's jerkin and made him yell.

All this took no more than a few seconds, but when de Wolfe sensed de Braose trying to pull his sword from under his foot, he swung out with his other leg and caught the man under the chin. De Braose staggered back, gurgling, and the coroner stooped to grab the lost weapon and hurl it away into the nearest bramble thicket.

In spite of the bleeding flesh-wound in his arm, Fulford still grasped the knife and, though Gwyn was holding him by the arms, the crack the officer had received on his head had halved his fighting abilities, especially as blood was pouring down from a cut over his right eye, almost blinding him.

Afraid that Fulford might still slide the dagger between Gwyn's ribs, John grabbed him from behind and put an arm-lock across his throat, doing all he could to crush his Adam's apple. He was only too well aware that his back was to de Braose who, like every man, carried a lethal dagger on his belt. He screwed his neck around to look out for the danger but, to his surprise, Jocelin had vanished.

Afraid to release Fulford until Gwyn had recovered, he had no means of pursuing the leader and the trio staggered back and forth in stale-mate for another half-minute, with Fulford beginning to go blue in the face from de Wolfe's grip on his throat. Gwyn resolved the situation by recovering enough wit to bring up his massive knee into Fulford's crotch with a blow that almost crushed his genitals. Unable to scream because of the arm-lock, Fulford's eyes bulged and he went limp. Afraid of some trick, John hung on for a little longer, but almost simultaneously he and Gwyn released their hold and stepped back. Fulford fell in a heap on the ground, gasping and groaning.

De Wolfe picked up the dagger, then turned to Gwyn, who subsided slowly to sit alongside Fulford, wiping the blood from his face with his fingers and holding his head with the other hand.

'Are you all right, man?' said the coroner, who had been in tighter scrapes than this one with his officer, but who was still concerned for his head injury.

Gwyn shook his head like a dog coming from water. 'Yes, I wasn't fated to be killed over a poxy treasure hunt. But that was a fair whack he gave me with that shovel handle.' He looked around him, blinking the last of the blood from his eyelids. 'What happened to de Braose?'

The sound of hoofs on the road was enough answer.

'He thought escape better than heroism, leaving his squire behind,' said the coroner, 'though he was good with a sword, I'll grant him that.'

Gwyn struggled to his feet and looked down at

Fulford. 'This one will live until he's hanged, but what about the others?'

They looked round at the mayhem in the area of crushed grass. The groom from the Close was now sitting up, holding his head in his hands, a large blue bruise rapidly appearing around his left ear. 'I'll be fine in a while,' he mumbled. 'But where's Wichin?' The other cathedral servant, who had been wounded in the arm, was found lying on his side behind the nearest large bush. He had lost a lot of blood, but when de Wolfe cut away his jacket, he saw that the wound was now full of clot and that the haemorrhage had stopped.

'I'll get him taken to the parish priest,' said a timid voice. Looking round, de Wolfe saw that Eric Langton, who had kept a safe distance during the fighting, had returned. He went off to find the priest and some help to carry Wichin to a nearby house to recover. David said that he would stay with him until the Archdeacon could send out a leech to see him and bring him back to the cathedral infirmary.

'What do we do with this fellow?' asked Gwyn, whose iron head had suffered no lasting ill-effects from the blow.

They looked down at Fulford, who was also recovering from the throttling and the scrotal insult. He had small red blotches in the whites of his eyes and his face was still slightly blue and swollen from de Wolfe's attempts to strangle him. He sat on the ground, one hand over the small cut in his arm, the other over his aching testicles, but his defiance was returning. 'Who in Satan's name are you?' he croaked. 'And what right have you to attack us? Don't you know that

that was Sir Jocelin de Braose whom you assaulted and drove away?'

De Wolfe's black and grey figure was hunched above him like a great crow. 'You ask us that, Fulford? I am Sir John de Wolfe, if we are bandying titles. You obviously don't know the King's coroner when you see him – and his officer.'

The man's confidence seemed to increase as the pain in his groin diminished. 'Coroner? What is this to do with corpses – except those you seem to produce yourself?' He pointed across at the bloody body lying on the other side of the hole.

Gwyn prodded him none too gently with his foot. 'Enough of your lip, man. The crowner will ask the questions.'

De Wolfe motioned to his officer to pull the man to his feet. 'You are a prisoner now. You will be taken back to Rougemont and lodged in the gaol there.'

'On what charge? You will regret this, Crowner, you are meddling in matters you don't understand.'

De Wolfe gave him a buffet on the ear. 'You impertinent devil! You forget your station in life, young man. A squire to some shiftless mercenary is of little account to me. As for dead bodies, you should know that another part of a coroner's duties is to safeguard finds of treasure trove, to keep them safe for the King from thieves like you.'

At this Giles Fulford remained silent, and Gwyn frogmarched him to the horses that were tied up some distance away at the edge of the little wood.

David had virtually recovered now from his bang on the head, and helped the coroner's officer to tie Fulford's hands to the saddle-horn with a spare thong.

'What about the corpse? Another outlaw, by the looks of his clothing,' said Gwyn.

Sullenly, the squire confirmed that the dead man was indeed another anonymous ruffian hired for the occasion, though from the quality of his fighting he must once have been a soldier.

'Let the village bury him here,' said de Wolfe. 'This time, I'll interpret the rules to accept that an outlaw is also outside the crowner's law and we'll do without an inquest.'

'What about the treasure hoard?' muttered Fulford. 'Are you going to leave that half-dug hole there for the village to steal whatever is hidden in it?'

At this, de Wolfe took a perverse delight in holding up the parchment, which Eric Langton had returned to him a few minutes ago. Holding it up before the man tied on the horse, he slowly ripped it in half and then in quarters. 'Written by my clerk the other night, especially for your benefit. There is no treasure, my lad – at least not in that hole!'

Fuming at the deception, and not a little uneasy at what the immediate future might hold, Fulford was led alongside Gwyn's mare and the cavalcade set off for Exeter.

chapter seven

In which Crowner John goes into the forest

They delivered their prisoner to Rougemont by late afternoon, giving him into the charge of Stigand, the obese and repulsive gaoler who reigned in the undercroft of the keep. Protesting violently, and promising retribution from on high, Giles Fulford was thrust into a filthy cell that lay off the passage that ran from an iron gate in the basement of the building.

This undercroft was partly below ground, reached by a short flight of steps from the inner bailey. It was divided in half by a dank, fungoid stone wall, the outer cavern being an open space, used for storage and as a torture chamber. There, ordeals, mutilations and the *peine et forte dure* were carried out. The rusted, barred gate was set in the centre of the wall, beyond which lay a dozen small cells and one larger cage.

De Wolfe gave no explanation to Stigand as to the reason why Fulford was to enjoy the sheriff's hospitality, and the gaoler showed no interest as he pushed a dirty jug of water, half a loaf and a leather bucket for sanitation into the cell with the new prisoner. When Giles demanded the attentions of an apothecary for the wound on his arm, Stigand took a casual look at it, shrugged and walked away.

De Wolfe had already discovered that Richard de

Revelle was out of the city until next day, so his intention to discuss the arrest of Fulford and the escape of de Braose was frustrated. Tired from a day in the saddle and the exertions of a fight, John was ready for a good meal, some ale and bed. He walked back across the inner ward of the castle with Gwyn, advising his old henchman to do the same, especially as he had a wide graze and cut on his forehead and was suffering a headache from the blow he had taken.

'Where will you get a bed tonight?' he asked, as the gates were shut and the Cornishman could not get back to St Sidwell's.

'Gabriel will find me a place in the barracks. I often sleep there if I can't get home,' Gwyn answered. 'I'll go down to the Bush to eat. I don't fancy the Saracen after today's performance.'

De Wolfe had the same desire for the tavern in Idle Lane, mainly to consolidate the healing of the tiff with Nesta, but he felt obliged to go home first, to see how the land lay as regards his wife's mood. But he and Gwyn were delayed again as they passed the wooden staircase to the keep entrance. A servant came to the rail on the landing above and called down, 'Sir John, the constable asked me to look out for you. He has an urgent message for you.'

Though the sheriff was the King's representative in the county, the castle had been Crown property since it was built by the Conqueror and its constable was appointed by the King. This was meant to avoid it being used as a base for revolt by the barons, who owned most of the other castles. De Wolfe and his henchman climbed the steps in search of Ralph Morin, and went into the main hall, where people were eating, drinking and making a general hubbub after the day's work.

As soon as he saw them, Morin got up from one of the tables and came across. He was a big man, almost the size of Gwyn, and his massive face was crowned with crinkled grey hair. He had a bushy grey beard with a fork in it that gave him the look of one of the Viking ancestors of his Norman race. He was an old friend of de Wolfe and they shared a dislike of Richard de Revelle, although Morin had to keep that well hidden as the sheriff was his immediate superior.

The constable invited them to sit with him and have a jar of ale as they talked. 'I saw you bringing in a man lashed to his saddle just now,' he began. 'Have you lodged him with that filthy old pig down below?'

De Wolfe told the story of the day's ambush in Dunsford and its connection with the death of Canon de Hane. Morin made a sucking noise through his teeth. 'De Revelle will have problems with that. He's quite thick with some of de Braose's friends out in the county.'

The coroner stared hard at him. 'Is something going on that I don't know about, Ralph?' he asked.

The constable refused to elaborate, saying he had heard only rumours, and he changed the subject by passing on his own news. 'While you were out jousting in the countryside today, a messenger rode in from Henri de Nonant's place at Totnes. It seems we have another high-class death, for during a hunting party there yesterday Sir William Fitzhamon fell from his horse and was killed.'

The coroner stared at him again. 'Just what in hell's name is going on, Ralph? Only three days ago I was sought out by Fitzhamon, who complained about a violent dispute over land with Henry de la Pomeroy – and now he's dead!'

The constable shrugged his great shoulders. 'Hunting is a dangerous pastime, John. Men often fall from their horses and break either their legs or their necks.'

The coroner scowled in disbelief. 'Mother of God, these coincidences are becoming more than I care to accept!' He drained his mug and stood up. 'I suppose I have to ride down there in the morning to settle this new death – my backside is raw from the saddle with all these corpses about Devon.'

Morin rose to see him off. 'At least there's no reason to think that your favourite culprits Fulford and de Braose are involved in this one.'

'Don't be too sure of that, Ralph. I've heard – and you've just hinted at it – that Jocelin de Braose is a creature of some of those barons down in deepest Devon. I'm keeping an open mind on this.'

'Well, that'll be more than Richard de Revelle will be doing,' murmured the constable, as he walked de Wolfe to the door.

With that cryptic comment in his ear, the coroner went thoughtfully back to Martin's Lane.

Riding out in the early morning from the West Gate seemed to be developing into a routine, thought de Wolfe, as he and Gwyn trotted out once again in the grey dawn light of New Year's Day. This time, there was no messenger with them, as he had turned tail the previous afternoon and started back for Totnes, probably buying a pennyworth of food and lodging at some village on the way.

As they jogged westward along the tracks, John pondered on the differences between women. Last night, Matilda had kept up her unrelenting sullenness, glowering at him whenever he had tried to make conversation to heal the breach between them. Even her habitual fascination with tales of the county aristocracy, which was usually grist to the mills of her snobbery, seemed to have evaporated: his news of the death of William Fitzhamon and the extraordinary behaviour of Jocelin de Braose, who had tried to kill her husband that day, failed to stir her from her sulks. By contrast, when he had given up the effort and gone to the Bush Inn, he had found Nesta her normally affectionate self, quite recovered from her passing fit of jealousy. In fact, she was even able to tease him about his infidelities, poking fun at his sexual stamina and hoping, for her sake, that his rutting abilities would not be overtaxed.

He smiled ruefully to himself as Bran's great legs ate up the miles to Totnes. He was stuck with Matilda, he had to accept that, but he was damned if he was going to spend the rest of his life worrying about it and enduring decades of domestic torture when women like Nesta and Hilda were able to offer him such amiable company and delightful passion.

Gwyn trotted alongside him in companionable silence, aware after twenty years with de Wolfe that this unfathomable man often needed to be left well alone, when he wished to churn something over in his mind. What it was, he didn't know, nor did he much care: he was content to do what his master asked of him, even follow him into the jaws of hell. Gwyn's domestic life was simple: he had a pleasant wife, who fed him, bedded him and had given him two boisterous children, never caring where he had been, whether it was to Dartmoor or Damascus.

This time, though, it was to Totnes Castle, twenty miles from Exeter, which took them three hours' riding. They were met in the bailey below the great stockade by Henri de Nonant, who gave Gwyn into the care of his steward and brought de Wolfe into the hall, a substantial wooden building at the foot of the high mound. The lord of Totnes conducted him to the fireside, where he was fed and wined after the cold rigours of the journey.

'We have the unfortunate lord's body in the bed-chamber next door,' he said. 'His son is here, waiting to claim it and take it back to Dartington for burial, but I know that your new crowner's rules insist on some formalities before that can be done.'

His tone reminded de Wolfe of Richard de Revelle's dismissive attitude towards coroners. 'What happened to him?' he asked tersely.

'He didn't return with the others from the hunt, so his reeve went looking for him and found him dead on the ground in the forest. His horse and hounds were wandering nearby.'

'Any injuries on him?'

'An obvious wound on the head, and I am told his neck seems broken. The ground is as hard as flint from the frost, as you know yourself.'

'Anything else?'

'When a number of the hunters went out there to retrieve the body, some noticed blood on an overhanging branch within a few yards of where he had fallen. It seems that he must have misjudged the height and struck his head on a bough. Naturally he was not wearing a helmet for hunting, only a cap.'

De Wolfe grunted, a favourite form of response he had picked up from Gwyn. Experienced riders had a sixth sense for overhanging trees and an old hunter like Fitzhamon would be unlikely to have been so careless – but the coroner had to admit that it could have happened that way.

After his refreshment, de Wolfe beckoned to Gwyn and they followed de Nonant into a small chamber off the hall. A still figure lay on a palliasse on the floor, covered by a linen sheet. A youth stood brooding by its side, his head bowed until they came in. 'This is Robert, Fitzhamon's only son,' explained de Nonant. 'We all feel for him in his loss.'

De Wolfe murmured something about having met the lad recently and expressed his own sympathy, none the less genuine for its brevity. Fitzhamon's heir nodded grimly to the coroner, but said nothing.

John advanced to the bed and Gwyn pulled back the sheet to chest level. The dead man looked much the same as he had in life, apart from his eyes which were closed as if in natural sleep. A white cloth was draped over his forehead and when de Wolfe pulled it away, they could see dried blood matting the white hair at the crown of the head. The coroner and his officer crouched down one on each side of the bed and de Wolfe parted the hair with his fingers. 'A deep tear in his scalp, running back to front, with bruised edges,' he commented aloud, motioning to Gwyn to lift the corpse from the bed.

Robert Fitzhamon turned away to look through the window-slit, as his father came up into an almost lifelike sitting position. But as de Wolfe took his hands away from the corpse's head, it rolled sideways in a most unlifelike fashion, lolling at an unnatural angle. Gwyn gave one of his grunts and the coroner placed his hands alongside the ears, to waggle the head on the neck.

'Broken, as you suggested,' he said, looking up

at de Nonant. The baron assumed a knowledgeable expression. 'Being hurled from a large horse after a blow against a tree is enough to snap a neck.'

De Wolfe pulled down the sheet and examined the rest of the body, arms, legs and trunk, dragging up the undershirt to see the chest and belly. 'Not another mark on him,' he muttered. As he was doing this, Gwyn supported the corpse with one hand and prodded about in the head wound with the fingers of the other. 'Let him down. We can cover him again and leave him in peace,' commanded the coroner, rising to his feet. He turned to the boy. 'You wish to take him home for burial, I presume. I will have to hold a short inquest for the sake of formality but I can do that within the hour.' He turned to de Nonant. 'What happened to the First Finders? We need them, and anyone else who has any knowledge of this affair.'

De Nonant looked dubious. 'His reeve, who accompanied him on the hunt, is still here, and one of the two men who went with him to find Fitzhamon. The other returned to his village with his own master, I cannot recall who. The only others were our hunting party who went out afterwards, but they could know nothing of the accident. Of those, only myself and Bernard Cheever are still in the castle.'

De Wolfe sighed, thinking that the King's Justices who made up the rules for the holding of inquests had little idea of the difficulties of trying to carry out their orders. In a static village, where none of the inhabitants ever went anywhere, it was easy to assemble everyone who might know about a death, but where barons and knights were concerned, with all their equally mobile companions and servants, it was impossible to stick to the letter of the law.

'Well, get everyone who might have even the most remote knowledge of this death together in the bailey as soon as you can. We will have to move the corpse out there. Then you, Robert, can arrange for a litter to take it to your home.'

The younger Fitzhamon came to life. 'Is it necessary to parade my father's body outside in the bailey, Crowner? Can he not rest here in peace and dignity until I can make arrangements for travel?'

De Wolfe shook his head, but spoke gently. 'I'm sorry, the jury must be able to inspect the body and see the wounds before we can reach a verdict. It will be very brief.' He turned again to de Nonant. 'I need to see where this happened. Can someone take us to the spot?'

The best person to do so was Ansgot, the dead man's reeve, and within minutes he was riding once again along the route he had taken two days before, followed now by de Wolfe, Robert Fitzhamon and Gwyn. They crossed the river and came to the place where the body had been found. He pointed to a place behind dead ferns where the frosted grass had been trampled by many feet. 'He was there, Crowner, lying crumpled on the ground, face down, chin tucked hard against his chest.'

De Wolfe examined the spot, but found nothing of any significance.

'What about this tree?' he snapped. Ansgot walked a few paces back the way they had come and pointed up to an old oak, twisted and gnarled, its bare branches contorted into a variety of shapes. 'This one here. It has blood upon it where a piece of bark is missing.'

Gwyn walked his mare up to the tree and, the tallest man there, measured his head against its height. 'True, it comes to my face. Fitzhamon was shorter than me, so he could have struck it with his crown.'

Robert looked away in distress. To be where his father had met his death so recently was harrowing to the boy, who had loved and respected his father, even though he had been a stern and undemonstrative parent.

De Wolfe moved to Gwyn's side and looked up at the offending branch. 'There's a smear of blood upon it – and a sliver of bark is missing at that point,' he conceded.

Gwyn was silent and de Wolfe looked sharply at him. Even though the Cornishman had not said a word, after years in his company the coroner could sense that he was not satisfied. 'Well, what's the problem?' he muttered.

Gwyn raised his bushy eyebrows and looked pointedly towards Robert. 'I want to look at the body again,' he murmured, through his moustache. 'Look at the direction this branch grows – across the track, not in line with it.'

De Wolfe took the hint and they rode back to the castle, the subdued boy following in the rear.

In the bailey, Fitzhamon's corpse had been brought down, still covered with the white cloth, and placed on two boards on trestles from the hall. A dozen people were assembled for the inquest, and young Fitzhamon, de Nonant, Bernard Cheever and Ansgot joined the circle around the bier. Before they began, Gwyn went with the coroner to the body. They lifted the sheet and spent a few moments in muttered conversation. Those nearest saw Gwyn again put a finger and thumb into the wound and show some tiny object to de Wolfe. They also looked long and hard at both sides of the head, turning it this way and that on the floppy neck. Then the officer stood back and called for silence for the King's coroner, who took over the proceedings.

'All here know the deceased for Sir William Fitzhamon but, for formality's sake, I will have this confirmed by his son and heir. Robert Fitzhamon, is this the body of your father?'

Robert assented in a low voice and de Wolfe continued, 'Equally, we can dispense with presentment of Englishry, as Fitzhamon's Norman blood is known far and wide.'

At this point Henry de Nonant interrupted, in a tone of bored impatience, 'Is there any need for this charade, Crowner? We are all aware that presentment was intended to discourage the assassination of our Norman forebears by treacherous natives. It is surely outdated now, but it can never have made sense in hunting accidents among Norman companions anyway.'

De Wolfe glared at him, the corners of his mouth downturned in his mournful face. 'Your sense of history may be correct in that strife between Saxon and Norman has all but vanished – but assassination is still with us. And I have good reason to believe that this is what has happened to William Fitzhamon.'

He tried to explain it to Richard de Revelle that evening, but with little success, as there is no one as deaf as those who do not wish to listen. 'It is a murder, carefully designed to look like an accident.'

The sheriff, leaning back in his chair behind the document-strewn table, was derisive. 'John, you see deception and conspiracy behind everything! I still question whether the death of that canon was anything other than suicide, in spite of your protestations. Now you come with this fanciful tale of murder, when it is patently obvious that the damned fellow fell from his horse!'

In an effort to keep his temper, the coroner marched around the chamber in Rougemont's keep. 'For the last time, will you just listen? First, someone deliberately put a knife across the fetlock of the reeve's horse so that Fitzhamon was left alone on the hunt. Then he was found dead, with a head wound and a broken neck.'

'What do you expect on a man who rides his head into a tree and gets tossed off on to the frosty earth?' snapped de Revelle.

'Great God! I've told you already, he didn't ride into that tree. The wound went from back to front, but the branch and its conveniently bloody part ran across the track, so the wound was at right angles to where it should have been!'

De Revelle made a noise redolent with scorn at the coroner's deductions, but John ploughed on. 'Furthermore, the tree was an oak and my officer picked a piece of beech bark out of Fitzhamon's head wound. Does beech bark grow on an oak tree?'

The sheriff made another dismissive noise. 'A trivial matter. Who ever heard of evidence from a scrap of wood? There was blood on the tree, wasn't there?'

'No doubt from someone who dipped his finger in Fitzhamon's blood and smeared it on the place where he pulled off a sliver of bark – oak bark!'

'Fantasy, John, sheer fantasy! I think it was a mistake, my recommending you for this coroner's appointment, you have too vivid an imagination for sober legal purposes.'

De Wolfe became more incensed than ever. 'Recommended me? I was given this job by the Chief Justiciar – and with King Richard's agreement! I needed no help from you, Sheriff. Do you need reminding that for certain reasons you were held out of office yourself for many months? You are still on probation now, as far as loyal subjects are concerned.'

De Revelle became incandescent with rage and leaped to his feet. 'You may not talk to a sheriff in that way, damn you! You meddle in things that are beyond your understanding. Fitzhamon died in a hunting accident, understand? Leave it at that.'

'He was struck on the head with a beech bough, brother-in-law. How do you explain that?'

'His neck was broken, too. How do you explain that?'

De Wolfe leaned on the table and glared into his brother-in-law's face. 'By someone taking his head in their hands when he was unconscious from the blow and wrenching his neck till it snapped!'

'Pah! More fantasy?' yelled de Revelle.

'No, marks on each side of his head! When we returned from the forest, enough time had elapsed for the bruising to come out on the side of his neck, behind the ears and on the temples where strong fingers had dug into the skin. Do you get fingermarks, identical on each side, from hitting a tree, eh?'

Though he had no rational explanation, de Revelle engaged in a repetitious tirade against the coroner's sanity, which left de Wolfe unmoved. 'So what are you going to do about this murder?' he demanded.

'Do? I'm going to do nothing. There is no murder, you great fool.'

Seeing that it was useless to continue arguing, de

Wolfe contented himself with an oblique threat. 'Well, his son Robert Fitzhamon now knows his father was killed – and, child though he may still be, he has a fair idea why it happened. When he discovers a possible suspect, he will Appeal him and then you will have to do something. If you don't, I'll go with young Fitzhamon to the King's justices and Hubert Walter. If necessary, we'll follow the King to France and petition him. There may be aspects of this matter that will bring him back post-haste to England.'

The sheriff glared at de Wolfe, but there was a shadow of concern, almost of fear, in his eyes. 'You meddle in things that are outside your competence,' he hissed, his voice tremulous with anger. 'Have a care, John.'

'It's you who should watch where you place your feet, Richard – and your loyalties,' he replied, taking a blind shot at obscure intrigues of which he could only guess. To further wrongfoot the sheriff, he suddenly changed the subject. 'To go from one violent death to another, what are you going to do about yesterday's episode? Unfortunately the prime suspect ran away, but I brought you back one villain, who lies in your gaol below.'

De Revelle's temper subsided, to be replaced by a triumphant smirk. 'I'm afraid he doesn't, John.'

The coroner glowered at him suspiciously. 'What do you mean? I delivered Fulford myself into Stigand's hands.'

'And I released him today – myself! You had no right or cause to arrest him. You attacked him without warning, killed his servant and chased off his master, who was unarmed.'

This time, it was the coroner's turn to explode.

'Unarmed! Only because I was treading on his bloody sword! And what possessed you to free Fulford? Either he or de Braose killed the canon – or they did it between them.'

From that moment on, there could be no intelligible exchange between coroner and sheriff. They stood almost nose to nose across the table, yelling recriminations at each other. The man-at-arms guarding the sheriff's chamber stuck his head round the door, thinking murder might be being done, but when he saw the clamorous tableau, he went back hastily to his post, thinking discretion the better part of valour.

After a few moments of futile shouting, de Wolfe decided that he was wasting his time and, without another word, stalked out of the room, with de Revelle still shouting insults at his back.

The coroner's next port of call was his own house, and by the time he had walked briskly through the cold streets from Rougemont to Martin's Lane, his anger at the sheriff's intransigence had faded, to be replaced by a thoughtful consideration of what in God's name was going on in Devon this New Year. It was becoming obvious that political intrigue was afoot, from the oblique threats of various people, but it was difficult to know who was friend and who was foe.

When he had talked privately to Robert Fitzhamon after the inquest, the boy seemed hardly surprised that his father had been killed deliberately. He explained to de Wolfe the intentions that the elder William had expressed to Henry de la Pomeroy to seek out the Chief Justiciar if the encroachment on his lands was not halted. 'I don't know exactly what had been going on, but in the past few months I gathered that some of

the barons and landholding knights had invited my
father to join them in some dubious enterprise. He
had refused, and as he spoke of this in the same breath
as of his loyalty to King Richard, I suspect that some
new rebellion was being mooted, which he declined
to support.'

As he pushed open his street door, de Wolfe thought
this a possible explanation for the murder, though it
seemed somewhat extreme. Brutus heard him arrive
and came up the passage from the yard, wagging
his tail, followed by Mary with an equally welcoming
smile. She helped the coroner pull off his riding boots,
then hung his baldric and sword on the hook in the
vestibule. Jerking a thumb towards the hall, she made
a wry face. 'You'll have little joy there tonight, Master
Crowner,' she whispered, 'so I'll get you something
substantial to eat. At least it will help you to pass the
time this evening.' With that she vanished back to her
kitchen and, with a sigh of resignation, John pushed
open the inner door to the hall.

Matilda was in front of the fire as usual, sewing by
the light of two tallow lamps on a bracket alongside her
chair. She was as uncommunicative as usual, offering
nothing but a curt word or two in response to his efforts
at conversation.

Soon Mary brought in a large earthenware pot of
mutton stew with root vegetables, and a loaf of hot
bread. Silently, Matilda came to the table, and as
they ate and drank, de Wolfe made another effort
at conversation, telling her again of the murderous
death of William Fitzhamon. Finally this struck a spark
of interest in her as, almost reluctantly, she gave him
a recitation of Fitzhamon's family connections, who
his wife was, how many children he had and more

from her compendious store of knowledge of the noble members of Devon society, to which she had an envious yearning to belong.

De Wolfe briefly had hopes of her coming out of her black mood, but he made a fatal mistake when she asked him whether anyone had been arrested for the crime. 'No, and your brother won't accept that it was a murder. He claims it was a simple hunting accident.'

From there it was all downhill: Matilda worshipped her brother and felt he could do no wrong. She still would not accept that he had been a sympathiser of Prince John in his rebellion, which had ended so ignominiously the year before – even though he had been prevented from taking up the sheriffdom for months after being first appointed, which spoke for itself. 'If Richard says it was an accident, why should you deny it?' she snapped, her power of speech returning in full.

'Because I was there, and examined the body, and he was not,' de Wolfe retorted, stung into more unwise comments by the unfairness of her reasoning. 'And he has released that Fulford man I arrested yesterday, without any explanation.'

'The sheriff knows more about what goes on in this county than you,' Matilda declared crossly. She got up and walked back to her chair by the hearth, pointedly turning her back on him and refusing to answer him when he tried to placate her again.

De Wolfe endured a few minutes more of her sulks, standing by the fire to warm his back, but as she refused even to look up at him when he spoke, he marched to the door, put on his walking shoes and cloak and slammed out of the house. He had intended going out in any event and made his way not to the Bush but to the Archdeacon's house in the close.

These were the slack hours before the night-time round of services and John de Alencon was reading a small leatherbound book in his bare room. Dressed in a grey cassock, his thin face looked grave in the light of three candles burning on his table. 'The Bishop is back and takes a very serious view of the behaviour of both Roger de Limesi and his vicar. He has committed Eric Langton to appear before a Consistory Court next week and is deciding whether to take any action against my brother canon.'

De Wolfe put in a word for the junior priest, as best he could. 'He did all that was asked of him in this matter of entrapping Giles Fulford – which also flushed out Jocelin de Braose. But that fool of a sheriff has let Fulford go free and he is at large somewhere in the city, no doubt sheltered by his friends.'

He then related to de Alencon the events of the past day and the death of Fitzhamon. 'There is treason abroad, John, I smell it. Have you heard any rumours that might confirm this?'

The Archdeacon pondered a moment. 'Rumour is the right word, old friend. Nothing tangible, just whispers and hints now and then – but they have been rife ever since the last attempt failed.'

The coroner shifted uneasily on the stool he had drawn up to the table. 'Is there anything we should do about this – or anything we *can* do, with no proof at all?'

The Archdeacon shook his head slowly. 'Watch and listen, that is the best course at the moment. You need to be careful, John, your allegiance to the King is well known and may not be to everyone's taste.'

'You are just as loyal, so what about you?' objected de Wolfe.

'I have the protection of the Church, but you are out in the harder world.'

'The Church was of little help to Thomas Becket against the secular power,' said John wryly.

De Alencon smiled sadly. 'That was a long time ago and things have changed. But we should reckon up who is likely to be for us and who against.'

'Your own bishop was sympathetic to the rebels last time. How is he placed now, I wonder?'

The Archdeacon shrugged. 'I think he will wait to see which way the wind blows strongest. In the last treason, Hugh of Nonant, Bishop of Coventry, was the moving force behind Prince John, but I doubt if our Bishop Henry will wish to follow his example.' He sighed and closed his book carefully. 'I find it strange that he leaned that way before, being brother to William the Marshal, who is nothing if not the King's man.'

'What about the barons and knights hereabouts? Which way will they lean? I know my dear brother-in-law would join them if he dared, even though his fingers were burned last time.'

'Certainly Ferrars and de Courcy would be loyal. Henry de la Pomeroy is very suspect, especially as his father came to his death from following the Prince. Gerald de Claville and Bernard Cheevers are also doubtful characters in that respect. Fitzhamon was a king's man – and look what's happened to him.'

They sat in silence for a moment, each deep in thought.

'Do you really think that Prince John would try again so soon?' asked the priest. 'It was a special opportunity for him last year, when no one expected that Coeur de Lion would ever get out of Germany alive.'

'The King doesn't help his own cause by staying out of England like this,' admitted de Wolfe. 'He's left Hubert Walter in a difficult position. Though he is well liked, he's forced to employ extortionate measures to fund Richard's campaigns against Philip of France, especially as the country has not yet recovered from paying off the ransom.'

John de Alencon agreed. 'And he insisted on reinstating that damned Walter Longchamp as Chancellor, a man everyone hates – though, thank God, he stays out of England with the King. All these things foster discontent. Our good Richard is too soft-hearted, except on the battlefield. Look how he forgave his brother for all the harm he did. Other kings would have had his head or his eyes for much lesser treason.'

They fell silent again. 'And none of this helps us solve our local problems,' sighed the Archdeacon. 'Who killed poor Robert de Hane and William Fitzhamon? Maybe they have no connection whatsoever.'

'And we still have no clue as to the whereabouts of this treasure, if it still exists,' said de Wolfe glumly. 'Thomas de Peyne has found no sign of that second parchment in the archives.'

'I care little for treasure – the Church in Exeter hardly lacks for money, though it becomes increasing difficult to resist the King's calls for donations.'

The coroner stood up, ready to leave. 'With the sheriff unwilling to apply the law, for reasons of his own, I have a good mind to apply my own brand of justice,' he said, and with this cryptic remark he left the Archdeacon to his reading. Once again, he did not make for Nesta's tavern but went further down the close to the canon's house, where Thomas had his meagre lodging. Going down the side lane to the yard, he ordered a surprised servant, cooking in the light of an open fire in the kitchen, to find his clerk and send him out.

A moment later, a dishevelled Thomas appeared, looking as if he had just risen from his mattress. 'Throw a cloak about you and go up to Rougemont to find Gwyn. He will probably be drinking with Gabriel in the soldiers' quarters. Then bring him down to the Bush, where I will be waiting.' He turned on his heel but, as an afterthought, he called over his shoulder, 'And tell him to buckle on his sword!'

It was an hour to midnight when the coroner's team arrived outside the Saracen Inn on Stepcote Hill. It was round the corner from the Bush, on a steep slope leading down towards the city's west wall. A thatched roof came down to head height on the outer walls, pierced by shuttered windows and a low door from which came the grumble of voices and the occasional shout and peal of laughter.

The trio stood to confer under the crude painting of a Moorish head, the inn sign of the Saracen.

'He doesn't know you by sight, Thomas, so go in and look around,' commanded de Wolfe. He was wearing a wide-brimmed black pilgrim's hat and had his dark cloak pulled up high over his shoulders, but his height and his hunched posture made this token disguise of little value in a city where he was so well known. Gwyn gave the clerk a shove through the half-opened door. 'Go ahead, and act the hero for once!'

De Peyne vanished, and the other two walked round the corner of the building to be out of the way, but within a minute Thomas was back again. 'He's there, laughing and drinking, though he's got one arm in a cloth tied up to his neck. That black-haired woman is with him.'

De Wolfe was satisfied that his guess had turned out to be right. Giles Fulford was banking on the reluctance of the sheriff to hold him prisoner, and risked appearing in public, until the city gates opened next morning. 'You know what to say, Thomas,' he said. 'We discussed it in the Bush just now.' Again the timid clerk, torn between fear and glory, slid into the tavern and pushed his way to the middle of the big smoky room where de Braose's squire, one arm in a cloth sling, was holding forth to a group of men clustered around Rosamunde of Rye. Thomas's tongue ran furtively around his lips as his eyes fell on her, and he imagined what it might be like to bed her. He had about as much chance of that as becoming the Pope, though, when his poor body was compared with hers. Boldly dressed in blue silk, with her glossy black hair rippling down her back, she stood with Fulford's sound arm firmly wrapped around her shoulders, another man alongside her doing his best to press himself against her.

Thomas tore his eyes reluctantly from her to get on with his business. Sidling up to the squire, he nudged him, and when Fulford looked down in annoyance, he said, 'A man outside asked me to give you a message, if you are Giles Fulford.'

Fulford was more interested in cupping Rosamunde's left breast, and snapped, 'What man? What message?'

Thomas, almost enjoying his acting role now, shrugged. 'I don't know. He looked like a priest, but muffled up. He gave me a ha'penny to tell you he doesn't want to show himself in here but that you might be interested in a lost parchment.'

Giles pulled away from the woman. 'If it's Langton, I'll kill him, the treacherous bastard, leading me into a trap like that,' he snarled. 'Where is he?'

'Around the corner of the inn, on the right,' offered Thomas and, as Fulford stalked to the door, he melted away to the back of the room where another exit was frequently used by patrons who wished to relieve themselves in the yard.

He ran round the back of the inn and, from a safe distance, was just in time to see a scuffle in the half-darkness, lit only by the intermittent light of the moon and a glow from the cracks in the shutters. Hesitantly, he came nearer and saw that Gwyn had Fulford pinned against the wall, with the edge of his sword across his throat.

The coroner had the wrist of the man's uninjured arm in the iron grip of one hand while the other brandished a dagger that he had plucked from the squire's belt. 'Come on, my lad, you won't escape from us as easily as you did from the sheriff,' grated the coroner. With that, Gwyn spun Fulford round, put his head in an arm-lock and lifted him off the floor as easily as if he had been a sack of turnips.

Fulford was unable to speak or shout as the coroner's officer half carried, half dragged him up the hill. He began to kick the Cornishman's legs, but de Wolfe produced a short hempen rope from under his cloak, which he had borrowed from Edwin at the Bush. He quickly lashed this round the prisoner's shins and tied a knot, then used the free end to carry the bottom half of Fulford clear of the ground.

They hurried him up the hill and turned right into Idle Lane. Beyond the Bush was a patch of wasteland, with winter-dead weeds and, at its edge, a trough, a long stone bath hollowed out for watering horses. Diagonally opposite was a livery stable: now shut for the night, a pitch flare still guttered on its wall, throwing a dim, flickering light over the area. Gwyn dumped his burden flat on the ground and stood over Fulford with the point of his sword resting on the man's throat. With one arm bound in a hessian sling and his legs tied together, the squire was as helpless as a trussed chicken.

'Yell as much as you like,' invited de Wolfe. 'The folk in the Bush have been told to take no notice.'

'You're mad!' croaked the squire, his blond hair tousled and his tunic crumpled from the struggle. 'The sheriff will have you hanged – and if he doesn't, there are a dozen others who will do it for him.'

The coroner stared down at him calmly in the faint light. 'You are of little account, Fulford. A squire, a mere hand-servant to a minor knight. Who cares about you? The sheriff only wants to get you off his hands, he's not concerned whether you live or die as long as you don't do it on his premises.'

'What do you want from me?'

A half-moon slid out from behind the clouds and its pale light fell on the scene. Thomas shivered, reminded of a miracle play depicting the angels of doom hovering over a sinner.

'Who killed Canon de Hane? Who killed William Fitzhamon? Who is employing your master Jocelin de Braose? That will do for a start.'

A stream of foul language and abuse was the response so Gwyn kicked Giles in the ribs to end the flow. 'I thought this was about a search for treasure,' gasped the squire.

'The death of an inoffensive old priest is about treasure,' snapped de Wolfe. 'Now, talk or face the consequences.'

Again there was a tirade of denial, mixed with blasphemies and threats of vengeance. De Wolfe stepped to the horse-trough and looked down at the layer of ice on the water. 'Thomas, get a stone from the waste and crack this up.'

In a moment, black water was glistening in the trough, with angular pieces of ice floating on top.

Without further orders, Gwyn dropped his sword and bent over Fulford. With one ham-sized hand grasping a knot of clothing at his throat and the other gripping the rope around his legs, he lifted the victim up and dumped him into the filthy water. His face was still above the surface and yells and oaths rent the night air, but his tormentors were unmoved.

'Did you kill the canon?' snarled the coroner. The foul language continued and, at a nod from his master, Gwyn pushed Fulford's head under the water and held it there as the man thrashed about, bubbles bursting from above his face. Then he hauled him above the water and waited for the coughing and spluttering to subside.

'Who killed Robert de Hane and Fitzhamon?' asked de Wolfe relentlessly. He was no sadist, but the image of the old canon revolving slowly at the end of a cord in his own privy hardened his heart, as did the recent memory of the boy Fitzhamon standing over his father's body.

It took two more dunkings before Fulford broke, by which time he had inhaled enough water and shreds of sodden hay fallen from horses' mouths to render him semi-conscious.

He was freezing and shivering and Gwyn was afraid that he might die before his determination cracked, but he was young and strong enough to survive. When he had recovered sufficiently to speak through chattering teeth, de Wolfe waved Thomas close to act as a third witness; later he must write it down from memory on his parchment rolls.

The gasped confessions were short and fragmented. When Fulford was quiet, de Wolfe stood back. 'He's no use to us now. Take him back to the Saracen and toss him through the door. Let his friends there warm him up, I'll not have the Bush fouled by such as he.'

CHAPTER EIGHT

In which Crowner John threatens the sheriff

It was well after midnight by the time de Wolfe and Gwyn walked back up the steep slope of the drawbridge of Rougemont. The clouds had cleared to allow the week-old moon to shine unfettered and the high, rounded archway of the gatehouse gleamed against the dark masonry. A shivering soldier lurked in the doorway of the guardroom, wishing himself under his bed-rugs in the arms of his wife.

'You go off to your palliasse, Gwyn. There's no need for us both to lose more sleep,' growled the coroner. He made off across the inner bailey towards the keep, while his officer trudged to one of the bastion towers in the wall where a dozen men-at-arms slept in the lowest chamber.

Another sleepy guard jerked himself awake at the entrance to the keep, wondering what had brought the coroner to disturb the Sheriff at this time of night.

A dozen servants and assorted lodgers were sleeping in the hall, wrapped in their blankets around the smouldering fire, though one man was still eating and drinking at a table with a tiny tallow dip for light.

De Wolfe ignored him and walked heavily into the sheriff's chamber, where de Revelle's steward was snoring on a mattress in the corner. The sheriff's bedroom was through an inner door, but de Wolfe made no effort to wake the servant or to tap on the panels. He pushed it open and walked in, indifferent to what he might find. Unlike the previous occasion when he had found Richard in this same bed with a whore, his brother-in-law was alone.

John unceremoniously kicked the corner of the low bed. The snores changed into a strangled grunt and the sheriff sat up, wild-eyed and confused. 'Who's there? Steward?' he called.

'Not your steward, it's the *King's* coroner.' He deliberately emphasised the word 'king'. Richard struggled up to a full sitting position, his nightshirt falling off one shoulder. 'What the hell do you want, John, in the middle of the night? Have you at last gone really mad?'

A candle-stump was still burning on a side table. De Wolfe went across to it and lit another from its flame, to give a little more light. 'I've just had a conversation with your friend Giles Fulford. He has told me a few interesting things, in front of two witnesses, one of whom is now committing it all to writing.'

The sheriff's eyes were two shining beads in the candlelight. 'Fulford? Are you still obsessed with that fellow? I thought he would have gone back to his master by now.'

'Not until the gates open, Richard. You should have thought of that when you let him go. Anyway, he kindly informed me that he was present when Jocelin de Braose strangled Canon Robert de Hane. He helped string the poor man up to his privy roof.'

De Revelle had recovered enough of his wits to start to bluster. 'And you woke me just to tell me this nonsense? Why should he confess this to you?'

'Because Gwyn of Polruan put him to the *peine et forte dure* in a horse trough in Idle Lane. It's a well-known method of arriving at the truth – one often employed by you, as I recollect.'

The sheriff was back to full consciousness. 'Torture! Are you expecting me to accept anything obtained under such duress?'

'It was good enough for you a few weeks ago when you pressed that silversmith to confess to rape. What's wrong with it now, that you want to reject it?'

De Revelle struggled out of the low bed and stood up, pulling a blanket around his shoulders. 'You've totally lost your senses, John! I hereby relieve you of the writ of coroner. Go home and take some physic for your fevered brain.'

De Wolfe sat calmly in a folding chair in the middle of the room, one with a curved leather seat and back. 'Don't be so stupid, Richard. My writ from the burgesses was confirmed by the Chief Justiciar and the Chancellor. You have no say in the matter. Good God, man, we were appointed partly to keep you sheriffs in check, so you have no authority over us whatsoever.' He held up a restraining hand in the gloom, as de Revelle was about to launch into another tirade of abuse. 'Fulford also told me that de Braose was at Totnes on the day when Fitzhamon was killed. I suspect he had a hand in that too, but it was what he said about you that really interested me.'

De Revelle's mouth, which had been open to rail and rant, shut abruptly. Then he spoke almost quietly. 'What did he say about me? I know nothing about the death of that old priest in the Close.'

For some reason, de Wolfe believed this, but he had other matters to pursue. 'He said that you were a frequent visitor to Totnes Castle and to Berry Pomeroy, that you and the lords of that area were getting very thick indeed. Just as you are thick with our Precentor and even the Bishop.'

De Revelle glared at his sister's husband. 'What does that mean? I am sheriff of this county. I am obliged to visit every part of it, and am well known to all its barons, lords and knights.'

'All those who favour Prince John, it seems. I hear no reports of your visiting the Ferrars, the de Courcys, the Courtneys, the Raleghs, the Inghams ... all the King's men.'

'That is ridiculous. What are you trying to accuse me of?'

De Wolfe pointed a long finger at his brother-in-law. 'There is rebellion in the air, Richard. I know it, you know it, and many others know it. That is treason against the King and many will hang for it, if it's not stopped. Do you wish to be one of them, Richard?'

The sheriff threw his blanket around him imperiously, as if he was a Roman emperor. 'You are a fool, John, and a dangerous fool. You have no proof of any such treason. Your imagination runs away with you. Did your precious Fulford tell you revolt was afoot?'

'He told us that de Braose was collecting and training men-at-arms from both England and France. Some came in quietly by sea through the Channel ports – I know that Dawlish was one.'

'Any baron is entitled to a fighting force of his own. I asked you, did this Fulford say that rebellion was imminent?'

'Not in so many words, but he gave me enough intelligence to start me on my way to get confirmation – a job you should be doing, if you are so loyal to the monarch you represent in this part of England.'

'Don't lecture me on loyalty,' flared the sheriff. 'It would be better if the King came home, paid some attention to his kingdom and stopped bleeding it dry. He sells privileges, honours and charters like apples in the marketplace – he said he would sell London itself if he could get a good enough price.'

De Wolfe felt his anger rise. 'A fine attitude towards the master whose lieutenant you are over thousands of his subjects. You make Fulford's words more credible every time you open your mouth.'

De Revelle stepped forward angrily towards the coroner, but John leaped from his chair and towered over the other man. 'You let Fulford go free and now he has confessed to having been involved in the killing of that prebendary – and, I suspect, the death of William Fitzhamon. He was caught red-handed trying to steal treasure, too, which by law belongs to the royal Treasury – and yet you, the keeper of the King's peace in this county, refuse even to arrest him.'

Woken by the shouting, the old steward put his head fearfully round the door, but his master screamed at him to get out. Then he yelled at de Wolfe, 'You have no proof at all of this man's guilt. You torture some false confession from him when all he has done is dig a hole in a wood in some poxy village. Is that such a heinous crime, eh?'

He kicked the chair in which de Wolfe had been sitting, tipping it over with a crash. 'I'll not put the man in my gaol! If he doesn't die of your assault upon him, he can ride out of the city in the morning where he'll be safe from your lunatic actions.'

De Wolfe moved towards the door. 'Very well. I felt

I should give you a last chance, Richard. As soon as I have collected a little more evidence, I will go to Winchester or London to tell what I know to the Royal Justices and to Hubert Walter. Fitzhamon intended to do that and I owe it to his memory – and to his young son – to finish what evil men prevented him from completing.'

As he pulled open the door, the Nero-like figure of the sheriff spat a last warning at him: 'Have a care, John! For my sister's sake – and Christ knows she has suffered enough from you – I must warn you that you are on a path that could lead to the gallows.'

The coroner glared at his brother-in-law from the doorway. 'Then maybe we will hang side by side on the same gibbet, Richard,' he said, slamming the door behind him as he left.

That next morning, the second short day of 1195, saw several urgent conferences in the county of Devon, mostly conducted in low tones with many a cautious look over the shoulder.

Well before dawn, shadowy figures could be seen entering the Bishop's palace behind the cathedral, and a keen observer might have recognised both Canon Thomas de Boterellis and Richard de Revelle going in to see Bishop Henry Marshal, who had recently returned from Gloucester. Soon after first light, the first two could have been seen galloping away along the road westward out of Exeter, with a pair of men-at-arms as escort.

Shortly before this, the coroner had been meeting the Archdeacon in the square chamber at the base of the north tower of the cathedral. In the opposite chamber of the south tower, used as the Lady Chapel, a group of priests and choristers was celebrating the early Lady Mass, but the bell had not yet begun to ring for prime, the first main service of the day, so John de Alencon had time to confer with de Wolfe and Hugh de Relaga, who had accompanied the Coroner to the cathedral. Hugh was a corpulent, cheerful fellow, addicted to colourful, showy clothing. An astute and successful wool merchant, he had been elected by his fellow burgesses as one of the two city Portreeves, the leaders of the civic administration. Unlike the other Portreeve, Henry Rifford, Hugh was an ardent King's man, and with de Wolfe, the Archdeacon and John of Exeter, the cathedral Treasurer, formed a firm core of support for the Lionheart amid those whose loyalty was suspect. They stood in a tight group in the deserted chamber, the pale dawn light creeping through the tower windows and adding to the glow cast by the candles on the two small altars of St Paul and the Holy Cross behind them. The coroner explained briefly what had gone on during the previous night. 'We made Giles Fulford tell us what happened to poor Robert de Hane. Although Fulford was the man that de Limesi and his vicar dealt with, it was his master Jocelin de Braose who was behind him. I lost him at our ambush at Dunsford, which made me suspect that he was the leading spirit in this search for Saewulf's treasure.'

De Relaga was slightly bewildered: he had not been privy to the whole story and de Wolfe had to give him a quick summary. 'That's the background,' he ended. 'But last night I could see that we would lose our only hope of knowing what happened as the thrice-damned sheriff had let Fulford free to leave the city this morning. So Gwyn persuaded him to tell the truth.'

'And that was what exactly?' asked the Archdeacon.

'When de Braose and Fulford dug up that Saxon brooch, it made them believe even more in the existence of the main treasure. When de Limesi failed to find any other parchment that would lead them to it, they decided to force its whereabouts from Robert de Hane. They beat him, then tried strangling him slowly into submission – but he suddenly died on them, poor old man. To avoid unnecessary problems, they hung him up to look like a suicide.'

While the coroner talked, de Relaga pulled his red cloak more closely about him in the chill air of the damp tower. He had been called from his bed too early to array himself in his usual finery, but his outfit was still in bright contrast to the sombre clothing of the coroner and the priest. 'But what has this to do with Richard de Revelle's refusal to arrest this Fulford?' he asked.

'Because de Braose and his squire Fulford are leaders of the mercenary gang that's being hired by the would-be rebels out there in the countryside, I suppose he feels obliged to protect them.'

De Relaga groaned at the possibility. 'I thought we had seen the last of this treachery last winter, when the King crushed the remnants of John's vermin. Now you think it's boiling up again?'

'There's no other explanation for the sheriff's behaviour. He as good as told me so last night. I admit that the Lionheart is his own worst enemy, leaving the country so soon and trusting that the Justiciar can keep the lid on the discontent that these hard taxes undoubtedly foster.'

The Archdeacon snorted. 'These nobles who are turning traitor are just using that as an excuse. They want more power and they see a better chance of getting it through the Count of Mortaigne, if they can seize the throne for him.'

The Portreeve was rapidly catching up with the situation. 'But surely Hubert Walter is well aware of what's going on? He has spies all over the country.'

'England is a big place, and he can't be everywhere at once,' replied the coroner gruffly. 'I suspect he anticipates attempts at revolt, but it would help him a great deal if he was given actual names and places.'

Hugh shook his head sadly. 'I can hardly believe that people we know well would defect again so soon. And although de Revelle was sympathetic to the Prince last time, he never actually fought for him. That's why he was allowed eventually to take up his sheriff's appointment, especially with people like Henry Rifford and the Bishop to support him.'

'The same goes for Henry Marshal and Thomas de Boterellis,' commented de Alencon. 'We all know that they sailed fairly near the wind, but never actually paraded their sympathies on the streets. Not like the Bishop of Coventry, who was the revolt's true leader.'

'Hugh de Nonant!' grated de Wolfe. 'A kinsman of the lord of Totnes, Henri de Nonant – who I suspect is also up to his neck in this. It was during his hunting party that William Fitzhamon was murdered. I'm beginning to think that the whole affair was organised as a cover for his killing. Which brings us back to de Braose and Fulford.'

'Do you think de Nonant is the prime mover of this treason in Devon?' asked John de Alencon.

The coroner looked at him mournfully. 'Who can tell? Henry de la Pomeroy is the biggest landowner, but my guts tell me that they are all in this together.'

'We have no proof of anything against any of them yet,' pointed out the Archdeacon. 'You claim, I'm sure correctly, that both our canon and Fitzhamon were murdered, but you have only a confession made under duress about de Hane, which is nothing to do with any rebellion.'

'You've got de Revelle's strange partiality towards Fulford, presumably because he is a tool of the rebels,' objected de Relaga.

'We could certainly do with better evidence,' conceded de Wolfe. 'But I am quite ready to ride to Winchester to talk to Hubert Walter.'

'Give it a few days to see if more hard fact comes to light,' advised the Portreeve. 'In the meantime, don't walk down too many dark alleys, John. Keep that ginger giant of yours close at hand with his fists and his sword!'

The weather had turned fine, but was bitterly cold as John de Wolfe left the cathedral and walked across the Close towards his house. The piles of earth dug out for new graves had frozen into rock-like heaps that blocked some of the paths and, with the rubbish, old timber and the hawkers' stalls that were scattered around the cathedral precinct, it was something of an obstacle race to navigate into Martin's Lane. Though Mary had given him some mulled ale and bread before he left to rouse Hugh de Relaga, de Wolfe couldn't resist going into his house for a better breakfast. He found Matilda huddled at the table, a heavy cloak thrown around her nightgown and her dishevelled hair wrapped in a cloth like a turban – Lucille had not yet wreaked her witchcraft upon it. She was eating coarse porridge from a wooden bowl, and a large loaf, butter and cheese lay on the boards in front of her.

She muttered a grudging greeting and carried on eating. Whatever turmoil and alarms came along, nothing spoiled her appetite, which accounted for the thickness of her features, the loose skin under her eyes and the solidity of her frame and limbs.

De Wolfe had had no chance in the early hours to tell her of the events of the night and something told him to keep quiet about his suspicions of her brother's loyalty. Mary came in with his hot porridge, fresh milk and more steaming ale, the only hot drink available on a freezing day like this – mulled wine could hardly be served at breakfast. 'Thomas came in while you were out, Sir John,' she reported, careful to be formal and respectful to him in the presence of the mistress. 'He had a message, but I told him you would almost certainly be going up to the castle when you had eaten, so he went away.'

'Do you know what he wanted?'

Mary opened her hands to him in a gesture of doubt. 'He said something about royal fish, whatever they are.'

'The evil little pervert is out of his mind,' muttered Matilda, breaking her silence at the chance to malign the clerk. John held his tongue, but he knew what Thomas had meant, even if he was surprised that the matter had arisen. As soon as he had eaten, he left the house and walked up through the streets to Rougemont. It was Sunday, but there seemed to be no lessening of the market activities, with stalls along High Street selling meat, fish, bread, dairy products and vegetables, all tailored to the season of the year. Much less was available in midwinter compared to later on, but anything that could be cooked or preserved was raucously advertised by the yells of the stall-holders and the keepers of the small shops under the covered ways formed by overhanging upper storeys. Between the fixed stalls and the shops, hawkers stood hopefully with trays and boxes of goods, or with live fowl and ducks struggling under their arms, everything offered for sale to a potential buyer, after the inevitable haggling over a price.

Black John strode past them all as if they did not exist, deep in thought about the ominous political situation, the prospect of a revival of Prince John's abortive rebellion. Although a coroner had no official stake in such matters, de Wolfe's intense loyalty to the King overrode any confinement of his actions to dead bodies, treasure and sanctuary-seekers. Last March, he had been at the sieges at Tickhill in Yorkshire and at Nottingham, the last castles to hold out for the Prince. He and Gwyn had volunteered, itching for action, to help regain these for Coeur de Lion. The King himself had hurried to Nottingham within days of landing at Sandwich in Kent, after his imprisonment. De Wolfe remembered his sovereign setting up a gallows outside the castle walls and hanging a few captives, which rapidly persuaded the garrison to surrender. As he strode up to Rougemont, he wondered whether the same tactics might be needed soon outside the castles at Totnes and Berry Pomeroy.

At the top of the stairs in the gatehouse, he pushed aside the sacking door and went in to the usual scene of Thomas writing at the trestle table and Gwyn perched on the window-ledge, eating and drinking. The little clerk, his thin nose red with cold, held up a parchment. 'I recorded all that Fulford said last night, Crowner. It's written here, as you ordered. I've even got that savage over there to make his mark on it where I've written his name. You can sign it here, if you want to take it to the Justiciar.' He offered his quill to de Wolfe, who, with some pride, carefully inscribed his name at the bottom of the document, the only words he was able to write.

He threw down the pen with studied carelessness. 'What's this about fish, Thomas?' he demanded.

'A sturgeon, Crowner, a big one! Stuck in a pool on the ebb tide near St James's Priory, where there are salmon traps. The prior sent a message with one of the fish-sellers early this morning.'

De Wolfe was intrigued: this was the first time he had been called upon to carry out one of the oddest tasks of a coroner. As well as looking into treasure trove and fires, he had to investigate catches of the so-called 'royal fish', which were sturgeons and whales. If they were found within the realm of England, these became the property of the Crown. Both were prized and valuable, the sturgeon for its flesh and roe and the whale mainly for the oil it provided for lamps, as well as its flesh, if it was fresh enough.

Gwyn looked up from his loaf and cheese. 'Very strange to have a sturgeon come up-river in winter. They usually arrive from the ocean to spawn in the spring.' The Cornishman came from Polruan, where his father had been a fisherman, and he considered himself an authority on anything that had sails, rudder or fins.

'Maybe this fish is an ignoramus like you, who can't tell January from March,' suggested Thomas, always quick to insult his partner. De Wolfe held up a hand to quell the inevitable squabble. 'That's enough! Let's get down there and see this beast. The rest of the day may be busier.'

As they went out, he muttered to his henchman, 'Gwyn, keep your eyes open and your hand on your sword. After our encounter with Fulford last night, there are people who would gladly see us dead.'

CHAPTER NINE

*In which Crowner John deals with a fish
and a mill-wheel*

The ride was quite short down to the banks of the
river Exe where the sturgeon was trapped. Between
Exeter and the port of Topsham was the small priory
dedicated to St James, founded over fifty years earlier
by Earl Baldwin de Redvers, sheriff of Devon, who had
held Rougemont against a siege by King Stephen for
three months. Though he could never have met him,
de Wolfe didn't like the sound of Baldwin, possibly
because he had fought against his king – for the
Empress Matilda, the namesake of John's wife. The
coroner's team trotted down the mile and a half to
the priory, following the track to Topsham, parallel
to the river. A small place, it housed only a prior and
four monks. Near it was the sluice to a mill-stream and
a palisade of stakes in the river for catching salmon.

When they arrived, a couple of monks and their
prior were waiting outside, the latter an amiable, fat
man with a fiery red face that matched the bare skin
of his tonsured head. St James's was a Cluniac house,
so they wore the black habits of the Benedictine order.
The finding of a sturgeon was a welcome break even
on the Sabbath from the routine of their day, and they
walked with de Wolfe down to the riverbank, where

three fishermen were standing around a large muddy pool alongside the salmon trap.

The prior offered the obvious explanation. 'It was stranded by the falling tide. On the next flood, it will just swim away.'

The fishermen were scowling at the prior, whose honest meddling in calling the coroner had deprived them of a valuable catch. As a fisherman's son, Gwyn typically sided with them against the Church. He went over to them as they stood barefoot in the mud, their rough smocks girded up to their thighs, to discuss the strange phenomenon of a sturgeon trying to force its way up-river at the wrong time of year.

The fish was at least six feet long, its bony tube-like snout projecting in front of it like a sword. The pool was small and was draining away even more as the tide dropped, so that the fish had to swim in a tight figure-of-eight in the shallowing water.

'What's to be done about it, Crowner?' asked one of the fishermen.

John considered the matter sympathetically. He was well aware that, especially at this time of year, fishermen had a hard time, hovering on the brink of survival with the sale of fish the only means of buying bread. But the law of the land said that these fish were the property of the King.

'Who found it?' he asked.

One of the men claimed that he had discovered it when he came down at the start of the ebb tide to see what was in the fish traps. He was a sickly, middle-aged man, thin and undernourished. De Wolfe knew that whatever the fish fetched would go to the Royal Treasury, undoubtedly to be put towards more warhorses, arrows and armour for the distant battles in France. He came to a decision and turned to the prior. 'Although by law the whole value of the fish should go to the King, I realise that the labour of landing, gutting, butchering and selling must be recompensed. Therefore I decree that it be given to these three fishermen, who must get the best price for it. They must divide the proceeds in half, keeping one half for themselves and the other for the Crown.'

He glared at the three men, whose faces had lit up: they had had no expectations of getting anything at all from this valuable catch. They readily agreed and de Wolfe ordered them to give half the sale price to the prior, to be kept by him until it was collected when the Justices next came to Exeter. They would pay it in to the royal treasure chest kept in Winchester or the new Exchequer treasury at Westminster.

Gwyn was as pleased as the other men at de Wolfe's generosity and helped them to haul out the great fish, struggling and thrashing in its death throes. The coroner accepted the prior's invitation to meet his monks over a cup of wine in St James's, to which gathering Thomas managed to get himself included, much to his delight.

The air was still and icy when the four horsemen reached Berry Pomeroy castle at about noon. The smoke from the kitchen fires rose straight up to a pale blue sky that had a few high mackerel clouds. As the two soldiers of the escort walked all the horses to the stables in the bailey, they assured each other that there would be no snow to prevent them getting back to Exeter by nightfall.

Richard de Revelle and Canon de Boterellis were received at the door of the donjon by Henry de la

Pomeroy and conducted to his private chamber off the hall, where first they warmed themselves by a good fire after their frigid journey, then were fortified with hot food and wine. The sheriff's visit had been arranged days before, though his bringing the Precentor was an emergency move triggered by the events of the night. Henri de Nonant and Bernard Cheevers were there too, as previously arranged, to talk to de Revelle, and the five men stood around the hearth as soon as the travellers were refreshed.

'I brought de Boterellis to report on what Bishop Henry learned in Gloucester and Coventry last week,' began the sheriff. 'But what happened last night is of more immediate importance to us – and to all who support the just cause, if my damned brother-in-law goes whining to Hubert Walter.'

De Nonant, the big-boned lord of Totnes, waved a hand towards the bailey outside. 'We know what happened. Giles Fulford rode in here just before you, as he left Exeter the moment the gates opened. He's still wheezing from dung-water in his lungs from that horse trough.' He spat noisily into the fire, perhaps a comment on Fulford's inability to keep out of trouble.

De Revelle was put on the defensive, feeling blamed for his inability to control the Exeter end of this conspiracy. 'How in hell could I foresee that this idiot squire would go straight to his favourite ale-house when I released him from gaol? He should have kept in hiding until he could leave the city, not lay himself open to kidnap. Though that was something no one could have dreamed of – only my devious brother-in-law could have thought up a move like that!'

Pomeroy's sour face regarded him with distaste, his drooping moustache following the downturned corners of his flabby lips. 'For Jesus Christ's sake, de Revelle, can't you control that man? You're the sheriff! Why don't you lock the bastard up or hang him?'

Bernard Cheever, ever the conciliator, came to de Revelle's aid. 'Come on, Henry, de Wolfe's the King's crowner – and he's married to Richard's sister! This has to be done with subtlety.'

The blunt lord of Totnes brought them back to the main issues. 'The damage is done – no use crying over spilt milk. John de Wolfe guesses there is another rebellion in the wind and that some of us are involved. He has no proof, unless the sheriff here has admitted anything, so we have to make sure that the coroner doesn't find any further evidence and that he won't go running to the Justiciar or the King about it.'

'He's well in with both of them, more's the pity, since they were all in Palestine,' muttered Richard. 'When Hubert Walter was here last month, they had their heads together a great deal – though, thank God, that was before any of our plans were known to de Wolfe.'

Henri de Nonant turned to the priest, who had been silent until now. 'What news did the Bishop bring from Gloucester, Precentor?'

Thomas de Boterellis considered his answer carefully, his small dark eyes peering gimlet-like from the folds of his fat face. 'Things are moving, but slowly. Your kinsman, Hugh de Nonant, who was deprived of his bishopric in Coventry, is being allowed by the King to purchase a pardon for the sum of two thousand marks.'

Pomeroy laughed cynically. 'The Lionheart would sell his grandmother for the price of a quiver of arrows.'

'But not his mother!' quipped Cheever, and bitterly they all agreed. The old Queen, Eleanor of Aquitaine, was the only person who could control her wayward sons. It was largely due to her rapid return to England, when Richard had been locked up in Germany, that the Prince's attempt to seize the throne from his elder brother had been demolished.

The Precentor carried on with his news. 'Hugh de Nonant thinks it politic to stay in Normandy for the time being, so we lack a strong leader at present.'

'What about another bishop?' asked Cheever. 'Henry Marshal of Exeter, for example.'

Boterellis shook his big head. 'He's too timid. If it falls flat again, he doesn't want to follow the Bishop of Coventry. And he's in an awkward position as brother to William Marshal, who has always been a King's man – whichever king it is.'

Pomeroy glared around at the others. 'So where are we now? Are we having a rebellion or not?'

'A number of barons about England are once more sympathetic to the Prince's cause,' replied the lard-faced priest. 'We have probably the strongest group here in the south-west. But it is so soon after the fiasco of last winter that many are treading softly. I'm sure that enough will rally eventually to the Count of Mortaigne, but it is too soon to declare openly yet.'

De Nonant brought them back to the current problem. 'All the more reason not to let this wayward crowner let the badger out of the bag! What's to be done?'

The lord of Berry Pomeroy took the initiative. 'He must be silenced, either by threats or violence. Why are we so concerned about some piddling pensioned-off ex-Crusader?'

Richard de Revelle was less sanguine about the county coroner. 'Much as I dislike the bloody man, I have to admit that he is able enough – tenacious, stubborn and cunning! And with that hairy Cornish savage watching his back, he can outfight any two men that I know.'

'Then we'll send five against him,' snapped Pomeroy. 'If he's a danger to us, get rid of him.'

'Can't we blackmail him somehow?' suggested the less bloodthirsty Bernard Cheever. 'Murdering a coroner, especially one who's a personal friend of the Archbishop of Canterbury and of the King, is a sure way of calling attention to ourselves.'

The sheriff responded quickly, anxious to avoid being involved in the assassination of Matilda's husband. 'I agree – and there may be a way of keeping his mouth shut. His Achilles' heel is his fondness for women. I've a plan which might just work! I'll put it into action as soon as I get back to Exeter tonight.'

Henry de Nonant was scornful of de Revelle's confidence. 'This de Wolfe sounds too hard a nut to crack that easily. We must have an absolutely foolproof strategem to keep him silent. What about those two adventurers we hired to recruit and train our mercenaries? De Braose did a good job on Fitzhamon, even if his squire let us down.'

Pomeroy went round with a flask to refill their wine cups. 'They're too fond of private enterprise for my liking. Their foolery with buried treasure led to the killing of that canon of yours, Boterellis, and hence to the crowner dousing Fulford in a trough last night to make him talk. If it wasn't for that, we wouldn't have this trouble now.'

Cheever, a smaller version of Hugh de Relaga in that

he was dressed in bright-coloured tunic and mantle, acted as middle man once again. 'If it was their fault that we have a problem, let's see if they have any suggestions to put it right.'

A servant was dispatched to fetch the pair from the hall, and soon they appeared. Jocelin de Braose's curly russet hair contrasted with the dark green cape he wore over his brown woollen tunic. Thomas de Boterellis, who knew the whole story of the treasure hunt, noticed that his cape was secured at his shoulder with a fine gold brooch of Saxon design.

Behind him stood Giles Fulford, slimmer and fairer than his master, dressed in a uniform-like leather jerkin and serge breeches. He looked flushed and constantly had to suppress an irritable cough that came from deep in his chest.

Henry de la Pomeroy had recruited de Braose to find and train a small army of mercenaries for the antici-pated revolt, but had not seen him lately. Pomeroy had instigated the murder of Fitzhamon to prevent him telling tales to the Justiciar but had naturally kept well away from the hunting party at Totnes. He was curious as to how it had been achieved. De Braose was quite ready to enlighten him. 'First we had to get Fitzhamon's bowman out of the way. Giles here damaged a hamstring on his horse before they left Totnes, so the reeve had to walk it back and leave his master to hunt alone. We tracked him and got ahead of him.'

'How did you get him from his horse?' demanded Pomeroy.

'Giles lay face down on the ground with an arrow held up in his armpit as if he'd been shot. When Fitzhamon came along the track, he dismounted to see what was wrong. As he bent over the supposed body, I came up behind him and cracked him over the head with a branch. Then we broke his neck while he was unconscious – he didn't feel a thing,' he added, with an unpleasant smirk.

In a hoarse voice, between coughs, Giles Fulford finished the unsavoury story. 'We carried him back near a tree with a low branch and left him on the ground. I reached up from my saddle, broke off a strip of bark to make it look as if he had struck the branch, then smeared some blood from the wound on his head on to the branch.'

De Revelle sneered at their pride in their ingenuity. 'And then you fools ruined it all by choosing an oak tree after hitting him with a beech club! And leaving bruises all over his neck!'

De Braose's face reddened to match his hair. 'Would you ever have thought that this damned crowner would notice that? I never heard of such a thing and I'm sure you haven't!'

The sheriff looked around at the other faces, almost as if to seek admiration of his brother-in-law's abilities. 'I told you what a cunning bastard he was!' he complained.

De Nonant brought them back to the present. 'We need to prevent de Wolfe from running to tell tales to Winchester or London. The sheriff is averse for some reason to slitting his throat, so we need to try a less fatal means. Have either of you young bucks any ideas?'

The conversation went to and fro for some time, with heads together and the wine flask circulating freely. Eventually, they pulled apart and de Braose and his squire left, the latter still coughing and wheezing like a broken-winded horse.

Soon, the precentor and the sheriff prepared to go, to reach Exeter before dark. As he left, Richard de Revelle said uneasily, 'I don't like it, but it may have to be done. But only if my suggestion fails to work.'

As soon as he was out of the door, Henry de la Pomeroy muttered to his cousin Bernard Cheever, 'And if they both fail, then three feet of steel in a dark alley will have to be the answer.'

That Sabbath day was a busy one for the coroner. After spending the morning down on the river at St James, he was called again in the afternoon to Exe Island, just outside the walls, where a body had been recovered from beneath the wheel of a mill. The coroner and Gwyn went to the edge of the leat, a narrow canal dug from the river upstream that brought water down to the mill via a crude wooden sluice-gate. The wheel was of the undershot type, where the water pushed against the lower edges of the large vanes, rather than dropped upon it from a chute above. During the morning, the wheel that drove a fulling mill inside the wooden building had ground to a halt, which often happened when debris, usually branches or the occasional dead sheep washed down from Exmoor, became jammed in it. This time, the miller's men had found a human obstruction and dragged it out on to the bank.

When the coroner arrived, the corpse had already been identified as a middle-aged man living in a hovel in Frog Lane on the island. He had been seen last on the previous afternoon, leaving a tavern in Fore Street, already drunk, but clutching a gallon jar of cider.

'A real tippler, he was,' said the miller to John de Wolfe. 'He used to work here, but he was never sober so he was thrown out. God knows how he lived – begging and stealing, I suspect.'

There was little to see on the body, except a few scratches where the skin had rubbed against the rough wood of the wheel. Gwyn tried his drowning test, which he had used successfully a few weeks earlier at a shipwreck at Torbay. As the body lay on the frozen grass alongside the leat, he pressed hard with two large hands on the chest and was gratified to see a gout of fine foam exude from the nostrils and mouth.

Satisfied that it had been a simple drowning, de Wolfe held an inquest there and then. The man had been a widower, but a twenty-year-old son was discovered to make presentment of Englishry by swearing that his father had been a Saxon, so there was no question of a murdrum fine. The miller and his two assistants, who had recovered the body, half a dozen workmen and a few locals from the mean shacks on Exe Island were rounded up by Gwyn for a jury, and within half an hour the inquest had been convened and concluded. The verdict was accidental death, it being assumed quite reasonably that the drunken man had fallen into the river further upstream and drowned, his body being washed later into the leat when the sluice was opened.

'There is no question of the wheel being deodand,' declared the coroner to the mystified jury. 'The wheel was not the object that caused death, it was merely the obstruction that trapped the dead body.'

One member of the jury – the miller – understood the significance of this and breathed a sigh of relief. Anything that caused death, such as a dagger or even a runaway horse, could be declared deodand by the coroner and confiscated for the Crown. Carts, or even a single wheel from a cart, might be confiscated, leaving the owner without a means to earn a living. The miller had heard of instances where a mill wheel had been confiscated and sold, if a live person had been crushed or drowned by it.

Having handed over the body to the son for burial, John and Gwyn walked back to the Bush for a drink and a gossip. Though tempted to stay with Nesta for the evening, the coroner decided that he had better go home and make an effort to keep Matilda in a moderately tolerable state of mind.

CHAPTER TEN

In which Crowner John meets a woman in distress

The forecast of the two soldiers at Berry Pomeroy that there would be no snow was correct – but they had not anticipated the rain that came down the next morning. In the early hours of the first Monday of the year, the frost was washed away by steady rain. The streets of Exeter became a slime of mud and rubbish with slippery cobbles exposed here and there.

As Crowner John made his way up to the castle, a torrent of dirty water ran down the hill towards him from the gateway. It trickled into the outer ward to add to the morass of churned mud that covered the wide space between the high castle walls and the wooden stockade that enclosed the outer bailey. As he looked to his left on the way up to the drawbridge, he saw the residents of the outer zone squelching between the huts and lean-to shanties that housed the men-at-arms and their families. Urchins ran around semi-naked with mud up to the knees, and women muffled in shawls tried to keep their firewood dry as they stoked their cooking stoves in the doorways of the flimsy shelters. Oxen and horses plodded through the mire, some pulling large-wheeled carts, adding to the chaos of what was a military camp combined with

an inner-city village. Ignoring the rain that began to
trickle down his face and off the end of his big nose,
de Wolfe strode the last few yards to the shelter of the
tall gatehouse.

As he was about to climb up the narrow stairs to his
chamber, Sergeant Gabriel appeared at the guardroom
door and saluted.

'Sir John, the sheriff wants you to attend on him as
soon as you arrive.' He coughed diplomatically. 'By the
way he said it, sir, I reckon it's urgent.'

De Wolfe grunted and walked out into the rain
again. The inner ward was filthy too: all the rubbish frozen into the ground these past two weeks
had now floated to the surface. He trudged moistly
across to the keep and reached the hall with some
relief, although entering feet had made the floor
within the entrance almost as muddy as it was outside.

Ignoring the noisy throng milling around, he loped
to the sheriff's door and nodded to the guard as he
went in. A clerk and a steward were in the chamber,
talking to Richard de Revelle and thrusting parchments under his eyes. For once, instead of making
the coroner wait, as soon as the sheriff laid eyes on
him, he hustled the other two out and commanded
the guard not to admit anyone on pain of death. He
slammed the door shut and walked over to the window
embrasure, the furthest point from the door and the
least likely place to be overheard. Here two wooden
seats, like shelves, had been built into the thickness
of the rough wall below the window-slit. De Revelle
sat down heavily on one and pointed to the other. De
Wolfe lowered himself and the two men sat hunched
towards each other.

'John, we have some serious talking to do. We parted at cross purposes last time.'

'Matters seemed very clear to me, Richard. You confessed to treachery against the King and conspiring with rebels.'

'I did nothing of the sort! Listen, you are my sister's husband and for that I feel a considerable obligation towards you. Especially that of trying to keep you alive.'

'Keep me alive? More likely the other way round.'

'I think not, John. The danger to you is much more immediate.'

'Is that a threat, Sheriff?' asked de Wolfe darkly.

'Not from me, no. But from now on you are in considerable peril. Probably more so than on your precious Crusades and foreign wars.' He changed his tone, attempting a reasonable, wheedling persuasiveness. 'Look, you always proclaim yourself a true servant of the King. I feel exactly the same.'

'You have a strange way of showing it,' observed John sarcastically. 'You came pretty near hanging last year. You almost never became sheriff and now you're setting off along the same dangerous track again.'

De Revelle scowled, but managed to keep his temper. 'I said I was a loyal king's man, like you. But which king? Last year, we all thought Richard was either dead or soon would be. It was doubtful, even after the ransom was paid, whether Henry of Germany would let him go. After his release, they tried to recapture him and only missed his ship out of Antwerp by hours. We were getting ready to put John on the throne, as it was a reasonable expectation that Richard would never get back.'

De Wolfe glowered at his brother-in-law. 'Well, you

were all very much mistaken, weren't you? What's this to do with me?'

De Revelle reached out and grasped the coroner's forearm. 'John is going to be the next king – it's only a matter of how soon. Join us, and use this great loyalty of yours for the right sovereign!' The sheriff became more animated as he warmed to his theme. 'Richard has never taken the slightest interest in England. He's spent only a few months here since he was crowned. All he does is screw taxes from the people to support Normandy and his vendetta against Philip of France – England is nothing but a colony! Prince John would change all that, be a true king of England. And you would have someone better to whom to offer your allegiance.'

De Wolfe pulled away his arm sharply. He was angry, and his anger was the worse because he knew there was a core of truth in what the sheriff said. 'The King is the King, damn you!' he shouted. 'Richard is the man crowned and blessed by God as sovereign lord of England. Both of us swore knights' oaths to serve him to the death. Until he dies, or willingly hands the Crown to someone else, he is our one and only king. Any deviation from our loyalty is treason!'

De Revelle sighed. 'You're a fool and it will be the end of you! Is that your last word?'

'I'll see you dead – I'd slay you myself – before I'd let you talk me into treachery, damn you!' snarled the coroner.

De Revelle stood up and looked down at him, his narrow face working with emotion. His pointed beard jerked like a dagger as he spoke rapidly and spitefully. 'Then it must be done another way, John. If I am to try to save your life, you must give up any notion of riding off to Winchester with your rumours of rebellion and other gossip. Do you understand?'

De Wolfe looked at him in amazement. 'Go to hell, Richard! I'll do exactly what I think is right. How do you imagine you can stop me? With your little sword?'

De Revelle flushed and swallowed hard to control himself. His lack of prowess in all things martial was well known and he was excruciatingly sensitive about it. He had always wanted to be a courtier, in the political arena, not a warrior. But de Wolfe's insult made it easier for him to spit out his ultimatum.

'Your scandalous private life is well known, especially to my spies. If you do not agree to keep quiet, I'll see to it that Matilda is told not only about that drab you visit in the tavern, but also about Hilda, wife of Thorgils. And, for good measure, that Welsh woman will also be told about her rival in Dawlish!'

De Wolfe jumped to his feet and looked down at his brother-in-law in amazement. Then he did something that the sheriff had not expected. He began laughing uproariously, and was still laughing as he passed the astonished guard at the door.

That afternoon, de Wolfe attended the funeral of Canon Robert de Hane. Although it was over a week since his death, the cathedral Chapter had waited this unusually long time before burial because of the absence of the Bishop, who was to conduct the mass for the dead. The freezing weather had allowed the body to lie in its coffin without putrefaction.

As he watched it lowered into a deep hole below

a paving slab in the apse behind the high altar, the coroner cursed the sheriff for not arresting the two men who had killed de Hane. He had no idea where Jocelin de Braose and his squire were at present, but suspected that they were being sheltered somewhere in the west of the county, probably at Totnes or Berry Pomeroy. As coroner, he had no legal power to seize them, so there was little that he and Gwyn could do except by subterfuge, as at the ambush in Dunsford, which could hardly be repeated.

After the funeral, he met John de Alencon briefly in the nave. The other canons passed them on the way out and most nodded a greeting, except Thomas de Boterellis, who studiously ignored them. In the distance, de Wolfe saw the remote figure of the Bishop making his way back to his palace and he wondered how deeply Henry Marshal was involved in the budding rebellion.

He told the Archdeacon about the sheriff's attempt to suborn him into the conspiracy and his ludicrous threat of blackmail. De Alencon smiled wryly at these venal matters, which were outwith the experience of a truly celibate priest. 'I gather that your amorous affairs are an insufficient threat to you, John?'

'The man is insane to think that they are anything more than a passing irritation!' snorted de Wolfe. 'My only concern is how he got to know about the lady in Dawlish. He must pay informers about the country to spy on me, as he claimed.'

The Archdeacon gazed up the nave at the great choir screen of ornately carved wood, as if seeking inspiration from on high. 'What is to be done, John? Will you ride to Winchester, as you intend?'

'I'll have to. This affair cannot continue unchecked.

But I'd like some firmer evidence to give Hubert Walter. I'll wait a few more days to see if anything turns up, though the bloody sheriff is watching my every move.'

John de Alencon laid a hand on the coroner's arm. 'I've warned you before, John. Be careful. These men are playing for high stakes and will swat you like a fly if they can. Look what happened to Fitzhamon and poor Robert, lying there in his box.'

With yet another caution ringing in his ears, de Wolfe walked back through the rain to his house in Martin's Lane.

At the midday meal of fried pork, onions, bread and some rather shrivelled stored apples, Matilda was in what her husband called an average mood. She had no spontaneous conversation, but at least answered his questions and comments civilly, even if her voice conveyed a total lack of interest in him and his doings. The only slight spark of curiosity he could strike from her concerned the funeral of Robert de Hane: she wanted to know who was present, if any wives had been there and, if so, what they had been wearing. As he had no answer to her last questions, she subsided into apathy again.

Later, as there were no hangings or mutilations at which he had to be present, he walked with Gwyn to Bull Mead, out of the city beyond the South Gate. On the meadows between Holloway and Magdalen Streets, which led away to the east, jousting lists had been set up and a minor tournament was being held that day. In his prime, de Wolfe had been a keen competitor in the sport that maintained and honed fighting men's skills between real battles. He had won many a joust

– and the prize money and sometimes the favours of a woman, which went with victory.

Both he and Bran were now too long in the tooth for this violent and often fatal sport, but he still enjoyed watching the spectacle. In former years Gwyn had acted as his squire and they both studied the new young men with a critical eye, as they thundered towards each other down each side of the wattle fence, trying to unhorse each other with a clash of lance on shield. Thankfully the rain had stopped, but the tourney field was a quagmire of churned mud under the horses' hoofs, and when a man was unhorsed, he became a greater figure of derision because of his mud-plastered ignominy.

The two former Crusaders spent an hour or two sitting on the benches of the primitive viewing stand, the sights and sounds of combat rekindling memories of battles gone by.

When the early winter dusk began to close in, the tournament came to an end and the crowd dispersed. Gwyn trudged off to his home in St Sidwell's, leaving de Wolfe to make his way to the Bush. At that hour it was almost deserted, but as soon as he entered, Nesta bustled across from the kitchen door and seized his arm to pull him to an empty corner, as far away from the few customers as possible. De Wolfe saw that her face was flushed and that her hazel eyes were sparkling with indignation. Hurriedly, he searched his conscience for some recent transgression, but he soon learned that her anger was not directed at him. 'I've never heard such impertinence!' she hissed. 'That rheumaticky old fool that is steward to the sheriff had the gall to come here earlier with a message from his master!'

Mystified for a moment, realisation dawned on de Wolfe. 'Oh, God, I never thought he'd stoop to such pettiness!'

The pretty alehouse keeper glared at him. 'You know what he said, then?'

'It was about Hilda, no doubt?'

'Yes, it was about bloody Hilda! It's bad enough knowing that you're unfaithful to me without having it bandied all about Exeter! What's going on?'

De Wolfe pulled her gently to his table by the hearth and, as they sat down, Nesta signalled to Edwin to bring the coroner his usual quart of ale. The old potman, who had been hovering uneasily in the background, keeping clear of his mistress's fiery temper, grinned with relief and hurried to his barrels.

John explained Richard de Revelle's attempt to blackmail him, and Nesta, with the volatility of spirit that went with her red hair, soon saw the ridiculous side of it and began giggling over the jug of ale that they shared.

'A good job we had this out between us the other day, John. I'd have hated to have learned it first from the sheriff!' Then she had a more sobering thought. 'But if he's been so vindictive as to tell me of your exploits with the ladies, he'll be even more certain to go sneaking to your wife. She won't be so forgiving as me, I'll be bound.'

'She's known about you for years, love.'

'The whole of Devon knows about us, John. But what about Hilda? Does Matilda know she's on your list of conquests?' Even Nesta couldn't resist the slightly bitter remark.

De Wolfe tried to shrug this off, but he had a nagging suspicion that he was in for a hard time with his wife.

As the light faded, the tavern began to fill when men came in at the end of the working day. Nesta had to bustle around, chivvying the cook and the serving-maids, so eventually de Wolfe went with leaden feet back to his gloomy house near the cathedral. As he pulled off his cloak and his wet, leaky boots in the vestibule, Mary put her head around the passage to the yard. She pointed at the inner door to the hall and rolled her eyes heavenwards, then vanished. Even Brutus slunk after her, his tail between his legs.

De Wolfe sat before the fire in the cowled chair usually occupied by his wife. His old hound had crept back in and lay now at his feet. Simon, the aged man employed to cut wood and tend the fowl and garden pig, had carried in a pile of logs sufficient to last the night. Mary had brought him a stone flask of Loire wine, the last of those bought from Eric Picot before he had disappeared last month. Thus stocked up, he prepared to pass the long evening alone, as a westerly wind moaned outside and spattered rain against the shutters. He heard the outer door slam as Mary left to visit her mother in Rack Lane, leaving him in peace to contemplate the events of the past few hours.

As Nesta had anticipated, his brother-in-law, having had his attempt at blackmail so scornfully rejected, had vindictively gone ahead and revealed John's indiscretions. It was not the old steward who had called but de Revelle himself, while de Wolfe had been at the jousting that afternoon, to poison his sister's ear against her husband.

As John sat moodily before his hearth, sipping warm wine, he recalled the final show-down with Matilda earlier that evening. After his visit to the Bush, he had expected a blazing row, foul words, maybe something thrown at him and then a few weeks' ostracism and certainly banishment from their cold marital bed, to all of which he was well accustomed.

But this time it had been different. He did not know exactly what de Revelle had said to his sister, but he suspected that he had embroidered the bare truth considerably and probably added some political lies to the issue of infidelity. Whatever it had been, Matilda had stood before him in the hall, grim-faced and flinty-eyed, but not in the expected raging temper. De Wolfe remembered the actual words she had used – they had been so few.

'My brother has told me of your evil, John de Wolfe. I am ashamed to be burdened with your name and I am leaving you this moment. You no longer have a wife and I never wish to see you again.' She had stalked past him towards the door, her square, high-cheekboned face white with suppressed emotion. Then he noticed Lucille lurking in the shadows near the door, already dressed for outside. She held a cloak, which she draped over her mistress's shoulders, then picked up some large bundles tied into cloths and followed Matilda to the vestibule.

'Where are you going, for God's sake?' he asked, tracking them to the front door. Matilda ignored him, but as she stepped outside he saw Sergeant Gabriel and two men-at-arms standing in the lane as an escort. As they walked away, Gabriel risked giving him a shrug of supplication and pointed his finger in the direction of Rougemont. A moment later, they had vanished into the gloom of the lane, lit only by the farrier's torches opposite.

Hardly knowing whether to be mortified or relieved,

de Wolfe came inside and slammed the outer door. Instantly Mary appeared from the passage, where she had been eavesdropping.

'She's left me, girl,' he said, almost incredulously.

'No such luck, Sir Crowner!' said the maid cynically. 'She'll be back some time. You're too good a catch for a woman her age to let slip through her fingers.' She followed him back into the sombre hall, which somehow seemed all the more cheerless now.

'I presume she's gone to her brother at the castle,' he muttered.

'Yes, I heard her talking to Lucille about it – that ugly witch is delighted you're in trouble and that she's now going to live in a manor house'

'What manor house?' he demanded.

'They're going to stay in the sheriff's rooms in Rougemont for a day or two, as Lady Eleanor has gone home, then they are travelling down to Revelstoke to live there indefinitely.'

De Wolfe gave a roar of sardonic laughter. 'By Christ, that makes me feel better already! Matilda and Eleanor living in the same house! There'll be murder done within a week. And Revelstoke – your friend Lucille will go mad there with boredom. She might as well be on the moon as that lonely place on the cliffs.'

Revelstoke was the sheriff's ancestral home, in a remote spot on the coast near Plympton in the west of the county, where both he and Matilda had been brought up. Richard had another manor near Tavistock, which his haughty wife preferred.

'Did you hear anything else between them, Mary?' he asked.

'No, I was out buying fish when the sheriff called. All I heard later was that your wife will be sending

Lucille back some time to collect all her clothes and belongings.'

Now, as de Wolfe sat alone with his hound and his wine, he mulled over the implications of this unexpected turn of events. He had little doubt that Mary was right, and that in the fullness of time Matilda would return. What else could she do? Divorce was well-nigh impossible and a woman of forty-six had no other prospects, other than buying her way into a nunnery. That was always one possibility, given Matilda's religious leanings, but John felt this was too good to be true.

Looking on the bright side, he had little to concern him. The house was his, bought with money left him by his father and from the accumulated loot of a dozen wars. He had wisely invested money in Hugh de Relaga's wool export trade and he had a steady income from his share of the manors at Stoke-in-Teignhead and Holcombe. In fact, he could never have been appointed coroner unless he was financially independent: the Justiciar had laid down that every knight so elected must have an income of at least twenty pounds a year, which was supposed to make the attractions of embezzlement less appealing. With Mary to satisfy his stomach, and Nesta his heart and loins, he felt ready to wait out Matilda's latest protest – and if she chose to take the veil, good luck to her!

As he drank and dozed by the fire, he thought half-heartedly of going down to the Bush to tell his Welsh mistress the latest news, but sleep overcame him. As the wind moaned outside, he began to snore gently as Brutus edged nearer the dying logs.

De Wolfe must have slept for several hours, though

as the nearest clock was in Germany, it was only later that he calculated from the cathedral bell that he must have awakened around the tenth hour. His final dream seemed to contain an insistent knocking, and as he opened his eyes groggily, he realised that someone was hammering on his street door.

He climbed to his feet and sleepily threw some small sticks on to the fire, which had crumbled to glowing ashes. Brutus lazily hauled himself to his haunches as John stumbled across the cold stones of the hall, pulling a grey house-cape more tightly around his shoulders against the damp chill. A tallow dip guttered in its bowl on the long table, and he lit the wick of a new candle in passing to light himself to the front door.

The knocking continued with greater urgency, and he wondered who it could be. Not Mary, for she would spend the night with her mother, as she did once a week, coming back early in the morning to prepare breakfast – and she would have known that the door was never locked, as would Gwyn or Thomas.

He lifted the big iron latch and held up the candle, as the farrier's flares opposite had burned out. The rain and the wind had died down and his candle flame survived the remaining breeze to show a muffled figure on his doorstep. Mindful of the Archdeacon's warning of assassins, he held the door only partly open, until he realised that the figure was female.

'You are Sir John – the Crowner?' asked a tremulous but still attractive voice.

'I am indeed. And who are you?'

'My name is Rosamunde – Rosamunde of Rye, they call me. Can I speak with you, Crowner, please? I am in trouble.'

The fitful candlelight fell on a beautiful face, half

hidden in a deep hood – though even this poor view showed something wrong with one eye. Though the chivalrous de Wolfe would have helped any woman in trouble – even an old hag – one with such a voice and the face of a sultry angel was irresistible.

He pulled open the door and beckoned her inside. This was the woman who had been involved with Giles Fulford and probably Jocelin de Braose, but somehow he doubted that she had come to stab him to death. He escorted her into the hall and over to the hearth, where the sticks were now burning briskly, throwing light across the room. Brutus stood to look at the new arrival then, sensing no danger, wagged his tail slowly and lay down again.

The woman, tall and straight, was still shrouded in a heavy cape that fell to her feet. 'I know you have heard of me, Sir John, in not very favourable circumstances.'

As they stood eyeing each other from either side of the fire, she lifted her hands and threw back the pointed hood of the mantle, revealing a cascade of glossy black hair that gleamed in the firelight. She also revealed, on the smooth features of her full-lipped face, a large bruise that discoloured the eye lids and the upper part of her left cheek. 'Look at this, Sir John – and these!' Rosamunde slid the mantle from her shoulders so that it fell to the floor. She wore a bright green silk kirtle with a deep round neckline, unlike the modest tops of the dresses he was used to seeing. The silk strained across her full breasts and was pulled tight at her waist by lacing at the back.

He dragged his attention back to what she was showing him. Down both sides of her long white neck were red scratches, obviously from fingernails, and above her collarbone, partly obscured by the edges of her dress, were recent blue bruises.

'I have been bady used, Crowner, and this is only the half of it! I know I have a reputation but I still deserve the protection of the law.' She gave him a look of supplication from her large eyes, which glistened from under half-lowered lids. Her lashes were darkened with soot and her lips reddened with rouge.

De Wolfe moved closer to her, partly to study her injuries but also in a spontaneous gesture of sympathy. 'Who did this to you, girl?' he demanded.

'Jocelin de Braose, the swine! You must know that I am the woman of his squire, Giles Fulford. His master decided that he wanted to bed me too, and when Giles was away today he forced himself on me – look here!'

Her hand had been on her right shoulder and now she pulled it away to show that the green silk had been ripped from the back of the neck to the seam of the long bell-shaped sleeve. As she took her fingers down, a large flap of the bodice fell forward to expose most of her right breast. 'The other is the same, Crowner,' she said, in her low voice, pointing with a slim finger to the group of penny-sized bruises on her bosom and around the large brown nipple.

Interested though he was in wounds and injuries, the details of these bruises were not foremost in de Wolfe's mind as he gazed down at her seductive body – especially as her face and lips were within inches of his own. He swallowed and dragged his mind back to this unique situation. 'Where is de Braose now?' he rumbled. If the renegade was inside the city, maybe he had a chance to trap him, even though Gwyn was locked outside the walls until morning.

But Rosamunde did not reply and, suddenly, alarm bells began pealing in his head. Before he could step back, she put an arm around his neck and kissed him full on the lips, her bare breast pressed to his chest.

The next moment, she threw herself on the floor at his feet and screamed, 'Rape, rape!' at the top of her voice. As she did so, she was busy pulling down the other side of her kirtle top and dragging up her skirt so that she was naked to the waist. For some seconds, which seemed like minutes, de Wolfe was paralysed with surprise. Though in battle his reflexes were instantaneous, this had been so unexpected, so outrageously bizarre, that he stood gaping at her performance in that empty house.

Except that it proved not to be empty: the hall door crashed open, four men burst into the hall and ran across to seize him. He struggled, but he had nothing, not even a dagger, with which to defend himself, his weapons being in their usual resting place in the vestibule. His old hound jumped snarling against the first intruder, but a heavy kick in the ribs sent him yelping into a corner.

Two ruffians grabbed his arms from behind and held him in a vicelike grip, while the other two men came to stand before him. They were Jocelin de Braose and Giles Fulford, who came up close and sneered in his face. De Braose gave him a heavy punch in the stomach, which would have doubled him up, had he not been held by the men behind. 'That's part payment for Dunsford, blast you,' he snarled. He was followed by Fulford, who gave de Wolfe a double slap on either side of his face, which almost knocked his head off. 'And that's for near-drowning me, Crowner. I'll pay you for the rest later!'

For a moment, de Wolfe thought that they were going to kill him there and then, but when his head cleared after the blows, reason told him that if this was a simple assassination, there would have been no need for Rosamunde's play-acting.

She picked herself up from the floor, the two men making no attempt to help her. Calmly, she dropped the hem of her skirt and pulled up the top of her kirtle to cover her bosom, pinning it back in place with a small brooch she produced from a pocket in her cloak, which she picked up and threw around her shoulders. De Wolfe found his tongue at last, though his lips were swelling from the blows he had taken. After a stream of oaths, which aroused the admiration of the two thugs holding him, he muttered thickly, 'What do you bastards want of me? You've already committed two murders, which will bring you a hanging – and you tried to steal the King's treasure! Are you asking to be hanged three times?'

De Braose thrust his round face with its rim of red whiskers close to him. 'What's the penalty for ravishing this poor girl, Crowner? One hanging will be enough to stretch your neck.' He gave de Wolfe another prod in the belly as he spoke.

The coroner shouted back, with a voice like a bull, 'And who is going to try me on this laughable load of perjury that two criminals and a painted whore will trot out?'

'Painted whore? Yes, Crowner, that's paint from her lips that's on your own, you dirty old bastard!' sneered Fulford, his thin, fair face contorted with hate.

'You ask who will try you?' replied de Braose. 'The sheriff in his court, of course. This was partly his idea, as his stupid first idea to shame you with your mistresses had no chance of success. Everyone knows what a randy old goat you are, even your pig-faced wife.'

'Don't speak of my wife like that! She's worth a thousand like you, you putrid bucket of shite!' roared de Wolfe, adamantly determined that he was the only one entitled to insult Matilda.

De Braose lifted his hand to strike John again, but thought better of it and turned to the woman. 'You've got your story straight, have you?' he demanded. 'We're all going up to the castle now to throw this stubborn fool into the cells, unless de Revelle can talk some sense into him.'

Rosamunde, her mantle now wrapped around her, said nonchalantly, 'Don't worry about me. My acting's better than yours. And if we ever do this again, don't be so enthusiastic with your fists and your nails, you sadistic bastard! You nearly pulled my dugs off, making those bruises!'

Ignoring her complaints, the squat de Braose turned back to the coroner. 'I'm to give you a last chance, de Wolfe, though I truly hope you won't take it as I want to see you hang.'

The Coroner glared at him, wishing he could get his hands around that thick neck. 'And exactly who says you're to offer me this last chance, whatever that is?'

'Henry de la Pomeroy, though surely you know that already. I am to tell you that if you agree not to cause any more problems for the rightful campaign to put a better king on the throne of England, we'll not even take you from this house to Rougemont. You can remain as coroner and continue that post under the new King.'

He stopped to see if De Wolfe had anything to say,

but the coroner waited in silence and de Braose finished his ultimatum. 'But the complaint of this woman will remain hanging over you, backed up by four men's sworn testimony, in case you get any ideas about backing out of the bargain in the next month or so. After that it won't matter – John will be on the throne anyway.' He waited for an answer and got it straight away.

'Of course I'll not keep quiet, you fools,' de Wolfe shouted. 'Why are you going through this ridiculous charade of a ravishment? Why not kill me now and then run away, as you did with the old canon and William Fitzhamon? That would stop me taking the news to the Justiciar, without all this mummery.'

De Braose shrugged indifferently. 'I agree – but Pomeroy and de Revelle think that a murdered coroner might raise some eyebrows in Winchester or London. The next thing we know, some of the King's Justices might be sent down here to snoop around. But the quick trial and disposal of a lecherous ravisher would attract little attention.'

Fulford motioned to the two roughly dressed mercenaries, who had been recruited probably from outlaws. 'Come on, he's said no, let's take him to the sheriff.'

Jocelin made one last appeal to de Wolfe. 'You realise that, once outside that door, you are accused and damned in the eyes of the city and county as a rapist? There's no going back!'

For answer, de Wolfe spat accurately into his face and received another crippling blow in the belly, followed by a punch to his face that split his upper lip. Then he was dragged, struggling, towards the door and into the lane, followed by the soulful eyes of his hound, who still hid in the furthest corner.

CHAPTER ELEVEN

In which Crowner John goes to gaol

At least de Wolfe was spared the ignominy of being marched as a prisoner through the streets of Exeter in daylight. It was approaching midnight as they climbed the slope to Rougemont, and as the rain and wind had returned, there were few to see or care about a tight knot of men hurrying to the castle.

The two surly ruffians had released de Wolfe's arms after one had lashed together his wrists with a length of rope. Using the free end as a leash, he allowed him to walk closely in front of him, with Fulford, de Braose and the woman going ahead, the other man behind.

Apart from an astounded guard at the gatehouse, who had been earlier told by de Revelle that de Braose was to be admitted, they saw virtually no one on their journey. De Wolfe, although he felt as though he was acting out some awful dream, realised that he had to bide his time: it would be pointless to call for help to any casual citizen they passed. The sheriff was the power in this county and all law enforcement, such as it was, drained back to him, which was why the rebels needed him on their side. Aid for John de Wolfe would have to come from outside Exeter, and tonight was not the time to find it.

They reached the undercroft of the keep and clattered down the steps into the almost pitch black interior. On the further side was a faint light, where Stigand had a small banked-down fire. He had his living space in one of the arched vaults, which he had blocked off with a crude wooden partition. Behind it was a filthy mattress and some cooking pots. Fulford kicked him awake and, when the grotesquely fat gaoler had come to his senses, he grudgingly lit some horn-lanterns and stumbled ahead to the iron gate closing the cell passageway. With a clatter of keys and mumbled curses, the gate squealed open and Stigand led the way to the first cell on the left, the door of which was open. De Wolfe was thrust inside and the rope taken from his wrists before the door was slammed and locked. There was a barred grille in the wooden panel, and de Braose's face peered in.

'You won't be alone for long, Crowner. The sheriff wants a word with you – about arrangements for the hanging!' Pleased with his wit, he walked off laughing.

De Wolfe knew every cell in this prison: he came here several times a week to record Ordeals and mutilations. He felt his way in the dark to a thick slate shelf built into one wall of the tiny room and sat down, ignoring the protests of the rats he disturbed in the dirty straw on the floor. His belly ached from the blows he had received and his bruised face and torn lip stung, but otherwise he was unbroken and unbowed. He had been imprisoned several times before, in worse places than this, both in France and England, but then he had been a prisoner-of-war rather than an alleged criminal ravisher. He cursed his own lack of suspicion of the woman on his doorstep, but on reflection he could see no way of anticipating such a devious plot. He had thought that someone might try to stick a knife in his back, but not to trap him in this way. It could only work, of course, because of the sheriff's monopoly of power, and he tried to think of some way in which this could be frustrated – but no inspiration came. A few minutes later, he heard voices, and lights bobbed towards the passageway. He heard the outer gate creak open and close on its rusted hinges. Then his cell door was opened.

Richard de Revelle stood in the entrance and behind him de Wolfe could see the other three conspirators. The two strong-arm men had gone, and Stigand had been sent out of earshot.

'This is a sorry state of affairs, John,' said his brother-in-law unctuously. 'I always knew you were overfond of the lusts of the flesh, but never thought you'd be driven to rapine!'

'Spare me your nonsense, Richard. I doubt this was your idea, you don't have the brains for it.'

The sheriff smiled sardonically at him. 'This hasn't been your day, has it, John? Your wife leaves you for good, because of your shameless adultery with God knows how many women – and within hours, you indecently assault this poor girl. I suppose her undoubted attractions were too much for you.'

'It's not so long since I caught you in bed with a whore, Richard, but I was foolish enough not to arrange for perjured witnesses to be present.'

The sheriff stiffened with annoyance, but no one there cared a whit for his morals. 'This is your last chance, John. You are still my relative-in-law, more's the pity, so I regret this situation for the sake of my sister. But, as you are too stubborn to join us, my reputation and my life are at risk if you are allowed to ride off to London with your misplaced loyalties.' He looked over his shoulder as if seeking support for his final words.

'You know what my answer will be to that!' The coroner shouted his reply as loudly as he could, so that anyone nearby could hear it, even if it was only the few other miserable prisoners further along the passage. 'I denounce you, Richard de Revelle, as a traitor to the King you have sworn to serve and a rebel against the Crown of England! You will be hanged for that – though you may be blinded, castrated and gutted first. That's my answer!'

Though de Braose, standing just outside the door, guffawed at this, the sheriff did not take it so lightly. De Wolfe could see his Adam's apple rise and fall beneath his small beard as he swallowed nervously. 'Nonsense, man, you have no proof – not a single witness to implicate me. Even if you were able to blab to someone, where could you go now with these wild tales? Winchester and London are far away for a man imprisoned for rape.'

'So what do you intend to do with me, brother-in-law? Get Stigand to poison me tonight – or cut out my tongue tomorrow to silence me? That would be effective, as you know I couldn't write my denunciation of you!' He even used his private longing to be literate to goad the sheriff.

De Revelle was becoming more rattled as he realised the enormity of the path he was being forced to take. Getting rid of a king's coroner was not as easy as getting rid of a common criminal. Coroners did not just vanish from the face of the earth without questions being asked at the highest level. He was now irrevocably launched on this escapade, but the further he went the less he relished it.

John sensed this, and deliberately provoked his brother-in-law with mockery. He raised his long chin and pointed to the black stubble on his neck. 'When you hang me, before all those good burgesses and churchmen, do you think the knot should be on the left or right, eh?'

Jocelin de Braose could see what was happening and stepped forward angrily. 'Come on, Sheriff, leave him, he's trying to make fools of us!'

'Too late, God did that years ago!' sneered de Wolfe. De Braose raised his arm to strike the coroner, but then realised that he was not being held or tied. He stepped back hastily and pulled his dagger from its scabbard.

'That's it, hack the crowner to death,' invited de Wolfe. 'That really would intrigue the Chief Justiciar and the Lord Marshal.'

Richard de Revelle was almost at the end of his tether at this taunting mention of the most powerful members of the royal court. 'Stop this, de Braose! Remember your place. You are nothing but a hired sword and you have no say in these matters.' He turned back to the prisoner with a final entreaty. 'I beg you, John, consider your position through the night. Otherwise this woman will Appeal you for ravishing her at the County Court tomorrow. We have four witnesses to your indecent assault – and have an apothecary who will say that he examined her and found her grievously bruised about the private parts. Within days you will be accused, convicted and hanged. I am powerless to stop this once you set foot in the Shire Hall tomorrow morning.' Then, as if afraid to hear any more than would unnerve him, the sheriff stepped back, slammed the door, and yelled for Stigand to lock up.

With plenty to occupy his thoughts, de Wolfe lay back on the cold slate slab, wondering if the inside of a tomb was as hard and as dark as this bare stone.

Though Richard de Revelle had enjoyed same malicious delight in telling his sister about her husband's infidelities, he had not anticipated the consequences. He had thought that she would give de Wolfe hell on a grander scale than usual, but not that she would leave home immediately and saddle herself on him. Matilda had always idolised her elder brother, but in spite of his outward show of affection for her, he had from childhood thought her a plain and sulky girl, whose sourness had grown as she got older. To have her ensconced, bag and baggage, in his already cramped living quarters at Rougemont was too much – especially at a critical time like this. And to have that evil-eyed, buck-toothed French maid there too was intolerable. He had had to evict his steward from his outer chamber to sleep there himself, give his bed to Matilda and have a pallet brought in for the maid. Thank God he could get rid of them in a few days' time when he took them down to Revelstoke – though his spirit quailed at the prospect of telling his wife, Eleanor, that she was to have permanent lodgers. Perhaps one of them would move out to his other manor near Tavistock, but de Revelle could foresee serious domestic trouble stretching into the infinite future.

But was there going to be an infinite future for him – or even much future at all?

As he lay sleepless on his steward's lumpy mattress in the early hours of the morning, de Revelle felt increasing apprehension at what the coming day – and weeks – would bring. He felt that he was launched on a slippery slope over which he had no control. The grand idea of rebellion had seemed excitingly attractive in the planning stages, when conspirators had gathered over jugs of wine to change the face of England. But now that he was in danger of being forced to hang his own brother-in-law, who was a king's officer, a friend of the Justiciar and the monarch himself, that impersonal plotting seemed far removed from less palatable reality.

De Revelle had come near to disaster before, less than a year ago. He had always craved the status of high office, and being sheriff of a far western county so remote from the centre of power had not satisfied his ambition. He had never found favour at the court of either Henry the Second or his son Richard. Every effort he had made to gain a post in Winchester or Westminster had been frustrated. Perhaps he had become paranoid about it, but he sensed personal snubs and rejection from every quarter, especially since the old King had died in 'eighty-nine. Two years ago, when he heard rumours of the Count of Mortaigne's aspirations to seize the throne in the absence of his brother Richard, he had seen a chance to nail his colours to a different mast and hopefully be repaid for his new allegiance with preferment under a new sovereign.

Thankfully, as it turned out, he had not gone too far down this road before it collapsed under him. By the time the old Queen, Eleanor, had mobilised action against the rebels, shortly before Coeur de Lion was released from captivity, de Revelle had been promised the sheriffdom of Devon through the influence of barons sympathetic to the Count. When the revolt crumbled, he had been brushed with the same tar of disgrace as the other rebels, and his elevation to sheriff suspended. This was when Henry de la Pomeroy's father had been driven to suicide. Only the casual, irresponsible pardon granted by the King to his brother and most of the rebels got Richard de Revelle off the hook and eventually allowed him to take up the sheriff's post.

Now the whole cycle appeared to be beginning again, and as he lay on his cold bed he wished that he had stayed content with his lot. The worm of ambition still wriggled within him, but the last day or two had made him doubt that the price he paid in anguish was worth the tenuous prize at the end.

At the meeting in Berry Pomeroy, two days before, he had put forward his feeble plan to shame de Wolfe into silence as a desperate attempt to avoid the present situation dreamed up by Bernard Cheevers and de Braose of having the coroner in gaol for alleged rape so that he could be judicially strangled! For the sheriff, the situation had snowballed into a nightmare, out of control and irreversible. He tossed and turned, and cursed – the curses aimed as much at himself for becoming so involved, as at de Wolfe for being such an iron-headed, stubborn fool, yet a fool who commanded respect for his loyalty, as compared with de Revelle's own repeated treachery.

Before sleep born of exhaustion claimed him, he had a last waking nightmare: he had to face Matilda in the morning and tell her that her husband was now a ravisher as well as an adulterer, and that by the end of the week she was likely to be a felon's widow.

*   *   *

As always, it was impossible to keep anything quiet in the small city of Exeter. Soon after dawn the rumour went around like wildfire that Sir John de Wolfe, the coroner, was in Rougemont gaol, though as yet no one knew why. When he came off duty, the guard at the gatehouse had told his drinking friends the news, they had told their wives, and as soon as the stall-holders and hawkers flooded through the opened city gates, the gossip flashed through the city like fire through a cornfield.

Gwyn heard it when he was buying a slab of cheese at a stall just inside the East Gate as he came in from St Sidwell's. Astounded, he hurried towards the castle and overtook Thomas de Peyne, who was limping as fast as he could up the hill, after hearing of his master's plight from a cook in the close, who had been out to buy butter for breakfast. Anxiously, they both went through the gate, noticing that the guards had been doubled. No one had orders to prevent the coroner's staff from entering – and, anyway, Gwyn would probably have throttled anyone who tried to stop him. They dived down the steps to the undercroft, Thomas hobbling and hopping to keep up with the Cornishman's determined strides. The gate to the cells was locked, so Gwyn thundered over to Stigand's cubicle, where the gross gaoler was boiling something in a pot. 'Open that bloody gate, you fat toad! I have to see to the coroner at once.'

The bloated Saxon looked up from his cooking with a sneer. 'No one is to speak to him, I have strict orders.'

Gwyn was in no mood to discuss the matter. He grabbed the shoulders of Stigand's dirty smock in both hands and jerked him clear off the ground. Shaking him violently, he hissed in his face, 'Listen, you bag of slime, open that gate or I'll twist your head off!'

Convinced in an instant, the repulsive guardian of the prison almost ran across the gloomy vault, with Gwyn prodding him all the way, Thomas following behind. When, hands shaking, the gaoler had manipulated his keys to let them in, Gwyn grabbed them from him and ordered the clerk to lock the gate. 'We don't want this bladder of lard running to raise the alarm,' he snapped. Turning to the cell door, he peered in and found de Wolfe's face within inches of his own on the other side of the grille. 'We'll have you out in a moment, Crowner! Thomas, bring those keys here.'

During the night de Wolfe had had plenty of time to think. 'No, Gwyn, that's not the way. The guards may have let you in but they certainly won't let me out. In any case, I'm not going to run from my own city. If you try to force a way out, you'll be trapped too.'

He explained quickly what had happened and how he had been tricked by Jocelin and the others. Gwyn was all for seeking out de Braose and dissecting him with a blunt knife, but again John restrained his violent inclinations. 'You must stay free, it's vital – and you, Thomas. You are my only link with the outside. Gwyn, you must go quietly out and straightaway ride into the county to alert those barons and knights we know are loyal to the King. Lord Ferrars, and Reginald de Courcy – you remember them from that business of Fitzosbern a few weeks ago. They will spread the message to others they know. Tell them that a rebellion is brewing again and that Pomeroy, Cheever and de Nonant are behind it in Devon.' Something kept him from including the sheriff in his list. 'Say that I have been falsely accused of a felony to keep me quiet and need assistance straight away. That will be sufficient to bring them post-haste into the city.'

He turned his face to his clerk, his gaunt features dirty and more unshaven than usual, and bent to lower his great height to the aperture. 'Thomas, go to the Archdeacon with the same story as fast as your little legs will carry you. Also tell him that the men who killed the canon are behind this. Now go, both of you, and don't get caught or I'm done for!'

He moved back into his cell to forestall any argument from Gwyn, who would have been willing to demolish the gaol stone by stone to free his master. But the big man had recognised the urgency in the coroner's voice and did as he was told. 'Get going, dwarf, down to the Close.' He opened the gate and gave Thomas a push to send him on his way. Stigand tried to follow, but Gwyn grabbed him by the collar and dragged him up to the large cell at the end, where three ragged men waited to be hanged the next day. Unlocking their gate with Stigand's keys, he thrust the gaoler inside and locked up again. He marched out, oblivious to the yells and screams of the fat sadist as the condemned felons worked off their anger on him.

He caught up with the limping clerk after a few yards, and they walked with exaggerated casualness to the gate, then hurried down to the town to do as they had been bidden.

Meanwhile, the sheriff was steeling himself for the show-down with his sister. Though he normally ate at the top table in the hall, this morning he ordered his steward to serve it in his office chamber. Resentful at being banished from his sleeping place, the man banged mugs and dishes on the table with surly indifference, but de Revelle was in no mood to worry about servants. Lucille had been sent to eat with the other maids in the kitchen, and as soon as the food was laid out, he dismissed the steward.

Then he tapped on the inner door and called Matilda to breakfast. There was no answer and he knocked harder, then harder again. With foreboding building, he put his head around the door and saw that she was sitting on the edge of the bed, fully dressed, staring fixedly at the narrow window-slit. Eventually, after several invitations, which became more terse as his frayed patience became thinner, she rose and walked past him without a look or a word.

'Bloody women!' he muttered under his breath, but chivalrously held the only chair for her to sit, while he took a stool opposite. Though Richard had little appetite, incredibly Matilda had none. She broke some bread and made a pretence of eating, but mostly sat with her head lowered. He noticed tears welling from inside her thick eyelids, but no sound came from her as he summoned up courage to tell her about her husband.

Pouring a little heated ale into her already full cup, he cleared his throat. 'Matilda, I have some disturbing news, I fear.' She made no response, but the two trickles down each side of her rather flat nose reached her upper lip. De Revelle failed to understand the depth of her apparent grief at her husband's infidelity. He knew that she had been well aware of his long-standing affair with the woman at the Bush Inn – he had heard her on many occasions taunting de Wolfe with the 'Welsh whore', as she was wont to call her. Why she should be so ravaged by the disclosure of his adultery with the

Dawlish wife was quite beyond him, as she had often accused John of affairs with women other than Nesta. But thinking of the often irrational behaviour of his own wife, he mentally shrugged it off as a typically female aberration.

The problem still remained of breaking the worse news to her. 'During the night, a terrible thing has happened, Matilda dear. I see no way of breaking it gently. John is in the castle gaol, beneath us. He has been accused of ravishing a woman of the town. That she is little better than a harlot makes little difference, as there were four witnesses and the girl insists on Appealing him at the County Court this morning.'

Her head came up slowly and she fixed him with a blank stare, the like of which he had never seen on her before, neither in childhood, nor since. For a moment, he feared that she had gone quite mad. He gabbled on, beginning to be gripped by the fear of being in the company of someone mentally ill. 'I have to hold the court, Matilda, I have no choice. This is none of my doing, this Appeal comes from that woman, supported by her friends who caught John in his lecherous act! I am only carrying out my duty as the King's sheriff in this county.'

There was a crash as Matilda's chair went over backwards. She had shot to her feet, glaring at him, her lips quivering, but she said nothing. White-faced and shaking, she went in to the bedroom and closed the door. Unnerved by her behaviour, he approached the door timidly and tapped again. 'Are you alright, sister? Shall I send for your maid?'

There was a pause, then her voice came, low but steadier than before. 'I shall be at the the Shire Hall to support my husband.'

With a sigh, de Revelle turned away, wishing for a world made up only of men. Then his other troubles avalanched back into his mind and he wished himself anywhere but Devon, preferably Africa or Cathay.

ChAPTER TWELVE

In which Crowner John goes to the County Court

The intermittent rain had turned to sleet as the wind went round to the east, but the cold and wet did not dissuade scores of people crowding into the Shire Hall before the tenth hour that morning. The large bare room, with its muddy floor, was crammed with spectators and many more pushed and shoved at the archway that was the only entrance. The low platform at one end was the only free space, with its couple of chairs, some benches and stools for the officials.

As the distant cathedral bell marked the hour, two small processions met outside the keep and merged to march the few yards to the courtroom. One came up from the undercroft, with Sergeant Gabriel leading John de Wolfe, followed by two men-at-arms. It tagged behind the other coming down the steps from the keep. Constable Ralph Morin walked before Richard de Revelle, then came Precentor Thomas de Boterellis and the two Portreeves, Henry Rifford – whose daughter had been raped a month ago – and Hugh de Relaga. At the end walked Matilda and Lucille, both heavily cloaked against the bitter weather.

Gabriel's battleworn face was grim as he escorted a respected friend to what might be a fatal verdict.

Though of a much lower station in life, he had been a soldier like de Wolfe, and had shared common experiences both in the Holy Land and nearer home. The old warrior did not believe that Sir John was guilty of anything and strongly suspected some plot of the sheriff, whom he detested. Thankfully, he had not been ordered to shackle the coroner to take him to the Shire Hall, as was the usual practice. He would have refused, even if it meant the most drastic punishment.

As it happened, Ralph Morin had bluntly told the sheriff beforehand that he was not prepared to put de Wolfe in chains and, with his weakening resolve about the whole conspiracy, de Revelle had not pressed the point.

When the procession reached the wide arch of the hall, the chatter of the crowd ceased and a path opened up as the onlookers drew back. The silence was unnatural, as prisoners were usually subjected to jeers and cat-calls, even missiles, and the respectful hush was far more impressive than cheers or shouts of encouragement. As the escort walked into the hall, a few hands went tentatively out from the throng to touch de Wolfe gently as he passed.

Pale-faced, the sheriff led the way on to the dais and stood in the centre, while other dignitaries, clerks and men-at-arms ranged themselves on either side. There was a moment's confusion as de Revelle invited his sister to the platform, but she shook her head angrily and went to stand with her maid in the front row of the crowd, behind her husband, who was led by Gabriel and another soldier to a point directly below the sheriff.

The crowd packed in even tighter, those around

the doorway shoving to get out of the icy rain and to be within earshot. John stood outwardly calm, his black hair dishevelled and bits of straw sticking to his crumpled grey over-tunic, as those on the platform shuffled and muttered among themselves, the two clerks to the court waving parchments at each other. Ralph Morin stood behind the sheriff, a head taller and with a face like thunder. On the opposite side of the hall to the door, Jocelin de Braose, Giles Fulford, Rosamunde of Rye and a furtive man, who was presumably the apothecary, stood uneasily within a ring of Morin's soldiers, as if they were to be protected against the wrath of the crowd. Not far away, standing with Thomas de Peyne, Edwin and one of the maids from the inn, was Nesta, her face drawn and tearful.

After a few moments, the sheriff sat down on his central chair while the Portreeves and the Precentor subsided on to benches on each side. Then a thin figure in a flowing black robe pushed his way through the crowd at the door. The Archdeacon stepped up, uninvited, to the dais and sat down alongside Hugh de Relaga, his expression suggesting that he would tolerate no challenge to his right to be present.

Richard de Revelle raised a hand to his chief clerk to begin the proceedings. The sheriff was dressed more soberly than usual, as if he wanted to avoid drawing any more attention to himself than necessary. He looked very ill-at-ease and he studiously avoided eye-contact with his sister or her husband as they stood below him. The clerk cleared his throat and held up a parchment roll to read the indictment.

'Whereas this woman, Rosamunde, daughter of Ranulph, commonly known as Rosamunde of Rye, currently domiciled in the city of Exeter in the county of Devon, has brought her Appeal in the proper form to the Sheriff Court of the said County of Devon. The said Rosamunde alleges that she is aggrieved by the felony of ravishment, committed against the common law by one John de Wolfe, knight of the said county, within his dwelling in Martin's Lane on the third day of January in the Year of our Lord eleven ninety-five. And that the said Rosamunde prays and appeals for justice for the said hurt against John de Wolfe, in the due manner prescribed by law.'

He stood back and rolled up his document, looking across at the sheriff for the next stage of the proceedings. With increasing reluctance, now that the awful consequences of his ambition were almost upon him, de Revelle rose to his feet and was about to open his mouth, when a familiar deep voice boomed from below him.

'Before we even start this nonsensical charade, let it be known that these proceedings are invalid and above the law! The alleged crime of rape is now one against the King's peace and is a Plea of the Crown, to be tried by the King's Justices. All that could be done here is to record the so-called evidence and present it to them at the next visit of the Eyre of Assize.' Having delivered his first broadside, de Wolfe fell silent but continued to scourge those on the platform with his deep-set eyes.

The two clerks clucked and shrugged, and looked again at the sheriff for enlightenment. He grasped at this legislative conundrum as a temporary diversion from the looming responsibility of condemning his sister's husband to the gallows. He hauled himself to his feet to speak. 'This court still has jurisdiction! Though there is now an alternative through the royal courts, this woman has chosen the ancient and traditional path of Appeal and she has every right to pursue it. Continue with the trial, clerk!' He sat down again heavily, with his hand nervously plucking at his beard.

No one asked the prisoner whether he pleaded guilty or not and the clerk motioned for the soldiers to bring over the Appealer and the main witnesses, who stood in a line alongside de Wolfe, but with a man-at-arms between them and him in case a free fight developed.

The older clerk, a grey-headed man with a large red nose studded with old abscess scars, took up another parchment. 'Do you, Rosamunde, daughter of Ranulph, bring your Appeal against this prisoner?'

The woman threw back her hood so that her eye, now blacker than ever, was clearly visible. 'I do, sir! He ill used me by both assault and ravishment.' Her voice was strong and bold, but instantly it was matched by another, harsh and just as loud.

'You lying whore! Repeat that with your hand on the Scriptures and earn everlasting damnation!'

It was no priest speaking but Matilda de Wolfe. There was a buzz of consternation in the hall and the sheriff blanched even further. How could he accuse his own sister of contempt of court or have her ejected? His mouth opened and closed, but as she said no more he decided to ignore the interruption and carry on.

The witnesses were called one by one and lied solemnly and persuasively, apart from the leech, who was a bag of nerves. Neither de Wolfe nor his wife made any disturbance as the fabricated story unfolded. Rosamunde claimed that the previous evening, she had been going about her lawful occasions in the city, returning from devotions in the cathedral to the high street. If necessary, she declared, she could even call a priest as witness to prove that she had been kneeling at the altar of St Edmund at about the ninth hour. In the cathedral Close, she had heard footsteps behind her and, when passing through the narrow Martin's Lane, a man called out to her. Knowing him for Sir John de Wolfe, the county coroner, she had no apprehension, even when he urgently asked her to step into his house nearby, on a matter of great importance to do with her friend, Giles Fulford. Worried and unsuspecting, she did so and as soon as they were inside, he fell upon her, kissing and groping at her bodice. She resisted fiercely and tried to scream, but he struck her in the face several times and forced her to the floor, tearing her upper clothing and scratching her neck.

Rosamunde sobbed dramatically before the court as she went on to describe how he had abused her bosom and then lifted her kirtle to ravish her forcibly against her will. She had kept up her screaming as best she could and was saved from further rapine and possibly death by her friends hearing her cries for help and bursting into the house.

Then Giles Fulford, who described himself as Rosamunde's 'protector', and his master Jocelin de Braose, gave a melodramatic account of how they had arranged to meet the woman at the corner of High Street and Martin's Lane, but she had failed to appear at the appointed hour marked by the bells. Then they heard violent screams from a nearby dwelling and entered to find de Wolfe in the act of ravishing the girl. Finally, the weedy, shifty-eyed apothecary falteringly described how the other witnesses had brought Rosamunde to his apothecary's shop in Curre

Street* for her bruises and scratches to be bathed and anointed. He catalogued these and said also that, as they demanded, he examined her nether regions and confirmed rough usage and bleeding. He even produced a crumpled piece of cloth with small bloodstains, which he said he had used to clean her thighs, as the law on rape required physical evidence of venereal injury. There was a murmuring in the Shire Hall when the evidence was finished, some impressed with this lucid tale of lust, the majority regarding it as a transparent fabrication.

The sheriff, who had been chewing the inside of his lip to shreds during this recital, dared to drop his eyes to meet the brooding gaze of John de Wolfe. 'You have the right of reply to this charge,' he croaked.

The coroner drew a deep breath, ready to blast his brother-in-law from the platform with an overwhelming denunciation of his witnesses and his loyalty. Even though it might not be believed at first, it would sow the seeds of doubt about the sheriff's integrity and help to delay matters until Gwyn could mobilise support for the Lionheart from the county. He refused even to countenance the possibility of being summarily convicted and hanged. But he was about to receive one of the greatest surprises of his life, as the nervous de Revelle repeated his question. 'What do you say to this serious charge?'

'He need say nothing – I will say it for him!' The grating voice of Matilda rose high-pitched above the murmuring as she thrust aside a man-at-arms with her burly shoulder and, dragging Lucille behind her, stood alongside her husband. 'This harlot and these so-called

* Now Gandy Lane.

witnesses are audacious liars and must be punished for flagrant perjury!'

Richard de Revelle felt as if an iron band was squeezing his head. What was he going to say to his own sister, who only yesterday had left her husband because of his adultery and was now trying to excuse his rapine?

He struggled to get his mouth working. 'I realise that it is only natural that a faithful wife should attempt to—'

'Shut up, brother, or you will hear more than you desire! I say now that this is a foul conspiracy and that all these people are lying. There never was any ravishment of this strumpet. She insinuated herself into our house by deception while her accomplices lurked outside to bear false witness.'

There was a general clamour in the court, which the castle constable quelled by the powerful use of his lungs, aided by some of his men who laid about them with staves. When relative quiet had been restored, a furious Jocelin de Braose shouted at the bench, 'She should be thrown outside! What value is the braying of a wife about her husband's innocence? What does she know about it? She was not there.'

Matilda de Wolfe turned majestically upon the angry speaker, her square face jutting like the prow of a ship. 'Indeed I was there, you evil man! You chose the wrong night to perform your tricks – and the wrong house. Had you but known it, there is a window-slit high up on the wall between hall and solar. And I was in that solar and heard all that passed – and saw much of it, too.'

A buzz of consternation rippled through the crowded hall.

'The woman insinuated herself into my house on

some pretext about this de Braose swine assaulting her,' continued Matilda, in a voice like a rusty nail being drawn across slate. 'She wanted my husband to obtain justice for her, and began to show him her fabricated injuries. He was too gullible to see what she was about until it was too late. The harlot pulled down her clothing, which she had already torn, and fell to the floor shouting, 'Rape!' Her accomplices must have been waiting at the door for her signal, as they entered within the space of a few heartbeats!'

Again a wave of gasps and murmuring passed across the hall like a squall at sea, but soon subsided so that they could hear the next act in this drama.

De Braose was sneeringly dismissive. 'A likely tale! The desperate gamble of a woman who tries to save her husband from a hanging. Why do you waste our time listening to this, Sheriff?'

That was too much even for de Revelle, though he was a creature of those who employed de Braose. 'Be silent, sir! That is my sister of whom you speak in such a rude manner! Though I agree that the testimony of a wife in these circumstances, though laudable, cannot be accepted without good proof.'

'I will give you proof, brother Sheriff,' snapped Matilda, with quivering passion. 'First, let the Archdeacon or Precentor, as senior men of God here, make me and these villains all swear an oath on the Testament that what we say is true. It may well be that hell-fire holds no terrors for them, unredeemable sinners as they are – but have you ever known me break a vow to Christ?'

There were more mutterings and contemptuous noises from Fulford and his master, but Matilda had more up her wide sleeve. 'Take also the testimony of

my handmaiden Lucille. She was at my side in the
solar and can vouch for every word I say. And, lastly,
I challenge you to test me by seeking my description
of the clothing these three wore last night – none of
which they now display.' She glared up at her brother
triumphantly. 'Neither my maid nor I have ever seen
these scum before – nor have we seen them since last
night. Yet if you seize the clothing they wore then –
especially the green silk that that harlot was wearing
– you will find that it tallies in every particular with a
description I can now give, for Lucille and I anticipated
that we would not be believed.'

There was turmoil both along the front of the court
and on the platform, where everyone seemed to want
to shout at everyone else. From the body of the hall,
there were yells of 'Let him free!', 'Lock the bastards
up!' and 'Adjourn, adjourn!'

The soldiers struggled to prevent Jocelin and
Rosamunde from bearing down on Matilda and
her maid, a scuffle that John de Wolfe tried to enter,
but Gabriel and his men managed to keep everyone apart.

The sheriff was left on the edge of the dais, helpless
until order was restored, again mainly through the
bull-like bellowing of Ralph Morin and the efforts of
his men. The Archdeacon and both Portreeves came to
speak in de Revelle's ear and even the constable came
across to whisper vehemently at him. Uncertainly, the
sheriff shook his head, but Matilda, who had been
watching him intently, stepped close to the edge of
the platform and spoke up to him in a low voice that
could be heard only by those very near them.

'I can speak of other matters I heard from the
solar window, brother, some concerning you and your

recent activities. Do you want to hear those in public? For though yesterday you told me matters about my husband that made me hate him, my respect for you has now also turned to contempt.'

At those words, Richard felt as if a pitcher of icy water had been thrown over him. He knew suddenly that he was beaten, and what mattered now was how much he could salvage from the wreck, such as his own career and possibly his neck. The instinct for survival was strong in de Revelle and he threw up his hands and shouted for order, supported again by Morin and others.

'In view of the controversy that appears to surround this evidence, I have no choice but to adjourn the court.' He looked down at the accusers. 'In fact, I strongly recommend to the Appealer and her witnesses to reconsider their plea, which seems to have substantial evidence to the contrary.' He hesitated, but a glare from Ralph Morin convinced him that he had no alternative. 'Similarly, the accused is released, though of course the Appeal might be revived in the future.' At that, there were a few sardonic laughs from the hall, but the sheriff, now desperate to cut short any chance of open exposure of his part in the plot, plunged on, 'The court will disperse and all parties may take their ease.'

He turned to leave the dais, but de Wolfe's voice rang out like the crack of a whip 'No, Sheriff, that's not good enough!'

Everyone froze and watched, with bated breath, as the two main actors confronted each other again.

'These two men cannot be allowed to walk free once again. They are accused of the murder of Canon Robert de Hane, of the murder of Sir William Fitzhamon –

and the attempted theft of treasure belonging to the King. All these are Pleas of the Crown, and I demand that they be committed to prison to await the King's Justices.' He paused and looked to his left, pointing at the accusers. 'I care nothing for the whore and the leech, they are of no importance, but those two men must be brought to justice!'

De Revelle hesitated again, for he was supposed to be part of this conspiracy, set up by Bernard Cheever. Now he was being asked to arrest his co-conspirators, but a few seconds' quick thinking told him that they would be better off incarcerated in Stigand's cells, than allowed to ride off to tell Pomeroy and Cheever of his own duplicity. As he hesitated, Ralph Morin bent near him and snarled in his ear, 'I'll not let those men out of the city, say what you will, Sheriff!'

With mutiny threatening on all sides, de Revelle nodded.

There was an immediate struggle in front of the platform, as a delighted Sergeant Gabriel waved his guards on to de Braose and Fulford and submerged them in a welter of arms and legs, from which they emerged bruised and pinioned.

'Get them out of here!' screamed the sheriff, terrified of what they might shout about him, now that he had abandoned their cause.

As the guards bundled them out into the inner ward, de Revelle hurried from the platform and vanished, leaving John de Wolfe at the centre of a milling crowd pressing in to congratulate him and to assure him that they never believed the foul slander – though some of the same folk would have happily turned up to watch him dangle from the scaffold if matters had turned out differently.

As soon as he could escape their attentions, he looked for the remarkable Matilda, to thank her for her intervention and to take her home to Martin's Lane. But she had vanished as rapidly as her brother, along with Lucille, without saying a word to him.

As the crowd jostled their way out of the hall, he saw Thomas and the trio from the Bush hanging back and hurried over to them. Although Nesta was always diplomatic enough not to flaunt their affair away from the tavern, she clutched his hand and, with tears in her eyes, told him of the waking nightmare she had suffered since the news broke at dawn.

'I'll come down later and tell you all about it,' he promised. 'Now I must find Matilda – I suppose she's gone home.'

Nesta shook her head at him. 'I doubt it, John. It's not as simple as that.'

She was right. When de Wolfe got back to Martin's Lane, Mary, who almost alone in the city had known nothing about the drama, told him that there had been no sign of the mistress. Mystified, he wondered whether to go back up to Rougemont to see if she was still with her brother, when John de Alencon and Hugh de Relaga tapped at the door and came in. They discussed the fiasco in the Shire Hall, then settled to work out the significance and what should be done next.

'You wife certainly turned the tables, John. Whatever the present problems are between you, she proved that the marriage bond is unbreakable,' said the priest, with a touching faith in the sanctity of an institution that he could never experience. De Wolfe had a niggling feeling that this explanation was too simple, but let it pass. 'At least we have the killers of your canon in custody again, though whether the sheriff will do anything about them remains to be seen.'

The Archdeacon had been near de Revelle when his sister had warned him. 'I think our sheriff is having second thoughts about his attachment to this nascent rebellion. He was always a survivor and I suspect he's searching for some way to escape his affiliation to Pomeroy and his crew.'

Hugh de Relaga, resplendent as always in a red tunic with a mustard-coloured cape and puffed cap to match, had a shrewd mind, which he turned now to the problem. 'We may be able to use that to our advantage,' he offered. 'It depends on how much you want to see your brother-in-law hanged, John.'

'What d'you mean?' asked the coroner suspiciously.

'If de Revelle is keen to save his skin and perhaps even his post as sheriff, he may be willing to co-operate in bringing about the downfall of the traitors in our county. There's nothing we can do further afield, but surely we can spoke the wheel of Pomeroy and de Nonant.'

De Wolfe saw the way his mind was working. 'Yes, we should have Ferrars, de Courcy and perhaps Ralegh here today or tomorrow, if Gwyn has done his job. They can muster a large number of men between them – and the rebels have now lost their mercenary leader, this bloody man de Braose.'

De Alencon, a man of peace, looked puzzled. 'How can the sheriff play a part in this?'

The deceptively amiable de Relaga, though a successful merchant, had always longed to be a man of war and now aired his martial yearnings. 'If he wants to grovel for a pardon, then he might be used to lure

Pomeroy and de Nonant away from their strongholds where they might be seized. We don't need more castle sieges, like Tickhill and Nottingham last year.'

De Wolfe was dubious and resentful about this proposal. 'Wait! Why should the swine get away with it? He's a traitor, he's been a traitor before and he's not to be trusted.'

'He's your wife's brother, John,' said the ever-forgiving Archdeacon.

'To hell with that! He was all for hanging me an hour ago, now you suggest that I hand him the olive branch.'

'Turning the other cheek, John,' de Alencon reminded him mildly.

'What about the Bishop, Archdeacon?' asked Hugh. 'There's more than a rumour that he has sympathy for Mortaigne.'

'Like Richard de Revelle, he wants to be with the winners, not the losers. So far, I suspect he's only put his toe in the water. If he finds it too hot, he'll back away. But there are more fervent supporters in the cathedral precinct. One was in the Shire Hall today, one who has aspirations to be a bishop himself if Prince John succeeds.'

They all knew he referred to the Precentor but, at the moment, that seemed a low priority.

As they left to go, John promised they would meet again when Lord Ferrars and the others arrived. Then he climbed up to the solar and found it empty of all Matilda's possessions, clothes, embroidery and crucifix. Baffled, he walked to the slit in the partition wall and found that, by looking down and across, he could just see part of the area where Rosamunde had performed her act the previous night. Mary was clearing ashes from the hearth and he could easily hear her singing softly to herself and talking to Brutus, so Matilda's claims about eavesdropping were quite feasible.

Feeling filthy from his night in gaol, he broke his twice-weekly rule by going to the backyard and washing in a bucket of lukewarm water, using soap made from goat's tallow and beech ash to remove the grime, and to have an extra shave with his specially honed knife. Mary found him clean clothes and dropped his prison garb into a cauldron of boiling water to kill the lice and fleas. Then the faithful girl set out some food for him, leaving him feeling clean and well fed, but very uneasy about many things, especially the whereabouts and mood of his wife.

He had the rather mortifying feeling that the spirited defence she had put up for him stemmed from some other cause rather than love of her husband.

CHAPTER THIRTEEN

In which Crowner John talks to his wife

By mid-morning, de Wolfe could wait at home no longer: he was fretting about where Gwyn might be in his search for supporters and also had concerns for Matilda. He recognised the irony of the situation in that after years of suffering her moods and avoiding her at every opportunity he was now brooding over her welfare.

Hunched again in his wolfskin cloak, he strode through the cold, wet streets, met with salutes and smiles from those who knew about his abortive trial. His tower chamber was deserted as his officer was away, and after the relief of seeing his master freed, Thomas had gone back to his relentless search for the missing treasure plan in the Chapter House library.

Coming down again to the inner ward, the coroner was accosted a dozen times as he crossed to the keep, the most vociferous congratulations coming from Gabriel, who with great satisfaction had now locked up de Braose and Fulford.

In the hall of the keep, he ran a similar gauntlet of acclamation and escaped into the sheriff's chamber, to find it empty. The steward was happily restuffing his palliasse with fresh straw, having reclaimed it from the sheriff. 'Sir Richard has gone out, sir, I don't know where,' he said. 'The ladies have gone too. A man-at-arms was sent with a handcart to take their belongings somewhere.'

Briefly, de Wolfe wondered if Richard de Revelle had galloped away into the sunset to escape his problems, but it seemed improbable. Now he might have the chance to redeem himself once again, and with two manors and a wife in the county he was hardly likely to become an outlaw or abjure the realm.

As for Matilda, the transfer of her beloved clothes and finery on a handcart meant that she was not far away – and the only alternative to Martin's Lane was her cousin's house in North Street, unless she'd gone to live in sin with the fat priest at St Olave's, he thought cynically.

There was no way that he was going to brave his wife in her cousin's house, as that woman was far more objectionable even than Matilda. He made his way back to his own dwelling, feeling strangely incomplete, with an uneasy sensation of being cast adrift even if it was from the exasperating but familiar presence of his spouse.

In the vestibule, he threw off his mantle and boots and strode into the hall, determined to get a pint of red wine inside himself before Mary brought him his dinner. Inside the door he was brought up sharply, amazed to see Matilda standing stiffly at the end of the long table. She wore her outdoor clothes, even to a thin leather hood, which was still damp with rain, over her cover-chief. He hurried across to her, hands outstretched, but she stiffened and stepped back from him. He saw that her face was wet beneath the eyes and that it was not due to the rain. 'I wanted to thank you for what you did this morning,' he said humbly. 'You may have saved my life.'

Matilda lifted a hand in a gesture of dismissal. 'I must talk to you, John,' she said jerkily. 'I have come to plead with you.'

Her husband felt momentarily bemused. Surely he was the one at fault, and should be pleading her forgiveness for philandering, especially in the light of her public support for him? Why should she plead with him? He tried to get her to sit by the fire, but she refused and continued to stand like a granite statue in the centre of the hall. 'I did what I did today because of my brother. It was not right that you should suffer for his sake.'

Light began to dawn on de Wolfe. He knew that Matilda had always looked up to Richard, not so much because of their blood tie but because he was ambitious, literate, the holder of the highest post in the county and an even more rabid social climber than she. Now his sister had discovered that he had feet of clay, and was little better than a traitor to the King he represented. She had never accepted that his temporary fall from grace a year ago was anything but some jealous conspiracy against him – but this time, she must have heard something with her own ears that had demolished her idol. In a leaden voice, she soon confirmed his reasoning.

'Last night, I returned with Lucille to collect the rest of my clothes. The housemaid was not here, and you were fast asleep, so we went to the solar to pack my possessions.' Her voice faltered. 'I did not wake you, as I did not want to see you, John. Then that woman came in and I heard all that transpired, how she tricked you and falsely feigned a ravishment. Those evil men entered, having obviously been waiting outside for her signal.'

She swayed slightly and John took her insistently by the arm. This time she did not resist as he led her to her usual chair by the fire. He sat opposite and waited.

'All that was bad enough, but that Jocelin's sneers about my brother were far worse. Though I have tried to shut it from my mind, it is useless! I have to admit to myself that Richard has again allied himself with the King's enemies. I am mortified, John, I hate him for it, yet I fear for him. He is a fool. The ambition that I admired in him is so overweening that it will destroy him, unless he can somehow be protected.'

Her voice became stronger and more agitated as emotion seized her, and she reached across and grasped his arm. 'My pride pulls me another way after what was revealed about you and those women. Not that I was ever ignorant of it, as with most wives. But to be told about it by my brother and to have his servant sent like an errand-boy to flaunt it in the face of your tavern-keeper was too cruel of Richard. I know now that it was a feeble attempt to force your mouth shut over his treachery, but it cut me to the quick.'

She sobbed and passed her dangling sleeve across her eyes. 'Then to conspire to have you convicted of rape, just to try to buy your silence, was ten times worse and I hate him for it – but I fear for his life, John!' Matilda sniffed loudly and clutched his wrist more tightly. 'Help us, I plead with you! Do what you can to save the fool from himself!'

De Wolfe wished the ground would open to swallow him up. Always embarrassed by any show of emotion, the sight of his normally hard-bitten wife in tears, pleading with him for her kinsman's life, made him cringe – yet another part of him softened into a genuine sympathy for her anguish. Burgeoning affection was too strong a description for his feelings – she had been too flinty an adversary for too long for that to be so – yet, almost against his will, his hand fell on hers and he squeezed it awkwardly. 'Of course, I'll do what I can, Matilda. The man's weak, he turns with whatever wind blows strongest. I never trusted him and I'll never trust him again – but, for your sake, I'll do what I can. There may be a way to save him, if the idiot will do as he's told.'

Her face lit up through her tears, which now cut rivulets through the white powder on her pudgy cheeks. 'He'll do it, John, I'll see to that. When I've finished talking to him,' she went on grimly, 'he'll do anything that's asked of him!'

She stood up abruptly, returning to the old Matilda he knew, with a look on her face that spoke of a hard time ahead for her brother. 'Lucille!' she yelled, lifting her face towards the narrow slit of the solar high above their heads. 'Lucille, we're going at once.'

As he followed her to the door, de Wolfe sighed. The veil that had been lifted to give a moment's glimpse of her inner self had fallen again, and the wife he knew and suffered was back.

At the street door, John asked his wife to return home, but she refused. 'Not yet, John, it is too soon. I need to see this crisis through and set my mind in order first. I detest all men at the moment, you and my brother. I will stay with my cousin for the time being.'

She sailed off with the smirking French maid in tow and de Wolfe hoped for her sake that her new-found confidence about her brother's fate was not too optimistic. Personally, he was unconcerned as to whether or not de Revelle swung from a gibbet, which was no less than he deserved – but somehow he wished no further misery for his wife, whose brightest star had just been dislodged from the heavens.

He watched them vanish round the corner, heads bent against the icy wind that blew a mixture of rain and sleet down the narrow passageway that joined the high street to the Cathedral Close. When he went back inside, he saw Mary peering from the passageway to the yard. 'Has the mistress gone?' she asked. 'I kept out the way. The look on her face when she arrived would have turned an angel to stone.'

De Wolfe smiled wryly. 'For the first time in years I felt sorry for the woman.' He sighed. 'Now get me my dinner, girl!' he boomed, and with a return of his usual spirits, he gave Mary a kiss and a smack on the bottom.

The cathedral bells continued to mark the hours, with the coroner becoming more and more impatient for Gwyn's return. He ate his meal, typical winter food of salt fish and boiled pork, but it was after the second hour of the afternoon before hoofs and neighing outside told of the arrival of horses at the farrier's stable opposite.

Soon the hall was bustling with large men, all wet, hungry and thirsty. Mary bustled about with ale and wine, and brought in all the food she could lay her hands on. The arrivals were Gwyn, Lord Guy Ferrars, his son Hugh, Reginald de Courcy, Walter Ralegh and Alan de Furnellis, the last two being landowners from the south of the county. De Wolfe's woodman, Simon, was dispatched into the Close and soon returned with the Archdeacon.

A groom from the farrier's ran all the way to Rougemont and came back with the constable, as Ralph Morin was a direct appointee of the King.

After they had all warmed up and refreshed themselves, they sat around the refectory table for a council-of-war. First of all de Wolfe related all that had gone on, especially the devious plot to prevent him going to the Chief Justiciar with news of the embryo rebellion. Mindful of Matilda and his promise, he played down the involvement of the sheriff and made it sound as if Richard de Revelle had been manoeuvred and manipulated by the arch-plotters into a situation from which he could not escape. From the looks on some of the listeners' faces, it was plain that they had doubts on this score, but other matters were more urgent.

'How ready to move are these traitors?' snapped Guy Ferrars, the most powerful of the barons present. He was a large-boned mass of a man with a florid face half hidden by a brown moustache and beard. Though he was utterly loyal to King Richard, he was an arrogant, intolerant man, a Norman to his fingertips, who should have been born more than a century before so that he could have carved out his own empire as a Marcher lord. His son was cast in the same mould, though he was too fond of drink and women ever to be the man his father was.

'They have a force of mercenaries – and seem to have employed many outlaws as foot-soldiers,' replied John. 'There is no way of telling how many men they have, without spying on their camps, but at least we have their commander in gaol, this Jocelin de Braose.'

'We need to nip this in the bud as soon as possible,' said de Courcy, another powerful figure in Devon. Older than the others, he was completely bald, with his hair on his face, where a narrow grey rim of beard was joined by a wispy moustache. He and Ferrars had fallen out badly over the recent death of de Courcy's daughter, who had been going to marry Hugh Ferrars, but to the coroner's relief, they seemed now to be the best of friends.

'We must catch the leaders unawares, if possible,' grunted Ferrars. 'Use the same dirty tricks on them as they tried on you, de Wolfe. We don't need a pitched battle between armies, if we can help it.'

There were murmurs of agreement from Ralegh and Alan de Furnellis who, after years without strife in the region, had no wish to disrupt their comfortable life if they could avoid it.

This was the opening the coroner was seeking. 'I think we have the opportunity to do that. Richard de Revelle, as we know from his past history, is at least well known to them, and until the news of today gets widely abroad he is still *persona grata* with them.'

'How does that help?' objected the elder Ferrars.

'We need Henry de la Pomeroy and Henri de Nonant out of their castles. They have set this plan in motion to silence me. It has failed miserably, but they don't yet know that. If the sheriff sends them a message demanding an urgent meeting about the coroner, at some point well away from their refuges, then we may ambush them and cut the serpents off at the head.'

They discussed this for some time, and found no fault with it, as long as it could be pulled off.

'But is it legal?' queried Ralegh, a black-browed man rather like a watered-down version of John de Wolfe.

'To hell with it being legal!' shouted the short-tempered Hugh Ferrars. 'Is treason legal? These swine should be pulled apart by horses – hanging's too good for them.'

'Well, let's catch them first,' cut in the mellow

voice of reason, coming from Alan de Furnellis, a younger manorial lord from near Brixham. 'It should be put into action tonight. Once they learn that this de Braose is in prison, they'll not trust the sheriff, who was supposed to protect the plotters. You know how fast bad news travels around these parts.'

De Courcy looked over at John de Alencon. 'How does the Church stand in this, Archdeacon? The Bishop is well known not to be impartial in this affair.'

'I think he has dreams of Canterbury if Prince John succeeds. Certainly Hubert Walter would not last five minutes under a new king and would be lucky to keep his head on his shoulders. But at this stage, I doubt Henry Marshal wishes to cross the Rubicon of treason – not until there is a clear signal that he would be on the winning side.'

After further discussion they decided that they would immediately approach the sheriff and put an ultimatum to him: help us or else!

With the prospect of armed conflict the next day, the visitors decided to stay in Exeter overnight. Ferrars and de Courcy had houses in the city, and while the other two went off to find quarters in a tavern, the remainder set off for Rougemont and a show-down with Richard de Revelle.

They found him in his chamber, sitting behind his table, his rolls and parchments lying neglected in front of him. When they marched in unannounced, the sheriff jumped up in alarm, white-faced and convinced that this deputation of Lionheart's supporters had come to arrest him.

This was the first time that de Wolfe had seen him since the débâcle in the Shire Hall and Richard had difficulty in looking him in the eye. He began a half-hearted explanation of how he had been misled by de Braose and the woman, but the coroner cut him short and, without directly accusing him of complicity in the plot, set out their proposals for ambushing the leaders.

The sheriff tried to evade the issue and claimed that he had no knowledge of Pomeroy's or de Nonant's involvement and that he would have no influence upon them. Exasperated, as time was passing, de Wolfe turned to Ferrars and de Courcy.

'I think I should explain the situation to my brother-in-law in private,' he said acidly. 'As you might guess, there are family considerations in this, relating to my wife.' Then he almost dragged his brother-in-law into the adjacent bedchamber and shut the door firmly.

'Understand this and understand it quickly, Richard!' he grated. 'If you want to keep your life – and possibly your sheriffdom – you will do exactly as we ask, without question.' Richard tried a last-ditch attempt at indignation. 'A few hours ago, John, you were in danger of your own life. After all, I have only Matilda's word on this and she may be inventing the whole scene to protect you, as de Braose suggested.'

De Wolfe restrained himself from punching the idiot on the nose. 'Your sister is distraught, not so much at the peril I was in – she cares little for me – but for your betrayal of her. Love turns quickly to hate, Richard, and you hang by a slender thread held by Matilda. She heard de Braose implicate you as a rebel. She has pleaded with me to give you a chance to save yourself. If you fail to grasp it in both hands, she will add her denunciation to mine. The end of the track has come for you, man. You have no choice, if you want to keep your eyes, your testicles and your head. So choose now!'

He ground out the words with brutal urgency and the sheriff nodded miserably, his spirit broken. They went back into the outer chamber and began to make practical arrangements. Within the hour, Sergeant Gabriel galloped off alone for Berry Pomeroy on the best horse available, hoping to cover most of the journey before nightfall.

Whatever the next day might bring, John de Wolfe had a very good evening and night. Shaking off the concern, tinged with guilt, that he had for Matilda, he went down to the Bush to eat, and did not return home until after breakfast. In the tavern, he was again besieged by well-wishers and was bought enough ale and cider to fill the famous horse trough outside. Eventually, he was able to settle down by the fire with Nesta at his side and enjoy a whole duckling fried in lard, followed by bread and honeycomb. After he had told his mistress all the events of that eventful day, she snuggled up against him, the terrors of seeing him accused of a felony and facing execution gradually receding.

'Would you have been in any danger if Matilda hadn't spoken for you?' she asked.

'It would have been a damned sight more dangerous,' he grunted. 'I had only Gwyn's pilgrimage to other supporters of the King to rely on – and they didn't get here until this afternoon. I'd certainly have been convicted by that slippery charlatan in the castle. Whether they'd have got me to Magdalen Street by the end of the week is another matter.' One of the roads out of the city to the east, Magdalen Street was where the gallows tree was planted.

The Welsh woman was quiet for a moment, trying to crush the image of her pinioned lover twitching at the end of a rope, as the oxcart tumbril was driven from under his feet. She shuddered, though she had seen it many times because the twice-weekly hangings were a source of public entertainment in every town.

He dipped his fingers in a bowl of water that Edwin had placed on the table and wiped the duck fat from them with a cloth. Then he slid a hand under the table and ran it up her thigh, feeling the warm flesh through her linen kirtle. She prodded him playfully with her elbow. 'You've had quite a week for women, you old rake,' she murmured. 'First Hilda, damn you, then fair Rosamunde of Rye!' She leaned nearer and whispered in his ear, 'You didn't do it, did you?'

His caressing hand gave her a hearty pinch. 'No, madam, I did not! Though I'll admit she's a very bedworthy girl. But I like my women to be co-operative. I don't think rape would be to my liking.'

An hour later, he gave her a demonstration of what he meant in her little room upstairs, from which they could hear the paying guests snoring and muttering on their straw pallets.

ChAPTER FOURTEEN

*In which Crowner John congratulates
his clerk*

The message that Gabriel took to Henry de la Pomeroy
was for an urgent meeting with Richard de Revelle at
noon next day. The spot chosen was the ford across
the river Teign near the village of Kingsteignton,
about half-way between Exeter and Totnes. The sergeant was deliberately vague about the reason for the
meeting, claiming that the sheriff told him nothing
more. However, he let it drop that it concerned the
coroner, whom he said had been convicted of rape
and thrown back into gaol to await sentence. Pomeroy,
with ill-grace, agreed to send a message to Henri de
Nonant at Totnes and to Bernard Cheever early next
morning and to bring them to Kingsteignton at the
appointed time.

Although Gabriel had expected to escort them to
the meeting, he was sent back to Exeter after being
fed at daybreak – but he went no further than the
ford over the river to await events. The river was
narrow there, above the tidal reach, and trees came
down almost to the banks on either side. An hour
before noon, as far as he could judge from the grey,
sunless sky, he heard a whistle from the eastern side
and, on going into the woods, he found a large force

of his own men arriving, together with his constable, the coroner and his officer, and the nobles that had assembled in Exeter the previous afternoon.

The sergeant confirmed that Pomeroy and his accomplices had taken the bait and immediately Ralph Morin began to set his ambush. A score of mounted men-at-arms were sent over the river to hide on each side of the track, having been ordered to keep well hidden in the trees. Others fanned out along both banks and again melted into the forest edge, together with all those from Exeter except Richard de Revelle and one escorting soldier, who sat on their horses in full view on the eastern edge of the Teign.

After an hour's wait, a group of helmeted riders appeared on the opposite bank and stopped in the shadow of the trees. Four were obviously guards; the three others wore richly coloured cloaks over their tunics. They waved to the sheriff, who waved back, and both groups moved down the banks into the water of the ford.

There was a sudden blast of a horn and the pounding of hoofs as Morin's soldiers raced down the track behind the new arrivals. A host of other armed riders appeared from between the trees and all converged on the visitors. They pulled their horses round in consternation, but found no way out as yet more troops appeared behind the sheriff, cutting off any escape across the river.

There was no fighting. The ambush force slowly closed in to a wide circle around the seven men, none of whom had even unsheathed his sword in the patently hopeless situation.

De Revelle splashed his horse across towards them

with de Wolfe, Guy Ferrars and the others coming behind.

As the sheriff neared the ambushed riders, he stopped suddenly. 'These are not the ones!' he shouted. 'We've been tricked!'

In a moment it became apparent that the men were ordinary soldiers from Pomeroy's garrison. The helmets with nose-pieces and the chain-mail aventails covering everything but the face allowed recognition only at close range – and the borrowed finery of the cloaks completed the deception.

'We were told to escort the sheriff to Berry Pomeroy, if he proved to be alone,' grunted the leading man-at-arms, who had played the part of Pomeroy. He seemed unconcerned at being captured as, knowing nothing of what was going on, he had just done as his master had told him.

Frustrated, the leaders of the Exeter force pulled their horses together for a conference. Immediately the sheriff was on the defensive, claiming stridently that he had played his part as well as he could and it was no fault of his if Pomeroy's cunning mistrust had thwarted their plans.

There was nothing to be done except turn tail and go home.

'We're not going to put Totnes and Berry Pomeroy under siege with the forces we have locally,' barked Guy Ferrars. 'Let Hubert Walter or the King decide what's to be done.'

There was general agreement on that, as no one wanted to start a private war in Devonshire without royal backing.

'Let these men go back to their master,' suggested Ralph Morin. 'Seven men are not going to make much difference to a national uprising – and they will tell Pomeroy and his gang that the secret is well and truly out.'

De Wolfe cursed, but agreed with the constable's logic. 'I suspect that many a sympathiser will have second thoughts now, when it's realised that, within days, Winchester will be told of what's going on down here,' he said resignedly.

The men from Berry Pomeroy were sent on their way, with a message to their lord that heralds would leave that day to take the news to the Justiciar and the King's Justices.

'That should give them a few sleepless nights!' said John. 'Either they'll have to buy their pardons with a huge fine to the Exchequer or stock up their castles for a long siege. I suspect the first choice will be cheaper.'

Frustrated at being deprived of a fight, they wheeled their horses round and began the soggy journey back to the city.

Before the King's supporters dispersed, a last meeting was held in the sheriff's chamber in Rougemont. The main purpose was to make it abundantly clear to Richard de Revelle that they all knew of his recent questionable behaviour and that he was on probation for an indefinite period. Typically, he turned and twisted and made excuses, mostly by attempting to claim that he had had dialogue with the rebels only to spy out their membership and their intentions. No one was convinced by his feeble justification and Guy Ferrars summed up for all of them. 'If it were not for the pleading of your brother-in-law, who quite naturally wishes to spare his wife such shame, we would denounce you to Hubert Walter and let him take what action he sees fit. As it is, we shall look the other way for now, but any whisper of further impropriety will condemn you. Do you understand?' Having had this rubbed in in several ways, de Revelle was left in no doubt that he would have to walk strictly in the paths of righteousness from now on, under the eagle eye of John de Wolfe.

When the meeting dispersed, he was left alone with the coroner in the chamber, as darkness fell outside. Awkwardly, he began to mumble some thanks, mixed with excuses, but de Wolfe cut him short. 'Forget that for now, but I'll be watching every move you make, Richard. More to the point, I want to know what we are going to do about those murderous rogues that are in the cells beneath us.'

The sheriff wanted to do nothing with them, having allowed one of them to go free once before, but he dared not again show such partiality, or even apathy, with the Damocletian sword of the loyalists hanging over him. 'What do you suggest, John?' he said diplomatically. 'Have you really got solid evidence against them?'

'A confession from Fulford, witnessed by three people, written down soon after by my clerk,' snapped de Wolfe. 'True, it names Jocelin de Braose for both killings, but his squire was with him on both occasions and must be a partner in the crimes. And as for the attempt to steal Saewulf's treasure, I saw them both with my own eyes – and then they both tried to murder the King's officers who challenged them. There is enough there to condemn them three times over.'

After his dramatic downfall, de Revelle's cunning was returning quickly. He saw a chance to wash his hands of the affair, even if it meant an about-turn from his previous attitude. 'Then these are Pleas of the Crown, John! You should present them to the Justices in Eyre when they next come. You've wanted that privilege so often and now is your chance to employ it.'

The sheriff was wrong if he thought he had managed to hoist the coroner with his own petard, as John had already fully intended to prevent the sheriff fudging the matter through his own County Court. His concern was to make sure that de Braose got his just deserts, and there were considerable risks in waiting months for the Justices to trundle down to Exeter. Escape from gaol was a stock joke in most parts of England, where a considerable proportion of those committed for trial never appeared in court. The cost of guarding and feeding prisoners fell on the tax-payers of the city and that, together with bribery of guards and the dilapidated gaols, made escape a common event. Many prisoners reached sanctuary and abjured the realm, the rest either vanished into the forest to become outlaws or slipped away to other parts of the country and began a new life. De Wolfe had no intention of letting Jocelin de Braose slide back to his old haunts in the Welsh Marches, after the brutal killings he had perpetrated.

Looking at the weak, evasive sheriff, he could see that he would get no help there. He sensed that de Revelle still had one eye on the possibility of Prince John eventually coming out on top and wanted to avoid any acts that might put himself on a blacklist with any new government and its supporters in the West Country. The germ of an idea was wriggling in the coroner's mind. He left Richard to lick the wounds of his injured self-esteem and walked back to the chamber high above the gatehouse.

Gwyn was there, eating as usual, having given up trying to get home to his family before the curfew. They spent some time going over the momentous events of the past couple of days. De Wolfe suspected that if he had been convicted and sentenced to be hanged, his faithful Cornish giant would have torn down the gallows to prevent it. As they sat talking, they heard the familiar erratic tap of a limping leg coming up the stairs. 'The midget priest seems in a hurry tonight,' grunted Gwyn, as the sacking curtain flew aside and Thomas hopped into the room. They could see that he was in a state of great elation, his ferret face alight with excitement.

'I've found it, Crowner!' he squeaked, groping in the scruffy cloth bag he used to carry his pen, inks and parchments. He hurried up to the table, where a couple of tallow dips threw a pool of light, and carefully unrolled a parchment, which protected a loose inner page, stained and mottled with age. 'After all these days and nights, I found it! The missing directions to Saewulf's hoard!' He could hardly speak, such was his agitation.

De Wolfe rose from his stool to look, while even Gwyn forgot to bait the little clerk and came across to the table. Though neither man could read it, they looked with fascination at the frayed piece of treated sheepskin, on which faded brown ink was partly obscured by rings of fungus and scattered yellow foxing.

'Are you quite sure this is the genuine document?' asked the coroner.

'And where did you find it, dwarf?' boomed Gwyn, secretly proud of his colleague's tenacity and success.

Thomas rubbed his spiky hair ruefully. 'I fell asleep

in the archives this afternoon and slipped off that high stool,' he admitted sheepishly. 'I hit my head on the leg of the desk and lay there for a moment in pain. Then, as I was looking up from the floor, I saw that on the under-surface of old Roger de Hane's desk this outer parchment was stuck with blobs of bone glue. I pulled it off and inside was this ancient piece of vellum.'

They looked at it again, silently. 'So what does it say?' asked Gwyn.

Thomas ran his finger along the faint words, being careful not to touch the fragile membrane. 'Sixty paces, each of four shoe-lengths, sighted from the west tower wall, in line with the outer corners. Mark the spot, then twenty paces towards the largest yew. A leg's length deep.' They digested this for a moment. 'It doesn't say where, and there's no mention of Saewulf or a village priest or even a treasure,' complained Gwyn.

'The vellum is torn off close above and below the actual writing,' explained Thomas, indignant that his marvellous discovery was being challenged. 'Someone has ripped the directions from a longer document – maybe it fitted the original that de Limesi told us about.'

The coroner was less critical than his officer. 'Given what we know about the finding of the brooch and the whole story of Saewulf – and that this parchment was deliberately hidden under de Hane's desk – I'm quite sure that it's genuine. Well done, Thomas. Your diligence will be rewarded somehow.'

As the clerk basked in his master's approval, Gwyn still wanted to know how the message was to be interpreted.

Exasperated, the quicker mind of the clerk enlightened him. 'It has to be Dunsford church, surely. The directions are clear enough, as long as we don't use your huge feet for a measure – they would take us twenty yards beyond the spot!'

As he dodged a swipe from the redheaded officer, de Wolfe pictured the place where they had ambushed Jocelin and Fulford. 'The wooden tower is square, so we look along the line of the end wall and go sixty paces. That takes us again into the rough ground over the hedge.'

'What about the tree, Crowner?' asked the clerk. 'This was written over a hundred years ago.'

'Those yews live for ever. Probably the big one was there in the time of Jesus Christ,' said the coroner confidently.

Gwyn rubbed his huge hands. 'Shall I go for a shovel?' he asked gleefully.

Finding Saewulf's treasure was so easy as to be almost an anticlimax. On the evening Thomas found the vellum, de Wolfe went to the Archdeacon's house to give him the good news. De Alencon decided that the Bishop had better be told, as it was one of the rare occasions on which Henry Marshal was actually in his palace at Exeter. The Archdeacon and the Treasurer, John of Exeter, had already made sure that the news of the discovery of rebels in the county had been circulated all around the cathedral precinct. Although no names were mentioned, except those of Pomeroy and de Nonant, there was plenty of nose-tapping and smirking at the knowledge that a few residents of Exeter would be keeping a low profile for some time to come – including some around the cathedral.

The coroner and the Archdeacon made a brief visit to the palace, the largest house in the city, which nestled behind the south-east end of the cathedral. De Wolfe made it clear to Bishop Henry that even if it was found, the ownership of any treasure would have to be decided by his inquest and it could not be taken for granted that any of it would necessarily belong to the Church.

A rather distant and abstracted bishop listened politely, then agreed to leave everything in the hands of the coroner and decided to abide by whatever decision he made at his inquisition. When they left the palace, John de Alencon again arranged to provide servants and horses from the Close, as they had at the time of the ambush. They would to go again to Dunsford in the morning, armed with pick, shovel and baskets, in the fervent hope that this time there would be more to find than a single Saxon brooch.

The cavalcade that arrived next day at the little village contained three canons, attired in plain travelling clothes. Apart from the Archdeacon, the Treasurer felt obliged to be there too and Jordan de Brent also accompanied them, the archivist agog with enthusiasm for this bit of diocesan history come to life. De Wolfe, Gwyn and Thomas were naturally the leaders of the expedition, which might well end in an inquest, and the remaining three were servants from the Close.

The village priest was overawed by the arrival of such senior colleagues from the cathedral and watched, along with half the village, as the servants unstrapped the tools from the packhorse. Within minutes, the measuring began and the rotund Canon de Brent was flattered to be used as having an average stride – de Wolfe and Gwyn were judged too tall for accuracy. The jovial prebendary marched across the rank grass of the neglected churchyard along a line sighted by the coroner, who stood with one eye closed at the rear of the old tower, shouting directions at de Brent to veer left or right.

The priest came up against the rough hedge at forty paces and had to wait until a hole was hacked through the dead brambles, hazel branches and weeds for him to proceed into the rough copse beyond. At the sixtieth pace, a stake was hammered into the ground, then Gwyn took a sight-line from it to the prominent yew tree a hundred yards away. Off went the canon again for twenty paces and stopped. With a ragged cheer from a few throats, a second stake was knocked in and the digging began, Gwyn joining the cathedral servants in throwing up red earth, thankfully a few feet clear of the roots of several small trees.

To allow for errors in pace-lengths and direction, they cut a six-foot circle through the soil and, within a few minutes, the four men's efforts took them thigh deep. It was David, the groom who had been with them at the ambush, who made the first contact. He was working at the edge of the two-yard excavation when his wooden shovel, a copper band riveted to the edge, gave out a clanging noise as it hit something. 'A pot, sirs! A big one,' he shouted, after he had bent to scrape away soil with his hands. A few minutes later, two large earthenware pots, rather like amphorae, were dragged from the earth. They had broken ring-handles near their necks and the wide mouths were stoppered with wooden plugs covered in thick red wax.

As they were hoisted up to the coroner and the canons, the other diggers made sure that there were no others in the wall of the pit. 'They're damned heavy, Crowner!' said the groom happily. 'I reckon there's more than a brooch in them this time.'

Though de Wolfe had intended taking them back intact to Exeter before opening them, the beseeching looks on all the faces, from that of the Archdeacon to the village idiot, were such that his resolve was weakened.

Right opposite the church, across the track that lay at the bottom of the steep path from the church door, was an alehouse, the one they had used during the ambush. The woman who brewed and sold the ale was only too happy to let them use her single room to open the jars, and most of the population of Dunsford either crowded in behind them or peered from the doorway.

Gwyn cracked off the hard but brittle wax of the first jar and used his dagger to lever out the wooden stopper, which had softened with age and dry-rot.

'Tip it gently on to the floor,' commanded John and the audience watched with amazement as a cascade of coins poured out. The majority were silver, pennies from a dozen different Saxon mints, even a few Roman coins – but a number were gold, dulled by time and damp, but which shined up on being rubbed with a finger. While Gwyn watched the heap with an eagle eye and kept off any villager tempted to stretch out a hand, de Wolfe examined some of the golden coins. 'This says 'Offa Rex' – that's an old one,' he said.

The know-all Thomas peered over his shoulder and pointed out the crude Arabic lettering. 'Made for the Eastern trade, copied from the Kaliphate of Al Mansur,' he said importantly, which earned him a poke in the ribs from Gwyn.

That first jar contained only coins, and the coroner made a rough guess that they amounted to probably seven or eight hundred. When Gwyn up-ended the other amphora, half the contents were similar coins, but an assortment of brooches, rings and pins also slid out on to the earthen floor. Most were gold or silver, but a few had red and green gems embedded in the intricate metalwork. No one there had seen such wealth, not even the cathedral Treasurer had seen as much at any one time.

'This Saewulf must have been a very rich man, John,' murmured the Archdeacon, whose ascetic other-worldliness was still impressed by such a display of precious metal.

While Gwyn carefully scooped up all the treasure and replaced it in the jars, de Wolfe ordered a celebratory jug of ale for the team before they returned to Exeter. The Archdeacon promised the village priest of Dunsford that if any of the value came back to the diocese, he would not be forgotten – not least for having to fill in two large excavations in his wood, which belonged to the Church.

'At least that avoids one complication,' said the coroner. 'It was found on Church land, not that belonging to the manor, so we don't have to negotiate with the Fulfords over this.'

Ironically, the manorial lord of Dunsford was related to Jocelin de Braose's squire, Giles, but John was sure that they would not wish to associate themselves with their notorious kinsman.

With the jars safely strapped to the packhorse, the procession made its way back the seven miles to Exeter. De Wolfe's mind jumped between treasure trove, Matilda's intentions and his developing plans for dealing with de Braose.

That night, there was no sign of his wife in Martin's

Lane, and though he spent the evening at the Bush he came home to sleep, feeling strangely lonely on the big mattress in the solar. Huddled under sheepskins with a wide bear fur over the top, he missed the snorts and grunts that previously had been a source of nagging irritation. He was under no illusions that he had developed a fount of affection for Matilda since the crises of recent days. It was just that, since returning from Palestine two years before, he had become too dependent on the stability of a well-accustomed routine. He tossed and turned in the cold chamber, wishing now that he had stayed with Nesta – and his mind strayed occasionally to the blonde Hilda, who was forbidden fruit for at least a month or two.

Finally, before sleep eventually claimed him, he looked ahead with interest to the morning, when he would hold the inquest on Saewulf's treasure. In the four months since he had become coroner, he had never before had cause to enquire into such a hoard. The instructions as to coroners' duties and rules were so scanty that he had considerable latitude as to how to conduct the inquisition. He wondered if he should just record all the facts and let the King's Justices deal with it in the future – but no, to the devil with them, he thought. I'm the coroner, I'll make my own decisions.

In the morning, he used the Shire Hall for these deliberations. The sheriff kept well out of the way, as he had no obligation to be present, but the castle constable was there. The persons present at the excavations yesterday were all called as a jury, even the priests. For once, the inquest was a fairly private affair, and took place on the platform of the hall where Gwyn had placed a trestle table purloined from the castle kitchens. The two Portreeves had heard of the find and were there, as were a few of the other canons. Some off-duty soldiers and a handful of townsfolk were standing at the foot of the dais, gawking at the glint of gold and silver, but for once yesterday's expedition had been kept fairly quiet.

Before the inquest, John and his clerk had sorted all the coins into groups by metal and value, and had laid out the jewellery separately. Then Thomas had laboriously recorded the numbers of coins and descriptions of all the brooches, rings and pins. Some of the brooches were large, circular hoops several inches across, used for securing a cloak at the shoulder by pulling the corner of the cloth through the ring. The weight of gold in some of these was considerable and scales had been borrowed from an apothecary to weigh each item. The value of the pieces with gemstones would remain unknown until a craftsman could examine them.

The inquest was simple, mainly because de Wolfe had no idea what needed to be said, except to decide upon the disposition of the hoard. 'The value will have to be assessed by coiners, goldsmiths and silversmiths,' he said, after the usual preliminaries were over. 'We have no idea of the purity of the precious metals here, or of the value of the jewels. The whole treasure may have to be taken to London for this to be proved, even though the equivalent value, or part of it, may return to Exeter.' He looked without avarice at the fortune gleaming on the table.

'Now, though Saewulf intended this treasure to be given to his family if he died – as indeed he did – he did not abandon it or lose it. He left instructions that if the hoard could not reach his descendants, it should be given to the Church.'

John of Exeter, the cathedral Treasurer, spoke up. He was an open-faced man of fifty, with iron grey hair. 'Does that not constitute the testament of Saewulf, which still pertains today? I don't see that the passage of a century makes what he willed any the less valid.'

De Wolfe thought about this for a moment. 'I agree that maybe Saewulf's intentions remain the same. But, remember, they were made under a different race of kings, and a different system of law was introduced after the battle of Hastings. We have no reason to abide by what Saxons intended before they were conquered.'

Gwyn made one of his threatening noises in his throat, but no one took any notice as his Celtic aversion to the Norman conquest was as well known as his dislike of organised religion.

'I could therefore decide that this hoard be declared treasure trove, found in the soil of England, all of which soil belongs to King Richard, in which case the entire value would go to the Crown.'

There was a silence as every ear strained to catch his next words.

'However, given the will of Saewulf and the fact that the hoard has lain in Church ground ever since its concealment, I feel the most equitable course would be to divide the value into two equal parts, one to go to the King, the other to the diocese of Devon and Cornwall for them to use as they see fit. That is my verdict.'

'Just like the bloody sturgeon last week,' muttered Gwyn, but everyone else seemed satisfied with this compromise. De Wolfe gave the treasure into the keeping of Ralph Morin, to be locked up in the strong box of Rougemont, which was kept in the sheriff's chamber. Though he did not expect de Revelle to get up to any more bad behaviour for a considerable time, de Wolfe made a mental note to check the treasure at intervals against Thomas's detailed list, until it was sent to London for valuation.

As he left the Shire Hall, the coroner looked across the inner ward to the entrance to the undercroft of the keep, where Jocelin de Braose languished. His next priority was to do something drastic about that evil man, and within the hour he was on Bran's back, riding with Gwyn to Dartington to see the bereaved family of William Fitzhamon.

CHAPTER FIFTEEN

In which Crowner John uses an old glove

As he was too late to return to Exeter that night, John de Wolfe stayed again with his family at Stoke-in-Teignhead, but wisely returned straight to the city next morning with no diversion into Dawlish. He had a long discussion with his officer about his intentions as far as de Braose was concerned, as the plan might well endanger Gwyn's future livelihood. However, the Cornishman, though doubtful whether the coroner's proposition was possible, was happy to go along with it, if it was accepted by the other parties.

As soon as they arrived in Exeter, John lost no time in putting his plan into effect. They rode straight up to Rougemont and collected Thomas from the gatehouse, to act as witness and recorder. Mystified, the little ex-cleric hobbled after the other two, across the inner bailey down into the undercroft.

Gwyn roused the dozing Stigand from his pile of straw and prodded him across to open up the gaol gate. Inside the passage, which stank of damp, mould and human ordure, de Wolfe peered through the door grilles until he found Jocelin de Braose and Giles Fulford in adjacent cells. The blubbery gaoler, his face still mottled from the bruising he had suffered a few days before, went to unlock Jocelin's door, but the coroner stopped him. 'What I want to say can be done from here!' he grated.

Peering through the bars, he saw the man sitting on the slate slab, hands on knees, staring towards the voices. He was filthy, and a reddish stubble grew on his cheeks inside his rim of beard. As soon as he saw the coroner, he leaped to the door and shook the bars, screaming abuse at him. From the next cell, Giles Fulford also began yelling at his master to know what was going on. Stigand battered with his cudgel on Fulford's door for quiet, and gradually the pandemonium subsided. The coroner waited patiently until he could speak.

'Jocelin de Braose, you will certainly be hanged if the due processes of law are applied to you. Your crimes are Pleas of the Crown and the usual course would be to present you before the King's Justices when the next Eyre of Assize reaches the city. The sheriff wanted to try you in the County Court, as you so foully engineered for me – and that would mean a hanging within a week.'

Jocelin's foul language had abated as he considered this menu of certain death. Then he said, 'The sheriff! De Revelle wouldn't let me be harmed. We have powerful protectors in the country.'

'Not any longer, young man. The sheriff has seen the error of his ways and is now fully a king's man. And your patrons in Berry Pomeroy and Totnes will be too anxious to save their own skins to concern themselves with you. They now have a rebellion that is as flat as a griddle cake on Shrove Tuesday.'

There was silence from inside the cell, but from next door Giles Fulford called out angrily, 'I heard that, Jocelin! It's a trick, don't believe them.'

De Wolfe walked a few steps further up the passage and glowered through the next grille. Another grimy face beneath tousled fair hair glared out at him. 'I should keep a still tongue in your head, Master Fulford,' said the coroner evenly. 'It was that same tongue that condemned your master, with a little lubrication from some cold water.'

'It was a lie! You forced me under duress. None of it was true.'

'Tell that to the hangman! Maybe he'll believe you, for I won't,' snapped de Wolfe. He moved back to de Braose's cell. 'But there is a third way for you – for both of you.'

De Braose looked suspiciously at the coroner, his round face scowling. A prison louse was crawling down a hank of red hair hanging near his left ear but he ignored it, though his neck and hands were spotted with bug bites from the infested straw.

'What new trick is this, Crowner? If we're going to be hanged, then leave us in peace. Don't come gloating and tormenting us.'

For reply, de Wolfe fished in the inner pocket of his riding cloak and pulled out a glove. It was an old one he had brought from home for the purpose. Reaching through the bars, he lightly smacked Jocelin's face, dislodging the louse, then he dropped the old glove at his feet. 'I challenge you, Jocelin de Braose, to trial by combat to the death. If you win, you and your squire may go free.'

The auburn-haired man stared at him through the square aperture. 'They all said you were a madman and they were right! How, in the name of Mary Mother of God, can a crowner challenge a prisoner to trial by battle?'

Fulford yelled from next door to know what was going on, and de Braose answered, at the top of his voice, 'This crazed man wants to fight me to the death!'

'It's better than hanging,' shouted Fulford.

De Braose glared at the coroner and waved a hand dismissively, turning to go back to his stone slab. 'Go away, leave us in peace.'

De Wolfe explained calmly, 'I have just challenged you, not as crowner or even as a law officer of any kind. I did it in my role as champion for an aggrieved party who has laid an Appeal against you.'

De Braose came back to the door. 'A champion! How in hell can you be a champion? For whom?'

'A minor who, because of his tender age, can't prosecute his Appeal in person. You must know as well as I that it's normal practice for women, the infirm and those under age to appoint a champion.'

'I know that, Crowner! But whom do you claim has made this ridiculous gesture?'

'Robert Fitzhamon – for you foully murdered his father and he wants both justice and revenge.'

There was momentary silence. 'I deny it, there's no proof at all of that. My squire's so-called confession was made under duress.'

'Then you can prove that in combat. Fight me and win, and you demonstrate your innocence by my death – it's a common procedure. Forget that I'm coroner, just think of me as an old Crusader, slow in the mind and weak in the sword-arm!'

Jocelin was thinking of the fight near Dunsford church a few days before and had no illusions about de Wolfe's prowess with a broadsword.

'I will allow you to use Fulford as your squire. My officer Gwyn of Polruan will be mine.'

'Are you really serious about this, de Wolfe?'

'You killed an inoffensive old priest after beating him up for the sake of treasure and then made a young lad fatherless to suit your scheming masters. I can't fight them at the moment, so I'll make do with you.'

De Braose was scornful. 'You'd not catch me by surprise again as you did in Dunsford. I'd kill you, Crowner.'

De Wolfe was philosophical. 'Maybe you will, maybe you won't. Let's see, shall we?'

'How is this to be played, then? The challenged has the choice of weapons.'

'Choose what you will – but lance and shield are usual. If we're unhorsed, then let the sword decide it.'

'That suits me, Crowner, if you let me use my own horse. I'll kill you on the spot.' He raised his voice. 'D'you hear that, Giles? We're going to be free, thanks to the crowner's wish to commit suicide.'

The reply was an exultant stream of foul language, but held a note of sudden optimism, natural from a man whose only expectation five minutes before was of having his neck stretched on the communal gallows.

As they climbed the steps out of the undercroft, de Wolfe muttered to his two retainers, 'Now to convince Richard de Revelle that it's legal – not that he's any expert on legality.'

Matilda was still holding out at her cousin's house and de Wolfe made his usual pilgrimage to the Bush tavern that evening. The news of the trial by combat had not yet leaked out, though he knew that by tomorrow the whole of Exeter would be agog with the prospect of their coroner fighting a man accused of two murders.

Nesta was distraught at the thought of her lover putting his life in danger. 'He's so much younger than you, John! From what I saw of him in the Shire Hall, I'd not put him above twenty-five years.'

They sat as usual at his table by the side of the hearth. He put his arm around her shoulders and squeezed her. 'Are you convinced that I'm senile and past it, my love?'

She looked up at him with her big hazel eyes, worry creasing her smooth face. 'You could be killed, John. What would I do then?'

'I could be killed every day of my life, Nesta. A fall from a horse, a sudden ambush by a dozen outlaws – even stabbed by a jealous husband!'

She jabbed him in the ribs with her elbow. 'Stop it, John! But be serious. Though you've been a fighting man for twenty years, this de Braose is young and fast. And what about Gwyn? He's not so nimble as he was – and getting too fat.'

De Wolfe shook his head. 'Gwyn's not fighting Fulford. They are to be our squires, looking after the arrangements – and picking up the dead bodies.'

'What happens to Fulford if de Braose is defeated?'

'It means that they were guilty, so he'll hang.'

Nesta sighed. These violent Norman traditions were so different from the Welsh laws, where restitution was the object, not revenge and death. 'I won't sleep until all this is over, John. When and where will it happen?'

'Three days from now, at the tourney ground on Bull Mead. De Braose will be given a chance to ride his horse and get familiar with the lists on the day before.

It wouldn't be fair to take him stiff and cramped from a cell and put him straight on the back of his steed without some loosening up.'

Nesta shook her head wonderingly at the madness of men. 'You look on this as some kind of game! I can't understand you, playing with death as if it were some kind of entertainment.'

He looked grim. 'We can't take the chance of seeing these two go free again. I still can't trust the sheriff – but apart from him, there are so many ways of evading justice, especially when months may go by until the king's judges come.'

She brooded for a while, staring into the fire and imagining life without her man. 'Did de Revelle agree to this?'

'He's in no position to deny it. He put up only a token opposition to my proposal.'

'What did he say?'

'He objected that for trial by battle there are supposed to be five summonses in the county court before combat can be accepted. That would take weeks, so I told him I was using my powers as a king's coroner to abrogate this rule.'

'Can you do that?'

'No, not as far as I know! But no one here knows any different, without getting a ruling from the king's judges – and that can't happen in time. Anyway, the sheriff has no power to reject an Appeal – and I brought a letter written by Robert Fitzhamon's priest confirming that the boy wishes to Appeal de Braose and appoint me as his champion due to his minority.'

The inn-keeper clung more tightly to his arm. 'I fear for you, John, I really do! What about Bran? That great horse is getting old like you. Can he be relied upon?'

'As long as he can still run in a straight line, that's all I ask of him.'

With misgivings mounting with every passing moment, Nesta resigned herself to three days and nights of constant worry over this great beanpole of a man, with the black hair and dark jowls, whom she loved so much and was now afraid of losing because of some stupid masculine ritual.

John de Wolfe lost no sleep over the coming joust. Though he was optimistic about winning, he was not complacent about his survival, for the loser would die, that was for sure. He was fatalistic about his chances, as he had learned to be over a score of years when Irish, French, Moorish and even English adversaries had brought him near to death on many occasions.

He made sensible preparations for the event, but did not let them interfere with his daily duties. Indeed, a whole day was occupied with riding to Okehampton and back to inspect and hold an inquest on the body of the victim of a violent robbery on the highway. However, he made time to get to the livery stables to check Bran's shoes and to purge him of worms with an extract of male fern. Gwyn sharpened all their weapons with a whetstone and checked over the chain-links on John's hauberk. Then they went down to the tilting-ground at Magdalen Street to watch Jocelin de Braose and his squire practise. True to his word, the coroner had arranged with Ralph Morin to allow the two men several hours' freedom, under guard, to practise at Bull Mead with their own horses, which had been stabled near the Saracen. He had even sent palatable food to the gaol, in place of the muck that

Stigand provided, as he wanted no complaint that he had fought a malnourished, prison-sick opponent.

For an hour, Gwyn and he sat on the two ranks of benches that were fixtures on Bull Mead for the upper-class spectators on tournament days. They watched de Braose as he charged at the quintain, a post carrying a horizontal swivelling arm with a fixed shield hanging from one arm and a heavy bag of sand dangling from a rope on the other. The attacker would ride his horse at the device and strike the shield with his lance, dodging the violent swing of the bag, which could knock him off his horse if he was too slow.

Then Jocelin and Fulford made mock charges at each other down each side of the tilt, a long barrier of hurdles made of woven hazel-withies stretching across the field, the ground on each side beaten into bare earth by the pounding hoofs of the heavy destriers. At practice, they carried the usual flat-topped shields, but only leather armour as they were using long wooden poles with flat ends rather than real lances. After a dozen passes, the clash of pole on leather-covered wood led to two successful unhorsings, both by de Braose against his squire, who picked himself up bruised but unbroken.

A number of spectators watched, including Morin's guards, some old men dreaming of battles gone by, a few women with urchins running around with toy swords, and several cripples and beggars with nothing better to do. They were silent most of the time, knowing that the two combatants were criminals who would be fighting for their lives in a day or two – though each time Fulford crashed from his mare, there was a low murmur of anticipation of a broken neck or back.

After the quintain and the tilting, the two men practised sword-play for half an hour, until the men-at-arms hustled them off the field and marched them back to Rougemont, past the drying racks for serge cloth that stood in almost every empty space around the city walls.

'That de Braose is good with a lance. You'll have to watch him,' admitted Gwyn grudgingly, as they walked back to the South Gate. 'And he's got a powerful swing with a broadsword. I thought they might have tried to escape when they had horses under them.'

'Ralph had that in mind – that's why he had twenty soldiers there, half a dozen of them mounted. But they could hardly fight through them with only a long broom-handle for a lance and deliberately blunted swords.'

'A pity they didn't try, then maybe you wouldn't have this risky business to contend with,' grunted Gwyn, who was secretly worried about the coroner's chances in the coming combat.

De Wolfe slapped his massive back cheerfully. 'Come on, Gwyn! We've beaten much better men than these many a time in the past. I'm not ready to hang up my arms and sit by the fire yet.'

The day of the trial began wet with a fine drizzle, but by mid-morning it had stopped, though it was misty and miserable. 'At least the ground will be soft, for those who fall from their mounts,' said John. 'Hitting frozen mud can kill you, without needing a lance in your guts.'

He and Gwyn were at the tourney ground in one of the arming chambers, a grand name for two rickety thatched sheds that were built at each end of the

double tier of viewing benches. Thomas de Peyne
was lurking nervously in the background, frequently
making the sign of the Cross and saying prayers for
the preservation of his master's life – and for his soul,
if he lost. Jocelin de Braose and Giles Fulford were
under guard in the other shelter, going through the
same routine as John and his officer. The constable of
Rougemont had sent down a couple of soldiers with a
handcart to carry the armour and weapons for the two
combatants. De Wolfe, of course, was using his own,
tried and tested in many a conflict, while de Braose had
been loaned accoutrements from the castle armoury,
his own being in Berry Pomeroy.

As Gwyn helped his master into his fighting kit,
they could hear the increasing clamour of the crowd
outside. Everyone in Exeter and some of the surrounding villages knew of the contest and as many
who could get away from their labours were there.
Some merchants and craftsmen had even given their
workers a couple of hours' freedom to come to the
Magdalen Street arena.

'Sounds as if half England has turned out to see you
kill de Braose,' observed the Cornishman, as he helped
de Wolfe pull his gambeson over his head. This was a
long quilted garment, padded with wool, to underly
his chain-mail and buffer any impacts.

'I don't think they care who gets killed, as long as
there's plenty of blood for a spectacle,' replied the
coroner cynically.

Putting on the heavy hauberk was more difficult,
but John's was an older type with only three-quarter
sleeves, making the hundreds of chain-links sewn to
the canvas a little lighter than the full version, which
had long arms ending in mailed gloves. Neither man

mentioned the possibility of defeat, but they had been through this routine many times and each knew the other's thoughts. De Wolfe wondered what would happen to Matilda if he was killed. He had not seen a sign of her since her outburst in the Shire Hall and then her pleading with him to save her brother's life and reputation. Presumably, if he survived this, she would eventually return home. He wondered if she would come to see today's battle – which, with increasing certainty, he had to admit might have been a foolish act of bravado.

'We're not wearing the full battledress, are we?' asked Gwyn, looking at the metal leg greaves that Ralph Morin had included in his cartload of armour.

John shook his head. 'This isn't going to be a day-long conflict, Gwyn. A quarter-hour should be more than enough to see one of us vanquished, so I don't think legs are going to be a target.'

'That bloody Fulford used them as a target last time – but he hasn't got a shovel today,' grunted Gwyn, with an attempt at humour. He hung a sheet-iron oblong over the centre of de Wolfe's chest on top of the chain-mail and tied the leather laces around his back to hold this heart protector in place. Then de Wolfe pulled on his coif, a thick woollen bonnet, and tied it under his chin, before donning his round helmet, which in recent years had replaced the conical one. It had a larger nasal projection than the earlier models and a chain-mail aventail was suspended from its edge. This hung down like a curtain all around the back and sides of his neck and covered his chin up to his lower lip.

'What about this?' asked the Cornishman, holding up a rather creased linen garment. It had once been white, but years of wear and exposure had given it a greyish-yellow tinge.

'Yes, why not?' said John. 'If I'm to win or lose, they may as well see me in my father's surcoat.' He slipped it on over his head, and as it fell to cover him from shoulder to knee, a savage wolf's head was displayed across his chest in black embroidery.

Gwyn stood back to examine his handiwork critically, walking around his master to make sure that all was perfect. Spurred leather boots over long stockings with cross-gartering completed the outfit, apart from thick gauntlets with metal plates sewn on to the backs of the hands and fingers. Satisfied, Gwyn hung a heavy leather baldric over the right shoulder, coming down diagonally to support the great sword hanging from a thick leather belt, which he buckled tightly over the wolfish surcoat. 'You could shave with that edge now,' commented Gwyn proudly, pointing at the sword, which had also belonged to John's father, Simon de Wolfe.

'What about the lance?' growled the coroner, hefting the eight-foot shaft of seasoned ash. He looked carefully at the shielded hand-grip about a third of the way along and at the iron tip, which had a small crosspiece behind the spear-head, to prevent it going too deeply into the flesh of the target and becoming difficult to withdraw.

'I've ground the point finely,' said Gwyn. 'You could impale a bluebottle on that.'

Everything seemed in order, and without any more delay, de Wolfe went out of the shed where Gabriel was standing anxiously by Bran, who was unconcernedly eating some crushed grain from a bucket. They were out of sight of the crowd, who stood in a double line well back from the tilt, which was about two hundred paces in length. The excited talk and shouts merged into one buzz of noise as de Wolfe was helped up into his stallion's saddle, Gwyn giving him a foothold with two hands, against the extra weight of his hauberk. The destrier had no armour, apart from a token leather facepiece from its ears down to its muzzle, with some iron plates riveted to its front to protect its forehead. Gwyn handed up the lance and then the shield, made of toughened linden wood covered in a double layer of thick boiled leather, again crudely painted with a wolf's head.

'All set, Sir John?' asked Gabriel anxiously, and when de Wolfe nodded, he vanished around the corner of the hut to the front of the bank of benches, placed opposite the half-way mark of the tilting fence. Here, on the second row of planks, were the upper-class spectators, with Richard de Revelle and Ralph Morin in the centre. The two Portreeves were there, Hugh de Relaga looking unhappy at the prospect of his friend and main business partner in jeopardy of his life. Surprisingly, as the Church officially frowned upon jousting and tournaments, several canons and lesser priests were perched on the benches, swathed in black cloaks over their vestments, trying to look inconspicuous. The Archdeacon and the Treasurer, as well as Jordan de Brent, were there. The rest of the benches were taken by various burgesses and guild-masters, and several women were present, looking forward with no apparent horror to seeing mortal wounds.

As de Wolfe walked his horse round the corner to the front of the benches, he scanned the occupants and his eyebrows went up momentarily when he saw Matilda there, sitting wooden-faced next to her brother. She was dressed in black, an unusual colour for her, and he wondered whether this was preparation for widowhood or for entry into a nunnery – or possibly both. Slowly she turned her head towards him and their eyes met. There was no expression in hers, but gradually she raised her hand to him in a salute, the significance of which eluded him – she might have been wishing him good luck or saying farewell.

At each end of the benches, beyond the two arming chambers, a double line of spectators reached in either direction to the ends of the central fence, and on the further side, a similar crowd was lined up, being importuned by hawkers, beggars and soothsayers, all taking the opportunity of a captive crowd to do business.

In the moment he had before the sheriff began the proceedings, de Wolfe's eyes searched anxiously for Nesta, but he could not pick her out from all the other women in the crowd.

'I make one last supplication to you,' came Richard de Revelle's voice, and de Wolfe jerked his eyes back to the sheriff. From the other end of the seating, Jocelin de Braose had approached the centre, dressed almost identically to himself and seated on a large black gelding, much younger than old Bran. He wore no surcoat over his chain-mail, but Morin had seen to it that the armour and weapons were identical, so that no allegation of favouritism could be made.

The sheriff was standing up to make his speech and John could see that, in spite of his recent humiliation, he was already regaining his old arrogance and conceit. He decided to cut him down to size at once, to emphasise, at least to de Revelle himself, where his limitations of power lay. 'What supplication can there be, sheriff?' he boomed. 'This man has been Appealed for the murder of Robert Fitzhamon's father, which is only one of his sins. Either you let this legitimate trial by combat go ahead – or he goes back to gaol to await the King's Justices, who will surely send him to the gallows and commit his body to rot on the gibbet thereafter.'

De Braose looked sharply at John, then back to de Revelle. 'Much as I revile de Wolfe, I agree with what he has said,' he cried, in ringing tones. 'There is no alternative. I have your word, Sheriff, that when I defeat him, I and my squire will go free. What more can a man ask, when he has been unjustly accused of a crime of which he is innocent?'

Richard threw up his hands in resignation. 'So be it. You may continue this ill-advised course of action.'

Secretly, he was relieved that it had come to this, and he fervently hoped for victory for his brother-in-law, not from any tender feeling towards him but because he suspected he would get hell from Matilda for years if he allowed her husband to be killed – and also it would be useful to get rid of de Braose, who might be a danger to himself, knowing as much as he did of de Revelle's involvement with the rebels. He spoke his last words with some relief. 'This is not a tournament nor jousting for sport! This is trial by battle and you may fight as you please to the death.'

He sat down with a bump and Archdeacon John de Alencon could not resist rising to his feet to hold up a hand in solemn benediction and to murmur a prayer for righteousness to triumph – and for the repose of the soul of the defeated. Thomas, standing near the arming shed, was almost in tears as he jerkily crossed himself.

Ralph Morin, as the senior military man present, rose and pointed to de Braose. 'You will go to the east end, your adversary to the west. When I drop this white kerchief, you may begin,' he rumbled. 'You may make as many passes as you wish. If you are unhorsed you may remount, if you can. Otherwise, there are no rules. You will fight, tooth and nail if needs be, until one of you is dead.' He remained standing until the two horsemen had trotted off to opposite ends of the long wicker fence, their squires running behind them until they all turned to face each other.

The crowd fell silent. They were used to tournaments and jousting where, not infrequently, fatal injuries occurred, but trial by combat, where death was mandatory, was becoming uncommon. Certainly, the sight of their county coroner, a well-known and respected former Crusader, fighting an alleged murderer as champion for a thirteen-year-old boy, was unique, and the city held its breath while they waited for the Constable to make his signal. Even the clouds seemed to stand still while everyone watched for the cloth to drop.

There was a flutter of white and then a pounding of hoofs. The two horsemen hammered along opposite sides of the tilt, lowering their lances as they went. De Braose's steed was faster than Bran and the point where they met was to the left of the viewing stand.

Both lances met the shields simultaneously with a tearing thwack, as the leather on both was gouged. De Braose attempted to lift his spear-tip at the last second to hit John in the face, but the coroner lifted his shield at an angle to protect his head and caused the lance to slide off sideways. His own caught de Braose's shield squarely over his breast and the great weight of Bran, with the spear held vice-like in de Wolfe's muscular arm, jerked the other man back, almost pushing him back over the raised cantle at the rear of the saddle. In a fraction of a second, they had thundered past each other and slowed down towards the further end of the tilt.

The crowd relaxed slightly, some yelling encouragement, others cat-calls, as the more knowledgeable of them knew it was a foul to aim for the face in a tournament – though, admittedly, this was a fight to the death with no holds barred.

As soon as de Wolfe got near the end of the barrier, he turned Bran in a wide circle to avoid losing speed and immediately galloped back down his side of the list. De Braose, who had slowed almost to a stop to turn his horse around, was at a standstill when he saw the coroner pounding down at him from the other end. Caught unawares, he lost a few seconds in cruelly spurring the gelding into action and was not up to speed when de Wolfe bore down on him, again well beyond the centre-line. John's lance again caught him four-square on the shield and crushed it against his chest, knocking him clean off his horse into the mud. There was a great yell from the crowd and all those on the benches stood up to get a better view.

Bran's great bulk hurtled on under its own momentum for twenty yards until de Wolfe could pull him round. By that time, de Braose had picked himself from the mire, miraculously without any apparent injury. His well-trained horse had stopped short and wheeled around to canter back to his fallen master. As the black gelding came up to him, Jocelin put a foot in the stirrup and scrambled back into the saddle – no mean feat considering the forty pounds of chain-mail on his back, which spoke well of his youthful fitness. There was a roar of congratulation from the crowd, who even-handedly applauded his remarkable recovery, just as earlier they had condemned his foul.

As he remounted, Giles Fulford had raced up the side of the tilt and handed up the fallen lance to his master's right hand. De Wolfe was now alongside on the other side of the tilt. He made no move against de Braose while he was getting back into the saddle, but suddenly de Braose made a sudden jab with his lance across the hurdles, catching the coroner in the ribs. The attack was futile, as without the force of a galloping horse behind it, the spear was easily blocked by the chain-mail and caused nothing more than a bruise. The crowd booed and hissed at this unsporting violation, again ignoring the fact that anything was acceptable in this mortal combat.

The wolf-emblazoned fighter ignored the jab and cantered away down to his end of the field, again making a swift turn and accelerating back towards Jocelin de Braose. This time, the younger man had learned his lesson and imitated de Wolfe's manoeuvre, so that they were both up to full speed when they met. Whereas de Braose had raised his lance to John's face on the first encounter, this time he unexpectedly dropped it, and as he took the impact of the coroner's weapon on his shield, he deliberately plunged his own spear deep into the neck of de Wolfe's stallion.

With a dying scream as the iron tip tore into his spine, Bran's front legs collapsed and he pitched his rider over his head. Landing with a crash, with his great horse almost on top of him, de Wolfe was not as lucky as de Braose had been a few moments earlier. He turned through half a circle in the air and landed with one leg under him. Almost as if everything was happening in slow motion, he heard the bones in his left shin snap as it took most of the impact. Though the fracture saved his head and chest, the pain was agonising for a moment, then faded. His overwhelming feeling was for his horse, his beloved Bran.

'My horse! You bastard, de Braose, you swine!' he heard himself rave at the sky above. The crowd seemed to agree with him, as there was a great tumult of abuse from all sides against this unscrupulous act. The fight to the death was between the men, not the horses, and the spectators screamed their hatred at de Braose. In their anger some tried to run across to the tilt, but Morin's men-at-arms rushed along the line and forced them back.

The great stallion was kicking spasmodically in his death throes, eyes rolled up, showing only the whites, the legs thrashing as the lance still lay embedded in his spinal cord. De Wolfe realised suddenly that the death of his horse might be the prelude to his own demise for, seconds later, he saw de Braose scrambling over the hurdles, sword in hand. There were yells on every hand, mainly from the crowd but also from Gwyn and Giles Fulford, as they raced back from either end. De Wolfe tried to get up, but his leg collapsed under him, bent at an unnatural angle. He got as far as his knees and managed to draw his sword, but de Braose was already upon him.

'Fight to the death, you said, Crowner!' he exulted. 'You've had your wish, but it's you that's going to do the dying!'

As de Wolfe crouched on his knees, ineffectually holding up his sword towards the redheaded attacker, he thought what an ignominious end he would have, after surviving all those years in so many conflicts. Then, in the split second before Jocelin lifted his weapon to strike, he was suddenly at peace, his only regret being that he would never again lie with Nesta or Hilda. With poor Bran gurgling and jerking alongside him, he prodded upwards feebly and deflected the first slash that de Braose made.

The sneer on the young man's face was worse than the fear of impending death. 'Still fighting, Coroner? Then try this one!' He lifted his blade high above his head and stepped back to make a swing that could cut de Wolfe in half.

John closed his eyes automatically and felt a heavy thud against his arms. Puzzled, he could not understand how that could be his death agony and opened his eyes to find de Braose spitted on his sword, the blade passing up between his thighs, through the slit in his hauberk. The man had fallen forward, his face on John's shoulder, blood pouring from his mouth and nostrils, his body twitching a little but with nothing like the convulsions that the huge stallion was making alongside them.

Bewildered, de Wolfe pushed at the body, causing ferocious pain in his leg, but he managed to roll de Braose off him on to the ground. John's sword was still between his opponent's legs, the pommel level with Jocelin's knees. A foot of the blade had entered near his genitals, the point being somewhere up in his belly.

In de Wolfe's muddled mind, all this seemed to have taken hours, yet it could have been only seconds. The next thing to confuse the shocked coroner was the sight of a manic fair-headed man vaulting over the barrier and coming straight at him with a dagger in his hand. With sudden apathy, John's resignation to suffer a violent death returned and he sank back on to his haunches, the pain in his leg monopolising his senses.

But Giles Fulford never reached him. A hairy whirl-wind erupted into the gap between the blond squire and the coroner, as Gwyn arrived from the further end of the tilt. Though Fulford struck out with his dagger, it sliced harmlessly across the Cornishman's thick leather cuirass. He never had another chance to stab, as Gwyn's bulk struck him with the force of a runaway horse. He was smashed to the ground with the coroner's officer on his back and de Wolfe, still half stupefied by his fall and the events of the past half-minute, watched as Gwyn's huge hands pulled back the blond head until there was sharp snap as the neck broke.

'That's what you did to Fitzhamon, you swine!' he muttered, as he let the dead man's head drop into the mud. By now there was pandemonium all around. Those on the south side had seen everything that had happened and were running across, swamping the few soldiers who tried to keep order. On the north side, the fence had obscured the last acts of the drama and all the spectators there were now lined along the tilt, peering over the hurdles at the mayhem on the ground. Gwyn ignored everyone, turned to de Wolfe and cradled him in his arms.

'My leg's gone, but otherwise I'm all in one piece,' murmured the coroner, trying to ignore the pain in his calf.

Tenderly, Gwyn picked him up and sat him on the ground so that his legs were now straight out in front, which immediately relieved much of the pain. 'You're too heavy even for me to carry, Crowner,' he said. 'We'll get Gabriel to fetch a cart to take you home.'

John looked around him at the two corpses and his dead horse, now lying pathetically still. He reached out and gently touched a hairy foot that lay alongside him. 'What, in God's name, happened after that bastard speared my poor Bran? He was just about to skewer me to the ground!'

Another voice came from the ring of people that had appeared around him. 'It was your stallion that saved you, John,' came Ralph Morin's deep tones. 'Just as that evil fellow was going to strike, the horse gave a last massive spasm with all his legs and kicked the bastard down on to your upraised sword.'

'I feel sure that the Almighty had a hand in that,' said John de Alencon, who knelt down solicitously to look at the fractured leg. 'Who else would have ordered things so that a dying horse would avenge itself upon its killer?'

De Wolfe grunted, his normal frame of mind rapidly returning. 'I think I was an old fool to so rashly put myself forward as a champion,' he muttered ruefully. 'Gwyn, if I ever think of such a thing again, be sure to tie me hand and foot, will you?'

As they waited for Gabriel to organise a cart to take him home, he became aware of a silent figure standing over him. It was Matilda, who in her black cloak and white cover-chief already looked like a nun. 'Are you in pain, husband?' she said shortly, her face still devoid of any recognisable emotion. He murmured some dismissive words and watched her uneasily. 'I will come home and tend to your needs until that leg mends,' she said grimly. 'That girl Mary has no idea how to look after an invalid.' Then she turned away and walked off towards the city gate with her brother, who was inwardly singing with delight at the way matters had turned out.

As the soldiers waved away the crowd, Gwyn and Thomas stayed close to the coroner. 'If you're stuck in bed for a month or so, I'll bring you some decent ale from the Bush every day,' promised Gwyn. Not to be outdone, his little clerk, who was nearly crying at the thought of how close his master had come to death, offered to give him reading and writing lessons to pass the time.

The handcart came with Gabriel and two men-at-arms to push it, and Gwyn and the sergeant gently lifted de Wolfe aboard, with a couple of gambesons under him for padding. From his elevated position, John could see Richard de Revelle and Matilda vanishing in the distance, and he wondered what married life now held in store for him.

'I think you ought to look the other way as well!' grunted Gwyn, pushing the cart round.

Coming from the other end of the field directly towards him were two women, walking hand in hand. One had rich auburn hair, the other was a pale honey-blonde.